When she stepped into the garden, the heel of her shoe sank into the moist earth, still soft from the previous evening's rain. Despite the warm afternoon sun, a million tiny droplets of water rested on the lush petals of the roses.

It was such a soothing feeling to walk among the rose bushes, occasionally stopping to touch the velvety smoothness or to smell the heady fragrance of a bloom.

Bethany was reaching out to caress the petals of a crimson rose when she heard her name called. Her finger struck a thorn. "Ouch," she mumbled, and lifted her finger to her lips to thwart the pain.

She looked up to see Wilder walking toward her. "You startled me," she said, rubbing the pinpoint injury with her thumb.

"Sorry. I didn't mean to make you prick your finger. Here, let me see."

Before she could back away, he grabbed her hand in both of his and held her slender finger up for inspection. His touch was warm, soft, firm. They stood close together, hands touching, eyes meeting. He slowly brought her hand up to his lips and kissed the injured finger.

Gasping, she allowed him the familiarity. Her heart seemed to swell in her chest. A shudder of longing raced through her veins. Wilder pressed the finger to his lips once more, letting his tongue gently caress the tip. His eyes held hers, and Bethany felt ablaze with more desire than she'd ever experienced. . . .

GLORIA DALE SKINNER

GEORGIA FEVER

ZEBRA BOOKS
KENSINGTON PUBLISHING CORP.

ZEBRA BOOKS

are published by

Kensington Publishing Corp.
475 Park Avenue South
New York, NY 10016

First printing: July, 1992

Printed in the United States of America

On the one hundredth anniversary of the Homestead Steel Mill Strike, I dedicate this book to all Americans, union and non-union, who work in our factories, plants, and mills, but especially to Lester, Donna, Jim, Shirley & Alen, and Susan & Jody. Thank you for giving us products Made in the USA.

Prologue

Homestead, Pennsylvania:
February 1892

Wilder's body burned. He groaned and his heavy lids fluttered upward. Though his vision was blurred, he caught a glimpse of his brother.

"Did they cut off my leg?" His throat was dry and his voice raspy as he asked the all-important question. He was in so much pain he couldn't be sure of anything.

"No, it's still there," Relfe said.

"Thank God," Wilder whispered, but beneath the sheet that covered him, his hand automatically slid down his thigh, seeking proof.

"I don't know how much good it's going to do you. Someone did a thorough job of beating you up. The man who found you lying in the snow thought you were dead."

Relfe's candid remark didn't make Wilder feel any better. "How bad am I?"

7

"I won't lie to you. The news isn't good. In time, your ribs should heal." He paused. "The doctor doesn't know if you'll ever use that leg again."

With glaring pain, Wilder remembered hands that closed around his arms as tight as steel bands, holding him down while gloved fists punched his face and stomach. He remembered booted feet catching him in the ribs, lifting him off the ground. He remembered his own piercing scream of pain torn from his throat as a hammer caught him just below the knee.

Wilder shuddered and shook off the offending images, replacing them with raw anger. He looked up at his brother and said, "Don't worry. I'll use my leg again to stomp the hell out of those—" Wilder tried to rise, but Relfe grasped his shoulders and forced him down. He lay back, panting and sweating. He didn't have the strength to fight.

A chuckle from his brother increased Wilder's anger. He felt as if he lay under a blanket of red-hot coals, his chest so heavy and tight he could hardly breathe. There wasn't a muscle in his body that wasn't taut with pain and Relfe was laughing.

"What's so damn funny?" he muttered, trying not to breathe too deeply.

"You. Thinking you can fight the whole goddamn labor union."

"I only want five of them."

Relfe sobered. Placing a gentle hand on Wilder's shoulder, he said, "That's how many attacked you. Did you recognize any of them?"

"Hell no! But I'll know them if I ever see them again," he swore.

"Well, you won't get the chance for a while. As soon as you can travel, I'm sending you south to recuperate. I think it's best if you're out of town for a couple of months. With all this talk of a strike, it'll only get worse before it gets better."

"I don't understand," Wilder said, touching the puffy swell of a tender bruise below his eye. "I was on their side."

"That's not the way the steelworkers see it. Maybe it's time you accepted that."

"No, I—" Wilder tried to rise again and felt a sharp pain in his chest that took his breath away.

Relfe touched his arm affectionately. "Lie back and rest. You don't need to upset yourself. For once, you're in no condition to argue with your big brother. We'll talk again when you're feeling better. Don't worry. If I have to spend every dime of our inheritance, I'll find the bastards who did this to you."

Chapter One

Eufaula, Alabama:
May 1892

"This has to be the most beautiful garden in the world," Bethany said.

"Yes'um," the tall, gangly gardener said as he stood looking at the spectacular array of color before them.

Mid-morning sun warmed Bethany's cheeks as she smiled. She'd worked hard to keep the tradition of the mansion intact. That included making sure The Georgia had the best-kept grounds of all the homes in Eufaula. For the last five years, she'd followed the routine her father had set over twenty years ago, when after the war the family home became The Georgia Restaurant and Inn.

"You do an excellent job, Seth," she told him. "I'm lucky to have you."

"Yes'um," he said, bobbing his head as he scratched behind his ear. "And I'm proud to be here."

She took off her gardening gloves and handed them to the older man. "I think I have enough roses for today. I'll let you put the tools away."

Seth picked up the shears and the clippers and stuffed them in his gardening apron. "Yes'um," he said, and gave her the basket of cut roses.

"Don't forget to check at the mercantile to see if that new fertilizer has come in. Let me know if it has. I want to read what the packaging has to say before you use it."

"I'll check on that right now," he said.

While Seth ambled away, Bethany continued to stand in the garden with her head tilted upward, enjoying the warm sunshine. She didn't know how long she'd been standing there, when strong arms slipped around her waist from behind and jerked her around, making her spill the basket of roses.

"Stanley!" she cried, looking up into the face of her attacker. "Let go of me this instant!"

"Don't pretend you don't want me to do this," he said with a confident grin on his face.

Bethany gasped in outrage as Stanley's wet lips touched hers. His muscular arms pinned her body to him, and his big hands kneaded the soft flesh of her back.

Shock gave way to anger. Bethany twisted and turned, trying desperately to break Stanley's forceful hold. With no alternative left, she closed her teeth around his bottom lip and bit down hard.

Stanley howled and quickly let her go. His hand covering his mouth, he muttered words that made Bethany's ears flame red. She spun around to flee, only to be jerked back against his chest.

"You little bitch! I'll show you how—"

Bethany's open palm cracked against Stanley's cheek, cutting off his words, snapping his head backward. She was ready with another slap, when a loud round of applause sounded behind them. Bethany and Stanley stopped struggling and turned around. A man leaned against the stone pillar of the portico a short distance away, grinning as he clapped.

Although her breathing had slowed its erratic pace, Bethany's chest heaved painfully. Abruptly, Stanley let go of her wrist. She pushed away from him, her gaze refusing to leave the stranger's handsome face.

"I thought I might have to step in and save your honor," the stranger said, limping toward them. "I guess not. You seem to have done an excellent job of taking care of yourself."

The man's accent immediately dubbed him a Yankee. In spite of the praise he'd handed out, Bethany knew Stanley wouldn't have turned her loose had the man not gotten their attention.

"We were just having a little fun, isn't that right, Bethany?"

Turning quickly, she saw Stanley putting away a bloodstained handkerchief. She shuddered and involuntarily reached up to scrub her lips with the back of her hand. Looking back to the stranger, she saw him lift his eyebrows as if to question the other man's statement. Even though she was angry, she couldn't make a bigger scene here in the middle of The Georgia's rose garden. It infuriated her to have to do it, but she had no choice. She had to let Stanley off the hook for now.

"I think it's time you left, Stanley," she said in a tight voice, hoping her expression let him know she detested him.

Her breathing even once more, Bethany reached up and smoothed back the dark blond hair that had fallen away from her neatly coiled bun when Stanley grabbed her. When she lifted her lashes and looked up, both men were staring at her. She found she couldn't think clearly in the face of the stranger's calm gaze and Stanley's satisfied smile.

"I'll be back around six to see Grace." He winked at Bethany. "You tell her for me." Stanley wiped his bottom lip with the back of his hand and gave the stranger a mere snub of a glance before turning away.

Shaking with anger, Bethany watched Stanley brush back his thinning black hair as he jauntily walked away, whistling. She ached to run after him and tell him what a loathsome man she thought he was. She wanted to kick him where women weren't supposed to kick men.

Bethany had disliked Stanley from the first time they'd met a few months ago. He had come calling on her his first week in town, and she'd let him know right away that she wasn't interested. To her dismay, he'd turned his attentions to Grace. Bethany had never thought Stanley Edwards was the right suitor for her sister. Now she was sure of it. Grace didn't know the kind of man she had fallen in love with, and Bethany intended to see that she found out.

Her gaze drifted over to the man who had helped her. He was watching Stanley walk away, too. She took a deep breath, and her hand crept up her chest to fiddle with the cameo pinned on the stand-up collar of her white blouse.

"I'm sorry you had to witness that deplorable encounter."

The stranger faced her and Bethany looked into the most incredible eyes she'd ever seen. They were a rare shade of twilight blue.

"You have no need to apologize. I'd just stepped into the garden when I saw that man grab you. I didn't know what was going on, so I thought I'd stick around to see if you needed help." His smile turned to a pleasing grin. "Looks like you took care of him quite nicely."

His voice was smooth and cultured, inspiring trust. Bethany smiled. "Stanley was most definitely out of line. Had you not interfered by making your presence known, I'm sure he wouldn't have backed down so easily. I do believe a thank-you is necessary."

Bethany hated admitting that to this stranger. It wasn't like her to not have control of a situation, especially one as dreadful as being accosted by her sister's fiancé. She should have known weeks ago that Stanley's stealthy attentions toward her would lead to a shocking incident such as today's. He didn't like to take no for an answer.

"Who was he? Some unwanted beau?" he asked, the friendly smile remaining on his lips.

Bethany frowned, tightening her features. Mid-afternoon sunshine fell across her face, causing her to squint. "No, Mr.—"

"Burlington. Wilder Burlington."

Immediately recognizing the name, Bethany cringed. Mr. Burlington was the guest they had been expecting. The Georgia usually handled overnight travelers en route between Atlanta and Mobile. Seldom did anyone register for more than a couple of nights, but Mr. Burlington had requested a room for two months. She hoped her tussle with Stanley wouldn't make him change his mind and move to one of the other inns in town.

Favoring one leg, Mr. Burlington bent to pick up the basket of roses Bethany had dropped when Stanley grabbed her. For the first time, she saw that he had a cane in his hand and remembered that he'd walked with a limp. There was something wrong with his leg, and here she was standing idly by and letting him clean up her mess. That would never do. Gathering the folds of her wide-striped skirt, she knelt beside him on the ground and picked up a rose, carefully laying it in the basket.

Bethany glanced over at the man. Straight hair the color of dried goldenrod fell across his forehead. His face had firm, defined features, with an aristocratic nose, high cheekbones, and finely sculpted eyebrows. His lean body was casually clothed in summer wool pants, held up by suspenders, and a white cotton shirt. He kept one leg straight and out to the side while the other supported his weight.

"I didn't want him to kiss me," she said when she couldn't stay quiet any longer. She wasn't one to tell strangers her inner thoughts or feelings, but she didn't want this man to believe such things were a regular occurrence at The Georgia or that she was actually interested in Stanley Edwards. "I was appalled he'd do such a thing. Especially in public. Grace could have seen him."

Raising his head, he stared into her eyes. "Who is Grace?"

Bethany's pulse raced when he looked at her, and she was instantly drawn to him. His cheeks were gaunt, his complexion pale, but he was still a very handsome man. "My sister. Stanley is her fiancé." She reached for another rose.

His eyes narrowed. The attractive grin faded and a scowl formed on his full lips. "You were kissing your sister's fiancé?" he asked.

"No! He was kissing me," she argued.

"And you think that makes it all right?" he asked tersely.

"Of course not," she defended herself. "I told you I was appalled that he'd do such a thing."

"So that's the reason you were struggling. You didn't want your sister to catch you in her fiancé's arms."

Shocked by his words, Bethany grabbed the basket of roses and got to her feet. He was misunderstanding everything she had said. "No! You've got everything all wrong. I didn't want the kiss, and I surely didn't want Grace to see it," she said, trying to vindicate herself.

Her hand tightened around the handle of her basket as she watched Mr. Burlington stand, relying heavily on the cane. He was thin, too thin, she thought.

"She'll find out sooner or later that you love her fiancé. If I were you, I'd find someone else to bestow my affections upon," he said in a disapproving voice.

His last words renewed Bethany's anger. How could he even imagine she loved Stanley? What an

17

outrageous statement to make! Stanley was despicable, and the last man in the world she could love.

Exasperated, she said, "You're not understanding what I'm saying." Bethany was trying to remain calm even though he was prejudging her.

"On the contrary. I understand very well." He laid the last rose in the basket and turned away.

Watching the handsome stranger hobble back toward The Georgia, Bethany fumed. But as soon as he was out of sight, she found herself wondering what had happened to his leg. The bad limp indicated more than a minor injury.

Bethany entered the house a few moments later and called for Kate, the housekeeper.

"Yes, ma'am," Kate answered, walking into the room with a dusting rag held in her hand.

"Mr. Burlington has arrived. Have Seth cut some bedstraw and lengths from one of the ornamental vines to go with the arrangement of roses in Mr. Burlington's room. We don't want it to look too feminine."

Kate's big brown eyes held steadily on Bethany's face as she nodded.

"Also," Bethany continued, "when you take the flowers up, I want you to introduce yourself and ask him about his wash. Unless he's changed his mind, Mr. Burlington will be with us for a couple of months. I'm sure he'll want you to take care of his laundry for him."

"What's he doin' here for two months?" the dark-skinned woman asked.

Bethany pursed her lips and handed Kate the basket of roses. "I'm not privy to Mr. Burlington's affairs. And I suggest you make it a point not to be, either."

"Yes, ma'am. I won't mess with his things." She shook her head. "Not me. I'll keeps his clothes and room clean, and dat's all."

"Good. If he needs anything, let me know," Bethany told her, then crossed the large marble foyer. She didn't want to lose Mr. Burlington to one of the other inns in town. The extra money would go a long way to putting a new roof on the house next fall.

Bethany passed underneath the stairway and went to a pair of beautifully carved doors set against the far wall. She inserted a key in a small lock embedded in the dark wood casing and opened one of the doors. Stepping inside, she climbed the private stairs to the third floor.

The Georgia, once a grand plantation mansion, was now a restaurant and inn. The first floor housed the restaurant, two offices, and a sitting room, and the second had four rooms for overnight travelers, which could accommodate up to twelve guests. The third level was Bethany and Grace's home, a large apartment with two bedrooms, a sitting room, and a sewing room.

Bethany hurried into her bedroom, poured water into the basin, and splashed it on her burning face. Opening the first four buttons of her high-necked blouse, she let the cool water trickle past her throat and through the valley between her breasts. When she looked into the mirror, instead of seeing her own dark green eyes, she saw twilight blue ones staring back at her, haunting her, troubling her with their presence. Wilder Burlington was attractive, alarm-

19

ingly so. His voice had been like a soothing balm in the aftermath of Stanley's crude behavior.

Angrily, she splashed more water on her face. She didn't have time to think about that man or ponder what he must think of her. There were more important things to do. She had to warn Grace about Stanley. There was no way she could allow her sister to marry the kind of man who would approach another woman and force a kiss on her.

Dabbing a small towel to her cheeks, Bethany cringed at the thought of what she had to do. For more than six years, she had been Grace's mother as well as her sister. Grace had been twelve and Bethany barely eighteen when their parents were killed in a boating accident on Lake Eufaula. Bethany knew she'd spoiled Grace by trying to make up for the loss of their parents. Because she had always put Grace's feelings above her own, it wasn't going to be easy to tell her sister that the man she loved was unprincipled.

The cool water had soothed her heated cheeks, but inside she was still hot with anger as she rebuttoned her blouse and fastened her broach. She shuddered as Stanley's words came back to haunt her. "Don't pretend you don't want me to do this," he had said, grinding the words between his teeth.

Bethany shuddered again and washed her mouth out with rose-scented soap, preferring the taste of the cleanser to Stanley's lips.

Still mulling over her approach to telling Grace about Stanley, Bethany took the stairs back down to her office on the first floor. She had neglected her record-keeping and office work for the last couple of weeks while she'd helped Grace with her wedding plans. Grace had wanted her wedding to be the biggest Eufaula, Alabama had ever seen, even including the glorious, entertaining days before the war. Now Bethany was going to do everything in her power to keep the wedding from taking place.

Bethany sank into the leather chair behind her oak desk. She could no longer put off the chore of trying to find enough money to go around. For a long time after her parents' death, the house had continued to flourish. Lately, though, it seemed to be going steadily downhill. There were some major repairs that had to take place in order for the house to remain in good condition.

She looked around her office, hoping for insight to the problem and inspiration for the answer. The ceiling in the room was twelve feet high, painted a buff-white and finished off with eight inches of beautiful hand-cut cornices, as were most of The Georgia's fifteen rooms. The large French windows stretched floor to ceiling, and the royal blue antique satin drapes that covered each side were tied back with gold braided roping.

Over the years, Bethany had managed to keep up with the small things in the house that needed replacing, but there just wasn't enough money for a new roof, paint for the exterior, and new china for the kitchen. It took the entire weekly income from the restaurant to keep up the grounds and replace worn-out items in the kitchen and the other rooms. The inn seldom took in more than enough money for wages for The Georgia's five employees. She could meet the weekly budget needs, but there never seemed to be enough left over to put aside for large repairs and general upkeep.

Looking at the ledger book, Bethany slowly shook her head. How was she going to come up with a solution to her problem? Margaret, her trusted friend and only office help, had advised her to raise the rates at the inn and restaurant, but she couldn't do that and remain in competition with the other two inns in town.

Margaret had also suggested she take out a loan with the bank and put her half of the house up as collateral. If she did that, Bethany was afraid she wouldn't be able to pay the money back and the bank would soon own The Georgia. She needed to make a decision soon, but she didn't consider either one of her options an answer she could easily live with.

The Hayward Mill, which was located across the Chattahoochee River ten miles away, was in the same condition. What little profit was made from the cloth they produced and sold went back into keeping the old machinery running. Bethany had considered closing the mill and selling the land, because the cloth manufactured in the thriving factories of the East was of a much better quality, but she knew the men needed the jobs to feed their families. It looked as if she might lose no matter how hard she was trying to win.

Her only hope, short of raising the rates for a night's stay at the inn, was a dry, hot summer. If the weather would cooperate with high temperatures, more families would travel south to the shore for a holiday. The extra money from Mr. Burlington's stay and a good summer season would give her enough money for the new roof. The other things would have to wait.

Bethany was still working on the books when Grace burst into the room, smiling. "Bethany, look at this exquisite gown I just bought for my honeymoon!" Her bright green eyes sparkled with excitement as she tore the top off a box and pulled the beautiful garment free.

Taking the evening dress from Grace's hands, Bethany looked at it closely. It was a lavender chiffon one-piece. The bodice and skirt had been lined with silk. Ornate roses were embroidered across the stand-up collar and cuffs. Bethany knew immediately the dress was very expensive. She tensed.

"Grace, how did you pay for this dress?" Bethany asked.

"Oh, I had Mrs. Stevens put it on our account."

"We don't have an account with her. Grace, we don't have the money to buy ready-made dresses. I've tried to explain to you—"

"Oh, Bethany, you know I need this dress. Mrs. Stevens agreed you could pay her a little each month." Grace playfully snatched the dress from Bethany. "Besides, with summer coming, we'll have more guests staying at the inn and that means more money."

Even though Bethany could make a dress just as beautiful, an hour ago she would have given in and let Grace keep the dress. But not now. Once she told her about Stanley, there wouldn't be a wedding or a honeymoon.

"Grace, I want to tell you something." Bethany paused, wishing she didn't have to do this, wondering if she had the strength to break her sister's heart.

"Don't be so serious, Bethany. I know you said we need a new roof on the house, but we'll have enough money for both. You can manage it." Sparkles and shimmers danced in Grace's eyes. "I have an idea. Why don't you come to St. Louis with us? You haven't left this place since Mama and Papa died. When they were alive, we always took a few days off each year and went down to the coast, but you never do."

Bethany cleared her throat. "Don't be ridiculous. Honeymoons are for two."

Laughing, Grace threw her arms around Bethany. "I just want you to have some fun."

Bethany embraced her sister tightly for a moment. Even as she cherished the bond that kept the two of them so close, she winced. Grace was too immature to see for herself what kind of man she was planning to marry.

"I have fun," Bethany finally said, knowing they were off the main subject. "You know how much I enjoy working in the rose garden."

"Notice you said *working* in the garden, not playing." Grace's eyes turned serious. "Maybe we should have sold this house when John Martin wanted to marry you and move us to California."

The memory of the heated argument she'd had with John Martin Sommers darted through Bethany's mind. He'd been furious because she had chosen The Georgia over him. She had never regretted her decision not to marry him, although she sometimes wished she had someone to confide in, someone to hold her close and kiss her and make ripples of delight prickle her skin.

She really didn't want to talk about this with Grace, so she said, "You know that John Martin and I had some differences we couldn't work out. We would have gotten married if he had agreed to live here at The Georgia."

Grace sighed and folded the dress. "Don't you think this will keep Stanley from looking at all the other pretty women in St. Louis?" she asked soberly as she replaced the gown in the box.

Bethany felt a tug at her heart when she saw how much her sister wanted to be the only woman in Stanley's life. As much as she hated to do it, this was the time to tell Grace that that would never happen. She didn't want to see the hurt and pain that would appear in her sister's eyes when she told her that just this very afternoon Stanley had cornered her and kissed her. But it had to be done.

Wrapping her arm around Grace's shoulder, Bethany spoke softly and said, "Grace, you just turned eighteen last week. You—"

"I don't want to hear it, Bethany." Grace pulled away, her mood changing abruptly. "You still can't believe that I'm all grown up now. I'm not a child anymore."

"Let me finish what I'm trying to say."

Grace's lips formed a pout, and she folded her arms across her chest. "No. You're going to tell me that Stanley is well past thirty and too old for me. I won't listen to that again. I'm going to marry him."

"That's not what I was going to say. Today while you were out—"

"I don't want to hear it, Bethany! I'm going to

marry Stanley. I don't want to end up an old maid like you!"

The sharp retort hit Bethany hard but she didn't flinch. In anger, Grace often said things she knew would hurt. Bethany always forgave her.

Brushing aside the truth of Grace's remark, Bethany said, "Of course you don't. Sit down. I want to tell you something."

"I don't have time. Stanley's coming over at six. We're joining the Mixons for dinner."

"Wait, Grace. We need to talk about this now."

"Forever the mother, Bethany. I don't need to sit down and talk, and I don't need a sister telling me what to do anymore. Stanley said I'm old enough to make my own decisions, and from now on I intend to."

Bethany should have known that Stanley was behind this rebellion. He was trying his best to turn Grace against her. "How am I supposed to treat you? You were still a child when Mama and Papa died. I—"

"That was six years ago! I'm a grown woman now," Grace interrupted fiercely. "I know what I'm doing."

"Not if you're planning on marrying *that* man," Bethany said angrily.

"You can't stop me!" Grace whipped up the dress box and ran out the door.

Sighing heavily, Bethany returned to her desk and sat down. Frustration knotted her stomach and a worry line creased her brow. Grace didn't want to hear anything bad about Stanley. What was she to do? She couldn't let her sister marry that man.

Closing her eyes, she felt the fatigue that had been building in her body for the last month. Bethany hadn't slept well a single night since Grace had excitedly broken the news of her pending marriage. And her work was suffering, too. With a sigh, she laid her head on her desk, thinking she'd rest for a moment, but she couldn't. The wedding had to be stopped. Grace had to be told. Now, all she had to do was come up with a way to do it. She'd wait up for Grace tonight. When Stanley brought her home, she'd tell her about today's incident.

"Excuse me, Miss Hayward."

Bethany's head popped up and her eyes met Wilder Burlington's. He stood in the doorway, staring at her. Her hand flew to rub the back of her stiff neck as she rose from her chair. "Yes, may I help you?" she asked, wondering if the stress she was feeling showed on her face.

"Are you all right?" he asked. He walked into the room, his presence commanding even though he limped.

"Yes," she assured him in a level voice, wishing her pulse would behave. "I'm really quite fine."

His eyes continued to question her. She looked down at her desk to avoid them. Catching sight of the balance sheet, she wondered how she could lie so easily. She wasn't fine! She was close to losing control of The Georgia, the mill—and her sister was planning to marry a womanizer.

"You don't look well." His intense blue eyes allowed her no escape.

"I'm a little tired." Was he happy now that she had admitted that? She didn't owe him an explanation

27

about anything.

"When I met you this morning, I didn't know you were the owner of this inn."

"Yes. Along with my sister, Grace," she said, suddenly worried he might have decided to go elsewhere after all.

Wilder leaned heavily against the velvet-covered wing chair and hooked his cane over his forearm. "According to the . . . ah . . . lady in the front office, I need your permission in order to change rooms. I'd like a larger one, and since I've registered for two months, I would think such a small request could be accommodated."

Bethany's eyes widened as she breathed a sigh of relief that he wasn't planning to go to another inn. "Well, of course you can have a larger room. It's unusual for anyone to register here for more than a couple of nights."

"I want complete quiet and rest."

Thinking of all the things she could accomplish with the extra income, she answered, "I'm sure you'll find that here."

"Really?" he questioned as he arched one golden-brown eyebrow, challenging her. "I'm beginning to wonder, after the little affair I witnessed this morning."

"Don't say that!" She moved swiftly from behind the desk. Her long skirts swirled around her ankles as she stopped in front of him. "How many times do I have to tell you I wanted no part of that kiss?" Why was it so important to her that this man believe her? He had for a while—until he found out that Stanley was Grace's fiancé. He wasn't giving her a chance.

"Oh, good, he found you," a woman called.

Bethany's gaze darted to the doorway where Margaret Hodge stood, her large frame almost filling the space. For twenty of its twenty-two public years, Margaret had been a part of The Georgia. After her parents' death, Bethany took over the management of the place, but she could have never kept it going without Margaret's help.

"Yes, he did. And it will be all right for Mr. Burlington to have a larger room." She looked directly at him. "The east wing is usually reserved for families of four or more, but because of your length of stay, we'll make an exception."

"Thank you," he said, with no real appreciation in his voice.

It bothered Bethany that when he looked at her, she had the feeling she was doing something wrong. Wait! He *did* think she was doing something wrong. He thought she was in love with her sister's fiancé. What a pious man he was. Even if she *was* leading Stanley on, who was he to judge her actions?

Lifting her chin proudly, Bethany said, "Show Mr. Burlington to room 202, Margaret. I think he would prefer the green room over the rose."

"If you'll come with me, Mr. Burlington, I'll get the key so you can settle in right away." The buxom gray-haired woman looked back at Bethany. "Kate has already gone home. The room he's in now won't be cleaned until tomorrow."

Her words sounded like a complaint, but Bethany knew it was just Margaret's way of speaking.

"Mr. Burlington was the only one registered for today, but I'll remember that should we have any unexpected guests show up," Bethany assured her.

With Margaret gone, Bethany turned back to Mr. Burlington, who still leaned against the chair. "Was there anything else?" she asked in an icy tone, still upset that he presumed to judge her and think she was in love with Stanley.

"Yes. Since I'm going to be here for a while, I assume we'll see each other every day. I want to dispense with the formality of Mr. Burlington and Miss Hayward and use our Christian names."

"I don't think that would be appropriate," she said stiffly, thinking he was deliberately trying to provoke or embarrass her.

He took a step toward her, his gaze staying on her face. "I'm afraid I have to insist, even though we haven't been properly introduced. I don't want to spend the next two months calling you Miss Hayward."

She didn't know when it happened, but her breathing had increased. "All right," she said, thinking it better to humor him than to oppose him. "If you wish, Wilder."

Using his cane, he moved closer to her, inching along carefully, as if he were approaching something dangerous. "Now tell me your name. I already know your sister's name is Grace."

Bethany's face suddenly grew hot, and a blush tinted her burning cheeks. She wanted to back away from him and move closer at the same time. She didn't understand her mixed feelings for this man.

"Bethany." She blinked rapidly. Why was she breathless? "My name's Bethany." He was standing too close to her, taking in every detail of her face as if he meant to memorize it. She scolded herself for remaining there and letting him do it.

"Bethany and Grace. Such lovely names for two beautiful sisters." His voice was soft.

Her heart hammered repeatedly in her chest. "Have you seen Grace?" she asked.

He nodded. "A short while ago. She almost ran over me in the foyer."

Fear gripped Bethany's throat, her stomach muscles tightened, and her head was spinning. If Grace found out about that kiss from anyone else, it would destroy her. "You—you didn't tell her about—"

"About your secret affair with her fiancé?" He shook his head. "No, I didn't tell her. That's for you to take care of."

"It's not an affair!" Bethany argued when she found her voice. "I was an unwilling recipient of that kiss. I don't want Stanley Edwards and I don't want Grace to marry him. I wish you'd believe me."

His gaze continued to travel languidly over her face. "You do sound convincing." With those words, he turned around and limped out of her office.

Chapter Two

Later that evening, Bethany went outside for her usual stroll in the garden before dinner. As she walked among the rose bushes with their beautiful blooms, Wilder Burlington entered her thoughts. It wasn't like her to think twice about a man. Especially one who could be so stubbornly arrogant. If she hadn't seen the likable side of him before he found out who Stanley was, she wouldn't be giving him a second thought.

For a while after John Martin had left, she had missed his humor and charm. She often thought of his warm kisses and caresses. Even now, she could bring to mind the tingle and excitement his touch had evoked. What was she doing wondering if Wilder's lips would give her the same pleasure? Such thoughts were ridiculous. She didn't even like the man. He was too presumptuous, too condemning, and too quick to believe his own interpretation of the scene he'd witnessed.

Without realizing it, Wilder had stirred feelings in

her reminiscent of those John Martin Sommers had aroused four years ago. Instead of foolish dreams of love and romance, she should be thinking of how she was going to save her sister from Stanley's clutches, and of how she could avoid taking a mortgage out on The Georgia or the mill.

She stopped and looked out over the gardens. May in southeast Alabama was alive with color. All the flowers and shrubs were in full bloom. The azaleas with their soft shades of pink and the tulips and lilies with their deep, dramatic colors were lovely. But the roses were Bethany's pride and joy. She loved to look at them when early morning dew touched their velvety petals and made them sparkle like thousands of diamonds. Nothing could bring a smile to Bethany's face faster than a bouquet of roses. The dining room might need china or the linens might be wearing thin, but one thing was certain: The rose garden was never without whatever it needed.

Everyone in Eufaula spoke highly of The Georgia's grounds. The town itself was rich in history, starting when the Creek Indians first cultivated the fertile lands on each side of the Chattahoochee River. Now Lake Eufaula was being touted as the fishing capital of the state, and that in itself brought many guests to The Georgia during the summer.

Leaving the gardens, Bethany walked up the steps to the large back porch. As she turned to sit down on the green velvet-cushioned rocker, she saw Wilder at the other end of the porch, lounging on a chair with his book facedown on his chest, his eyes closed.

Confident he was asleep, she studied him at

leisure. She had already noticed he was thin and pale, with the look of someone who had been seriously ill.

Bethany had to put a stop to her rambling thoughts about Wilder Burlington. But a moment later, she found herself wondering just what kind of name that was, anyway. He was a Yankee. That didn't bother her, although most of the townspeople didn't regard anyone from the North very highly. The war was still too fresh in their minds almost thirty years later.

Annoyed he'd crept back into her thoughts, she rubbed the back of her neck. There were more pressing things to think about than a man who would only spend several weeks in the comfort of The Georgia, then return to his own life. She had to tell Grace about Stanley, and she had to come up with the right words. Words that wouldn't alienate her sister and send her running back into the arms of a man who could never make her happy.

"Are you having fun staring at me?"

Shocked that she'd been caught, Bethany cleared her throat and said, "I wasn't staring," knowing good and well she was lying.

"Well, what do you call it in the South when you take five minutes to look over a man?"

Bethany gasped. "I—I was—" She couldn't think of a quick reply to exonerate herself.

"Oh," he said, rising from his chair. "The same thing we call it. Staring."

Grinning, Wilder closed the book and walked over to her. Even with the bad limp, he walked with a proud air, swaying his shoulders just enough to be attractive. His light sandy-brown hair had been combed away from his forehead and lay neatly to one side.

After having a moment to collect her thoughts, Bethany said, "I was just noticing that you look as if you've been ill. That you walk with a limp."

"Ah . . . my limp. How could you miss it? And to say that I've been ill is putting it mildly."

She heard a trace of bitterness in his voice. Her interest in him wasn't idle curiosity. He'd been on her mind too much, and he would be at The Georgia too long for her to treat him as an ordinary guest. "Do—did you have a sickness?" she asked somewhat apprehensively.

"Three months ago in Homestead, Pennsylvania, I was attacked by five men and left for dead." His voice grew soft. His eyes glistened and a faraway gaze crept into their depths. "I lived through the beating, the exposure, the broken bones and high fevers."

Bethany had the feeling he was seeing the incident all over again, reliving the terror, the helplessness of not having control.

"That must have been horrible for you," she said with empathy.

"It was, and unfortunately I'm reminded of it every day. I'm trying to learn to live with the fact I may always limp." He gently slapped the leg he always favored.

She wanted to tell him the limp in no way detracted from his masculinity. He was too attractive, too appealing. She wanted to cradle him in her arms and soothe the pain out of his eyes.

"Why did you choose The Georgia as the place to

recuperate?" she asked.

"Actually, my brother made the arrangements. I think one of his friends had stayed here and suggested it." Wilder moved closer. "Tell me why a house that's located in Alabama is named The Georgia?"

Bethany moistened her lips. "The house and grounds cover about four acres of the fifty-acre estate. Most of the land is wooded, except for a small pond. Ten of the remaining forty-six acres are across the Chattahoochee River in Georgia, where we have a textile mill. After the war, the mill was useless for a time and our livelihood was in jeopardy. My parents opened the house to boarding. Within a couple of years, it had evolved into a restaurant and inn. The house needed a name, so my parents decided to honor the land in Georgia by giving the house its name."

"Is the mill operational now?"

She nodded. When he looked at her with those arresting blue eyes, Bethany was tempted to break the control she held on her senses. He reached down for her hand, and she let him help her out of the chair and pull her close. He caressed her cheek with the back of his fingers, then raked his thumb carelessly across her lips.

"You're very beautiful, Bethany." His voice was tender, husky.

"You are very handsome," she admitted, knowing she should be appalled by such an admission, by the feelings he was creating in her. But how could she resist his eyes, his touch, his words? They held her spellbound. He was only going to be at The Georgia a couple of months. She couldn't afford to let her feelings for him go any farther than they were at this moment. If she didn't put a stop to this now, when Wilder left The Georgia, he'd take her heart with him.

"You see, Bethany, when you come close to dying, you realize how precious life is. Things that were important once suddenly seem trivial. The daring and reckless side of life loses its thrill and appeal."

Bethany had never done a reckless thing in her life. "Are you dangerous?" she asked.

"You be the judge," he whispered, and lowered his head toward her face.

With the tip of his tongue, he outlined her lips. She stood perfectly still as waves of sensations rippled through her. He smelled of shaving soap. His breath was warm and pleasant against her skin. She heard longing in his voice when he whispered her name.

Bethany wasn't sure she was still breathing when he raised his head and looked into her eyes. She swallowed, trying to catch her breath, trying to come up with a good reason for letting this man touch her in such a manner. Aghast at her behavior, she realized no excuse was acceptable. She'd allowed his forward attentions, and if he thought her a loose woman, she'd have no defense.

"I believe you are dangerous," she said, stepping away from him. "Excuse me, I have something to attend to inside the house." She turned and hurried away, but not before she heard a smothered chuckle coming from deep in his chest.

After Bethany disappeared into the house, Wilder returned to his chair and sat back down. Chuckling to himself, he opened the collection of Poe's short stories, then just as quickly closed the book. He must be crazy pulling a stunt like that. What had possessed him to taste her lips? He didn't even know her. She could have slapped him as promptly as she had the man in the garden. *But she didn't,* his inner voice told him.

He ran the pads of his fingers over his lips as he thought about her. She was a little taller than the average woman, slender and graceful in her movements. Her green eyes sparkled when she was angry with him. He liked that. Her white blouse and black-striped skirt were more conservative than he was used to seeing women wear, but somehow that classic look made her all the more appealing.

Maybe it was simply that it had been a long time since he'd been with a woman. Wilder shook his head. That could account for him being so forward, but not for Bethany being so desirable. He laid his head back and closed his eyes. His visit to the deep South was shaping up to be quite interesting.

It was close to nine o'clock, and Bethany paced back and forth across the spacious living room on the third floor, clasping her hands together, then releasing them again. Grace would be home any minute now. Bethany had spent the last two hours practicing how to broach the subject of Stanley to her sister, and she was still nervous. The red robe she'd tied securely around her waist showed the feminine figure that was usually hidden behind matronly clothing. Her long honey-blond hair fell thick and straight over her shoulders and down her back.

At last she heard the door open. Her chest

tightened and her throat felt parched. Telling Grace about Stanley wasn't going to be easy. Oh no! she cried to herself, when she heard voices. Stanley was coming in with Grace.

"Bethany, I'm glad you're still up," Grace said, hurrying into the room. "Stanley and I have something we want to discuss with you."

Bethany smiled at Grace, then, with reluctance, she turned her head to acknowledge Stanley. His lascivious eyes roamed over and down her body until she felt undressed beneath his leering stare. She felt a moment of victory when she noticed that his bottom lip was swollen from the bite she'd given him. Pulling her robe together at the base of her throat, she fixed him with an icy look before turning back to Grace.

"You sound excited about something. What's going on?" She joined Grace on the sofa, leaving Stanley to sit on the crewel-stitched wing chair.

"We were talking about the wedding and where we're going to live after our honeymoon." Grace turned to Stanley for support. He nodded his head. "Of course, Stanley had planned on our living in his apartment on Ashton Street, but it's so small there's hardly room to turn around." She looked at him once more. He flashed her a dazzling smile, and she hurried on. "So I decided we would live here at The Georgia with you." Her face beamed with happiness.

Bethany sat silently as she struggled to absorb this latest blow, trying to force a smile that wouldn't come. Looking quickly at Stanley, the smirk that twisted his lips confirmed her suspicion he had engineered this whole thing. She stiffened her resolve. Bethany wasn't going to be fooled by his cunning ways or get caught in the trap he was laying. He'd drawn the lines of battle, and she was prepared to fight him.

"I don't know what to say. This is such a surprise." Feigning confusion, Bethany stalled for time. Why did he have to get Grace so excited about things like this? But then, Stanley was smart.

Bethany grew hot with anger. She felt his eyes on her, daring her to tell Grace no. He had set this up so she would have to give in or else look bad in her sister's eyes.

"Tell me you'd love for us to live here." Grace grabbed Bethany's hands and squeezed them tight. Her eyes sparkled with joy.

Dozens of conflicting thoughts tumbled through Bethany's mind as she looked at Grace's innocent face. What was she going to do?

Half of the house belonged to Grace, and she would never tell her sister that she couldn't live there. But Stanley was another matter. Bethany couldn't tolerate having him in the house overnight, let alone live there. Why couldn't Grace have fallen in love with a decent man?

Choosing each word with care, Bethany began, slowly and gently. "Grace. The Georgia is your home and always will be. But we can't afford for you and Stanley to take one of the rooms we rent, and that would only leave your bedroom here on the third floor. There'd be no privacy here for you. Newlyweds need to be alone, so they can get to know each other." She paused to take a deep breath, swallowing the anger she felt toward Stanley for putting her in this situation. "We can discuss this more later. We have two months before the wedding."

Grace's eyes lost their joyful sheen, her smile faded. "I guess you're right. We wouldn't have much privacy living here with you."

"Half of this house belongs to you, Grace. She can't keep us from living here." Stanley's demanding reminder interrupted the silence that had fallen.

Measured contempt laced Stanley's voice, and Bethany felt a raw tension dominate the air between them. When she looked at him, Bethany saw in his dark eyes just how serious he was and she mentally braced herself. This unscrupulous man was going to fight her every inch of the way.

"Maybe she's right," Grace offered as she let go of Bethany's hands and turned to Stanley. "I've lived in this house all my life. I would like to live somewhere different for a change. And it would be more romantic if we were living by ourselves." Her last words were spoken softly and strictly for her fiancé's benefit.

"We'll talk about it later," Stanley cooed as he rose and took her hand. "It's late. Walk with me to the front door so you can lock up." Then he turned and with cold eyes said, "Good night, Bethany."

When at last the door closed behind the two, Bethany let her shoulders sag, dropping the controlled veneer she had worn. For several minutes she agonized over her decision to tell Grace the truth. She had waited all day. It couldn't be put off any longer.

Bethany knew by the look on Grace's face when she returned that Stanley had given her a hard time about where they would live. She hated to shatter her

42

sister's dreams, but there was no other way. She shored up her courage and said, "Before you go to bed, I'd like to talk with you about something."

"If it's about the wedding, we'll do it tomorrow, Bethany. I'm tired," Grace whined, and started for her bedroom.

"I'm sorry, Grace. This can't wait. Come sit down." Bethany took a seat on the rose-colored settee, holding her hands together tightly. Her mouth felt as if it had been wiped dry with cotton. She had to remain calm and keep control of the conversation.

Grace plopped on the small sofa beside her, huffing to show her disapproval.

"I have something to tell you. It's not easy to say, so . . . I'll just tell you straight. Stanley came to The Georgia today while you were out shopping and—and he grabbed me and kissed me." The last words were rushed past trembling lips.

"Bethany!" Grace exclaimed, jumping off the sofa. She stared down at her sister, an incredulous expression on her face. "What are you saying? What are you trying to do?"

"I'm trying to tell you that Stanley doesn't love you." Bethany rose and met Grace's stare. "He only wants to marry you to get his hands on The Georgia and the mill."

"You're lying!" Grace's eyes widened with horror. "How dare you say such things! Just because no man wants to marry you, you don't want me to have a husband, either."

"That's not true," Bethany denied the accusation. "Of course I want you to marry. You had several

43

beaus interested in you before Stanley started calling on you. I remember—"

"Wait a minute. Stanley came calling on you first, then dropped you when he met me. That's it!" Her eyes widened. "You're jealous. If you can't have him, you don't want me to have him, either."

"That's an unconscionable remark. I don't want Stanley." Bethany couldn't believe the things she was hearing. "I only want you to be happy, and I know Stanley can't do that."

"Don't lie, Bethany. Stanley's right. You'd do anything to keep us from getting married and living here. Well, we're not going to let you stop us!"

Tearfully, Grace ran from the room, and Bethany sank onto the sofa, wishing she had said more, said it differently, and wondering what to do next.

Chapter Three

"Well, if it isn't the sweet lady of the manor sitting on her throne," Stanley remarked as he strode into Bethany's office the next day.

Bethany pushed aside the stack of papers she was working on and turned cold eyes upon him. "I want you to leave. You're not welcome here," she said. After her heated argument with Grace the previous night, she wasn't in any mood to deal with him. She was afraid she'd attack him.

"I've got work to do." He chuckled lightly and ran a hand over his carefully styled hair. "I need to convince you to stop giving your little sister advice. You're confusing her."

"I don't have anything to say to you, Stanley. Please leave." Bethany wanted to put an end to the conversation before it started.

"Not this time." He placed both hands on her desk and leaned forward, bringing his face close to hers. "You and I have a lot of things to talk about." His voice was low and calculating.

Pushing her chair back from her desk, Bethany rose to get away from him. He smelled of a strong, offensively spicy cologne. "Go away. You're not wanted or needed around here."

He shook his head. "Not true. You and Grace need a man around this house. It's not safe for you here alone every night, taking in strangers the way you do."

"One loud scream would bring Seth running from the carriage house. Besides, the only person we're not safe from is you. We were quite happy before you came into our lives and we'll be happy when you leave. Now, get out of here." She kept her voice level even though she was furious with him.

"Seth's too old to scare anyone. But you're right about one thing, sweet Bethany. You'll never be safe from me. You were my first choice . . . but Grace will do for now."

His dark eyes bored into her, and it was impossible not to get his meaning. Being subtle was not Stanley Edwards's strong point.

Stanley moved closer to her. Bethany wanted to run, but she didn't want to give him the pleasure of knowing he frightened her. This was one unpleasant scene she couldn't avoid.

"Half of The Georgia belongs to Grace, and we're going to live here after we're married. It may take another week or two to bring her around to my way of thinking, but she'll agree. She always does." He laughed, and Bethany's skin pebbled with fear. "And you won't be able to do one thing about it. This is a big place. You and Grace need me to help you manage everything around here. I rather fancy myself owning the mill and a house this grand. I might even give myself a title." He took a deep breath, puffing out his chest.

Stanley had just confirmed her worst fear. He was only interested in becoming the owner of The Georgia and didn't really care about Grace. Bethany had hoped that even if he did like to flirt with other women, he might have one redeeming quality . . . truly loving her sister. Now she knew he didn't.

"You're a repulsive man. I've suspected for some time that all you wanted was to get your hands on this house and the mill. Well, it's not going to happen. I've upset your little plan by telling Grace what kind of man you really are. She knows what happened yesterday and it's only a matter of time until she breaks the engagement."

Bethany spoke with a confidence she didn't really feel. She wasn't so sure she could make Grace believe her, but she couldn't let Stanley know that.

Stanley advanced on her, and she stepped backward until he pinned her against the window. "Do you really think Grace will believe anything you say against me? She loves me."

Every nerve in Bethany's body prickled. He was so close his hot breath fanned her face. She wouldn't give him the pleasure of shrinking away from him again. That would only please him. She was not going to let him bully her—or marry her sister.

"Grace will listen to me," she said with budding confidence. "She's loved me a lot longer than she has you. I've been her mother as well as sister for the past six years. She has complete faith in me."

"The guardian angel swooping down to rescue the

little girl. Ah, that's you all right, my sweet Bethany. An angel sent from heaven. That 'don't-touch-me look' you always flash at me drives me crazy and makes me want to kiss you.''

As the last words left his mouth, he grabbed her upper arms and yanked her against his chest. His lips found hers and ground them against her teeth. Bethany struggled against his strength, feeling defiled by his touch. She heard a small cry of alarm and thought it her own, until Stanley released her and, out of the corner of her eye, she saw Grace standing in the doorway staring at them. Disbelief was written in her sister's bright green eyes. Her young face was drained of color and tears rolled down her pale cheeks.

"Grace!" both Stanley and Bethany exclaimed at the same time with equal surprise, and they started toward her.

"Don't come near me!" she screamed.

Had she let this happen? Bethany's heart felt as if it were breaking in two. She berated herself as she stared at her sister.

"Grace, honey, this is all Bethany's doing," Stanley said in a smooth tone, inching his way closer.

"Grace, don't listen to him," Bethany cried in desperation. Fear knotted in her stomach. The air left her lungs, and her throat tightened.

"Stay away from me!" Grace screamed. They both stopped. Grace sniffled, her tear-filled eyes darting from Stanley to Bethany. "How long has this been going on behind my back?" Her voice trembled. "How could you do this to me?"

"You don't understand. I can explain what happened," Bethany began.

"I know what happened. I saw it. You've ruined my whole life!"

"No, Grace, listen to me. I tried to explain this to you last night."

"I saw you kissing Stanley. That's all I need to know." Her gaze flew to him. He reached out to grab her but she pushed him, causing him to stumble backward. "I don't want to ever see either of you again," she shouted as she ran from the room.

"Why didn't you stop her?" Stanley demanded from behind Bethany. "This is all your fault."

Bethany faced him. Stay calm, she told herself. Remember, you're dealing with an unscrupulous man and a show of outrage will only delight him. Tell him what you think of him, but keep your voice low. "Get out of here and don't come back," she said coldly. "You're reprehensible, without a shred of decency. If you set foot on my property again, I'll have Sheriff Beale arrest you."

Stanley chuckled, his upper lip curling upwards. "Don't be so dramatic, Bethany. This is just a temporary setback. I'll go find your little sister and bring her back safely. We've got a wedding to plan."

Her skin burned with tension. "Leave my sister alone," she warned him.

A carefree chuckle rang from his mouth, "You don't frighten me, sweetie." He smirked. "Grace will be back in my arms as soon as I explain how you've been chasing me, begging me to leave her and marry you." He ran his tongue over his lips, then turned and strode out of the office.

Hot tears gathered in Bethany's eyes. Her lips

49

trembled, and she couldn't think straight, wondering what she was going to do.

She clenched her hands into fists. "I'll never let you win, Stanley Edwards," she whispered into the quietness of the room. "I'll find Grace before you do and make her believe me," she vowed.

He was slow and it wasn't easy, but Wilder made it up the twelve steps to the second-floor landing. Panting for breath, he denied the pain in his muscles and bones, thinking himself a fool for pushing so hard to gain full use of his leg. He leaned heavily against the rail and rested.

Sometimes he wondered why he put himself through it. So what if he limped the rest of his life. But even as the thought crossed his mind, he became more determined to force a complete recovery. He had defied the doctors' predictions by walking, and now he would show them he could walk without a limp.

Wilder tried to tell himself that wanting to walk straight again was a matter of pride, but in a dark corner of his mind he knew he'd never have the respect of his men at the steel mill if he wasn't whole. He'd been in management too long not to know how the system worked.

A small sound of scraping wood caught Wilder's attention and he glanced down the hallway. The door to his room was ajar. Wilder tensed. He remembered locking it. The fear that someone from the Steel Workers Union had found him rushed through his mind. Quickly, he looked around for a weapon. A vase of flowers and a brass cherub sat on a table at the top of the stairs. He picked up the cherub, feeling the weight of the brass in his hand, wondering if he was strong enough for a fight if there was more than one man inside.

His fingers gripped the cold statue, turning his knuckles white. The pain in his leg intensified and his breath grew short as he remembered the beating three months ago. Wilder rubbed his eyes and shook his head. "Not this time, you bastards," he whispered to himself. "You either kill me or be killed."

He moved to the wall and skimmed his way down the dimly lit corridor toward his room. Sweat popped out on his forehead, and he strained to hear something other than his own breathing.

When he reached the door, he listened but heard nothing. Could one of the maids have been in and left his door open? Still cautious, he peered around the doorway. In the shadowed gaslight, he saw Grace Hayward standing in front of his bureau, her hand digging into the pocket of the pants he'd shed earlier in the day.

Wilder blinked rapidly, for a moment unsure of what to think. He'd prepared himself for a fight. His breathing slowed as he watched Grace. When she found nothing in his pants, she opened the top drawer of the bureau and pushed aside his clothing. Her hand darted into the depth of the drawer and brought out his leather pouch. With shaking fingers, she pulled a wad of folded bills from the small sack and stuffed them down the front of her dress.

Furious, Wilder jerked the door wide and stepped inside, closing it firmly behind him. Grace gasped and flattened herself against the far wall.

"Oh! Mr. Burlington. You startled me. I—I—"

"You what?" He continued to advance on her, the pain in his leg making him mean.

"I—I was just putting your clothes away for you."

"I don't think so."

Her wild gaze traveled to the brass cupid held tightly in his hand, and Wilder saw terror in her expression. Softening, he threw the statue onto the bed. Still enraged that she'd steal from him, he reached down the front of her dress, pulling out the money.

"Is this how you and your sister make extra money?" he demanded. "Stealing from guests?"

"No! Of course not." She shook her head furiously. "I was going to leave you this in place of the money."

She fumbled in her pocket and brought out a wrinkled piece of paper. Her voice trembled with fear as she said, "It—it says that the bearer is owner to my half of this house. I—I don't have time to sell it properly."

In the dim light, Wilder looked over the paper. The note was handwritten, and it gave the bearer title to her half of The Georgia Restaurant and Inn just as she'd said. His anger cooled and he looked back into her eyes.

"Why?" he asked.

"I had to," she said desperately. "I must get away from this place and I have no money. I was going to take some from the safe and leave this for Bethany. But there isn't any money in the safe. I don't even know if we have any. I only know I have to be on the train that leaves at three o'clock this afternoon." She paused and moistened her lips. "If that's not enough, I'll do anything you ask if you'll let me have that money."

Wilder had a feeling Grace didn't know what she was getting into by making a statement like that to a stranger. He wasn't the least tempted by what the little witch was offering. Even if his leg wasn't killing him with pain, he wouldn't be interested in Grace. It was her sister who sent his blood racing with just the mere thought of her.

"I'll do anything," Grace said again, her bottom lip trembling.

All Wilder wanted to do was get rid of Grace as fast as he could and take his medication. But she appeared to be upset enough to go to someone else for the money, if he didn't scare the hell out of her by showing how dangerous her remark could be.

"Anything?" He let his fingers glide down her soft cheek, down her neck, stopping just above her breasts. Grace gasped but didn't say a word.

Wilder looked at her face. Her eyes were tightly shut and her teeth dug into her bottom lip. He moved his hand a little lower, thinking she would slap it away. But she didn't move. He cupped her breast and squeezed softly. Grace remained rigid.

"Do you like what I'm doing?" he finally asked, his voice rough. He was angry with her for letting him fondle her.

Grace shook her head but didn't open her eyes or voice a protest.

"Then why in the hell are you letting me do it? Damn!" he swore, and stepped away from her.

"Open your eyes. I'm not going to hurt you."

She opened her eyes and stared at him. "Is that all you want to do?" she whispered fearfully.

Wilder grimaced. "I didn't want to do that much." He sighed, bending down to rub the aching muscle in his leg. "Grace, you could get into a lot of trouble telling a stranger you'll do anything for money. Don't you know if you tell a man he can do anything, chances are he will?"

She took a step toward him. "I don't care. I'll do what I have to in order to get away today!"

He believed her. Grace was obviously too immature to know what she was saying, and the next man she propositioned might take her up on it. "Why do you want to leave?" he asked.

Her breath was choppy as she said, "B—Bethany has s—stolen my fiancé. I can't bear to s—stay here and watch them together."

Wilder felt a stab of jealousy that quickly turned to anger. Bethany had been so convincing with her appeals of innocence that he'd almost believed her. He'd *wanted* to believe she wasn't involved with Stanley. Damn. He'd tried to tell her that Grace would find out. He knew better than anyone that you shouldn't get involved with someone who's already spoken for.

"You can have the money. I don't want your house."

"No, please take it," Grace said. "I don't want it, either. Bethany runs The Georgia. It's really hers. I insist you take it for the money." She shoved the document back into his hands.

Wilder took the paper, then picked up the bills

he'd placed on the chest. There was a little over a thousand dollars in the roll. "This isn't enough money for half of this house."

"If it's enough to get me to Atlanta, it will do," she said.

"It will get you to Atlanta and keep you for a couple of weeks. But it's not enough payment. Tell me where you'll be staying, and I'll send more after I go to the bank tomorrow."

She shook her head. "I don't know yet. I've never been to Atlanta."

Wilder was tempted to take her by the hand and march her down to Bethany's office. But what good would that do when Bethany was part of the reason Grace wanted to run away?

"How old are you?"

"Eighteen last month. I'm old enough to be on my own."

"No, you're not," he answered gruffly, annoyed he was in this position.

"I am, too. Besides, I couldn't tell you where I'm going even if I knew. You might tell Bethany. I know she'll try to find me."

For a moment, Wilder wondered if she'd seen through his ploy to know her destination. He was certain Grace didn't know how to look out for herself. She'd proven that by letting him touch her. If he didn't want her telling another man she'd do anything for money, he'd have to see she had enough to live on until she came to her senses.

Wilder bent and rubbed his leg below the knee. "Before coming here, I spent several days in Atlanta. I stayed at The Magnolia Glen Hotel. It's a nice place. I want you to stay there so I'll know how to get in touch with you.''

She appeared to think about what he'd said. ''I'm afraid you'll tell Bethany.''

''I won't tell her. This is hardly enough payment for half this business. I'll make arrangements at the bank to have some money deposited into an account for you. If you want the rest of your money, I'll have to know where you're staying.''

Grace sunk her teeth into her bottom lip again. ''Give me your promise you won't tell Bethany.''

''I promise,'' he said, then took hold of her wrist and stuffed the money into her hand.

Chapter Four

"I looked for you for over an hour," Bethany said when Grace walked up to her in the rose garden later that day.

"Yes, I know. I saw you." Grace's words were clipped.

Bethany looked into her eyes and saw anger in them. "You could have acknowledged me."

"I wasn't ready to speak to you."

Moistening her dry lips, Bethany said, "Are you ready to listen to me now?"

Grace smirked. "I just sold my half of The Georgia to Wilder Burlington."

"What? You're not serious!" Bethany exclaimed, a prickle of fear crawling up her back.

"Oh yes, I am." Grace held out a piece of paper to her sister. "Here's the legal document to prove it."

Taking off her gardening gloves and laying them in the wicker basket, Bethany opened the paper. The noonday sun glared off its whiteness, making the print difficult to read. "This can't be true." Stunned, she looked at Grace's smiling face. "You couldn't have sold your half of the house . . . to Wilder Burlington. He's a stranger." She swallowed the lump in her throat. "I hope this is a joke."

"Do I look like I'm joking?" Grace's expression remained hard.

Bethany's hands closed as fear and frustration slowly mounted. The paper looked legal enough. It was in Grace's handwriting, and it stated she'd sold her half of The Georgia to Wilder. She knew that Grace was hurt and angry about Stanley, but this was pure madness.

"I asked Mr. Burlington if he would like to buy my half of The Georgia. He was more than happy to take it off my hands. I wrote two copies of this and signed them. He has the other."

"I didn't even know you knew Wilder!"

"Of course I know him. I met him when he arrived. He's a very nice man. And he was very sympathetic to me."

"I bet he was," Bethany said between clenched teeth, while icy fingers of doom crept up her back. "Oh, Grace! What have you done?"

"I've gotten you out of my life," she shot back tersely.

"You didn't have to sell the house in order to do that." This couldn't be happening. Her sister couldn't have sold her half of The Georgia.

"It seems this place is worth much more than I ever expected. But, then, you never let me know anything about our financial situation, did you? I've never known how much money we have." Grace's eyes were scathing. There was a proud lift to her shoulders.

"I don't know what you've been told, but The Georgia isn't making any money. We have enough to keep it going on a day-to-day basis, but right now we need money for some major repairs and it's just not there. Grace," she pleaded, "this is our home. We share its grandeur with others so we can afford to live here ourselves. What were you thinking?"

Bethany was losing control—of Grace, of The Georgia—losing control of her ability to remain calm in the midst of chaos.

Defiantly, Grace jerked her hands to her slim hips, her drawstring purse dancing from her wrist. "If this place isn't making any money, why did Mr. Burlington pay me so much for my half?"

"I don't know. I've never had the house evaluated. Forget about the money. It's not important. Is this thing legal?" She pointed to the document. "Did you have a lawyer handle this?"

"Of course not! A lawyer would have made a beeline straight to you. Mr. Burlington said as long as we both signed the paper, it was legal. I believe him."

For the first time in her life, Bethany wanted to shake Grace. "Do you know what you've done? You've sold your inheritance, your home! And to a stranger. Do you know what this means?"

"Yes," she said harshly. "That I'm no longer under your thumb. I can do whatever I want, and now I've enough money to do it with. You can have Stanley. You two deserve each other."

Bethany felt hot and cold at the same time. "I don't want Stanley!" Her words were a hiss. "I never have. I think he's a horrible man. He was forcing that kiss on me, and it wasn't the first time. I've tried to explain. Grace, listen to me." Her voice turned high and raspy.

"No, you're lying. Stanley's too handsome for anyone to resist, even my old-maid sister."

Bethany stared at her younger sister. "Why won't anyone believe what I say about Stanley?" Bethany asked, suddenly tired of fighting. Tired of accusations being made against her. Tired of having her honor questioned.

"Because you're lying. Just like Stanley lied when he said he loved me. You're both horrible people, and I hope I never see either of you again!"

Bethany grabbed Grace by the shoulders. "Get hold of yourself. You have to believe me, if I'm going to get us out of this mess you've gotten us into."

"My bags are already on their way to the station. I'm leaving and I'm not coming back," Grace said calmly. "I'm not in a mess. You are. You've lost control of me—and of The Georgia."

Maybe she had tried to control Grace, but only because she wanted her to be happy. In a desperate attempt to stop her sister from leaving, Bethany changed her tactic. "You're making way too much out of this." She tried to keep her voice level. "It was only a kiss."

Grace's expression softened. "No, not just because of the kiss. There's so much more. I want to get away from here, away from you."

"I've never tried to keep you here."

"Oh, Bethany, why do you make me say it?" Grace cried. "I don't want to spend the rest of my life here at this house. You never go anywhere or do anything."

60

Her voice was shaking. "I don't want to end up like you, without a husband and children, without love. I know there's more to life outside this house and I'm going to find it."

With the last whispered statement, Grace turned away. There was nothing for Bethany to do but let her go. She stood as if rooted to the floor as Grace walked out the door.

For a long time Bethany sat in her office with her head on her desk, buried in her arms. Stanley hadn't been able to defeat her but Grace had, with a few well-chosen words. It had been her choice not to marry John Martin and reject all other suitors for fear they would also want her to give up The Georgia.

The Georgia. Bethany's head popped up. Wilder owned half of her home. He must have taken advantage of Grace in her overwrought state of mind and forced her to sell. Bethany intended to get it back. She scrambled to her feet and hurried out of the room.

A couple of minutes later, Bethany beat on Wilder's bedroom door, but no one answered. She searched the house from top to bottom and all around the grounds, looking for him. She spoke to Mr. Fletcher, the other guest staying at the inn, but he hadn't seen Wilder, either. Finally, she gave up, leaving word with Margaret that she was going up to her rooms and she wanted to see Wilder the moment he walked through the door.

This is probably better, she thought, as she paced from one side of her living room to the other. She needed time to think and plan. Where was she going to get the kind of money Wilder had paid Grace?

Twelve thousand dollars was a lot. One possibility was the jewelry her grandmother had left her. The very thought of it tore at her heart, but she had to raise that money. Bethany had never had the jewels appraised, so she didn't know what they were worth. She seldom wore any of them because most of the pieces were intended to accompany the ball gowns and fancy dresses her grandmother had worn before the war. Surely Grandmother Hayward would have approved of her selling the jewelry in order to keep The Georgia in the family.

Bethany let out a long sigh. Even if the jewelry gave her part of the amount she needed, she would probably still have to borrow from the bank and use her half of the house and mill for collateral. It looked as if she were going to lose no matter how hard she tried to win.

"Where did Wilder get that much money?" she wondered aloud as she walked over to the window and looked out. In the few times she had talked with him, she had been given no indication that he had that kind of cash available to him. But now that she thought about it, she had noticed the clothing he wore was expensive, and he'd paid in advance for two months stay at The Georgia. And he was obviously wealthy enough to take time away from his work to come south to recuperate.

Rubbing the back of her neck, she wondered if this was some kind of cruel joke. Was someone toying with her sanity, not knowing that she wasn't as strong as she always pretended to be? Yes, she had wanted Grace to find out about Stanley, but the way she had found out was unfair to both of them. It had torn them apart. How was she going to win back Grace's trust and buy back their home?

Realizing she was teetering on the edge of the breaking point, Bethany knew she had to do something. If she kept up the pace she was going at now, she wouldn't even be coherent by the time Wilder arrived. The deed was done. She had to proceed from there.

Wilder slowly made his way down the stairs to the first floor. After he and Grace had finished their business, he'd taken his medication and slept off the pain in his leg. Now he needed to exercise it. He needed to talk to Bethany, too, but he could do that later. He was sure she'd have a few things to ask him about the sale of the house, but they'd just have to wait.

He didn't want Grace's half of The Georgia, and he intended to put Bethany's mind at rest about it by telling her she could buy it back. The last thing he wanted was to be caught up in a lovers' triangle. He couldn't help feeling a little angry that Bethany had lied so convincingly to him about her feelings for Stanley. Wilder was definitely attracted to her, but he refused to have anything to do with a woman who was in love with another man. He'd learned that lesson the hard way.

Deciding he had to rest before going any farther, Wilder leaned against the banister and hooked his cane over his arm. Four steps to go. A portly gentleman scampered up the stairs beside him, tipping his hat and calling a greeting as he passed.

Wilder scoffed to himself, remembering the times he had carelessly run up and down stairs as freely as the hefty man. Now he couldn't make it to the bottom without stopping.

He massaged the muscle in his calf and mused about what he had done. How had he let that little blonde persuade him to make a promise he didn't want to make? What was he doing getting involved in a family squabble? This was supposed to be a time for him to regain his strength, not get mixed up with two beautiful sisters.

The muscle spasms in his leg sharpened. He shouldn't be worrying about Bethany or Grace. In a few weeks he'd be back in Homestead, walking straight and looking for the bastards who'd left him for dead. That would make him forget about Bethany Hayward.

When Wilder made it to the bottom, his eyes immediately met the unrelenting gaze of Margaret Hodge. She strode to the middle of the foyer and stopped in front of him, her large frame blocking the door. He knew the woman didn't like him, but he had no idea why. He always made a point of being polite to her.

"Good afternoon, Mrs. Hodge." He greeted her with a forced smile.

"Miss Hayward wants to see you," was her only reply.

He leaned on his cane, and his mouth tightened. "I'll see her later."

Margaret put her hands on her hips and grunted loudly, "She wants to see you now."

Wilder thought that she'd probably raised fear in

64

the hearts of many a man with her thunderous voice. This woman was so different from the dignified Bethany Hayward.

He grimaced, deciding to take the easy way out. Right now, he could handle Bethany more easily than he could Margaret. "All right, I'll go see her now."

"She's not in her office. You'll have to go upstairs to the third floor. That's where she lives."

Anger shot through Wilder. "Maybe you haven't realized just how difficult—" His pride jumped in and he stopped. He wasn't about to admit to this woman how hard it was for him to climb those damn stairs.

Margaret walked over to a paneled door and unlocked it. "Through here," she said. "You can't get to the third floor from up there. The door's been nailed shut."

For a moment Wilder considered telling this bossy woman to go to hell, but he decided she was too old for him to be that disrespectful. He limped over to the door, wondering how he was going to make it up two flights of stairs.

The old cedar chest stood in the corner of a small closet. Bethany dropped to her knees and fumbled with the rusty lock until it opened. The clean smell of wood assaulted her as she dug through heirlooms, tossing some out and pushing others aside with care. At last she came upon a black velvet drawstring bag. Pulling it open, she looked inside. The gems twinkled in the darkness, teasing her with their glimmer. She felt a tug at her heart, knowing she had to part with her grandmother's jewelry. She re-knotted the strings and slipped the black roping over her hand, leaving it to swing from her wrist while she put the trunk back in order.

Her only coherent thought was to get the jewelry to the store so she could get some money and buy back The Georgia. She couldn't think beyond that point. When she opened the door to rush out, she was stopped dead in her tracks. Wilder stood before her.

"What's the big rush?"

Bethany backed away slowly, one step at a time, until she was a safe distance from him. "I've been looking for you," she said breathlessly. Her heart was pounding so loudly she thought for sure he must hear it.

He didn't take his gaze off her face. "I know. Margaret told me."

"You didn't answer when I knocked on your door a little while ago."

"I'd taken some medication and was sleeping. It's quite strong. I didn't hear you."

She didn't want him to use that soft, compelling voice. She couldn't think straight when those blue eyes caressed her face. He had coerced her sister. She had to be careful.

Closing the door behind him, Wilder asked, "What happened to you? You look like someone rolled you in dust."

Bethany immediately tried to tuck the loose strands of hair back into her bun. She looked down and brushed at the dust and dirt that clung to her dark green skirt. Embarrassed that she'd forgotten about her appearance, her cheeks grew warm with color. She could only imagine what she really looked like.

"I'm afraid I wanted to find you so badly that I was looking under beds and in the attic."

Wilder shifted his weight. "I'm flattered, but I needed the rest."

Pointing him to one of the wing-back chairs, Bethany walked over to the sofa and sat down, dropping the black velvet bag on the cushion beside her. The jewelers would have to wait until tomorrow. The room was growing dark with late afternoon shadows, so she turned up the lamp. The pool of light lent its warmth and comfort to the charged atmosphere between them.

Bethany took a deep breath and for the first time realized her head was throbbing with pain. Wilder didn't look as if he was feeling too well, either. He was pale and there was a trace of discomfort showing in his face.

"I want to buy back The Georgia. I'll add ten percent to what you paid Grace."

"Bethany, I don't want ten percent," he said quietly.

"Grace didn't know what she was doing. She thought I'd betrayed her." Her hands made fists. "And for a man like Stanley." The thought of it made her eyes burn with unshed tears. Nervous, Bethany rose and started pacing. Wilder might look at The Georgia as a business because of the restaurant and inn, but to Bethany it was so much more than that. It was her home. She couldn't let him own her home. She couldn't. Stopping in front of him, she demanded, "Why did you take advantage of her?"

Wilder stared up at her. "I didn't. Grace was caught between you and Stanley and needed a friend."

"Forget about Stanley. He's not important. You stole her inheritance," she accused.

Her words brought Wilder out of his chair so quickly that he stumbled as he rose. Bethany reached out to steady him.

"Don't!" he said harshly, his eyes a cold shade of blue. "I may be crippled, but I don't need your help to stand." He steadied himself with his cane and took a deep breath. "I have never stolen anything in my life." Anger laced every word, and his face was dark and brooding. "I paid Grace very well for this house. She was determined to get enough money to leave town. If she hadn't sold to me, it would have been to someone else."

"Grace wouldn't have willingly given up her home. You must have forced her to sell."

Wilder's eyes narrowed. "The only thing I did was keep her from making an even bigger mistake. She was ready to do anything for that money."

"I don't believe you," she said on a breathy note.

"I think you do." He paused, then opened his mouth to speak again, but promptly closed it and turned away.

Bethany gripped his arm and forced him to turn and face her once again. "Give me back The Georgia," she whispered desperately.

He grasped her wrist. Their eyes locked together, blue and green. Her chest heaved, waiting for his answer.

"No," he said.

Chapter Five

Bethany stepped out of the claw-footed bathtub and wrapped a large sheet of white cloth around her slim body. She usually splashed water from the basin on only her face in the morning, but after tossing and turning all night, her body felt bruised and battered. The warm soak had relieved some of the stiffness, but her soul was still numb.

As soon as Wilder left her sitting room late yesterday afternoon, she'd hurried over to the train station. The ticket agent confirmed that Grace had boarded the northbound train to Atlanta. She'd stayed at the station two hours, telling herself she'd take the next train and follow Grace, but after she calmed down she realized how foolish that would be. How could she find Grace in a city as big as Atlanta? She wouldn't know where to begin looking.

After drying herself, Bethany slipped into her red bathrobe, a gift from Grace last Christmas. Red had never been one of Bethany's favorite colors. Grace had explained that because of the time of year, she couldn't possibly have chosen any other color.

With the robe loosely tied about her waist, Bethany walked over to her dressing table and sat down. She had never really known her sister. How could Grace have sold her half of The Georgia to Wilder Burlington? And why had she felt the need to run away?

Bethany removed the top from her blue powder jar. She lightly dabbed the cotton puff to the powder before whisking it across her face. A knock sounded on the living room door, startling her.

"Grace," she whispered with excitement, dropping the puff. Last night she'd prayed her sister would realize the mistake she'd made in running away and would take the first train back to Eufaula.

Bethany picked up the skirt of her robe and ran barefoot from her bedroom, her long hair flying out behind her. Grace had come home, she thought. Now they could make some definite plans for getting The Georgia back into the Hayward family.

She beamed with unabashed pleasure as she threw open the door. Grace's name flew from her mouth.

"Sorry, but the name's Wilder."

Bethany's green eyes rounded in surprise as she stared at the man standing before her, dressed in a white shirt and dark trousers that were held up by suspenders. Beside him on the floor sat a large brown satchel.

"You! How did you get up here?" she asked breathlessly.

"The same way I came up last night—the stairs."

"Did Margaret unlock the door for you? I can't believe she would let you up here this time of morning." Bethany tried to show her outrage in her tone of voice.

"Margaret didn't have to. I have this." He held up a key, dangling it before her eyes. "Grace gave it to me before she left. She explained that your father had the front stairs sealed off years ago because guests frequently wandered up here, not realizing this was the family home."

Bethany grabbed for the key, but he quickly snatched it away and circled her in his arms. "You are a feisty woman, Bethany Hayward." A husky tint outlined his voice.

A clean shaving soap smell teased her. Her gaze traveled up his masculine throat, over his freshly shaven chin, lingered on his lips longer than she wanted, then sped upward to his eyes. He lowered his head, and Bethany knew she wanted him to kiss her. She must be going mad. The feel of his strong arms around her must be blotting out common sense, erasing all rational behavior. A chuckle rippled through his chest while he held her close.

"Oh," she exclaimed, wrenching from his grasp before she did something stupid. The amusement that lurked in his expression was unbearable. "Give me that key," she demanded, although her tone lacked any air of command. She merely sounded breathless.

She took a deep breath, cleared her throat, and tried again as she clutched the lapels of her robe together. "What are you doing here?" No one ever invaded the sanctity of the third floor unless they'd been invited. Bethany gained control of herself. Her breathing became calmer, her heartbeat steady. She'd never

71

been attracted to a man with whom she was also at odds. This new turmoil only added to the constant strain she had been under for weeks. Nothing had gone right since Stanley Edwards had walked into The Georgia three months ago. And now there was Wilder.

With an air of self-assurance, Wilder stuffed the key inside the pocket of his pants, picked up the small piece of luggage, and limped past Bethany without responding to her question.

"What are you doing? You can't come in here." Her voice was high-pitched, and for some reason her heart was thudding crazily. She wished he hadn't touched her. She wished it hadn't felt good to have his arms around her, his body pressed close to hers.

He lifted his shoulders with a shrugging gesture, while his eyes peered into hers. "Bethany, I now own half of The Georgia. That entitles me to Grace's key and her bedroom. I'm no longer a guest here. I'm now part owner."

Calm and coolheaded, Bethany always avoided a nasty scene. This time, though, it appeared she'd be instigating one. She clutched her hands together behind her back. Her insides churned with indignation as she fought for control.

"Mr. Burlington, I am an intelligent woman. However, I fail to see how you owning half of this house entitles you to occupy my sister's bedroom." At last her haughty air had returned, even if she did feel blatantly exposed standing in a Christmas-red bathrobe with her hair streaming down her back.

They stared at each other for an interminable

moment. Finally, in an unassuming manner, he stated, "Bethany, I own half of *everything*. The house, the land, the gardens, the restaurant, right down to the sheets and pillowcases that are put on the beds. Half of everything is mine—including the third floor."

Her mind awhirl with accusations, why was she standing there mute, letting him declare that what was once hers was now half his?

"You can't do this. I won't let you. There must be a law against this."

"Against what?" His voice took on an edge. "Your father's will gave Grace half of this estate with no strings attached."

"He didn't expect her to sell it," she shot back quickly.

"Then he should have stated so." His face was grim. "Believe me, Bethany, you have no legal recourse."

"There must be something I can do. Grace didn't know what she was doing. She thought I was involved with Stanley. She thought I'd betrayed her. She would never have sold if not for Stanley. Let me buy it back." Her words and voice were a plea.

Wilder looked at her with a softening in his eyes. For a moment she thought he was going to relent and say yes, but he only said, "Finish dressing. I'll meet you downstairs in the dining room. Don't keep me waiting too long. We have a lot of things to discuss." He turned and walked out, leaving his satchel where it sat.

"Don't do this to me," she whispered to his back,

but as he opened the door and walked out, he gave no indication that he had heard her softly spoken plea.

Wilder sat at a table in front of the bay window. Early morning sun filtered through the pastel sheers covering the window and streaked across the room like a dominant predator. Most of the other guests had already left the dining room. The portly man Wilder had seen before sat at one of the tables reading a paper. Not far from him two women sat having coffee and quietly chatting.

He was being a heel of the worst kind, Wilder decided as he glanced about the room. There was no reason to keep ownership of The Georgia other than the fact that he wanted to. When he'd gone up to the third floor yesterday afternoon, he had had every intention of selling The Georgia back to Bethany. He would have, too, but she'd made him so angry by accusing him of stealing the house and demanding that he sell it back to her. He wasn't of a mind to give in to her that easily. Even if he didn't want it, he didn't need her telling him he *had* to give it back to her.

After having a few moments to think about everything that had happened, he decided he wanted to keep his half of the house, at least until he went back home. He'd have no use for it in Pennsylvania, but while he was here he could use it to help him recuperate faster. He needed something to do, something to make him feel useful. Already he was tired of sitting around and reading. He needed something more to keep him occupied. If he worked a little each day, slowly rebuilding his strength, he should be ready to return to the steel mill by mid-summer. The doctor had told him to get plenty of rest but to exercise his leg at least twice a day. Doing things around the house should take care of that.

And, he thought, Bethany should certainly keep his mind in good shape. One moment she was all softness and prim and proper, the next she was fighting for what she believed was right. She was a beautiful woman, strong and self-assured. He'd never met a woman more desirable than Judith until he'd met Bethany Hayward.

"Bethany," he whispered her name as he turned to look out the window. Damn, she had looked good this morning with her honey-blond hair flowing over that red robe and her green eyes flashing angrily at him. Was she as innocent as she looked, as innocent as she declared? And why couldn't he get her off his mind? As much as he'd like to think he was keeping The Georgia to aid his recuperation, deep inside he knew that he liked the idea of having that small amount of control over the tempting Bethany Hayward.

Hearing voices, Wilder glanced around the dining room. Bethany had come in and was talking to the two women. She had changed into a dark skirt and white blouse with a banded collar, her usual attire. He smiled. Bethany didn't need fancy hairstyles and elaborately decorated clothing to enhance her loveliness. In some ways she reminded him of Judith. They were both beautiful and soft-spoken, with an inner strength that few recognized. Yet, he had the feeling that Bethany had a touch of rebel in her that he'd never seen in Judith.

He continued to watch Bethany as she left the women and walked over to speak to the man with the newspaper. Wilder listened as she told the man she looked forward to seeing him on his return trip. When Bethany approached the table, Wilder stood up, neither one of them speaking as she sat in the intricately carved wooden chair opposite him. Out of habit, she took the floral printed napkin, unfolded it, and laid it in her lap.

"Good morning, Miss Hayward."

Bethany looked up to see Ruth Mayland's familiar face and smiled at her.

"I haven't seen you in here for a long time. Are you here for breakfast?"

"Just coffee for me, Ruth, but perhaps Mr. Burlington would like something to eat."

Wilder looked up at the waitress and said, "I'll have the pancakes, and make sure the syrup is warmed." He handed the menu back to her.

"Stilman wouldn't allow anything to come out of the kitchen that wasn't perfect, Mr. Burlington," Bethany remarked after Ruth walked away. "It wasn't necessary to tell her to warm the syrup."

"Wasn't it?" he questioned. "How long has it been since you had breakfast in here, Bethany? A month, two, three? Has it been a year?"

"It's been a while, yes. But I'm sure—"

"Then you don't know whether or not the syrup is warmed before it's served, do you?" he concluded dryly.

Bethany squirmed in her chair as she cleared her throat. Certainly, he had her at a disadvantage, and she hated it. He was right. She hadn't eaten in the dining room since ... well, a very long time, preferring to dine in the privacy of the third floor.

"Let's get one thing straight." Wilder was clearly agitated. "No more of this stiff Mr. Burlington act. We are on a first name basis and it's going to stay that way. I intend to make you aware of my feelings at all times. If I think something is not being done properly at The Georgia, I will say so. Like it or not, I'm your partner."

"I'll never like you being a partner."

"Fine. You don't have to."

"What makes you an authority on how to run a restaurant?" she asked.

Wilder sat back in his chair. His eyes softened. "Nothing."

Arrogance suited him well. He smiled, and Bethany's temper burned hot.

"But I do know how to manage a steel mill. If I can keep two hundred and fifty men and their jobs organized and running smoothly, I should be able to handle what goes on in a kitchen."

Bethany harrumphed and took note of the fact that he'd just told her what he did for a living. It was a good thing the Hayward Mill wasn't included with the house. If Grace had sold Wilder her half of that, she might never get rid of him.

Since Wilder had tried to use intimidation, Bethany had to respond in kind. "You wouldn't last a full working day managing a kitchen. Don't try to convince me otherwise."

Wilder grinned. "Perhaps. We'll have to settle this by putting my words into action."

"Anytime you're ready, let me know. I'll give Stilman the day off and you can have your moment to shine."

Ruth approached with the coffee, so they fell silent. Bethany didn't know why she was sparring with Wilder, except for the fact that she found him more interesting and exciting than anyone she'd ever met. But even though he made her feel alive and energetic, she had to keep in mind that her main goal must be to buy back Grace's half of The Georgia. She couldn't afford to indulge in her interest in him no matter how badly she might want to. She wouldn't share her house. Her resolve to get Wilder out was stronger than ever.

When Ruth walked away, Bethany turned serious. "I want to buy back The Georgia."

"It's not for sale."

Their eyes held. "I'll add twenty percent to what you paid Grace."

"It's not for sale at any price."

Moving to the edge of her seat, she said, "Grace didn't know what she was doing when she sold you—"

A frown creased his brow. "Bethany, we've had this conversation before and it's getting old."

"You don't understand. I have to buy it back. The house has been in the Hayward family for sixty years."

"Half of it still is."

"You're not listening to me," she said in a desperate attempt to make him understand.

Wilder bent over the table. "I don't want to fight about this. I'm not selling. I didn't plan the trouble between you, Grace, and Stanley—"

"Don't mention that man's name to me!" she interrupted him.

"That's an abrupt change. How can you love a man one day and hate him the next?"

"Love?" she said with disgust. It was difficult not to raise her voice above an acceptable level. The knot of tension that had been in the back of her neck for days grew larger. She sat back in her chair, wondering if she should try one more time to make him understand.

Bethany placed her hands on the table and laced her fingers together in front of her. "I don't like Stanley Edwards. I never have. He moved to town a few months ago and came calling on me. I let him know I wasn't interested in him and he immediately turned his attentions to Grace. After they became engaged, about a month ago, he started making offensive remarks to me whenever Grace wasn't around. I wanted to tell Grace what he was doing, but I didn't want to hurt her, either. I hoped she would wake up and see Stanley for what he was. After he accosted me in the rose garden, the day you saw him, I tried to tell her about him. She wouldn't believe me. Yesterday he cornered me again, and this time Grace saw him kiss me." Her eyes pleaded for understanding. "Grace's heart broke into a million pieces and I couldn't do anything to keep it from shattering." She closed her eyes for a moment, and when she opened them she saw that Wilder had softened. "I hate Stanley Edwards. I don't know if I can ever forgive him for what he's done."

"I thought you were secretly in love with Stanley. I

79

knew he'd forced that kiss on you that day and that you didn't want Grace to find out. I thought it was because of the shame you felt in loving your sister's fiancé."

Bethany's head was throbbing with pain. "Grace didn't know what she was doing. Why did you take advantage of her?"

Wilder rubbed his forehead. "Bethany, I'm telling the truth when I say Grace would have done anything to get enough money to leave town." He kept his gaze on her face. "Anything."

Affronted, she said, "I can't believe that's true."

"It is. If she'd approached any other man, she would have probably ended up spending the night in his room."

"Stop this!"

She started to rise, but Wilder reached and grabbed her wrist, forcing her to stay in her chair. "No. You stop. I have no reason to lie."

Bethany felt as if every eye in the room was on her. With a heavy heart, she jerked her hand free and sat back in her chair. Had Grace wanted to leave that badly?

"As I said, like it or not, you have a partner. And being your partner gives me everything Grace had."

His voice was harsher than she imagined it could be, considering how gentle he'd been when he had first spoken to her that day in the rose garden. It was odd the way she kept going back to that afternoon. But she knew what it was. There had been magic between them the first time their eyes met. That intangible feeling that draws two people together and forces them to put aside all rational thought. He was undeniably tempting. But if she were going to keep control of her heart, her life, and The Georgia, she had to deny herself that alluring pleasure and fight Wilder every inch of the way.

With a steady hand, Bethany lifted the bone china cup to her lips and sipped coffee that had no taste. She should have been better prepared for this. Everything had happened so quickly that her head was still spinning. For a moment she wondered if she had the strength to fight Wilder and win. Her best asset had always been her ability to remain calm when those around her were drowning in chaos. This time, however, she was the one drowning and Wilder the one so sure of himself.

"If you must keep what you stol—acquired from my sister, so be it. I don't have to like it. I would ask that if you should ever consider selling, you'll come to me first."

Taking the time to look fully into her eyes, Wilder said, "You have my word. I'll not turn over ownership of The Georgia to anyone but you."

She believed him. "Thank you." Bethany took a deep breath and drank from her coffee again. Feeling calmer, she said, "Grace had very little to do with the operations of The Georgia, and I suspect you'd like things the same way. I will, however, keep you informed of what goes on, and should I think you need to be aware of a problem, I'll come directly to you."

Wilder wiped his mouth with his napkin, failing to hide the wisp of a smile that touched his lips. "You mean, I should be something like a silent partner? You'll take care of the day-to-day business and send me a report at the end of each month?"

"Yes, exactly." This was suddenly going better than she expected. "You're here to recuperate and shouldn't have to bother with such things. I'll be happy to send monthly reports when you return to your home."

Bethany was surprised to see his eyes light up with a generous smile and a genuine mellow laugh emerge from deep in his chest. He pushed back his chair and stretched the length of his legs across the hardwood floor.

"You are priceless, Bethany," he said after his laughter subsided. "The perfect southern matriarch, but unfortunately your reign is over. I'm going to be an active partner in what goes on around here. Every decision that's made will have my stamp of approval."

"But Grace never had any interest in The Georgia and you bought her half," she said when she felt herself losing control of the conversation.

"But Grace doesn't own it anymore. I do." He smiled. "And I have my own way of doing things. First, I'll move into Grace's old bedroom and free up the room I'm now using for guests."

Propriety leaped to her defense. "No!" Bethany spread both hands on the starched tablecloth. "Never. Up north where you come from, it may be perfectly acceptable for an unmarried man and woman to share the same apartment, but not here in our small town. I will not be subjected to such gossip. If you move in, I'll move out."

When she stopped, Bethany realized she had half risen out of her chair again. Damn him for making her lose her temper and raise her voice, capturing the attention of everyone in the dining room. She eased back into her chair.

Wilder sat stoically, watching her with those twilight blue eyes. There was something in his expression she couldn't read. Was it regret, doubt, or retreat? She wasn't sure.

"All right, Bethany, I'll back down on this issue—for now. For the sake of your reputation. But don't make the mistake of thinking I'll be so accommodating on other matters. Keep in mind that when you challenge me, it only makes me more determined."

Relief stung her skin, and she rubbed the back of her neck. She had won the first round but she was drained, weakened by the fight.

He didn't have to agree to her demands, and she knew it. "Thank you," she whispered, lowering her lashes so he couldn't see just how grateful she was. "I'll have Kate carry your things back to your room."

Nodding, he said, "The first thing we should do is call a meeting and introduce me to the staff. Let's do that before noon, so we'll have the afternoon to go over the records. It's time I found out just what it is that I bought."

Startled, Bethany looked into his eyes. She hadn't thought about the employees. What would they think? She leaned forward. "All right, but I'd like to tell Margaret privately. She's worked here for twenty years. It's like a home to her."

"I don't have a problem with that."

Bethany nodded her agreement and rose from her chair. Telling Margaret wasn't going to be easy.

"Don't make this seem like a prison sentence, Bethany. It's business."

"It might be a business to you, but to me it's my home," she said defiantly and walked away.

It was probably just as well that he wouldn't be on the third floor, he thought as he watched Bethany walk away. He had to fight to keep his hands off her. She was so strong, so beautiful, and so courageous that he wanted to hold her and make her his. He had the feeling she could set him on fire with passion if they ever came together. But he couldn't contemplate that for several reasons. His life was in Pennsylvania, and he knew Bethany wasn't the kind of woman he could play around with, then leave.

There were other things between them, too, not the least of which was his promise to Grace. If Grace decided against his advice of returning home in a couple of days, he hoped she would at least keep her promise and stay at the hotel he had suggested. She was definitely too immature to be completely on her own.

He was a jackass for not telling Bethany that he intended to give her back The Georgia when he left Eufaula. But holding on to it for now gave him a feeling of power over her that he wasn't yet ready to relinquish. Besides, the more he thought about it, the better he liked the idea of owning half of the house. His brother lived in the family home in Pittsburgh with his wife and two daughters. Even though he spent most of his weekends there, for some time he'd felt more at home in his rented apartment in Homestead than in Pittsburgh.

Wilder pushed his coffee cup aside as the waitress

placed a plate in front of him. Until he'd been attacked, he had never wanted anything permanent in his life. But now at thirty years of age, he found himself wanting something more.

With a heavy heart and slow feet, Bethany entered the front office. Margaret was in her usual place behind her desk.

Bethany ran her hands down the sides of her skirt and said, "I need to speak to you about something important, Margaret."

The older woman pushed her chair away from the desk, the large white collar on her printed dress accentuating her buxom figure. Her gray-streaked hair was styled into a tight chignon at the back of her neck, and even though she was nearing sixty, her face had the complexion of a much younger woman.

"Is it about that Mr. Burlington?" she asked.

Bethany stared at her, wishing she didn't have to tell her. "Yes."

"Go on. I'm listening." Her clipped words encouraged Bethany to continue.

"Yesterday afternoon Grace sold her half of The Georgia to Mr. Burlington."

"Hush your mouth!" Margaret said gruffly, then groaned and mumbled something else under her breath.

"It's true." Bethany leaned against the desk, a tired sigh flowing from her lips. "Grace thought I was trying to steal Stanley away from her, so in order to get back at me, she sold her half of the house."

"She thought you were after that no-account

scalawag?" Her eyebrows curled in puzzlement. "That doesn't make sense," she concluded. "Grace is the only woman in town young enough and fool enough to fall for that ill-bred Casanova."

Bethany smiled at Margaret's apt description of Stanley. "I'm afraid Grace's immaturity isn't the biggest problem. I've offered to buy Mr. Burlington out, but right now he's not interested. I was so worried about Stanley getting his hands on The Georgia that I left the back door open for someone else to come in and take it."

"What are we going to do?"

The older woman's question was simple yet so important. "If there was anything that could be done, you know I'd do it," Bethany said.

Margaret nodded. "Where's Grace?"

Bethany's eyes clouded. "She told me she was leaving town, but I don't think I really believed her until I went over to the train depot late yesterday. The man at the ticket counter confirmed she boarded the northbound to Atlanta. You had already gone home by the time I returned."

"If I'd known—"

Bethany smiled. "I know. I have to believe she'll come home today. She doesn't know anything about Atlanta. All of her friends are here in Eufaula. I have to keep faith that she'll come home," Bethany whispered, then turned away.

By twelve o'clock that day Kate, Seth, Stilman, Ruth, and the other two restaurant employees had been told that Wilder now owned half of The

Georgia. Bethany had remained regal in stature and manner as she made the announcement to the small gathering in the marble-floored foyer. None of her inner grief at losing Grace or control of The Georgia showed on the outside.

Wilder had surprised her by speaking a few words to the group, assuring them that he would be actively involved in the operations and they should feel free to come to him at any time. There were no questions when he finished, only a faint murmuring among the employees as they went back to their duties.

After the short meeting, Bethany and Wilder went immediately to her office. Bethany walked behind her desk and sat down, leaving Wilder to close the door, which he did with a bang.

"You've got to stop this, Bethany. I've had about all I can take of your aristocratic *noblesse oblige* attitude. I don't need—or want—your charitable or honorable conduct." His voice was rough and he leaned toward her in a menacing way. "You stood beside me in there, chin held high, quiet voice, playing the part of the perfect martyr." He inched closer. "I'm not in this to hurt you. I want to help you."

"Then give me back The Georgia."

"No." He walked back to the window, raking his hand through his hair. "Dammit. I'm not going over that again. I want to be a natural part of this place, and I want you to accept me as an equal partner. Don't treat me in such a manner again."

Bethany felt thoroughly rebuked. Astonished, in fact, that he had been so perceptive. "I'm sorry. It wasn't my intention to appear condescending."

Wilder straightened, pulling himself to his full height. He smiled knowingly. "Yes, it was. You're doing it again, right now. You're denying your anger and saying what you think I want to hear. Don't hide from me. Let me know what you really feel, like you did this morning when I wanted to move into Grace's bedroom. Vent your anger and get it over with. Don't harbor it because you're afraid you'll appear unladylike if you lose your temper." He rubbed his chin, his voice softening as he said, "We'll never make this work if we don't find some common ground."

It was a strange feeling. Wilder knew her better than she knew herself. He understood more than he had the right to know. She stared at his lean, handsome face and wondered how they were going to find common ground where The Georgia was concerned. This house was her life. She had given up John Martin for it, and she'd lost Grace in her attempt to keep The Georgia from Stanley. Wilder was an outsider, and she had to keep it that way.

"Why do you want to own part of The Georgia?"

He took so long in answering that Bethany was beginning to think she should repeat her question.

"I could give you a lot of acceptable answers, and they'd all be true. But the main reason is now that I have it, I find I have no desire to give it up."

Pushing aside the accusations she'd already thrown at him, Bethany accepted defeat. In time, maybe he'd change his mind. Clearing her throat, she said, "Very well. Let's go over the books now." She opened the drawer on the left side of the oak desk and took out two black ledger books, one for the inn, the other for the restaurant.

"You know, this is a large office. With a little rearranging, we could move an extra desk in here for me," Wilder said, looking around the room.

Over my dead body, she thought, as she calmly said, "There's a small room three doors down with a view of the fountain and the east gardens. It will make you a perfect office—and give us our privacy."

He smiled. "All right. We'll take a look at it when we finish here."

A short time later, Wilder closed the ledger book with a sigh on his lips. He looked at Bethany with keen, observant eyes. "How long have The Georgia's books looked like this?"

An insulted gasp caught in her throat. "These records are accurate," she answered.

"I don't doubt for a moment that the figures entered are accurate. You don't have what it takes to be dishonest. What I'm talking about is the balance. How long has The Georgia been losing money?"

She felt glad that he was upset because The Georgia wasn't making lots of money. Maybe now he'd be willing to sell. She suppressed the smile that wanted to stretch across her face.

"We're not losing money. We're just not making any extra. It takes every penny we make to keep the house and restaurant running."

"In this case, Bethany, not making money is the same thing as losing it. This place has the potential to be a profit-making business."

Bethany could almost taste victory as she wondered what Grace must have told him. She chose her words carefully. "I'm sure you expected more from your investment. But there isn't a lot of money to be made in an operation like this." Bethany shrugged her shoulders to emphasize her words.

"Really?" he asked as he sat back in his chair and stroked his chin.

She held her breath. He seemed interested. "Yes, it's true. If you bought this hoping to make a lot of money . . . well, it's not going to happen. As I told you, after the war my father turned the house into a restaurant and inn so we could afford to live here. He was happy with just enough money to go around and so am I."

"But you haven't had enough to go around lately, have you?"

Bethany pursed her lips. "Well, no," she answered honestly, hoping she wasn't backing herself into a corner. "The house is getting older and it takes more each year to keep up. We usually see improvement during the summer months. Spring rains leave the roads impassable at times. When it gets drier, business will pick up and give us a little extra. I'm hoping we'll have enough to put on a new roof and paint the exterior of the house."

Slowly, Wilder cupped his hands behind his head. "But no real profit?"

"Right. No profit to speak of."

"And what do you suppose we could do about that?" he asked.

Bethany lowered her lashes over her eyes for a moment. This was it. She looked back at Wilder. Willing her voice to stay calm, she said, "I'm still agreeable to buying you out." She couldn't have been more casual if she'd been talking about the weather.

"No, Bethany. You misunderstood me. I mean, what do you suppose we can do to have enough money to go around all year, not just the summer months?" His tone was quiet and calming.

With pursed lips, Bethany stared at the man she perceived to be a thorn in her side. She'd misread him . . . for the time being, anyway. Her skin prickled, her stomach lurched, "If we're not making a lot of money like you'd hoped, why would you want to keep it?"

"The Georgia can be a profit-making business."

Bethany swallowed the lump in her throat, along with the hopes of Wilder selling. Aching all over, she wondered how she was going to convince this man to give back what was rightfully hers. "It's not a business. This is my home," she insisted, her gaze burning into his.

"Correction. The third floor is your home. The rest of this house is The Georgia Restaurant and Inn, and I intend to see that it's run like a business. Bethany, if the business of The Georgia doesn't succeed, you won't have a home."

He was right. No matter how badly she hated to admit it. His words cut deep. Being calm and levelheaded, always managing unpleasant scenes, had been her strength. What was she to do when Wilder could take that away from her so easily?

"Look, Bethany, I didn't come here with the idea that I was going to buy this place. I needed a quiet place for my recuperation. There was no special reason I ended up at The Georgia. In fact, I think I told you my brother made the arrangements." Wilder stopped for a moment, a speculative look on his face.

"I suggest we go ahead and have the new roof put on and the house painted before the June guests arrive."

"There isn't enough money—"

"Don't worry about that. I have enough money to have the work done."

Bethany's temper rose. "I won't let you come in here and change everything, taking charge as if you own the place."

"I own half of it."

A knot formed in Bethany's chest. She wanted to dispute his words but knew she couldn't. Instead, she said, "Then we'll each pay half of the cost of the repairs."

His gaze caressed her face. "Where will you get—?"

"I have money of my own—that my grandmother left me." It was a lie, but only a little white lie, she told herself. As soon as the jeweler sold her grandmother's jewelry, she'd have more than enough to pay for her part of the repairs on the house.

"All right. Fine. I didn't mean for our conversation to get so heated." Wilder pushed back his chair. "You know, Bethany, you take offense too easily." He stretched his injured leg out before him and massaged the large muscle in his thigh.

"I'm only fighting for what's mine," she answered softly.

"So am I."

Bethany watched his hand as it moved up and down his leg, sometimes caressing, sometimes kneading the firm flesh. The width of his palm was wide, his fingers masculine, his nails neatly trimmed.

She looked at him to see if he saw her staring. He didn't. She noticed a tightness around the edge of his mouth that hadn't been there before. Bethany remembered his words about the attack and she shivered inwardly.

"Is your leg hurting?" she asked, unable to keep concern out of her voice.

"A little. It probably wouldn't bother me at all if I would take the medicine the doctor prescribed at regular times."

Bethany watched as he continued to rub his leg, a movement she found almost mesmerizing. "Why don't you take it?"

"It makes me so sleepy I try to do without."

He looked up and caught her watching him. Their eyes met. The way he looked at her changed the atmosphere in the room. Suddenly, there was an undeniable intimacy between them. One move was all it would take. If she reached for him, he would come to her. If he touched her, she would be his. One of them had to go forward with what was happening between them or it would be lost. Suddenly, Wilder looked away. Bethany let out a shaky breath.

He stood slowly. "The walks every morning and afternoon help. I think I've been overworking my leg today."

"Maybe you should go upstairs and rest," she said.

"You're right. I'll take a look at the room for my office later."

"I'm sure it will work for you. Why don't I have Margaret and Kate set it up?"

He agreed, then went upstairs.

Bethany rested both elbows on her desk and cradled her head in her hands. It was apparent there was a force drawing her to Wilder. Where was the self-control she'd been exercising for years? How long could she keep repressing the desire to touch him, to be held and kissed by him? At times she found him comforting, his presence necessary. Yet, most of the time she was willing to beg, borrow, or steal in order to get him out of The Georgia.

Chapter Six

Later that afternoon Bethany walked into the main office, where Margaret sat at her desk. "Has there been any word from Grace?" she asked.

"Nope." Margaret answered with more of a grunt than a word. "You know I'd tell you immediately if I heard anything from her."

Bethany sighed heavily. "Of course I do. In truth, I expected her to return today. I don't like the idea of her being in that big city by herself."

Margaret looked at Bethany. "Don't worry about Grace. She may be young and inexperienced, but she's strong. She'll come home when she's through spending all the money that Yankee gave her. She doesn't have anywhere else to go."

Bethany smiled fondly at the older woman. Margaret was right. Grace had nowhere else to go, but it might take a lot longer than she thought. Margaret didn't know how much money Wilder had given her. Goodness, it could take her years to spend it all. Bethany had never found out where all Wilder's money came from. He had said something about knowing how to manage a steel mill and organizing men. She supposed he worked in a mill.

Why couldn't Grace have sold him her half of the mill? She'd been so worried about her sister and losing control of The Georgia that she had been letting Wilder ask all the questions. She knew for certain now that he wouldn't sell his half of the house, but somehow, she felt that she could live with that if only Grace would come home. If she wasn't back by the end of the day, Bethany decided she'd walk over to the station again. Maybe Grace had come back to Eufaula but had decided to stay somewhere else. Bethany hoped that was true.

"That carpetbagger asked to see my records for the last three years," Margaret complained. "I gave him the key to the file cabinet and told him to go ahead and look. I don't have anything to hide."

Bethany smiled, feeling comforted by the knowledge that Margaret was on her side. "If anyone needs me, I'll be in the rose garden," she said before walking away.

When she stepped into the garden, the heel of her shoe sank into the moist earth. The previous evening's rain had left the ground soft. A million tiny droplets of water rested on the lush petals of the roses. The late afternoon sun was warm but had failed to dry up all the traces of the spring shower.

It was such a soothing feeling for Bethany to walk among the rose bushes, occasionally stopping to touch the velvet-smooth petals or smell the heady fragrance of a bloom.

There was no particular order as far as colors in the rose garden. Bushes with soft yellow roses blended beside vibrant reds, and roses with a hint of pink were nestled close to the subdued corals. This was what made The Georgia's rose garden so spectacular. Most gardeners segregated the bushes into sections according to color. Bethany was delighted that Seth had mixed them all together. From the cupola on the roof, the garden looked like one big beautiful bouquet.

Bethany didn't know how many different varieties of roses the garden had, but there were many. And as soon as new varieties were developed, she was one of the first to have the opportunity to buy them and add to The Georgia's growing number.

As Bethany walked in the garden, a question kept nagging at her. Why couldn't Grace have sold Wilder her half of the mill?

Bethany reached out to caress the petals of a crimson rose when she heard her name called. Instead of touching the petal, her finger struck a thorn. "Ouch," she mumbled, and lifted her finger to her lips to thwart the pain.

She looked up to see Wilder walking toward her. "You startled me," she said, rubbing the pinpoint injury with her thumb.

"Sorry. I didn't mean to make you prick your finger. Here, let me see."

Before she could back away, he grabbed her hand in both of his and held her slender finger up for inspection. His touch was warm, soft, firm. They stood close together, hands touching, eyes meeting, blue and green coming together in peace. He slowly brought her hand to his lips and kissed the injured finger.

Gasping, Bethany allowed him the familiarity. Her heart seemed to swell in her chest. A shudder of longing raced through her veins. Wilder pressed the finger to his lips once more, letting his tongue gently caress the tip. His eyes, his touch, the way he held her hand . . . his breath, his lips, set her ablaze with more desire than she'd ever experienced.

Swallowing hard, Wilder slowly let go of her hand and stepped away.

Bethany lowered her lashes, embarrassed by the way he made her feel. His touch lingered on her skin. She gripped her hands together, trying to dispel the tormenting feeling of wanting more. Why did his touch bring on such a hunger to explore those womanly feelings she'd always denied? What was it about him that made him different from all the other men who had been guests of The Georgia?

She lifted her head with a jerk. What was wrong with her? This was the second time she'd had the feeling of wanting to be with him. It must stop. He owned half of her house. He couldn't be trusted.

"I'm glad you're here. I want to talk to you about something," she said hurriedly to cover the awkwardness that settled around them.

"I'm listening." Wilder slipped his hands into the pockets of his camel-colored slacks. He looked better than he had when he'd left her office earlier that afternoon. The rest had taken the pinched look from his face.

"I believe you said you work in a mill?"

"Yes." A cautious expression covered his features. "I'm a manager at the Carnegie Steel Mill in Homestead. I've been there for ten years." His look turned pensive. "Why?"

"Most of the towns along the Chattahoochee River were burned during the war. Bridges, buildings, mills, dams, even the railroads were torn up and burned. The few mills that weren't destroyed have never regained their prewar status. That's why most of the South's cotton is now shipped up north or to Europe. After the war my father rebuilt his mill. But neither the machines nor our cloth is the quality of that in the North. Osnaburg, the cloth we make, is sturdy and coarse. The cloth is mostly used locally, and when the merchants stop buying, we shut down until more cloth is needed." She stopped.

"And?" he asked.

"I was hoping you might take a look at the mill and see if you can find a way we can improve our production and our cloth, and keep our employees working longer."

He smiled. "I learn something new about you every time I talk to you, Bethany."

"I'm afraid that's because I've been letting you ask all the questions."

"We can change that whenever you're ready." He paused, then continued when she didn't comment. "I don't know much about the textile industry or its machinery, but I'll take a look at the mill for you."

She could see that he was pleased she had asked for his help. Hope surged within her. "Good. I'll write a letter of introduction to the manager, then you can go over whenever you like."

"I'm sorry to interrupt, Miss Hayward," Seth said as he walked up to them, carrying a large sack on his shoulder. "I just picked up that fertilizer you've been looking for."

"It's all right, Seth. Mr. Burlington and I were through." She turned back to Wilder. "I'll have that letter ready for you by the end of the day."

Wilder nodded, and Bethany followed Seth to the toolshed. She needed Wilder at the mill, not at The Georgia. If this went according to her plan, he would spend some of his remaining time in Eufaula at the mill. She would be free of his soothing voice, those maddening blue eyes, and that desire to be closer to him.

Chapter Seven

"Three days," Bethany whispered to herself as she marked *paid* on the invoice for the fresh vegetables delivered earlier that day. What could Grace be doing in Atlanta? she wondered. She'd checked with the stationmaster several times, and he kept assuring her that Grace had not returned to Eufaula by train. But just to be certain, Bethany had visited two of Grace's friends yesterday. No one had heard from her.

Bethany pushed her paperwork aside and rose to look out the window of her office. An idea had come to her last night while she'd lain awake, and it hadn't left her thoughts for very long. If Grace wouldn't come to her, she would go to Grace. The only problem was that she didn't know where Grace was hiding. She would have already gone to Atlanta if she thought she could find her. Bethany didn't know any more about big cities than Grace did. As much as she hated the idea, she had to hire a private detective to find her sister. Three days was too long for her to be gone.

"Three days until what?" Wilder posed the question from the doorway of her office.

Startled, Bethany looked up to see him leaning against the door frame. A pair of black suspenders held up his dark blue pants and his blue striped shirt was buttoned tight. The casual clothing and his lackadaisical stance added to his handsomeness.

"You look as if you're going boating," she said, ignoring his question, forcing herself not to stare at him. She had to constantly remind herself that this man was the reason Grace was gone. "Isn't it a little late in the day for that?"

"I'm not going boating. I'd like to before I go home, though. Maybe you'll come with me," he added.

The grief she had felt so many years ago pressed against her chest and brought sorrow to her eyes. What used to be an enjoyable pastime now frightened her. Bethany brushed down the length of her skirt before she met his eyes. "No, I don't think so," she said softly.

"Why not?" Using his cane, he limped into the room and leaned against the side of her oak desk.

"My parents were killed in a boating accident on Lake Eufaula. I haven't been in a boat since then. I can't." The pain of loss had faded with time, but not so much that it still didn't hurt.

Leaving his cane leaning against the desk, Wilder walked to where she stood in front of the window. After a moment, he spoke. "I understand how you feel. It wasn't easy for me to walk down the street alone after I was discharged from the hospital. It was a big jolt to my ego when I realized I was actually afraid of something that other men and women did every day. It had always been a natural part of my life to walk home from the mill in the evenings. Even now, here in Eufaula, I listen for every little sound when I'm out walking."

It couldn't have been easy for a man to admit he was afraid. Bethany understood his feelings and was comforted by his confession. She admired Wilder for acknowledging his weakness in order to make her feel better about her own ... only he was strong enough to fight his and win. Bethany had never stepped on board a boat again.

Refusing to look at him, Bethany continued to look out the window at the beautiful lawns of The Georgia.

A gentle hand touched her shoulder, and she faced him. His eyes were glowing with warmth and understanding. "Why don't you think about the possibility of going boating with me?" He was using that tone of voice again, the soothing balm that caressed and gave her the feeling he cared like no other could. The one he had used that first day in the rose garden.

The firm "no" that was on the tip of her tongue was never spoken. He placed his hand under her chin and rubbed his thumb across her lips. Their eyes and their breaths held steady as they comforted each other.

"Don't make a decision right now," he said. "Just think about it."

A sudden desire to be kissed by this man filled Bethany, consuming her. The very thought of it was crazy, wild, but still she wanted it. With a will of its own, her tongue came out and swiped across her lips, tasting the trace of soap that his touch had left on her skin. She heard his breath leap at her action.

He slipped his hand down the slender column of her throat to the back of her neck, gently pulling her close. Bending his head, he lightly brushed his warm lips over hers. Her heart seemed to stop for a moment. The kiss was brief but surely the sweetest she'd ever experienced. The intimate contact stole the breath from her lungs and sent fire speeding along her spine. But it wasn't enough to satisfy the yearning that was burning deep inside her. She wanted—no, needed—more.

Wilder must have felt it, too, because his other arm slipped around her shoulders and slowly drew her to him, pressing her breasts against his chest. Then he lowered his open lips over hers. Bethany wasn't well schooled in the art of kissing, but nature had a way of letting her know the rules. She circled his waist with her arms and her hands inched their way up his back, her fingers gliding up and over his shoulders. When she felt the tip of his tongue, she parted her lips and accepted his gentle movements as he thoroughly explored her mouth.

A shimmering glow seemed to envelop her in its midst. Surely this was the closest she had ever been to heaven. Bethany trembled from the sheer victory of this moment being as good as she'd dreamed. She had always known there had to be more to kissing than the few she'd shared with John Martin, and Wilder certainly hadn't disappointed her. The kiss lingered a few moments more until, with reluctance, it ended naturally.

Wilder's hand tightened on her neck briefly before he whispered, "Very nice, Bethany. Very good." He turned her loose and stepped away.

Bethany didn't want the kiss, the embrace, to end. But she didn't know how to let Wilder know.

"Now, why were you counting days when I came into your office? Are you wondering when I'm going back to Homestead?"

Even though her skin felt flushed and her lips still moist, the magic of the kiss was gone. If their embrace had the same effect on him that it had on her, he chose to ignore it. Maybe he was right to do so. It brought them back to reality. Some way, she had to put a stop to the indisputable attraction that surfaced whenever he was near.

Turning away from him, she said, "No, that's not what I was thinking about." Her voice sounded tremulous. She rubbed the back of her neck where Wilder's hand had rested. Her skin was warm from his touch. "Grace has been gone three days, and I haven't heard one word from her. She must know I'm worried about her. I can't believe she'd do this . . . that she'd stay away from home this long."

"I don't think you give her enough credit for knowing what she wants." Wilder folded his arms across his chest and leaned against the desk again.

Giving him an impatient glance, she explained, "She just turned eighteen. She's never been anywhere on her own, especially a place as big as Atlanta. This is her home . . . the only place she's ever known." Bethany looked away from him. "She knows how much I care about her. She knows I've always put her happiness and well-being above my own. How could she do this to me?" Bethany swallowed hard as she looked into Wilder's blue eyes. "How could she believe I'd be involved with a man like Stanley?"

"I think you're forgetting she loved him. It wouldn't have been too difficult for her to think you loved him, too. I believed it for a time." He gave her an apologetic smile. "She saw him as a wonderful man. The kind any woman would want, including her sister."

He didn't convince her, and the fact that he was trying to worried her all the more. Bethany took a step toward him and stopped. "I suppose you could be right about that, but it doesn't make me happy. And it's time I did something more than walk around wringing my hands, wondering when Grace is coming home." She looked around the room, then walked over to the door and shut it before returning to stand in front of Wilder again.

"I talked with Sheriff Beale this morning. I wanted his help in finding Grace, but he told me that because of her age and the fact that she left of her own free will, they couldn't do anything." She pulled in her bottom lip and released it quickly. "I've decided to hire a private detective to find her." Anguish showed in her words as well as her eyes.

"No, Bethany. You don't need one."

That wasn't what she wanted to hear. His answer was so quick it surprised her. He hadn't had time to digest the idea, let alone think about what she said.

Wilder grabbed her shoulders. His eyes were so intense she couldn't escape them. "Drop this idea now before you spend any money. Believe me, she will come home when she's ready."

Bethany was tempted. Yes, she wanted to believe Wilder. The warmth of his hands on her arms heated her whole body. She remembered his kiss, the soft sensuous way his lips had explored hers. His eyes were pleading with her to listen to him. No, she couldn't let him persuade her differently. She'd try again.

"I know some detectives have a reputation for taking your money and never finding—"

"Bethany, don't."

"Don't what? Don't try to find my sister? I have to. She may be in trouble or hurt. Do you know how many things I've conjured up in my mind? I have to find her and bring her home." She couldn't keep the plea out of her voice.

She jerked away from him, and Wilder reached out to bring her back into the fold of his arms. Bethany whirled away from him. "Don't touch me! This is your fault. You gave her all that money. Grace doesn't know how to handle that much money. She doesn't know how to manage on her own."

He took her accusation well, standing quietly for a moment before speaking. "Grace is angry with you because she thought you were having a lovers' tryst with her fiancé. Stop worrying and give her some time to get over her first heartbreak."

Her arms fell heavily to her sides. "I can't! She's my sister. She's the only family I have. I don't believe she'd stay away like this if something wasn't wrong."

Wilder's leg throbbed with every beat of his heart. How had he let himself be talked into making that promise to Grace? His word used to mean something, but now he wasn't so sure. How could it be right to keep his word if it meant putting Bethany through so much pain? He bent over and rubbed his leg below the knee. He knew all about pain. He was an expert.

"Did you call me?" Margaret asked from the doorway of Bethany's office.

Bethany and Wilder looked up.

"No, Margaret," Bethany said with a pang of guilt when she realized how loud she must have raised her voice.

"I thought I heard shouting going on in here." Margaret cut her eyes around to Wilder. A frown formed on her brow, and she took a step inside the room. "Are you giving Bethany any trouble?"

"No," Bethany and Wilder said at the same time.

Wilder didn't know why Margaret had taken a dislike to him. He tried to be nice to her even though she was gruff and never had a smile on her face. But he had to admire the woman. If it was her job to take care of Bethany, she did it well.

"Are you sure, Bethany? I know I heard you raise your voice." Her gaze darted back and forth between the two.

"I did and I apologize for that, Margaret, but everything's fine."

Wilder could see that Bethany was under a lot of strain. He didn't like the idea of Margaret adding to it. His promise to Grace had put him in a distasteful position. Maybe it was time he made a trip to Atlanta and had a talk with the girl.

He walked over to the desk and picked up his cane, steadying himself. Dealing with the pain in his leg was a constant struggle. "Naturally, Bethany is upset because she hasn't heard from Grace," he said to

Margaret. "I think she could use a cup of tea. Would you mind?"

Her eyes narrowed as she settled her gaze on Bethany. "You want some tea?"

"Yes, Margaret, that would be nice. Thank you."

Margaret gave Wilder another searing look before leaving.

As soon as she was out of earshot, Wilder picked up where they'd left off. "Bethany, it's foolish to hire a detective. Don't do it. Give Grace more time."

She brushed a wisp of hair away from her face. "I've made up my mind. I'm going to walk over to the mercantile and have Mrs. Stevens place a call to Columbus for me. Surely there's an agency there. Now if you'll excuse me, I need to get back to work."

Bethany was good at dismissing people. Wilder started to ask her who in the hell she thought she was to dismiss him like a servant who is no longer needed. Instead, he merely pushed away from her desk and walked out of the office.

He admired her courage, her strength. He'd known she had both the day he watched her take on Stanley Edwards in the rose garden. And now she would fight just as diligently for her sister. Wilder stopped at the door. How could he not tell her he knew Grace was staying at the Magnolia Glen Hotel in Atlanta? How could he not? Because he'd given his word. And his word used to mean something. If he didn't get his job or the full use of his leg back, his word would be the only thing left that made him a man.

Wilder continued on out the door and limped up the stairs with difficulty. If he hadn't been in a great deal of pain, he might have succeeded in talking

Bethany out of this wild idea of hiring an investigator. She was a strong-minded woman, and it wasn't easy to sway her. He respected her but that left him defenseless. He didn't want to take advantage of her any more than he already had.

Damn, he wished he hadn't kissed her. That was a big mistake. But he had wanted to since the first time he laid eyes on her, and when she wet her lips the way she had, he couldn't resist the temptation.

If he had known Bethany wasn't in love with Stanley, he'd never have made that stupid promise to Grace. In fact, he would have done a lot of things differently.

He pulled the brass key out of his pocket, unlocked the door to his room, and hobbled inside. The long walk he had taken, together with the climb up the stairs, was more than his injured muscles could take.

Sweating, he picked up the bottle of medicine the doctor had given him and quickly gulped some of it down. Wilder hated taking the foul-tasting stuff and prayed for the day when he would be able to throw it away and walk like a man once again.

He limped over to the bed and lay down on the floral-printed spread. A low moan escaped his throat when he stretched his leg to its full length. He opened his eyes and looked at the ceiling. It needed to be painted, he thought.

What in the hell was he doing thinking about the ceiling? Bethany wanted to hire a detective! If he was a decent man, he'd tell her where her sister was. Maybe Grace would come to her senses in a few days and return. In the meantime, he felt like the worst kind of deceiver.

Shielding his eyes with his arm, he remembered the softness of Bethany's lips beneath his, the sweet taste inside her mouth. He liked the way she fit up against him, the way her warm breath caressed his face. She felt good in his arms, as if she belonged there. Those few moments with her had made him feel as if he were home. The heady smell of roses that lingered in the air had been an aphrodisiac.

He flung his arm to his side, and his eyes popped open. Sitting on the dresser was a slender crystal vase with three dark red roses in it. No wonder the smell had been so strong. Someone had placed fresh roses in his room while he was gone.

After a few more moments, the pain in his leg subsided. Why had he kissed Bethany? he wondered. Because he had wanted to. Because she possessed all the qualities he liked in a woman. She was strong and independent, yet soft and feminine. She moved with a quiet grace he found alluring.

Wilder had to be careful. He didn't want to fall in love with Bethany. She was a beautiful woman. She was as attracted to him as he was to her. He was sure of that. Even though she tried to hide it, he sensed in her an eagerness to know about love. No, falling in love with Bethany would mean commitment and forever. Wilder rubbed his tired eyes as the medicine took effect. He'd better get that notion out of his head right now. Grace's little stunt had already preempted that possibility. Bethany would be furious and unforgiving if she learned he knew where Grace was staying.

After lying there for a few minutes, an idea came to Wilder. As soon as he slept off the laudanum, he'd walk over to the mercantile and place a few calls of his own. If Bethany was going to hire a detective, the least he could do was see that she had the best. If a Pinkerton found Grace, he would be free of that damning promise.

Later that evening, Bethany sat on the medallion-back settee in her living room, her feet propped up on a crewel-stitched footstool. Resting on her knees was a pad of paper. In her hand she held an ink pen. A jar of ink sat on a small tray on the sofa beside her. She was practicing the art of calligraphy from a pamphlet she'd picked up at the mercantile. Once she learned how to do the letters, she planned to make new menus for the restaurant and save the expense of having a professional printer do the work. She had also thought about printing Grace's wedding invitations. Thank God that wedding would never take place now.

A sudden knock at the door turned her *S* into a *Q*. It had to be Wilder or Margaret, and she doubted the knock was from the latter. Margaret had been gone a couple of hours. Putting down the paper, she set the ink jar on the small Chippendale table in front of her.

As she hurried to the door, Bethany realized she had already relaxed for the evening. Her hair was down but braided, thank goodness. She'd already removed her shoes and stockings, leaving her feet and legs bare. She never let anyone at The Georgia see her in such a casual manner. The only time she relaxed her dress code was in the privacy of the third floor. Copying her mother, Bethany usually wore a white high-neck blouse with a dark skirt and pumps. "A lady isn't dressed until she dresses up," her mother had always said.

The knock came again, louder this time.

Wilder lounged against the door frame, looking exactly as he had when she last saw him, except for the fact he'd rolled up the sleeves of his shirt to just below the elbow. For a moment she simply looked at him, trying to come to terms with the fact that as much as she would have liked for Grace to be standing there, she wasn't disappointed that it was Wilder.

His gaze ran from the long braid draping over her breast to her toes, which peeked out from underneath the hem of her skirt. "I like your hair that way," he said. "You don't look so . . . untouchable."

"Don't say that," she snapped, as irritation immediately stole over her. His reference was too close to a statement Stanley had made about her, and Bethany didn't want anything to remind her of that horrible man.

"I'm sorry," he apologized, limping past her. "Looks like I said the wrong thing."

"No, I'm the one who should apologize," she said in a softer voice, closing the door behind him. "I didn't mean to snap at you. It's just that what you said reminded me of something Stanley had said to me."

"Then I'll apologize again. I can imagine some of the things that came out of his mouth."

"I don't want to talk about it. Thank goodness I don't ever have to see him again."

113

As she led Wilder into the living room, Bethany crossed her arms over her chest to ward off the chill that Stanley's name provoked. The gas jets were turned all the way up but the room still seemed too golden with light, too intimate for her to be alone with a man who had the power to set her heart to racing. When he took a seat on the small sofa, Bethany sat down in the rose-colored wing-back chair. She sat straight with her hands folded neatly in her lap.

"That long braid brings out the little boy in me. Makes me want to put my hands on it and pull." His eyes teasing, Wilder moved to the edge of the sofa and reached over and pulled so lightly on her hair that it felt like a caress.

The movement was meant to put her at ease, and Bethany accepted it for a brief moment before turning away. How could she respond so warmly to his teasing, to his touch, when she knew that he would enjoy the fruits of The Georgia until his leg had fully healed, then be on his way back north to his life there?

"Did you want something?" she asked calmly.

"You smell of roses," he said, completely ignoring her question. "That's the first time I've noticed the perfume you wear."

Bethany lowered her lashes, feeling very feminine, very intimate with Wilder, even though she knew she shouldn't be sitting here alone with him. "It was always my mother's favorite."

"It's pleasant. I've never noticed, because the fragrance of fresh roses permeates the air in every room of this house." He lowered his voice. "It suits you."

Willing her pulse to stay under control, Bethany answered with a "Thank you."

"I like your feet, too," he said, letting his gaze drop to the floor. "You have cute toes."

Bethany's gaze flew to her feet, then quickly back to Wilder's smiling features. She had cute toes? She looked again. Her feet were slender, her toenails neatly trimmed. "I'm sorry, I wasn't expecting anyone. I like to go barefoot in the evenings," she admitted.

His eyes twinkled. "So do I. Only my feet aren't as attractive as yours."

Bethany's throat tightened. Was it proper to talk about their feet? Somehow she didn't think so. All Wilder had to do was say a few words, and suddenly the atmosphere between them changed. He was smiling. A sweet, natural smile that pleased her. His hair and clothes were rumpled just enough to be attractive. He was charming, seductive, and she was responding. He had the power to make her feel at ease and forget propriety. She liked for him to tease her, to smile at her, to kiss her—and she had to fight him.

She pulled her skirt down farther as she crossed her feet at the ankles, trying to hide them from his view. "Did you come for a specific reason?" she asked in a more formal tone.

Sensing she'd allow no more forward behavior, Wilder sat back on the sofa. "I walked over to the mercantile late this afternoon and made a couple of calls to some friends. I have the name of the best investigator in the Southwest. If you insist on having a detective, I want you to call him." He pulled a piece of paper out of his pants pocket and gave it to her.

Surprise leaped into her eyes before she could hide it. She didn't know why he wanted to help her, but he was a little late. "I've already called someone. His name is James Lester and he's from Columbus, Georgia."

Giving her a thoughtful look, Wilder pursed his lips. "What did you find out about him? How long has he been a detective and how many cases has he solved?"

"He said he'd spent six months with the Pinkerton Agency in Atlanta. Apparently, he's just opened his office in Columbus, but he said that would work to my advantage because he's available to spend all his time looking for Grace."

Wilder sighed. "That's not necessarily true, Bethany. How much experience does he have? I mean, has he been a detective for six years or six months?"

"I didn't ask," she answered truthfully.

"Who recommended him?"

"Sheriff Beale. He happened to be in the mercantile talking with Mrs. Stevens when I went over." Bethany rose from the chair and looked down at Wilder with firm, unwavering eyes. "I know what I'm doing, and I don't believe I asked for any advice."

Smiling, he answered, "I guess you didn't. I hope he finds her, Bethany. I hate to see you worrying about her."

He seemed sincere, and she appreciated his earnest attempt to calm her fears. "I won't worry so much now that I know someone is going to find her for me."

"It's not easy to find someone who doesn't want to be found."

"Grace doesn't know anything about hiding. I'm sure Mr. Lester won't have any trouble."

"I hope you're right." Wilder rose from the sofa. "It's been a long day for me. I'd better go."

Bethany followed him to the door. She was angry with herself for feeling disappointed that he was going so soon. She liked being with him. She liked . . . No, she had to stop thinking that way. He would be returning to Pennsylvania soon. She had to keep that uppermost in her mind . . . not that easy smile she found so attractive . . . not the gentle way he spoke . . . and surely not those alluring blue eyes.

When Wilder opened the door he turned back to her and said, "Sleep well, Bethany."

Chapter Eight

The next morning Bethany looked up from her desk to see Stanley Edwards coming toward her. He raised a hand, smoothing his thinning hair. A lazy smile formed on his full lips, and anger immediately erupted inside her.

"What are you doing here?" she demanded. Margaret must be away from her desk, Bethany thought. Stanley would never have gotten past her.

"Is that any way to treat an old friend, sweet Bethany?" he asked as he flopped into a chair, propping his booted feet on the edge of her freshly polished desk.

Contempt laced her voice as she said, "Get out of here. You're not welcome at The Georgia." She saw that the vehemence in her reply elated him, and she tried to check her anger.

"Don't be so hostile, Bethany. It doesn't become your gentle nature. I'll leave when I have what I came for."

"What do you want? There's nothing of yours

here." *Oh, let me stay calm until he leaves,* she cried inwardly. The last thing she wanted to do was scream at this man, but right now it would feel very good to do it.

His laughter had a bitter edge as he made another swipe at his hair with his hand. "I'm tired of waiting around. I want to know where Grace is. We've got a wedding to plan."

Bethany rose from her chair. "Do you honestly think I'd tell you even if I knew?" The man was incredible, unconscionable.

"Don't lie to me," he said, his words almost hissing. "You and Grace were thick as thieves. There's no way she'd be gone this long without getting in touch with you. You're her mama, right?"

Stanley's callous words brought renewed heartache for Bethany. She and Grace had been close once, but Stanley had ended that. Grace had been gone longer than Bethany would have believed. But she couldn't give up hope that her sister would forgive her and come home.

"Thanks to you, I don't know where she is," Bethany said, trying to stay in control. "Because she thinks you and I were having a—a tryst, she's punishing me by not letting me hear from her."

Stanley jumped to his feet and leaned over her desk. "You're lying." His eyes squinted in anger. "She worshipped the ground you walk on. She wouldn't do anything without checking with you first. Including running away from home."

"You changed all that! Thank God she finally saw you for what you are. A nothing of a man. Now, I want you out of here, and I don't want you to come back."

Stanley's nostrils flared and his eyes took on a glazed quality. For a moment Bethany thought he might strike her. Instead, he regained control of himself and straightened. He smiled sneeringly. "I'd say we're even, sweet Bethany. Like two peas in a pod. No one wants you, either." His lips twitched upward in a snarl. "I haven't seen any men courting you. It's no wonder your sister thought you were after me. Maybe you should take a chance at a man while you can. I'm willing to teach you how a woman pleases a man."

He walked confidently around the side of the desk and stood before her. "See, it doesn't matter to me that you act and dress like an old woman." His voice lowered to a whisper and his eyes fell to her breasts. He smacked his lips. "I know what's hidden beneath all those high-buttoned clothes you wear. I know how your long hair falls over your shoulders like silk when you take it down from that dowdy bun. I know what those tempting lips taste like and how good you smell."

Bethany squeezed her hands together so hard they hurt. Her whole body trembled. "How dare you speak to me in such a manner! You disgust me. Get out of here before I send Margaret for the sheriff."

"Dear, sweet Bethany call for help?" He shook his head. "Never. You'd scratch my eyes out or knee me in the groin before you'd let anyone think you couldn't take care of yourself. See, I know you well." He laughed.

"Get out!" she said.

He reached out and grazed her cheek with the back of his hand, letting his fingers slowly glide down. It took all her willpower not to shrink from his cold touch, knowing if she did it would please him, knowing he wanted to frighten her.

"Do you hate all men? Bethany," he asked with a smirk twisting his wide mouth.

"No, just you," she said coldly.

"Ah . . . such a waste! A beautiful, spirited woman like you needs a strong man like me. You need to be tamed, sweet Bethany. Don't worry. It's not you I want right now. I need your sister first. I'll know when she's back, and I'll come running to comfort her."

He reached out to touch her again, but a quiet voice from the doorway stopped him.

"Touch her and I'll smash your face."

Slowly, Stanley turned around and faced Wilder. He pointedly looked down at Wilder's legs. A smirk formed on his face. "Think you can catch me?" he asked.

"Touch her and you'll find out."

Stanley sighed dramatically and stepped away, running his hand across his dark hair. He pulled at his collar. "I don't fight cripples. Besides, I don't want Bethany. I want her sister."

"Do yourself a favor and don't come back," Wilder said in an icy tone.

After giving Bethany a wink, Stanley walked past Wilder, deliberately knocking his shoulder against the man and making him stagger backward.

Bethany rushed to Wilder's side, grabbed hold of

his arms, and pushed him against the wall, holding him there with her body. By the time Wilder regained his footing, Stanley was halfway down the corridor.

"Let go," he mumbled angrily. "I'll teach that bastard a lesson he won't forget."

"No, Wilder, please!" Bethany pressed against him as her open hands slid up his chest and held him to the wall. She looked into his eyes and said, "He didn't hurt me and you're not hurt. He's not worth it."

Staring up at him, she thought Wilder might push her aside and go after Stanley anyway, but he didn't.

"Are you sure he didn't hurt you?" Wilder asked, placing his hands on her waist, fitting her body to his.

She nodded, breathing easier now that she knew he wasn't going to attack Stanley, feeling safe now that she was so close to Wilder.

A chill shook Bethany, and she squeezed her eyes shut for a brief moment. She felt dirty where Stanley had touched her. What a horrible man he was.

"You're a difficult woman to protect, Bethany Hayward."

"Why?" she asked.

Admiration showed in his eyes. "You do a good job of taking care of yourself."

Wilder didn't know how wrong he was. She was failing miserably in trying to protect herself from him. She was afraid she might be falling in love with him.

With his hands still on her waist, he gently pushed her away from him.

Embarrassed, feeling utterly rebuffed, Bethany

took a step backward. "Did you need something?" she asked, her voice stronger than she expected it to be.

"I wanted to let you know I'd be gone the rest of the day should the impossible happen and you need me for anything."

Bethany started to snap out an angry retort but changed her mind and simply said, "Fine."

He was right. She didn't need him, she told herself as he walked away. She had to keep telling herself that, because the more time she spent with him, the less Bethany believed it.

The mill came into view as the ferry rounded a bend and sailed toward shore. The L-shaped building was nestled among a group of towering pines. Even from this distance he could see the building was in a state of disrepair. The paint was peeling in places and the tin roof had rusted. It appeared that what he'd heard about the poor condition of the factories in the South was true.

Wilder paid the man and stepped off the ferry, his boots splashing in the shallow water. Over the sound of the gently lapping water on the river's bank, he heard the wail of working machinery.

His boots crunched on the gravelly rocks as he made his way to the front of the building. The door was open, so he stepped inside. The stifling heat, together with the loud buzzing and clinking noises, immediately reminded him of the steel mill. He hadn't been back there since his accident. Wilder closed his eyes and saw flames leaping from the open hearths and the sweat-soaked bodies of the steel workers. He smelled the stench of melted iron and burned wood. He heard the hammers as they clanked against the steel.

"We're not hiring."

Wilder's eyes flew open at the sound of the coarse voice. A short man of about fifty, dressed in ill-fitting clothes, stood before him. Wilder realized his hands had made fists, and he relaxed.

"I said we're not hiring. Got all the workers we need. Check with the West Point mills up river."

Wilder was surprised to hear such a gritty voice coming from a man so small. "I'm not looking for work." He reached into his jacket pocket and brought out Bethany's letter. "I'm here at Miss Hayward's request."

The man eyed him warily, then took the letter and read the contents. He rubbed his nose with the back of his hand as he studied the paper. When he looked up at Wilder, he said, "I reckon she done hired her a fancy man to take my place. I did the best I could fer her."

"I'm afraid you misunderstood," Wilder hurried to say. "I'm only here to look over the mill and offer suggestions on how you might make it more productive. I'm not here to take anyone's job."

The man wiped his nose again, and his eyes squinted. "You telling me the truth?"

Wilder smiled and extended his hand to the man. "You have my word on it. I'm Wilder Burlington."

"Carl Braxton. I been working for Miss Hayward near on to five years." He shook Wilder's hand.

"Mr. Braxton, I'm pleased to meet you. If you have

a few minutes to show me around the mill, I'd appreciate it."

"Sure, if that's all you need. I can spare the time."

Wilder didn't want to mislead the older man. "Well, I may have to come back again in a day or two. I'm not sure I can get all the information I need in one visit."

"What kind of information do you need?"

"I want to study the mill and how it works. There may be ways to improve production." Wilder took out his handkerchief and wiped sweat from his brow, then took off his jacket.

Braxton shook his head. "Only way to do that is to keep these old worn-out machines working."

A quick glance around the large room told Wilder a lot. "The building needs better ventilation. More windows would be a big improvement. It's hot as hell in here. The machinery is probably overheating."

"More windows?" Braxton sniffed again. "That might help keep 'em running."

"What else you have in mind?"

Wilder started rolling up his sleeves. "Let's take a look and see."

With a wisp of a smile, the older man led the way.

Bethany was counting out the week's wages for the employees when Margaret came to the doorway of her office and announced, "There's a man out here who says he's from Columbus, Georgia. Name's James Lester. Said you were expecting him."

Bethany hurriedly tried to collect her thoughts. "Yes. He's the private detective I spoke with

126

yesterday. Give me a few minutes to put this money away, then send him in. And, Margaret, I meant to tell you earlier and forgot, but if Stanley Edwards comes back to The Georgia, I want you to go for Sheriff Beale immediately."

"He bothering you?"

"He could become a problem. I just don't want him here now that Grace is gone."

"I'll see to it."

"Thank you," she said as she opened the lockbox and placed the money inside.

Margaret stood in the doorway a moment longer. "It's none of my business, but are you sure you know what you're doing, hiring this man and all?"

"It's the only thing left to do. I certainly don't know anything about trying to find her," Bethany said patiently, searching through the papers on her desk for the envelope that contained the only good photograph she had of Grace.

"All right. It's your business," Margaret muttered as she walked away.

Bethany looked at the gilded bronze and marble clock sitting on the mantel. Mr. Lester was early, and she was justifiably nervous. She didn't know what kind of questions to ask him. Maybe she should have engaged the man Wilder suggested and let him ask the questions.

"What am I thinking?" she said aloud. "I don't need Wilder. I can handle this myself and Wilder said as much." But in her heart, she knew how easy it would be to start relying on him.

The dark-haired middle-aged man entered her office almost at a run, his hand extended for the introductory shake. "Mrs. Hayward, I'm James Lester. I'm sorry I couldn't come this morning, but I got here as fast as I could."

She reluctantly grasped his hand and he pumped her arm eagerly. The scent of strong spices assailed her senses, and she drew back from his overpowering cologne. "Mr. Lester, I'm pleased to meet you, and it's *Miss* Hayward."

"I do beg your pardon, ma'am . . . uh . . . Miss Hayward. You can call me James if you like." He released her hand and stood back, smiling widely as he brushed his too-long hair away from his forehead.

"I'd prefer to use Mr. Lester if you don't mind."

"Whatever makes you comfortable. Now tell me about this sister you want me to find."

Bethany didn't know quite what to make of James Lester. He wasn't as professional looking as she'd expected. Not only were his clothes old and worn, but they were also dirty. And she suspected the heavy cologne hid his unwashed body odor.

"Please sit down, Mr. Lester." She pointed to the straight-backed chair in front of her desk.

Mr. Lester eased himself into the chair, keeping the smile on his face. From his jacket pocket he withdrew a fat, stubby pencil and a folded piece of paper. "Now, I need your sister's full name," he said.

"Grace Hayward."

"Ah . . . you may want to spell that for me." He cleared his throat and smiled nervously. Pink stained his cheeks. "Just to be sure I have it right."

Bethany watched the detective as he slowly wrote Grace's name, then taking another swipe at his hair with his hand, he continued, "I'm going to have to ask you a few questions. Some of them may be a little personal, but don't worry. Anything you say to me is confidential.''

Bethany wondered how many cases he'd worked on in his six months with the Pinkertons. He didn't seem as experienced as she'd expected.

"Now, Miss Hayward, do you have any idea where Grace might be staying?"

"No, of course not." She was a little shocked by the elementary question. "I wouldn't need you if I had any idea where she was staying. We have no relatives to contact, and I've spoken with all her friends here in town. The stationmaster confirmed that she boarded the northbound train to Atlanta.''

"Have you heard from her since she left?"

"No. Not at all.''

"Does she have a favorite place in Atlanta that she likes to go to?"

"No. She's never been to Atlanta before." Bethany rubbed the top of her shoulder. Mr. Lester was probably only asking the same questions any detective would ask, but to her they seemed so trivial. He was a nice man and seemed eager enough. He made notes on the piece of paper as they talked, but already Bethany doubted his ability to find Grace.

"All right." He looked up at her and smiled. "Can you give me a physical description of Grace?"

"This envelope contains a photograph of Grace taken earlier this year. I'm afraid her . . . fiancé is also in the picture. I've listed her statistics on the back.''

"Splendid," he said. "Is her fiancé missing, too?"

"No. He was here only minutes before you. No need to contact him. He hasn't heard from her.''

"I see." When he reached for the envelope, Bethany was once again repelled by the heavy scent of his cologne. He must keep a bottle in the pocket of his jacket and lavish it on himself when it started fading, she thought. Her gaze dropped to his hands. He chewed his nails. It was probably a nervous habit, like combing through his hair with his fingers. Uneasiness settled around her. Wilder's offer of help was beginning to sound better. A little voice told her to tell this man she'd changed her mind, to pay him for his time, and to send him on his way. But another voice told her she couldn't start relying on Wilder Burlington. Kiss or no kiss. In a few weeks, he would be heading back north.

She watched Mr. Lester open the envelope and look at Grace's picture. He let out a low whistle, unable to hide his appreciation. "She's beautiful," he declared.

"Yes, she is," Bethany agreed. Thinking of Grace's smiling green eyes and her sparkling laughter tingling on the air made Bethany ache to see her, to know that she was well.

Mr. Lester stuffed the picture back into the envelope and laid it on his lap. "Is there any chance she could have run off with a man?" He continued his simple questioning.

"No."

"Her fiancé . . . what would he say to that question?"

Anything that reminded Bethany of Stanley was a source of irritation. She hoped she never saw him again. Bethany swallowed hard. "He would tell you that she ran away because of me."

He continued making his notes on the paper. "How much money did she have with her when she left?" he asked.

Bethany winced and her nails dug into the palms of her hands as she clinched them. Another sore subject. "A lot."

"What? Fifty dollars? A couple of hundred? More?"

"No, no, much more than that," Bethany said, shaking her head. "Why does it matter how much money she had with her?" Her skin already felt as if thousands of little needles were sticking her, and his simple questions were driving her crazy.

Mr. Lester looked directly into Bethany's eyes. "It's important to know whether or not she had enough money to go anywhere in the world."

His words hit Bethany hard. She sobered. He was right about that and it hurt. "Yes, Grace had enough money to go anywhere she wanted to go." She couldn't—wouldn't believe Grace had left Atlanta. Bethany sighed with sadness as her anger against Wilder was renewed. This was his fault. If he hadn't given Grace so much money, she would be home where she belonged.

After several more questions about Grace, they discussed his fee. She would have to be frugal with the money she received from the sale of her grandmother's jewelry. Already, she'd planned to pay for her half of the repairs to the house with part of it. The rest would be used to find Grace. It would take every extra penny she could get her hands on to do this, but the money was insignificant. Grace had to be found at any cost.

"I guess that's enough for now," Mr. Lester said, rising from the velvet cushioned chair. "I'll get started on this right away. You say the stationmaster said he saw her board the train?"

"Yes. That's what he told me."

"And it was headed for Atlanta?"

Bethany nodded. "But it makes several stops along the way. She could have gotten off at any one of them."

He smiled confidently. "Don't worry, Miss Hayward. I'll find your sister for you."

Mr. Lester put his paper and pencil back into his jacket pocket. "I'll be in touch," he said as he backed out of the room.

Stanley Edwards waited a short distance down from The Georgia. He'd returned to tell Bethany he had decided to go to Atlanta himself to look for Grace, and he'd overheard her and James Lester talking. So Bethany had decided to hire a detective to find her little sister. He chuckled to himself. He always knew Bethany was too smart for a woman.

No doubt the detective would find Grace before he could, so he had no choice but to talk James Lester into double-crossing Bethany. It would take what little money he had left, but it would be worth it. In the end he'd have Grace, The Georgia, and the Hayward Mill. And if he was careful, he just might get between sweet Bethany's legs once before he killed her.

Stanley chuckled again at that thought as he took out his handkerchief and wiped the back of his neck. He wished the detective would hurry. The sun was hot as hell. If he didn't get out of the scorching heat soon, sweat was going to stain his clothes. He had on his best suit.

What would be the best way to get rid of Bethany once he married Grace? he wondered. He could give her small doses of poison as he had his first wife. No. He shook his head. Bethany was too smart for that. He'd do better to go with an accident. Falling down the stairs had killed his second wife. No reason to think it wouldn't kill Bethany, too.

At the sound of whistling, Stanley looked up the street. James Lester was heading toward him. A satisfied smile spread across Stanley's lips and he took a deep breath.

"Good day to you, sir," he said warmly as the man approached. "I couldn't help but notice you just left The Georgia. Are you staying there?"

"Oh, no." He smiled as Stanley fell into step beside him. "I was there on a matter of business."

"Truly? So was I not more than a few minutes ago." Stanley paused and chose his words well. "My fiancée lives there."

"Do say." Mr. Lester looked Stanley over carefully. "Miss Grace Hayward?"

"That's right," Stanley answered, his plan forming as he talked.

"I thought so. Miss Hayward gave me a picture of the two of you together."

"Bethany's quite distraught over her sister's disappearance."

"Oh my, yes. That she is. She's hired me to find her."

"Yes, she told me she was expecting you. In fact, I'm the one who suggested she call you." Stanley knew that a little praise went a long way.

"Really? So very kind of you."

"Maybe you can help me. I'd like to spare Bethany all the heartache possible. You know how weepy women can get. Why don't you come to me with all the information you find on Grace. It might be easier for Bethany to get the news from me."

Stanley saw the hesitation in the man's eyes before he shook his head. "Oh, I couldn't do that. It wouldn't be right for me not to give her the information. She's paying me."

Stanley reached into his pocket and pulled out a twenty-dollar note. "I'll do anything to spare my fiancée's sister. She's so dear to me." He pulled another twenty from his pocket.

"Well, I could use the extra money. My wife's expecting our third child."

"No need to make a hasty decision." Stanley had the man right where he wanted him. From here on out, it had to be this man's decision. "Look, here's the hotel. Why don't we go in and get out of the sun. I'll buy you a drink and we'll discuss it. How does that sound?"

"I do believe I am a bit thirsty."

"So am I. Let's go inside."

"I do need to ask you some questions concerning your fiancée," James Lester said as he stuffed the two bills into the pockets of his pants.

Smiling, Stanley said, "I'll be happy to tell you anything you want to know." He clapped the man on the back, and dust flew from his clothes.

Chapter Nine

The next morning Bethany was sitting at her desk when Ruth Mayland rushed into her office, tears streaming down her cheeks, her hands clutching the hem of her white apron.

"Ruth, what's wrong?" Bethany asked, rising to her feet, eyes concerned.

"It's that Mr. Burlington. He fired me!" Ruth cried.

"He what?" Bethany asked, an incredulous look on her face.

Ruth sniffed and wiped her eyes with the wrinkled apron. "Well, he told me I wasn't doing my job properly and to get out until I could learn how to do it." She sniffed again, loudly. "He's a difficult man to work for, Miss Hayward. He's not kind and patient like you are."

Bethany reached into the pocket of her black skirt. Pulling out a lace-trimmed handkerchief, she handed it to the crying woman. She didn't know what to say. Granted, Wilder was a forceful man when he wanted to be, but she couldn't imagine him being cruel, especially to someone as soft-spoken as Ruth.

"Stay here in my office while I go talk to Wilder. I don't know what's going on, but I'll get to the bottom of this." She took a deep breath. He'd gone too far. There was no way she was going to let Wilder upset or fire any of The Georgia's employees without her approval. "Try to calm yourself. I'll take care of everything." She patted Ruth's shoulder when she hurried past her.

As she walked out of the office, Bethany lifted her chin and prepared for the battle she was going to have with Wilder. She didn't want to be constantly at odds with him, but she couldn't let him take control. Maybe Wilder would start spending more time at the mill. At least in that area, he had some expertise. She didn't need his help in managing The Georgia.

There was no one in the dining room, so Bethany walked through the swinging doors and into the kitchen. The morning cook, Stilman, and the two other workers were standing quietly in a row listening to Wilder. His back was to her but she was sure that he knew she had come in.

"I don't want to see another chipped dish come out of this kitchen and enter the dining room," Wilder was saying. "I also expect the service to improve. You are paid to prepare delicious, eye-appealing food and to give excellent service. I won't accept less. If any of you disagree with what I'm saying, you're free to go. Stop by Miss Hayward's office on your way out and she'll give you a week's pay." He turned to look at Bethany, who stood behind him, then back to the three standing at attention, stiff as wooden Indians.

"No one's leaving? Good. Let's get ready for lunch." As the others hurried to their jobs, Wilder walked over to Bethany. "Any comment?" he asked dryly.

"Yes," she said tightly, her whole body burning with anger. "Follow me."

The nerve of that man. Her pumps clicked rapidly on the hardwood floor and her skirts brushed against her legs. The nerve of him to underhandedly force her to appear as if she were in agreement with what he just did. He'd left her no choice. She couldn't let the workers know that she and Wilder were in a disagreement over anything. That would be asking for trouble she didn't need.

They made their way through the main office and past Margaret, onto the marbled foyer and out to the large front porch. Bethany was steaming, and the heat from the sun didn't help. In the distance beyond the tall camellia bushes, she heard Seth singing in a languid voice as he worked in the garden. Any other time the gardener's crooning would have given her a restful feeling.

Bethany faced Wilder with a determined look. "When you said you wanted your day in the kitchen, I didn't believe you meant it."

He took a deep breath. "Bethany . . ."

"You can't go around firing my employees." Her voice was soft even though her words were laced with anger.

Wilder leaned against one of the massive Corinthian columns. "I didn't fire them. I told them if they didn't like what I said, they could leave."

"I'm talking about Ruth. She told me you had fired her. Is that true?"

He was calm, watching her possessively, paying too much attention to her lips. How could she continue to be angry with him when he looked at her like that?

"I told her she either does her job without complaining or she's out."

"So you didn't tell her she had to go," Bethany stated, breathing easier but still uneasy under his hot gaze.

"Not yet. But believe me, I'm tempted. I'm going to give her another chance simply because I don't think she's ever been taught the proper way to serve food. You don't pour half of the coffee in the cup and the other half in the saucer. And you don't argue with a customer about what they ordered."

Bethany gasped. "I don't believe you. Ruth wouldn't do that. Stilman wouldn't allow it."

"You're the unbelievable one, Bethany." Wilder moved closer, and she jumped back slightly. "You think that because you do your best at all times, everyone else follows suit. That's not true." His blue eyes darkened. "Some people need to know that if they don't do their jobs right, they're out."

Bethany turned away from him and walked to the edge of the porch. She leaned against the large column and looked out over the beautiful lawn. Bright shades of red and pink geraniums lined the walkways, lifting their petals to the warming rays. To the side of the house the roof of the portico was held up by the same design of Corinthian columns as the ones that graced the front, only smaller. Yes,

Bethany thought, she loved this house and expected everyone else to love it, too.

She had been only eighteen when she took over the management of the restaurant and inn. Her parents' friends and Sheriff Beale had suggested she sell it. They all said she was too young and inexperienced to run it. She had kept the house and proved them wrong.

There was a crick in the back of Bethany's neck that had been there for weeks. She'd tried to rub it out but it wouldn't go away. Wilder was right. She never gave less than her best no matter what she was doing. She thought everyone who worked at The Georgia had the same kind of pride in the tradition of the mansion that she had.

"Bethany," he called her name softly. "You've got to remember that only the third floor of this house is your home. The rest of it is a business and it must be run like one."

There was truth in what he said, but that didn't make it any easier to accept. "I'll go speak to Stilman. If he confirms what you say, I'll talk to Ruth," she said huskily, then turned away and went back inside without looking at Wilder.

In a matter of moments, Bethany had made her way back to the kitchen. Stilman stood over a steaming pot; one of his helpers was busy chopping carrots. He looked up when she walked in. She cleared her throat and said, "I'd like to speak with you for a few moments, Stilman."

Stilman followed her to the far side of the large kitchen. He was a short, heavyset man, his size showing his appreciation of good food. Bethany had been wary of Stilman when she first hired him more than three years ago, but she soon realized he was a great asset to The Georgia. His experience in the kitchen brought many guests back to the inn.

Bethany smiled at the gentle giant of a man and said, "I'm sorry we haven't talked in a long time. But with Grace leaving and Mr. Burlington coming, things have been hectic."

"I know all about the problems you've been having, Miss Hayward, and—"

"And what, Stilman?" she prompted him to continue.

"I didn't want to add to your worries." Stilman rested his hands on his round stomach, but his eyes never left her face.

Bethany felt a moment of trepidation. Was there something going on that she didn't know about? "Go on. Tell me the problem."

"You know that when I came to work here, I told you I didn't want to have anything to do with the administration. I have my own job to do and that takes all my time."

"Yes, I know. That's why I take care of the paperwork, the hiring—"

"And the firing," he said, interrupting her.

"Oh," she answered softly, sensing this was going to be one of those unpleasant scenes she couldn't avoid.

"Mr. Burlington made me realize I've held my piece long enough." There was a nervous edge to his voice but a look of determination in his eyes. "Ruth Mayland is a troublemaker and a bad influence on my other helpers. I was easy on her at first because I knew her husband ran off with another woman and she needed the work. We're tired of pulling her load. She's taken advantage of all of us at one time or another."

Bethany watched Stilman's features for any sign of vindictiveness. There was none. The only thing she saw in his expression was the same distaste she felt in having to be part of a conversation like this.

"Do you think she's willing to try harder?"

Stilman slowly shook his head.

Wilder had thought Ruth might improve with proper training, but it didn't appear Stilman wanted to give her another chance. "Did you tell Ruth if she didn't improve you'd have to speak to me?"

"The only thing I told her was to quit complaining and to stop expecting someone else to do her job for her."

Bethany took a long breath that ended with a sigh. "Thank you for being honest with me." She turned to walk away, but Stilman spoke again.

"Did you want to speak with me about something?"

She smiled. "I wanted to tell you I think you do a superb job. I'm very lucky to have you."

A wide grin stretched across Stilman's face.

Deep in thought, Bethany walked back to her office. Stilman had confirmed what Wilder had said and added more. Ruth had not been doing her job. He'd kept quiet because he didn't want to add to her problems and he knew Ruth needed the work. Bethany had to keep that in mind, too. But another thing was on her mind as she walked back into her office to face Ruth. Wilder expected her to take care of the problem, and she would.

Midday sun was overtaking morning shadows. The brilliant sunshine poured into Bethany's office, heating it. Ruth stood by one of the windows, her nervous hands twisting her apron into an unsightly wad. Tears had collected in her eyes. She had opened the windows but there was very little breeze to stir the humid air.

Ruth was at least ten years older than Bethany, with two children to care for. Bethany had hired her without benefit of work experience because her husband had left her.

"I didn't do anything wrong, Miss Hayward," Ruth said, vindicating herself from the start.

"I know you've been trying, Ruth." Bethany tried to smile but she felt too bad about what she was going to do. "I've talked to Mr. Burlington and to Stilman and given this some thought. I've decided to change you to the mill."

"Oh no, Miss Hayward! I can't do that kind of work. It's too hard. I'll get sick!"

Bethany ignored the plea in Ruth's eyes and voice, sitting down at her desk and writing out instructions as she spoke. "I'm asking that you be given a job keeping the mill and the office there clean. I'm sure you can handle it. The work will be easier and you won't have to deal with customers."

The older woman sniffed and rubbed her reddening nose. Her small brown eyes were swollen from crying. "You mean I won't have to smile at people when I don't feel like smiling?"

Looking up at her, Bethany said, "That's right. All you have to do is keep the place clean. You can do that, can't you?"

Bethany knew the ordeal was over when Ruth dropped the hem of her apron and the corners of her mouth lifted into a smile.

Chapter Ten

The restaurant of The Georgia was dimly lit with girandoles mounted to the wall between the windows, giving the gold-tone flocked wallpaper an intimate glow. A nervous flutter attacked Bethany's stomach when she saw Wilder sitting at a table waiting for her. He looked very handsome in his light gray suit. It had been several years since Bethany had sat at a dinner table with a man, and for some reason she felt strangely young and vulnerable. Shaking off the feeling, she continued on into the room, stopping to speak to several guests before making her way to Wilder's table.

Wilder's invitation to join him for dinner tonight had been more of a demand. He'd left word with Margaret that he wanted her to meet him for dinner at six. She'd thought about not showing up but realized that would be a childish way to behave, so she'd changed into a wine-colored satinet dress with beige lace on the fitted sleeves and stand-up collar.

"You look beautiful tonight, Bethany," he said as

he rose to greet her. "That dress is very flattering."

Wilder had caused a melting pot of emotions to erupt inside her. One moment she was angry and resentful toward him, then the next she was attracted to him, wanting to feel his comforting arms around her. She thanked him and took her seat at a table that overlooked the beautiful gardens.

A light rain was falling on the petals and leaves of the flowers and shrubs. There was something faintly mesmerizing about watching the tiny drops drench the greenery in the early evening twilight. Through the windowpane, it looked as if the flickering candle flame that danced on their table was actually sitting in the middle of the garden, the rain trying desperately to drown it.

"I'd like to think you're smiling because you're so happy to be having dinner with me. Any chance I'm right?" Wilder asked.

Unaware that she had been caught staring at the illusion, Bethany laughed lightly. "From this angle, it looks as if the candle flame is outside, fighting for its life against the rain."

Wilder smiled fondly. "It's good to see you laugh. Your eyes are sparkling."

"I haven't had much to laugh about lately. But now I feel better, knowing that Grace isn't going to marry Stanley and Mr. Lester is looking for her."

Leaning forward, Wilder rested his arms on the white tablecloth. "For your sake, I hope he finds her soon." He took a drink from his water glass, then asked, "Tell me, how often do you leave The Georgia?"

"Leave?" she asked, not certain what he meant.

"How often do you get away and go other places?"

"Oh, well, I walk over to the mercantile once or twice a week, and there's an elderly woman I visit every Wednesday afternoon, Mrs. Bloomfield. She lives one street over in the Seth Lore district of town. We usually sit on her front porch and have a cup of tea or glass of lemonade, depending on the weather. Why do you ask?"

He shrugged lightly. "I noticed that you seldom leave the property."

"Where is there to go? The Georgia is my life," she said softly.

"I'm beginning to believe that. How old are you, Bethany?"

"Twenty-four," she answered.

And he was thirty. Wilder sipped his water again and sat back in his chair. How had he let his feelings for Bethany go so far? He knew her life was here at The Georgia. He'd known right from the beginning how important this house was to her, yet he couldn't keep the seeds of admiration, desire, and love from growing. She was everything he could want in a woman. Bethany was loyal and compassionate to a fault. She was strong and courageous. And she was passionate, too. What could he offer her that she didn't already have? The Georgia was far grander than the family home where he lived with his brother in Pittsburgh.

As if all that weren't enough to make him cower, he was involved in a deceitful agreement with Grace and he couldn't forget his limp. If he were going to recommend himself to Bethany as a possible suitor, what could he offer? Love and children, but at twenty-four, if she had wanted those things, wouldn't she already have them?

"You're so quiet. Why?"

He shook his head. "No reason," he lied, not wanting to admit to Bethany that he was having such intimate thoughts about her. "Tell me, how did it go when you talked to Ruth?"

"I took the easy way out and moved her to the mill. I think she'll be happier there."

A soft light crept into Wilder's eyes and a smile spread across his face. Just what he expected from her. Everything about Bethany was exaggerated sweetness and softness, yet she was very strong and independent. "I'm not surprised. You're a true southern lady, Bethany."

"Me! Oh no, Wilder. I've tried hard to be like my mother, but I've missed the mark so many times. I have a trace of rebel that rears its ugly head too often."

"Then you've only missed it enough to keep you desirable."

Bethany lowered her dark lashes over her eyes. She didn't want him to see how much his words meant to her. She wasn't prepared for the personal slant of this conversation. When she looked back at him, she asked, "Why did you ask me to have dinner with you?"

"I have a couple of things I'd like to discuss with you. But why don't we order first," Wilder said as he motioned for the waitress.

"All right. What looks good to you tonight?" she asked as she picked up the menu.

"You."

Bethany glanced up at him and he wanted to kiss her. Right here. Right now. He was tempted to lean across the table and place his lips over hers. As he looked into her sparkling green eyes, for a moment he thought she might let him, but the waitress walked up and the magic of the moment faded away.

"I'll have the roast beef and vegetables," she said.

"Sounds good. I'll have the same."

When the waitress left, Wilder said, "I'd like for us to give a ball."

"What?" Bethany wasn't sure she understood him. "A ball?"

"Yes. I've heard about genteel Southerners with their cordial hospitality and lavish entertaining."

Bethany smiled and moistened her lips, intrigued by the handsome man seated across from her. She placed her hand under her chin. "You're talking about the bygone era of hoopskirts for the ladies and gallantry for the men. The war changed all that. Things are better than they were in the seventies and early eighties, but most Southerners are still trying to rebuild their homes and their lives."

"We can help them. For one night, let's bring back those days before the war." His voice was seductively low and a warm gleam sparkled in his eyes.

Bethany wanted to share his enthusiasm but knew it wouldn't be right. "I—I think it would be in poor taste to have a ball with Grace missing."

Wilder didn't take his gaze from her face. "Life goes on, Bethany. At least think about it. You work so hard to make The Georgia the most beautiful house in town, you should have the opportunity to show it off to the townspeople. I think planning a ball would be good for you—and for me. With so much going on here, I don't have time to sit around and feel sorry for myself because my leg hurts or because I still have the damn limp."

"I'll think about it," she promised as she smiled and waved good-bye to a guest who was leaving the dining room.

The thought of a ball and dancing with Wilder sent heat scorching through Bethany. Wilder had made her aware of how much she had missed being with a man since her breakup with John Martin.

It occurred to Bethany that perhaps Wilder wasn't going to walk out of her life. Her problem with John Martin Sommers had been that he wanted her to sell The Georgia, and she had refused. Wilder owned half of it and had made it quite clear he wouldn't give it up. But what would he do when it was time for him to return home?

While they waited for their dinner, Bethany kept the conversation light, with talk about the new roof and paint for The Georgia. There were still things they didn't agree on, but neither of them argued about it. When the food arrived, they both ate the delicious meal with a hearty appetite.

"Why don't we take a walk out in the garden?" Wilder suggested after they'd finished coffee.

"I think there's still a light mist coming down," Bethany replied, although it was too dark to be sure.

"Are you afraid of a little rain?" he asked, a grin lifting the edges of his lips.

"Are you teasing me?"

The shake of his head was the only answer he gave.

"You're serious. You want to walk out in the

garden, in the dark, in the rain." This time he nodded, then rose and extended his arm to her.

"What about your leg?" she asked, still trying to digest his unusual request.

"It's not bothering me at all."

There was a slow rising cadence to the beat of her heart. She looked down at her wine-colored dress. It was one of her best. Should she take the chance it would be ruined? Why not? Why not walk in the gentle rain with Wilder?

By the time they made it to the edge of the lawn, Bethany could hardly discern Wilder's features. Clouds had covered the moon and the lights from the house were dimmed by low-lying fog. The rain was very light, more of a mist. Bethany lifted her face and let the fine moisture caress her. She liked the warm pressure of Wilder's hand on her back as he guided her onto the stone walkway. She couldn't remember ever feeling so uninhibited, so romantic, so free.

"Did you grow up with the idea that you'd one day take over the running of The Georgia?" he asked after a brief silence.

"Heavens no! I wanted to be a schoolteacher," she said as they continued to walk.

"Your parents' death changed that?"

Bethany was silent for a moment. "Yes. I was preparing to start my first year teaching when they were killed." Loneliness and sorrow crept into her voice. Even after all these years, she still missed them and wondered how her life would have turned out if they had lived.

"Would you still like to be a teacher?" he asked in a low voice.

151

"No, I don't think so." Remembering her parents made her hug her arms to her chest, to fight the chill from within. "I couldn't give up taking care of this house. It's too much a part of me now." But even as she said the words, Bethany realized her conviction wasn't as strong as it used to be. Since Wilder had arrived, so many things had changed.

"Looks like you're cold." He stopped and slipped his arms around her shoulders and pulled her close. "Is that better?"

Can birds fly? All evening, she had wanted to be in his arms. When she was with Wilder, Grace didn't seem as far away and The Georgia didn't seem as important. Yes, being in his arms felt just the way she remembered. No, better. Warmer. Safer.

Her behavior was dangerous, crazy too, but she couldn't deny herself the extravagance. Bethany snuggled closer, her nose resting against his warm neck. It was slightly scratchy, with a hint of beard. He smelled of shaving soap. She inhaled deeply. With her lips, she caressed his skin with the slightest pressure.

The rhythm of his breathing increased, and his arms tightened around her. He must feel the way she did. Should she take the chance? Her heart pounded so loudly she could hear it. His fingers cupped her chin and lifted her face toward his.

Moisture sprinkled her eyes and cheeks as his lips covered hers, softly at first, then harder, more urgently. There was no time to breathe, only to feel. She responded to his hot kisses by wrapping her arms around his neck. Her hands slid to the back of his head and tightened in his damp hair while their bodies pressed closer and closer. When his hand found her breast and covered it, she welcomed his touch with a moan of pleasure. Through her layers of clothing and a lightly ribbed corset he palmed, massaged, and molded her breast with his hand.

Bethany trembled with desire. She should stop his amorous advances. She'd been told not to let a man be so forward. She shouldn't let him touch her breasts, but she wanted him to. She'd been waiting for his kiss, his touch, all evening. Just a few more seconds of this heady, rapturous feeling that draped her like clingy silk, then she'd pull away.

His lips left hers and traveled over her cheek and down her neck, the stand-up collar not letting him get very far. Wilder groaned and moved his lips lower. Finding her breast with his mouth, he gently bit into the damp clothing, searching. For the first time in her life, Bethany wanted to strip for a man. Her arms circled his head and she cradled him close to her breasts. His breath seeped through the dampened material and warmed her skin.

Somewhere in the back of her mind, she knew what she was doing was wrong. But it was so good. Count to three, then break, she told her fuzzy brain. One. Two. Three. Four. Five. Six. Seven . . .

A little shove at Wilder's chest was all it took. He let her go and she turned away, trying to catch her breath, fighting the desire to turn into his arms once again and beg him to show her how to love him.

"I didn't mean for this to happen," she finally said in a ragged voice.

"Neither did I. But I should have known it would before the evening was over. It seemed destined to happen. I wanted to kiss you. I want to make love to you."

Bethany felt his warm breath on her neck as he came up behind her and slipped his arms around her waist. She forced herself not to turn and look at him. The admission was out. She wished he hadn't said it aloud. She was compelled to respond.

Pulling away from Wilder, she faced him. The clouds had parted and a hazy half-moon lent a soft light to show his features. "That mustn't happen," she whispered, knowing she was trying to convince herself.

"I know. But that doesn't keep me from wanting it to." He put his arm protectively about her shoulder and prodded her forward. "Come on, we'd better head back and get out of these damp clothes. I don't want you catching a cold."

Bethany kept her arms tightly wrapped around her and let Wilder lead her back to the house. Even though he didn't hold her close, she was glad he was touching her. The sensual feelings he'd awakened in her weighed as a heavy burden on her shoulders. When he went back home, she'd have the knowledge that he wanted to make love to her. Maybe that would keep her warm when the chill of winter arrived.

Chapter Eleven

The next day Wilder took the early train into Atlanta. During the two-and-a-half-hour ride, he had time to think about what he was going to say to Grace. The first thing he was going to tell her was that he could no longer keep her whereabouts from Bethany.

Grace had had more than enough time to come to her senses and realize that her sister didn't have designs on Stanley, but Bethany hadn't heard a word from her. Surely Grace wouldn't want Bethany spending money on a detective who wasn't needed.

Wilder took a carriage from the depot to the Magnolia Glen Hotel. He wasn't familiar with Atlanta but knew from his brother that this hotel was one of the city's finest. A short chat with the driver confirmed that the hotel was in one of the best sections of town. That made Wilder feel better.

A quick glance around the lobby told Wilder that the grand hotel was showing its age. The magnificent chandelier, the wall tapestries, and the furniture showed that no expense had been spared when decorating the hotel. But now, years later, the velvet cushions on the settees were faded and worn. The woodwork lacked that fresh waxed gleam, and the wallpaper was dingy from smoke and age.

Wilder walked up to the rotund desk clerk and asked for Grace's room number. The man peered at Wilder over the top of his spectacles and said, "I'm very sorry, but I can't give you the number of the lady's room."

"Is she registered here?" Wilder asked.

"Oh, yes," the man assured him. "I'll be happy to send a message up to her, but it's against hotel policy to give out room numbers." He slid his eyeglasses farther up the bridge of his nose.

If he'd been thinking correctly, Wilder would have known that. "I understand. Would you please tell her Wilder Burlington is calling on her?"

The man wrote Wilder's name down, then pointed to a secluded area of the lobby where he could wait. Wilder felt better about Grace now that he knew she was staying in a well-supervised hotel in one of the better sections of the city.

A few minutes later Wilder heard his name called from across the room. He looked up and saw Grace hurrying toward him. She was wearing a richly fashioned dress of lavender silk. The skirt was ruffled and the layers of soft material seemed to float about her legs as she hurried toward him.

He rose and took her hands, squeezing them briefly before letting go. "Hello, Grace."

Her smile radiated happiness. "Wilder, I'm so

pleased you've come. I should have known you would."

"I'm glad I found you in. I wasn't even sure you'd be here, since I never heard from you."

"I meant to write. But I've been so busy. There's so much to see and do here . . . so many places to shop. Sometimes I can't believe I'm actually here. It's so wonderful during the day. I don't go out at night."

Wilder smiled. He wished Bethany could see how happy Grace was. She bore no resemblance to the frightened young woman who had cowered in his room and told him she would do anything for enough money to leave town.

"Why don't we sit here for a while and talk," he said.

Grace took a seat on the settee and Wilder joined her. "I guess you came to see me so you could pay me the rest of the money for The Georgia."

Her pearl drop earrings bounced against her neck as she spoke. Wilder could have easily guessed that she'd spent her few days in Atlanta shopping. The clothes and jewelry she was wearing wouldn't be found in Eufaula.

"I'll take care of that while I'm here, but, no, I came for a different reason."

Grace folded her hands across her chest and said, "All right, tell me."

"Bethany's worried about you. I want you to come home."

Her eyes grew wide. "You can't be serious. If Bethany's worried, I'm glad. I'm not going back. Ever." Her brows drew together and her lips formed a pout.

"Grace, Bethany doesn't care anything about Stanley. She never has."

"You don't know. I saw them kissing with my own eyes," she declared with certainty.

"No, what you saw was Stanley forcing a kiss on—"

"Why are you doing this?" she demanded, interrupting his sentence. "I know what I saw."

Wilder kept his tone low and his voice soft, but what he really wanted to do was shake her. "I know what I saw, too. The first time I met Bethany and Stanley they were struggling because Stanley was forcing his attentions on her."

"I don't believe you."

Her words came fast and furious, but Wilder could see in her eyes that she wanted to believe him. She simply wasn't ready. "I have no reason to lie about this, Grace, and you know it."

The pout remained. "Well, I don't have any reason to lie, either. And I'm not going back. I don't want to ever see Bethany or Stanley again."

"Grace, Bethany's worried sick about you."

"Bethany's always worried about me. That won't change by my coming home."

Wilder had a feeling that was true. Bethany had spent so much of the last few years caring for Grace and managing The Georgia that she had no life of her own. "Grace, your sister has decided to hire a detective to find you."

"What!" She scooted to the edge of her seat. "Oh, no! You didn't tell her where—"

"No, I've kept my promise. The only thing she knows is that you took the train to Atlanta. The stationmaster told her that much. I don't want to see her waste money on a detective. If you won't come home, at least write and let her know you're all right."

"No! No," she said, rising. "She'll come get me. You don't know Bethany like I do." Grace twisted her hands together, her eyes wild with fright. "I've got to go somewhere else. I've got to hide so she won't find me."

Wilder was astonished at how fast Grace went from the confident, happy young woman who greeted him to the frightened, nervous woman before him now. "Grace," Wilder took her hands in his, "stop this. Come back with me."

"No!" She jerked away from him. "I'm going to move to another hotel today. I—I'll use another name. That way the detective can't find me, right?" she questioned.

Feeling sorry for her, Wilder admitted, "It'll be harder for him to find you."

"You've got to keep your promise and not tell her where I am," Grace said in desperation.

"I can't do that."

"Then I won't tell you where I'm going," she said defiantly. "I'll be gone and no one will know where I am."

Wilder winced inside. No matter how much Bethany might want it, Grace was not emotionally ready to go home. Dammit! He never wanted to get mixed up with these two sisters. This wasn't his problem. Correction. It wasn't his problem until he bought The Georgia from Grace. Now he felt forced to continue his deception. If she wasn't going home, he had to keep in touch with her.

"All right, I'll help you get settled somewhere else if you—"

"Oh, Wilder, thank you!" She threw her arms around his neck.

Disgruntled with himself, he withdrew her arms. "Grace, listen to me." He held her upper arms tightly. "You have to promise to write Bethany and let her know you're all right."

"No . . . I . . . can't. I . . . she . . ."

Tears ran down her cheeks, and she babbled. Wilder gave her a gentle shake, forcing her to calm down and look at him. "If you want my help, you have to write Bethany."

The warm, dry days of late spring brought many guests to The Georgia, keeping Bethany and the employees busy. A couple of weeks after Grace left, Bethany received a short note from her stating that she was well. Bethany immediately mailed the letter and envelope to Mr. Lester at his office, hoping the postmark might help him locate Grace faster. She knew Atlanta was big, but surely it wouldn't take too long to find an inexperienced young woman.

Bethany had sold most of her grandmother's jewelry to a local merchant who promised to keep the matter quiet. For the first time in a long while, she had money in the bank. Enough to pay for her half of the repairs to the house and enough to pay Mr. Lester—if he didn't take too long finding Grace.

After the night Bethany had walked in the rain with Wilder, she found it easier to accept his presence at The Georgia. In fact, she came to welcome it, to rely on it. He took care of getting workers to paint the exterior of the house and to put on a new roof. But he seemed to deliberately avoid being alone with her, which bothered her greatly. If she were talking to Margaret, Stilman, or Seth, he joined them, but he never seemed to seek her out as he had in the past. Every time they were together, she wanted to touch him. She wanted to be in his arms once again—time and time again. Whenever he was in the room, her gaze didn't leave his face.

As the days passed, Bethany found herself feeling less confident that Grace would return on her own. Mr. Lester kept her informed by letter of his efforts to locate Grace, insisting that eliminating possibilities was progress. She couldn't argue with that, but Wilder did.

Several times, he asked her to discontinue the search. Wilder didn't want her wasting her money on the detective when Grace had written her, but Bethany told him she couldn't give up.

It was late in the evening of a warm night that Wilder came up to the third floor. He was limping badly and pain was etched across his face. Concern clouding her thoughts, Bethany helped him ease onto the small sofa. He kept his troublesome leg stiff and straight.

This was the first time he had let her witness his distress. She wasn't sure what to do. Reaching down, she lifted his leg and placed it on the sofa, thinking that might help. The light from the lamp seemed to bother his eyes so she turned it down, then sat on the sofa beside him.

"Your leg is hurting," she said, wanting him to know that she cared.

Scowling, he growled, "You have a remarkable grasp of the obvious, Bethany."

Momentarily stunned by his sarcasm, Bethany jumped back, her eyes blinking rapidly. She quickly realized it was the pain that was making him ill-tempered and she forgave him.

"Have you taken anything?" she asked. It hurt her to see him this way. She wanted to comfort him, to take away the hurt.

"No. I went to the kitchen looking for a good stiff drink and couldn't find anything. I don't suppose you have any good whiskey up here, do you?" he grumbled.

His beautiful blue eyes were glassy, and it frightened her. "No. Papa never allowed spirits in the house. Besides, you don't need a drink. Why haven't you taken your pain medication? This isn't the time for bravery."

He grinned halfheartedly. "I've been out for a couple of days. I have to take it less and less. I thought I could do without it completely. Like an idiot, I climbed up on the roof today to see if the workers were doing a good job, and I think I re-strained a muscle."

"Oh, Wilder!" Bethany gasped, suffering right along with him, feeling each stab of pain. "You should have gone to the doctor here in town."

It would serve him right if she reprimanded him for his foolishness, she thought. Instead, she went immediately for the laudanum.

"Here, take this," Bethany said when she returned.

She felt helpless, wanting to help but not knowing what to do. She didn't like the feeling.

"What is it?" he asked as he took the cup from her.

"A small amount of laudanum mixed with brandy and honey."

"I thought you told me you didn't have spirits in the house."

"I have a bottle of brandy for medicinal purposes only," she assured him.

He gave her a doubtful look and said, "This should take care of it." He took the medication from her and swallowed it quickly, then laid his head against the sofa once again. He closed his eyes. "If it doesn't kill me, I guess it'll make me feel better."

Bethany's heart felt heavy, her breathing laborious, as tightness formed in her chest. She wanted to soothe away the pain that showed on his handsome face. Instinctively, she sat down on the settee beside him and touched her palm to his forehead.

Wilder chuckled deep in his chest. "I don't have a fever."

She withdrew her hand, but just as quickly Wilder grasped her wrist. His gaze held steady on hers. "No, don't take it away. It feels good." He placed her warm palm against the hardness of his forehead and sighed gratefully. "Mmmm. That's nice." His hand caressed the length of her arm before falling back to the sofa.

Bethany studied him while he rested. He was regaining a healthy look. She also thought he had added a couple of pounds. As her hand stroked across his forehead and her fingers brushed his hair, Bethany knew she was falling in love with Wilder. Unfortunately, she didn't know what to do about it.

He seemed to like her, to respect her, but that was a long way from love. And she constantly reminded herself that his life was in Pennsylvania. Bethany couldn't help but wonder if that was the reason he'd been avoiding her since the night they'd taken a walk in the rain.

Her heart started pounding and her breath quickened, but Bethany kept her hand steady as she caressed Wilder's smooth skin. Did she want him to leave? Yes, it would be better if he did. When he was gone, she could forget about the way his eyes sparkled, the way he always smelled as if he'd just shaved. She could forget about his teasing smile and soothing voice. She could forget—but she didn't want to.

"Are you going to see the doctor tomorrow?"

A smile touched his lips although his eyes remained closed. "Why should I when I have you to care for me?"

"You may have done serious injury to your leg."

He laughed again. "No. I've been through four and a half months of hell and two major operations. Nothing else can be done for me."

"Your problem is that you don't take care of yourself," she scolded lightly. "Always walking, spending time at the mill, and doing things like climbing up on a roof. You don't rest enough."

Wilder opened his eyes and picked up her free hand. Carrying it to his lips, he kissed the open palm. His tongue sampled her skin, sending shivers of longing through her. The tightness in her chest returned.

As he held her hand to his lips, she noticed a scar

on the inside of his arm that she hadn't seen before. It started at his wrist, ran up his arm, and disappeared under his rolled-up shirtsleeve. And it wasn't the clean line of a surgeon's knife. It was rough-edged and jagged. The image of several men beating a lone man flashed through her mind. "The accident must have been horrible for you," Bethany whispered.

"Accident? Hardly. The men were waiting for me. They obviously knew my route home. Every time there's talk of a strike, someone gets hurt. This time it happened to be me." He closed his eyes again, his grip tightening on her hand almost to the point that she wanted to cry out. He cupped her hand in both of his and held it possessively to his chest.

"Do you want to talk about it?" she asked.

He shrugged. "Why not?" He opened his eyes and looked at her. "It was the middle of February, one of the coldest days of the year. I was walking home from the mill. I'd been at a management meeting, trying to talk my boss into listening to the union's demands. That's the hell of it. I was on their side. From out of nowhere, two men jumped me and shoved me to the ground. Three others piled on top of me and started punching me, while the other two held my arms. When I was too weak to fight they let me go, but not before kicking me a few times. Then one of them brought a hammer down on my leg." Wilder shuddered. He let go of her hand and straightened in the sofa. "I've said too much."

Bethany touched his cheek and smiled. "No. I wanted to hear about it." Her words were a caress. "I wish I could have been there to comfort you." As soon as the words were out, she regretted them. They

165

told far too much.

"I wish you could have been there, too. When it looked like I might lose my leg, the woman I was courting took off in search of a whole man. No cripple for her."

There was no sorrow or bitterness in his voice, but Bethany still felt prompted to say, "I'm sorry." How could anyone leave someone they cared about? How could anyone leave this man?

"Don't be." He lifted her chin and stared into her green eyes. "I'm glad I found out what kind of woman she was before I asked her to marry me." He caressed her cheek with the backs of his fingers. "I can't imagine *you* running away from a man because he might lose a leg."

She was afraid to speak, afraid she might say something stupid like she loved him, so she merely shook her head.

"Hold me, Bethany," he whispered huskily.

Her arms circled his back and she pressed his face against her breast. His arms slid around her waist and pulled her tight against him.

"I would never leave you," she whispered. "I would stand beside you."

Wilder lifted his head and closed his mouth over hers, his tongue moving sensuously against hers. He tasted of honey and brandy. Bethany welcomed his kiss. She had wanted it, but more than that she wanted to give Wilder comfort and healing. When she leaned into the kiss, Wilder startled her by pulling away.

"I'm sorry. I shouldn't have done that."

Bethany's breath grew shallow as the realization

hit that he didn't want to kiss her. That hurt. She looked away.

"Bethany . . ."

"Please don't apologize again for kissing me. It's really not very flattering." A trace of disappointment laced her voice.

Wilder touched her shoulder. "You misunderstood me. I shouldn't be here kissing you in this frame of mind. I came in feeling rotten, feeling like hell. I wanted to bark and growl at someone, and you were the only one I could think of who would let me do it. I didn't mean that I didn't *want* to kiss you. I do, Bethany. And I want to do a whole lot more," he murmured seductively. "But of all the people in the world, you are the one I don't want to hurt."

His gentle words broke through her defenses and she faced him. A light glinted in his eyes, making her warm with contentment.

He carried her hand to his lips, kissing each fingertip before letting his lips rest on her palm. She followed his lead, imitating each move and glorying in the shudder that ran through his strong frame. His response encouraged her. She stuck her tongue out and drew circles, tasting, savoring his tangy skin.

When she lowered his hand, his arm went around her neck and pulled her close so their lips met in a passionate kiss. Wilder's deft fingers pulled the pins from her hair and dug into its long, silken length. The kiss was demanding and searching, giving and receiving. It lingered and deepened as Bethany fed her desire to be touched and caressed. They gave and took equally, sufficiently.

Bethany felt as if she floated on the threshold of a

dream. Wilder gently pushed her back against the arm of the sofa, pressing his body against her. She accepted it, welcomed it. Her long skirt and petticoat tangled around her legs as he fit his body next to hers. Delirious, burning sensations covered her skin with delicious prickles. She wanted everything Wilder had to give, and she wanted to give him all that she had. The night was theirs, until a low moan of pain wrenched them apart.

Wilder jerked away from her and massaged the muscle in his left leg, pain visible on his face.

"What happened?" she whispered, gasping for breath.

"A cramp in my muscle."

"What do you want me to do?" she asked, straightening her skirts.

He glanced at her, eyes clouded. "Don't worry, it's all right. It doesn't hurt that bad." A smile stretched his pale lips.

She didn't believe him. "Yes, it does. Oh, Wilder, I'm so sorry." She put her hand over his, following the massaging motion. When she bent over, her long hair fell across his arm. "I wish I could take the pain away."

"You know, you're beautiful with your hair down. You shouldn't wear it in that bun. Hair like yours needs to be free." He stopped rubbing his leg long enough to push her hair behind her ear. "It's better now. Give me a smile. Kissing you did not bring on the cramp."

She gave him the smile he asked for. It wavered a little, but strengthened as their gazes met and held. When he looked at her like that, she wanted to please him. She wanted to touch him but was afraid of hurting his leg again.

He caressed her cheek with the tips of his fingers. "I think we got carried away with the kiss. You're beautiful, and you feel good in my arms. Right now, I want to kiss you again. I want to forget all the reasons why we shouldn't make love and do it, anyway." His eyes held steady on hers. "But I won't do that to you. You're not that kind of woman. And I don't want to change you. Your life is here at The Georgia and mine is at a steel mill in Pennsylvania."

She lowered her lashes. "If I hadn't hurt your leg, we would . . . be lovers by now."

He smiled. "Maybe. But I don't think so. You would have come to your senses."

Opening her eyes, she met Wilder's gaze. "Yes," she said, but knew she was lying.

A part of her was pleased Wilder thought so highly of her, but another part was aching for him to teach her more of the intimacies a man and woman share.

Chapter Twelve

The early morning sun was drying the dew as Wilder walked down the front steps of The Georgia. When he reached the bottom, he turned and looked back at the impressive building. Eight Corinthian columns graced the front of the house, with four more of the massive columns flanking each side. The grandeur of the house reflected the opulent life-style of the planter aristocracy in the South—a perfect example of a bygone era.

Wilder thought of his family home in Pittsburgh and had to chuckle. The Burlington house was considered one of the larger homes in the area, but it could in no way compete with this house. No wonder Bethany was so protective of The Georgia. No wonder he was having second thoughts about returning it to her when it was time for him to leave. No wonder he worried about leaving Bethany.

Shaking his head, Wilder started down the dusty road. He was pleased with the progress his leg was making, even if it wasn't happening fast enough for him.

With each week that passed, he was getting stronger, walking farther, faster. He wasn't using his cane anymore, but he still limped. Damn, that bothered him. According to the doctor, he was lucky to have the leg. He should be grateful, and he was. But he wanted more. He wanted to walk straight again.

Damn the whole labor union to hell, Wilder thought as he picked up his pace. They knew he was on their side. Why did they attack him? Why didn't they go after Frick? He was the one who didn't want to agree to any of their demands. He was the one who wanted the sliding-scale minimum reduced and the contract's termination date changed to December. Wilder had been trying to persuade Frick to listen to the workers.

The managers of the mill and the Amalgamated Association of Iron, Steel and Tin Workers had had a reasonable relationship until Andrew Carnegie hired Henry Clay Frick to supervise the mill. Wilder's hands made fists as he walked, each step a painful reminder of his limp, a reminder that once his brother found the men who had attacked him, he was going to beat the bloody hell out of them one at a time.

Wiping the sweat from his forehead, Wilder turned and started back. The roof and cupola were all he could see of the house. He really should tell Bethany that he planned to give it back to her. And not because he didn't want it. The fact was, he did. The longer he stayed and the more he saw of Bethany made him want to forget about the dark and drab, saloon-filled town of Homestead and stay in the spacious opulence of The Georgia.

With Bethany, Wilder thought as he slowed his pace and remembered her long honey-blond hair flowing down her back. He'd promised himself he was going to stay away from her, and he had. But it hadn't been easy. How could he keep himself from a woman who attracted him like a moth to light? It didn't matter that he felt he had no right to touch her as long as Grace stood between them. How much longer could he go on wanting her? When would he say to hell with Grace and Homestead be damned, and make love to her anyway?

He wanted to hold her. Yes, and he wanted to kiss her. He wanted to take her silky blond hair and crush it in his hands. He wanted to see her shoulders. Were they softly rounded or firmly arched? He wanted to look at her bare breasts, to touch and taste them, too. Did they taste the way she smelled, like roses? His hands ached to know the feel of her. Was her skin soft like fine cotton, smooth like satin, or textured like silk? The white long-sleeved, high-necked blouses she wore teased him, frustrated him, challenged him to find out what lay beneath.

Wilder stopped in front of The Georgia, took a handkerchief out of his pocket, and wiped the sweat from his brow. Just thinking about Bethany had him hot with desire for her.

There were so many things about her he admired, not the least of which was her excellent management of the restaurant and inn and the mill. He admired her strength, her courage, her loyalty.

"Damn," he said aloud. "What's there about her not to like?"

Thoughts of Bethany usually led to thoughts of

Grace. How much longer could he watch Bethany worry about Grace? How much longer could he let her pour money into the pockets of an incompetent detective? Why wouldn't she just accept the fact that Grace needed some time alone and wait for her to come home? But as soon as he thought that, he knew he was only trying to justify his own deceit. He would do the same if Relfe were the one missing.

He should never have made that foolish promise to Grace, but at the time, he didn't know Bethany was going to become so important to him. He didn't know Grace would stay away this long. He hadn't realized just how emotionally immature she was. If the only problem was Grace believing that Bethany never had any designs on Stanley, she'd already be home. But it was more than that. His visit with Grace had proved as much.

Grace didn't want to come home, and after talking with her a few days ago, he agreed that she wasn't ready to return to Eufaula. What a trap to be caught in. He hated deceiving Bethany. A woman like Bethany didn't deserve a sister like Grace—or a man like him, he thought, but that didn't keep him from wanting her.

It had been easy to cool his attraction to Bethany when he thought she was in love with Stanley. He'd been down that route before and knew the heartache it could lead to. There was no happiness in loving someone who belonged to another. He had learned that the hard way. He'd courted several women since Judith had told him she wouldn't divorce her husband and marry him, but Bethany was the only

174

one who'd made him forget Judith.

The more time he spent with Bethany, the more he saw her, the more Wilder was convinced he was falling in love with her. And he knew she wasn't indifferent to him. Wilder had loved once before, dearly, deeply. He recognized the signs and didn't know how much longer he could fight it.

After talking with Grace, he realized she wasn't any closer to coming home than she had been when she left. All this time, Bethany had worried about Grace while he stood by and offered reassurances that didn't really reassure.

Yes, he wanted to hold Bethany. He wanted to force her to get rid of James Lester. As for Grace, he wanted to turn her over his knee and give her the spanking she should have had years ago.

"It's not like you to come in so late," Margaret stated as Bethany rushed into the main office.

Bethany was usually in her office each morning by the time Margaret arrived at seven. She didn't consider herself late when it was only seven-thirty but felt the need to apologize anyway. "I'm sorry. I was up until after midnight getting the records in order. Wilder likes to look them over. I don't want him to find one number out of place."

"He won't," Margaret said.

Bethany looked over at the older woman and smiled. Even if she was gruff-voiced, Margaret was loyal to Bethany, and she appreciated it. "Thanks for the confidence."

"Here's his report from the mill. Said you could look it over, then if you had any questions to let him know."

Surprised, Bethany took the folder. "I knew he spent a few days at the mill last week, but I didn't expect him to put anything in writing. That wasn't necessary." Bethany felt a stab of disappointment. This was another example of Wilder's avoiding her. He could just as easily have discussed his findings with her. "What does it say?"

Margaret harrumphed. "That you need a lot more money than you got if you plan to make the changes he talked about."

"That's what I thought." Bethany's spirits sank. How could she put more money in the mill when she didn't have it to spend?

"It's not right, you know. Selling your Grand-mother Hayward's jewelry like you did. If that Yankee wanted a new roof, you should have let him spend all his money on it."

Bethany fingered the cameo that rested at the base of her throat. "Margaret, you know it was time for a new roof and fresh paint. I was going to have it done with the extra money we get during the summer season. All Wilder did was move up the date. I agreed. The jeweler said he would hold the pieces that don't sell right away and I can buy them back. Besides, I need that money for Mr. Lester, too."

"I know all that, but I still don't approve."

"I kept my favorite," she reminded Margaret as the pads of her fingers traced the sculpted profiled head of a woman. "I have no use for a diamond and emerald necklace. Besides, I'm sure keeping control

176

of this house would have been more important to Grandmother Hayward than jewels hanging around my neck." She sighed, feeling the weight of her problems dragging her down. "I'll take this into my office and look it over."

A few minutes later Bethany walked back into the front office. "Margaret, would you check the booking sheet for tonight."

"Something wrong?" Margaret asked.

"Maybe. Do we have every room booked?"

"No need to check the book. I know we have guests in every room. Why?" Margaret asked, rising from her chair.

"It appears we'll be overbooked, and it's my fault." Bethany sighed. "I forgot to give you this letter and have you post it on the booking sheet. The MacDonalds wrote a couple of weeks ago saying they'd be coming in tonight and for us to hold a room for them. I just found this in one of the restaurant files. I don't know how I could have misfiled it."

"Let me see that."

Margaret took the letter from Bethany and looked it over carefully. "I remember them. They've stayed with us before."

"I know." Bethany rubbed her forehead. "How could I have mislaid this?"

"Don't surprise me with all that's happened the last few weeks . . . that Yankee showing up and Grace leaving like she did. I'm surprised there haven't been more mistakes going on around here."

Worried, Bethany asked, "Any possibility one of the rooms will be vacated today?"

"Not unless that Yankee decides to go back where

he came from. Don't expect that to happen.''

"Not today, anyway.'' Bethany paused. "I know what we'll do. The MacDonalds are good people. We'll just put them in Grace's room. That will take care of the problem.''

Margaret pursed her lips and glared at Bethany. "I don't think that's a good idea. You can't start letting people stay up there with you. It's not right.''

"Nonsense. This is a business decision. I don't want to upset the MacDonalds or lose the night's rent. It will be perfectly fine. We'll do it and not say another word about it.'' Bethany turned and walked back into her own office. She had to get hold of herself. Margaret was right. She was letting worry over the things she couldn't control affect the things she could control. That had to stop.

"What does this remind you of?'' Wilder asked as he walked into Bethany's office later that morning. He pointed to his attire—white and blue pin-striped trousers, white shirt, and red suspenders.

She looked him over carefully. He was as handsome as she had ever seen him. She loved the way his straight hair fell across his forehead and the way his eyes twinkled with light when he was in a teasing mood. She'd never tire of looking at him.

"Clothes?'' she guessed, and they both laughed. "What's the matter? Did Kate forget to do your laundry?''

"You are especially beautiful when you laugh. You should do it more often.''

Bethany glowed inside from his flattering comment. Whenever he told her she looked beautiful, she felt beautiful.

Wilder walked farther into the office, a gentle smile on his face. "The last time I wore these clothes you said I looked as if I were going boating. Remember now?"

"Yes." A vague sense of trepidation descended upon her, and she pushed her chair away from her desk.

"Guess what?" He grinned sheepishly.

"You're going boating," she replied. Suddenly, her heartbeat sped up and her stomach felt odd.

"*We're* going boating," he corrected.

Shaking her head, Bethany said, "No, not me. I'm not interested. Have fun."

"Stilman's already packed a picnic for two." His voice softened. "I want you to come with me."

"I can't," she mumbled, and turned back to the papers on her desk.

"You're not a *can't* person, Bethany." He took hold of her hands and pulled her out of her chair. "Grab your bonnet and parasol. We're going down to the lake."

Holding back, she said, "I don't want to go to the lake. I never go to the lake." It was an inane thing to say but she couldn't think properly.

"You never go look at the boats? Don't you like to look at boats?"

"Not especially." Icy fingers of fear crept up her back. She had told Wilder that she hadn't been in a boat since her parents were killed. Hadn't he listened to her? The thought of going out into the water panicked her. "I—I don't want t—to go," she said,

179

stumbling over her words.

He managed to get her to the doorway before asking, "Why?"

"It frightens me," she admitted reluctantly.

Wilder put his hands on her shoulders and forced her to look into his eyes. "We don't have to leave the dock if you don't want to. We'll put the picnic basket on board and have our picnic right there in the slip."

"You're not serious? You'd do that?" she asked.

His eyes told her he would before his mouth formed the words.

Half an hour later, Bethany and Wilder arrived at the marina on Lake Eufaula. Bethany opened her lace-trimmed parasol while Wilder lifted the picnic basket from the carriage. They walked down the boardwalk until Wilder stopped in front of a white sailboat with a small cabin. *Scarlet Dove* was written across the side in bold black lettering. Several birds flew overhead, and she could hear the sound of children playing in the distance. The water was calm. The smell of fish clung to the humid air. A few people milled about the marina, some carrying fishing equipment, others toting picnic baskets with loaves of bread peeking out from underneath linen tablecloths.

Bethany glanced around the marina. Boats of all different sizes floated alongside the dock. The glare of the sun burned her eyes as she remembered waving good-bye to her parents on a day just like this one.

"This is it. I've rented it for two hours. What do you think?" he asked.

Shaking off the memory of the past, Bethany looked at the boat. She realized that the idea of getting into the boat didn't bother her at all, only the thought of taking it out into the lake where water would surround her.

Remaining rigid, Bethany squeezed the handle of her parasol, looked up at Wilder, and said, "I don't know why we're doing this."

For a moment he simply looked at her with that caring expression she'd come to know. Softly, he answered, "Because I know what it's like to be afraid, and I don't want you living with that feeling."

Bethany's breath caught in her throat. She knew in that moment, without a shadow of a doubt, that she loved Wilder Burlington. And even if he didn't love her, she knew he cared.

"I want to help you overcome your fear of being in a boat, being on the water. You're too strong a lady to let this get the best of you. You haven't always been afraid of boating, have you?"

Her chin lifted. Bethany hated admitting she was afraid of anything. She wanted to be too strong for fear. She'd tried to be. "No. I've been boating many times. Our boat was just about this size."

"Good. It would be a shame for you to deny yourself the pleasure and beauty the water has to offer because of some memories that won't go away. Come on. Let's climb on board."

Still not sure why she was letting Wilder talk her into this, Bethany picked up her skirts and allowed him to help her onto the deck.

"When you're comfortable on the water again, we'll take it out on the lake," he said as two young boys ran past them on the dock.

"I don't know." Confused, she looked away to

stare at the water. It was a dirty shade of blue, as if someone had stirred up mud from the bottom. "Just sitting here at the dock doesn't frighten me. I feel safe, but I don't know if I'll ever want to go back out there."

Wilder sat on a red cushioned seat and pulled her down beside him. He took her parasol, folded it, and put it beside his leg. "Why don't you tell me how the accident happened?"

His expression was gentle, caring. It had been years since she talked about that time, but the story was as fresh in her mind as if it had been yesterday. The only thing different was that it didn't hurt as much anymore.

"We were here at this lake on a Saturday afternoon. It was already late in the day, but Papa wanted us all to go out and fish. He always said you could catch more in the late afternoon when it's time for their dinner. Grace wanted to stay and play with a girl she'd met. I told Papa I would stay and watch her. So Mama and Papa went out alone. No one knows for sure what happened." Bethany's breath quickened as she talked. "They think my father had a heart attack and fell into the water while pulling in a large fish. The sheriff believes my mother jumped in to save him."

"That must have made you very proud of your mother."

She smiled, thanking him for understanding. "Today, yes. But not back then. I was very angry with my parents for leaving us alone. I was frightened. I didn't know what to do. One day I was a carefree young woman, and the next day I had to manage a large house and take care of my little sister. I did what I had to do, the best way I knew how. I still miss my parents. I often wonder what my life would be like now if they had lived."

Wilder gave her a teasing grin. "I think you'd be right where you are now, running The Georgia."

"Maybe," Bethany said, but she was doubtful. She remembered her father being just as possessive of the house as she was. No doubt he wouldn't have wanted her telling him how to manage it. She'd like to think that she would have married and have had children she could bring to play on the spacious grounds.

Bethany closed her eyes and breathed in the fishy air. It felt good to talk about her parents. She and Grace seldom mentioned them anymore. Time had a funny way of stripping clean the meaty memories and leaving them whitewashed.

She opened her eyes and saw that Wilder was watching her. Suddenly, it was difficult to concentrate on the past. "Tell me about Pennsylvania."

Wilder reached over, untied the sash of her bonnet, and took it off her head. When he laid it in her lap, their fingers brushed, their eyes met. Bethany felt a rush of heat. Embers glowed inside her and she wanted Wilder to bring them to life.

"I know the sun's still bright, but I want to look at you without the bonnet." He picked up one of her hands and held it in his. "So you want me to tell you about Pennsylvania. Let's see. Aside from our big cities and industrial towns with their ethnic differences, we have a lot of farmland and sloping hills. Pennsylvania is a state with very green, lush vegetation."

"And your home in Homestead . . . what's it like?"

Wilder chuckled as he gently squeezed her fingers between his. "I have a small three-room apartment in Homestead, where I live during the week. On weekends I usually go to the family home in Pittsburgh, which is about ten miles away. It's a nice comfortable home, not as big or as grand as your house."

"Your parents are still there?"

Wilder shook his head. "My mother died in childbirth when I was seven and my father died in a train accident ten years ago. My brother, Relfe, his wife Ester, and their two daughters live at the family home."

Feeling more relaxed, Bethany leaned back in the seat. She liked the warm pressure of Wilder's hand on hers. "Have you ever thought about getting married?" she asked, feeling close and intimate with him.

Wilder's eyes turned a dark silvery blue. "I knew that had to be your next question, but I didn't know whether or not you'd ask it. Since I've known you, you've asked fewer questions than any woman I know."

Should she let him off the hook? Bethany smiled to herself. Ordinarily, she never would have considered prying into anyone's private life, but she wanted to know everything about Wilder.

"If you don't want to talk about it . . ." she said, offering him a way out, even though she was dying to know.

"The only woman I've ever asked to marry me was already married," he said bluntly.

A grim smile touched his lips as a gasp escaped

past hers. What an admission! Bethany didn't know quite what to say or do.

Suddenly, the air was heavy. "No," she said quickly, fighting twinges of guilt for having asked. "You don't have to tell me anything. I was merely asking to be polite. This is really none of my business."

"I think it is." His eyes were caressing her face. Gently, he touched her cheek with the back of his hand, then he brushed away a strand of hair that had blown free of her chignon. "We never had an affair. It's important to me that you know that. Not because I wasn't willing, but like you, she had a very loyal sense of right and wrong, and she didn't cross over that line. We didn't plan to fall in love. It just happened from seeing each other at parties, balls, and a host of dinner engagements. Being unattached, I was often called upon to even out the dinner table.

"At the time our . . . friendship started, she was having some difficulty with her husband, but our love grew out of a mutual respect for each other. I did ask her to leave her husband and marry me. For a time it looked as if she might. In the end, she decided to stay with him, and now I know it was the right thing for her to do. The guilt she would have felt would have ruined any life we could have managed to have."

Wilder still had a great deal of respect for the woman. Bethany could see it in his eyes, hear it in his voice. What a woman she must be to still command this kind of admiration in a man like Wilder. A knot grew in Bethany's chest. Was it jealousy? Was that what she felt? Over a woman she'd never met?

185

Bethany remained quiet for a long time before she said, "I take it this is not the woman you were seeing when you were in the hospital."

He laughed ruefully. "No. This happened four years ago. I thought a lot about Judith when I was in the hospital and told myself I was going to see her when I got out. Living on the edge of death made me want to reach out for the best thing I'd ever known. But my recovery wasn't as fast as I'd hoped, and by the time I was released, I realized that I couldn't disrupt her life again. I'm sure she knew it, too. Although I received a polite note from her, she never visited me."

His eyes met hers in a strongly appealing way, and Bethany gave him a reassuring smile.

"My past is one of the reasons I was so hard on you when I thought you were in love with Stanley. I know what it's like to want someone who belongs to another." He cleared his throat and stretched out his leg. "So now you know the story of my life."

It was Bethany's turn to be silent. Her heart hammered in her chest, and her arms ached to pull Wilder close and tell him she loved him and wanted the chance to make him feel again the way he'd felt about this woman. But she couldn't say those things.

The warm sunshine beat down on her head, and the water lapped at the sides of the boat. She took a deep breath. The odor of fish and muddy water lay heavily around them.

It took courage for Wilder to admit his past. Bethany's personal life had always been very private, not something she discussed with anyone, but because Wilder had opened up to her, she wanted to tell him about John Martin.

"I guess most of us have similar lost loves in our past. For me it was John Martin Sommers. Our relationship was doomed from the start, not unlike yours with the married woman. He wanted me to sell The Georgia and move to California with him. I thought about it for a long time, but in the end, I knew my home was more important."

Wilder tried not to show how deeply her words disturbed him. Not that he hadn't known The Georgia was Bethany's life. But to hear her say she'd passed up marriage to stay at The Georgia made her sound cold, and he knew she wasn't.

Wilder picked up her hand again and held it, gently squeezing her fingers. "Have you heard from him since he left?" he asked.

"No," she answered softly. "I didn't expect to. California is a long way from here, and we didn't part on friendly terms. He made it quite clear there would be no second chance."

"Have you ever regretted not going with him?"

"Never," she answered, without the least trace of hesitancy in her voice. "We would have married if John Martin had agreed to stay and live at The Georgia. He didn't want any part of managing an inn, and I felt I couldn't leave it. Some of my refusal may have been because I wanted Grace's life to be as normal as possible. I wanted to give back to her the security that had been snatched away with our parents' death. I tried to give her back the mother she had lost."

"And now Grace doesn't need a mother. When she comes home, she's going to need a sister."

Wilder watched as denial, then resignation crossed her face. In that moment he realized that Bethany didn't want Grace to grow up. The hot June sun hung high in the western sky. It all fell into place. Grace hadn't run away because of a kiss. She was running away from Bethany.

"Would you go to Grace if you knew where she was?" he asked, even though he was certain he knew the answer.

"Of course. I'd go right away and bring her home." She scooted to the edge of her seat. "No matter what she thinks or what she feels about me, her life is here," she said desperately.

"No, Bethany. This is your life. The Georgia is *your* life. Remember that when she comes home."

"How can you say that? She's my sister."

"Maybe you need to do a little growing up, too. Accept the fact that, for whatever reason, Grace doesn't want to see you. And if Mr. Lester was going to find Grace, he'd have done it a long time ago."

An indignant gasp escaped past Bethany's lips. "How dare you say I need to grow up." She reached down, grabbed her parasol, and pushed it open with a snap. "And as for Mr. Lester, he'll find Grace. I know he will." She laid the cane of the parasol on her shoulder, leaving the canopy to drape across her shoulder.

Wilder sat back and smiled. "All right. I've been thoroughly rebuked. I didn't mean to get off on that subject, anyway. Tell me what you think about my idea of having a ball?"

Bethany opened her mouth as if to speak, then closed it. A moment later, she said, "You certainly know how to change the subject."

"I thought I should quit while I was ahead." He grinned.

"That's debatable," she answered, then laughed lightly. "However, as for the ball, I've given it some thought since we last talked about it, and decided you were right. The Georgia needs some gaiety. I think we should make the ball the last Saturday in June. Stilman and the other employees have agreed to help wherever they're needed. They thought it was a wonderful idea. Let's see." She started counting on her fingers as she proceeded, putting one down for each item she mentioned. "Margaret is looking into getting the invitations printed and delivered. Stilman is working on the menu. I need to check into getting musicians. And of course, the flowers will come from our gardens." She finished with a satisfied sigh.

Laughing, Wilder said, "When you start to organize, you don't stop until everything's done. I can't believe this. I thought I was going to have to sell you on the idea of having a ball. Instead, I find that you have everything under control."

"Once I started, I didn't want to stop."

She smiled, but Wilder could tell she was a little embarrassed by his compliment. He wanted to kiss her so badly his chest hurt from the weight of it. Bethany was beautiful. He loved the way the wind had ruffled her hair, freeing fine wisps to blow about her face. He wanted to pull her to him and press her head on his shoulder, her face against his chest. But Wilder knew the danger in that, so he settled for taking her hand again and holding it close to his chest. He wished he could tell her that he was falling in love with her, but now wasn't the time. There might never be a time for them. The mill in Homestead, his home in Pennsylvania, Grace, and The Georgia all stood between him and Bethany.

Looking into her eyes, he said, "It's not the right time to say what I really want to say. But I have to tell you this much. You are the most important person in my life right now." His gaze lingered on her face, his hands moving up and down her arms possessively. His voice turned husky. "You are a very attractive, desirable woman. There's an innocent air about you that's exciting, tempting, and sometimes intimidating. I want very much to make love to you."

"Wilder—"

"No, don't say anything. I said I *want* to make love to you." He shook his head. "I didn't say I was going to. I wouldn't do that to you. I know how you feel about propriety. If I didn't respect you and your reputation, I'd have moved up to the third floor weeks ago." He let go of her and reached for the picnic basket. "Let's see what Stilman packed for us."

"You've changed the subject again without giving me the opportunity to respond." He pulled out a napkin and handed it to her. She spread it across her lap. "I think you're afraid of what I might say."

Wilder handed her a small loaf of bread, then said, "You're right, I am. I don't want to hear that you have no tender feelings for me whatsoever and"—his gaze met hers—"I don't want to hear that you do."

Shocked by his last statement, Bethany settled back against the side of the boat, resting her elbow on the gunwale. Yes, she loved Wilder. She was sure of it. She hungered for his touch, his love, his attention, his approval. Just now he had given her a glimmer of hope that he might feel the same. Why wouldn't he want to know how she felt?

She started to ask why, then realized she knew the answer. If she had no loving feelings toward him, he didn't intend to try to change her mind, and if she did, he didn't intend to encourage her.

TO GET YOUR
4 FREE BOOKS
MAIL THE COUPON BELOW.

Heartfire Romance

FREE BOOK CERTIFICATE

GET 4 FREE BOOKS

Yes! I want to subscribe to Zebra's HEARTFIRE HOME SUBSCRIPTION SERVICE. Please send me my 4 FREE books. Then each month I'll receive the four newest Heartfire Romances as soon as they are published to preview Free for ten days. If I decide to keep them I'll pay the special discounted price of just $3.50 each; a total of $14.00. This is a savings of $3.00 off the regular publishers price. There are no shipping, handling or other hidden charges. There is no minimum number of books to buy and I may cancel this subscription at any time. In any case the 4 FREE Books are mine to keep regardless.

NAME

ADDRESS

CITY _____ STATE _____ ZIP

TELEPHONE

SIGNATURE

(If under 18 parent or guardian must sign)
Terms and prices subject to change.
Orders subject to acceptance.

HF 103

Heartfire Romance

GET 4 FREE BOOKS

HEARTFIRE HOME SUBSCRIPTION
SERVICE
P.O. BOX 5214
120 BRIGHTON ROAD
CLIFTON, NEW JERSEY 07015

Chapter Thirteen

June was easing to a close, bringing with it the hottest days of summer. The flowers were in full bloom, and the evening breeze became humid. Bethany sat on the window seat in her room, staring up into the starlit sky with its clearly defined half-moon. She had told herself she couldn't sleep because of the heat, but as the night's wind fanned her cheeks and stirred her hair, she knew that wasn't true. Wilder Burlington was on her mind.

They had settled into a comfortable, workable relationship while they put the finishing touches on the plans for the ball and went over his assessment of the Hayward Mill, but there remained an undercurrent of tension that never left them for long.

Many nights during the three weeks following their trip to the lake, Bethany had lain awake in her bed wondering what it would be like if Wilder was lying beside her. His kisses and caresses had given her a glimpse, a mere taste, of the pleasure a man and woman could share. She ached to know everything.

Sometimes during those lonely nights she wondered if she was destined to live alone and without love the rest of her life because she had rejected John Martin Sommers's proposal.

Bethany thought back over the men in her life since her parents' death. Several had tried to court her the past three years, including Sheriff Beale after his wife had died last fall. John Martin had come the closest to capturing her heart, but in the end, even he couldn't. Now here she was wanting Wilder to court her and he was refusing. And she knew the main reason was that his life was in Pennsylvania and hers in Eufaula.

Wilder had kept to his word. He hadn't touched her since that day on the boat. What would she do when he went back to Pennsylvania? When he had arrived back in May, he'd told her he planned to stay until the middle of July. It was now the end of June. Bethany closed her eyes, trying to block out the thought of his leaving in two weeks. "No," she whispered and rose from the window seat, too restless to stay there a moment longer. Maybe a walk in the garden would help settle her thoughts so she could sleep. She looked at the clock on her bedside table. It was two o'clock. She should be safe going out in her robe. Surely none of the guests would be up at this hour.

As she tied the sash of her Christmas-red robe, Bethany made her way down the first flight of stairs. On the second floor, she paused. For a fleeting moment she was tempted to go to Wilder's room. She picked up the skirt of her robe and hurried on down the stairs before she did something that foolish.

Bethany knew she should be pleased he was concerned about her reputation and that he thought of her so highly. But how much comfort would an unblemished reputation give her when she was old? Wouldn't it be better to have more of the memories like Wilder's hot breath seeping through the dampness of her dress and warming her skin? Wouldn't she rather remember the feel of his hands on her breasts than the pious knowledge that no man had ever touched her?

"No," she whispered again as she flung open the back door and escaped out into the night air. Picking up the hem of her robe, she ran down the steps, along the stone-covered pathway, and into the garden. When she passed under the vine-covered trellis, she stopped. With uneven breathing, she looked over the darkened grounds. A light film of perspiration clung to her skin. Why was she having such thoughts about a man who wasn't even pursuing her? A man who knew that one of them would have to give up a lot for them to be together.

The night was darker than she expected, but she slowly made her way to the swing in the gazebo. As soon as she sat down, Bethany thought she heard Wilder calling her name. Surely her mind was playing tricks on her.

"Bethany," she heard again as Wilder came into view. She rose from the swing to meet him.

"There you are. Are you all right?" Wilder hurried up the three steps to the platform.

He was shirtless and his pants were unfastened at the waist. His hair was attractively rumpled. "Yes, I'm fine. Wilder, what are you doing here?"

"I was looking out the window and saw you running into the garden. I thought something was wrong." His chest heaved with choppy breathing.

Bethany's gaze lingered on his bare chest. She might never get another chance to see him like this and she wanted to drink in the sight of him. She *wanted* to touch him. Realizing the direction of her thoughts, she turned away, walked back to the swing, and sat down. "No. Nothing's wrong. I just couldn't sleep, so I decided to take a walk in the garden."

Wilder glared down at her. His mouth tightened. "You weren't walking when I saw you. You were running."

Shrugging her shoulders, she said, "I was in a hurry, that's all."

He reached down and grabbed her shoulders roughly, pulling her from the swing and forcing her to face him. "You scared the hell out of me, Bethany. What was I supposed to think when I saw you running away from the house in the middle of the night?"

Momentarily stunned by his brusque behavior, Bethany gasped. "I have no idea what you were supposed to think. Now let me go. You're hurting me." She tried to twist away from him but he held fast.

His gaze was intense with passion. "Not until you tell me who you were running from?"

"Who?"

His fingers tightened around her arms. "Has Edwards been over here bothering you again?"

"Stanley? At two o'clock in the morning?"

196

"Dammit, Bethany, who were you running away from?"

"You," she whispered desperately. The moment she said it, she wished she hadn't.

"Me?"

She swallowed hard. "I was running away from thoughts of you. I couldn't sleep, so I came out here hoping the night air might help me forget about you."

He loosened his grip on her arms and slid his hands over her shoulders and up her neck, cupping each side of her face. He looked into her eyes.

"I couldn't sleep, either."

"Wilder, I don't know what's wrong with me, but tonight I was ready to go to your room and—" She stopped.

He pulled her closer. She could see in his eyes that his passion had turned from rage to desire. "And what?" he asked huskily.

"I don't know."

"Bethany?"

"I wanted you to hold me," she answered softly, knowing she was getting dangerously close to revealing what she felt for him.

Wilder slipped his arms around her waist and pulled her up tight against him. "Like this?"

She nodded against his chest. Her arms went around his back, her hands flattened on his skin. It was the first time she'd touched a man in such a manner. Her stomach muscles tightened. She wanted him to touch her the same way.

"What else?"

197

"I wanted you to kiss me," she whispered.

"Like this?" he asked as his lips met hers in a brief, sweet kiss.

He looked down at Bethany. She shook her head. Wilder pressed his lips to hers again, softly at first, but as the seconds passed, the pressure grew and Bethany responded, matching his intensity. She opened her mouth and offered her tongue to him. He moaned his approval and took it, sucking it into his warm mouth.

Her hands roamed up and down his back. Bethany loved the feel of his skin. She opened and closed her hands against him, her fingers kneading, working his flesh as she explored his lower back, his shoulders, and the muscles of his upper arms. She couldn't keep her hands still.

"Is this what you wanted?" he whispered against her lips.

"Yes," she answered in a breathy voice, fearful that he would stop and fearful that he wouldn't.

"And this?" he asked as his hand pushed her robe aside and covered the firm swell of her breast. He fondled and massaged her breast as his tongue darted to the inside of her mouth and out again, teasing her.

Bethany murmured his name with pleasure. The fine cotton of her nightgown in no way impeded the warmth, the excitement, the satisfaction of Wilder's touch. Her stomach muscles contracted with wanting. An ache for something more settled in the pit of her abdomen.

Wilder's lips left hers and moved down her chin, over her jawline, down her neck to the crest of her shoulders. He cupped her buttocks and pressed her up against him. Bethany felt something rock-hard. It felt good. It felt right. The hardness of his lower body eased the wanting, the hunger inside her, and heightened it at the same time.

"I want to make love to you, Bethany."

His voice was raspy with desire but she understood him. "Yes," she answered in the same passion-fed tone. "Show me how."

"Yes, yes," he answered as he continued to kiss her. He loved, craved the feel of her breast in his hand. She was soft yet firm. The weight of her breast was just enough to set him afire with passion. He pushed her nightgown away from her shoulder, kissing every inch of space afforded him. He was so hot for her he wanted to rip the garment from her, but respect for her stopped him.

Wilder was sure he'd never wanted a woman as badly as he wanted Bethany right now. He looked around the darkened garden for somewhere soft to lay her down. All he saw were rose bushes, shrubs, a stone walkway, and a gazebo with a wooden floor and swing. He knew in that moment that he'd never loved a woman as much as he loved Bethany. He couldn't make love to her here in the garden. He looked down at her. Moonlight caressed her cheeks, starlight sparkled in her eyes. The golden lights in her hair shimmered against the dark night. She's beautiful, he thought as he watched her straightening her gown and robe. No matter how badly he wanted her, he couldn't treat her like a common woman of the night. He loved her too much.

Groaning, Wilder pushed away from her. "Go to bed, Bethany." His voice was harsher than he intended, but it wasn't easy to tell his body no when the woman he wanted so desperately was willing.

"W—why? I don't understand."

He held the tips of his thumb and forefinger together and said, "I came this close to taking your virginity."

Bethany winced and looked away. What they'd shared sounded so crass when put into words. He sighed, and she faced him. "Are you going to apologize again?" she asked.

"Hell, no," he said without hesitation. "But, Bethany, you're too good a woman for what happened between us tonight. I can't treat you like a whore." He bounded off the gazebo and into the night.

Wrapping her arms around her, Bethany watched him walk away. Just maybe for this one night, she wanted him to treat her like one.

The night of the ball finally arrived. All the gaslights at The Georgia were turned on, giving the house a wonderfully festive ambiance. The night was hot so Bethany had ordered all the windows and doors left open to let in the tepid breeze.

Bethany wanted to check on everything one last time before she made her way up to the third floor to dress for the evening. Her first stop was the kitchen. Trays of food laden with little sandwiches, chicken pieces, and slices of beef and ham, as well as a vast assortment of cookies, cream puffs, and miniature pies, lined the counters. Everything looked beautiful and tasted delicious, too, she observed as she sneaked a bite-sized piece of cake into her mouth.

"How are things going, Stilman?" she asked as she picked up a napkin and wiped the creamy icing from her lips.

He turned and faced her with a beaming smile. In his hands he held a large silver tray filled with decorated tea cakes. "I haven't had so much fun since I was a boy in my grandma's kitchen. I'm ready for the party to begin." His angular face glowed. "Don't worry about the food. I have everything under control in here."

Bethany smiled and touched his arm affectionately. "I can see that. You've done a wonderful job."

Satisfied that her guests would be well fed, she walked into the dining room. The musicians she had hired were busy setting up their instruments. Some of the tables and chairs had been moved out and the rug rolled up to make room for a dance floor. The rest of the tables and chairs lined the perimeter of the large room to accommodate those who wanted to sit out a dance or just watch the others. On each table sat a silver bud vase filled with three roses and a delicate smattering of bedstraw. Bethany had sniffed and cut each rose herself. If the fragrance wasn't deep and heady, she'd move on to the next because only the best roses made it inside The Georgia.

After speaking with the leader of the group about the evening's music, she made her way to the large front porch. Bethany found Seth giving last-minute instructions to the young men who were to help him with the carriages.

"How are things going, Seth? Any problems?"

"No, ma'am. I dressed the boys up real nice." He

pointed to his helpers. Bethany gave an approving smile. Everything was working out just as she'd planned.

At last it was time to go up and dress. The excitement inside her was rampant. As she hurried back into the house, she ran right into Wilder.

They'd been so busy with preparations for the ball that they hadn't had time to feel awkward about what had happened between them in the garden. Even now she found that she wasn't embarrassed by what they'd shared. How could she be? It was so natural. She looked up into his eyes, and she knew she loved him with all her heart.

"I thought you'd be upstairs dressing by now," he said.

"I think I'm ready to go up. Everything seems to be in order and flowing smoothly. I want everything to be perfect. Tonight is special."

"For me, too, Bethany. Tonight proves we work well together."

That wasn't exactly what Bethany was thinking. "Yes, we do, although it took me a while to realize that." She smiled before looking past him, into the fading twilight. She knew that Wilder belonged here with her. But how was she going to make him realize that?

"Well, if you don't hurry, you're going to miss your own party."

"Oops . . . I need to check one more thing. I asked Kate to—"

"Anything you asked her to do, she did. Now go upstairs. I'll come up in a few minutes, then we'll come down together. All right?"

No, wonderful, she thought, answering him with a nod and a smile before walking past him and up to the third floor.

Bethany allowed herself the luxury of a rose-scented bath and, after drying herself, lightly dusted her body with a fine powder.

When she'd known the ball was definite, she had wasted no time in asking Mrs. Bloomfield to make her gown. For hours they had pored over patterns and material, until they decided on a bodice made of ruched taffeta, with leg-of-mutton sleeves and a matching wide belt. Bethany had wanted her usual high stand-up collar, but Mrs. Bloomfield insisted a low neckline was perfectly acceptable for a ball gown. The hunter-green taffeta skirt was knife-pleated down the front, with matching lace inserts finishing the rest of the full skirt. By the time the gown was finished, Bethany thought it was the most beautiful dress she had ever seen.

First, she put on her bloomers and summer corset, then covered them with her lace-trimmed corset cover and the black net skirt that Mrs. Bloomfield insisted she had to wear so the taffeta would rustle. Next, she stepped into the dress. She had trouble trying to fasten all those tiny covered buttons Mrs. Bloomfield had sewed up the back.

Bethany started to call out to Grace for help when she remembered her sister wasn't home. She dropped her hands to her side, a wave of sadness stealing over her. Grace loved parties. She would be so happy if she knew Bethany was giving one. "Home," she whispered. "Grace, why don't you come home? I'll try to make up for all the heartache Stanley caused you."

With less enthusiasm than she felt at first, Bethany arranged her hair into a small round bun at the back of her head, leaving out a couple of strands to frame each side of her face. When she was finally finished, she stepped back and looked at herself in the mirror. Her gaze went immediately to the neckline of her dress. She'd never shown so much skin. The scooped neckline was cut wide, showing most of her upper chest and shoulders, and cut low, showing the swell of her breasts. She needed a necklace, but the only piece left of her grandmother's jewelry was the cameo she often wore. For the first time, she wished she hadn't sold all of the jewelry.

Bethany turned when she heard a knock on her bedroom door. "Are you ready?" Wilder asked.

"I'll be right out," she answered, then gave a determined look back into the mirror. No, she wasn't going to regret anything she'd done. Selling the jewelry had kept her from losing control of The Georgia to Wilder. Because of that money, she'd paid for her half of the new roof and the painting, and new rugs had been ordered. The rest of the money would help her find her sister. The jewels had a far greater value now than they ever could have had hidden away in the cedar chest or hanging around her neck.

"I'm sorry I took so much time. Have you been waiting long?" Bethany asked, walking into the living room.

Wilder's eyes roamed hotly over her body, all the way down to her toes. "Bethany." His voice was a hoarse whisper. "You are absolutely beautiful . . . stunning. That dress is . . . perfect on you."

Bethany smiled with pleasure, even though she felt

a little odd. She'd never before shown so much of her body. "And you're very handsome." In fact, she had never seen him looking better, dressed as he was in his black evening suit. "It's a shame there aren't more occasions for a man to wear a cutaway jacket with tails."

His heavy-lidded gaze wandered over her face and down to the rise and fall of her breasts. "It's a shame I can't have you all to myself tonight," he whispered seductively.

Breathing choppily, she quickly turned her back to him. He didn't know how much she would like that. "Would you mind checking to see if I closed all the buttons?"

Wilder's chuckle was a little nervous sounding. "I was wondering how I'm going to keep my hands off you, and now you ask me to do this."

Don't try to, she thought. *Just let it happen.* Her skin prickled deliciously when he walked up behind her. She felt the movements of his hands and fingers as they went down her back, checking each button. His breath was warm against her neck, fanning the short hairs at her nape and coming closer and closer, until she felt his cool lips graze the crest of her shoulder. She shuddered with desire.

Before the evening was over, Bethany knew she was going to tell Wilder she loved him. It seemed destined to happen. He would be going back to his home soon, and she didn't want to wonder what it would have been like to spend the night in the arms of the man she loved.

For the first time in years, wondrous contentment flooded through her. She hadn't come to this decision easily, but now that she'd made it, she knew it was the right one. It felt too good not to be.

Later that evening, she stood and watched while Wilder danced with yet another pretty woman. With his limp he wasn't as quick and graceful as the other men on the dance floor, but not one woman had refused him.

She wasn't sure of the time, but it had to be well after midnight. And Wilder still had not asked her for a dance. Like him, she had danced with several partners throughout the evening: Sheriff Beale and his deputy, as well as the owner of the lumber mill and the owner of the bank; all were very nice older men. But she wanted to dance with Wilder. Jealousy was taking big bites out of her fun because he was giving all his attention to other women.

"I'm going to say good night."

Startled that someone had touched her arm, Bethany turned to see Margaret. "Oh, so soon." Bethany suddenly worried that she'd been neglecting everyone in favor of watching Wilder.

"Afraid so. I'm too old to stay up this late anymore."

She smiled at the large woman so prettily dressed in a blue-printed organdy gown. "Did you have fun?" Bethany didn't mean for it to happen, but her gaze drifted back to Wilder.

"Of course I did. Had a dance with the mayor. The ball was a wonderful idea. You're the one that doesn't seem to be having any fun."

"What? Oh, no." She laughed lightly as her eyes scanned the dance floor, filled with beautiful women in colorful gowns and handsome men in dark suits, all wearing happy faces. "I'm having a great time."

"You can't fool me. Don't even try. I've known you too long. You're not having fun because you've spent too much time watching that Yankee man dance with every woman here but you."

Bethany's smile faded as she met the wise eyes of her friend. "I was hoping it didn't show." Her gaze inadvertently drifted back to the crowd on the dance floor and instantly found Wilder in its midst. The woman in his arms wore a daringly low-cut gown and Wilder seemed to be enjoying the view.

"No one else has noticed because you've kept a lovely smile on your face all evening."

Margaret's words gave her some comfort, and Bethany admitted, "It hasn't been easy."

"I don't know what you see in that carpetbagger. Coming down here and trying to take your home away from you same as after the war."

"Margaret, you know Grace sold him—"

"Yes, I know what I was told," she interrupted Bethany with a scowl on her face. "Why don't you just go over there and ask him to dance?"

"What?" Her eyes widened with surprise. "You know I can't do that. Besides, if he wanted to dance with me, he'd ask."

The older woman hit Bethany across the shoulder with her white handkerchief. "I don't want to hear that. I've never known you not to go after whatever you wanted. I don't like his Yankee ways, but you've had stars in your eyes ever since he came here. Stop this foolishness and go over and ask him to dance before I do it for you."

"You'd do that, wouldn't you?"

"In the blink of an eye. If you want to dance with him, I'll go bring him over here and tell him you're ready to dance."

Bethany laughed and it felt good. "You know, Margaret, I'm very fond of you."

The older woman stuffed her handkerchief under her sleeve before saying gruffly, "Get on away from here and go find that man."

A fast tune eased to a close and a softer ballad started as Bethany scanned the crowd for Wilder. The woman in the revealing dress was hanging on to him. Maybe Margaret was right. If Wilder wouldn't come to her, she'd go to him.

The first bars of the song were well past when Bethany tapped Wilder on the shoulder and said, "Pardon me, but I think you promised this dance to me."

"So I did." Wilder gave the woman he was holding a charming smile as they parted. He took Bethany into his arms. Her dress rustled when his legs brushed against it, just as Mrs. Bloomfield had promised.

But nothing else happened as expected. Wilder held her stiffly, coldly, without the least bit of warmth or romance.

Bethany couldn't believe it. His body was rigid, his movements stiff and out of rhythm. He was holding her as if he were a young boy taking his first lesson. When she looked up at him, she saw that his features were tight and strained. Suddenly, she knew the problem. His leg had to be bothering him. Obviously, pride wouldn't allow him to show it when he was dancing with other women. With her, he didn't feel the need to pretend. The thought warmed her heart.

"Wilder, is your leg hurting you?" she asked when he caught her staring at him.

"No, my leg is fine."

He said the right words, but Bethany wasn't convinced because the tightness around his mouth was still very visible. "Wilder, I can tell you're in pain. You don't have to pretend with me. Why have you been parading all over this dance floor without a rest? Do you want to go back to taking medication?"

"What are you talking about?" He appeared amused by her suggestion. "Bethany, my leg is fine. I assure you, it's not troubling me at all tonight."

Her eyes peered deeply into his, searching. "Then why are you dancing with me as if I were a stone statue?" They were no longer actually dancing, just swaying in time to the slow tune.

"I didn't realize I danced that badly."

"You don't," she interjected. "I've watched you dance, but you're holding me as if you are afraid to touch me." Her voice had thinned to a near whisper as disappointment flowed through her. She loved him. The way he was treating her caused an empty, aching feeling deep inside. Bethany lowered her head, no longer able to look into his eyes.

With the tips of his fingers, he lifted her chin until her eyes gazed into his once more. "If I didn't know you better, I'd think that was a jealous remark. But since you're interested, I'll tell you why I'm barely touching you." His voice was low. He moved closer to her, his breath fanning her cheeks. "I can hold, touch, and dance with all the other women here because I don't have the slightest interest in them."

His voice became husky. "I want you, Bethany. I want to make love to you this very minute. If I hold you any closer, you're going to know just how much, and so will everyone else when you walk away. Do you understand what I'm saying?"

Bethany's breath grew short, her heartbeat raced in her chest. It was wonderful. He was feeling what she felt. Oh God, she prayed silently, if she were lucky enough, this night might end with her in Wilder's arms.

"Yes, of course I understand," she whispered hoarsely. They were swaying, not dancing, but she didn't care. She was touching him and that gave her a peace she hadn't felt since her parents died.

"If you continue to look at me like that, I'm going to press you close and then—" He looked at her with fire-filled eyes. His voice trembled as he whispered, "I won't be able to walk away from you without embarrassing both of us."

His words had the desired effect. Bethany wanted nothing more than to press as close to him as she could get, but she wanted to keep that private. They stopped moving and stood still in the middle of the floor; the music continued playing while others danced around them.

"Will you dance with me later, when we're all alone? When everyone else is gone?"

"We've been through this before, Bethany. I don't think you know what you're asking." He murmured seductively low, waiting for her response.

"Yes, I do. I know exactly what I'm asking." Her words were filled with all the emotion she was feeling. For once, she didn't try to hide her love. She knew what she was saying and doing. Taking a deep breath, she asked again, "Will you?"

He only continued looking at her with uncertainty. Something was wrong. If he wanted her as much as he said he did, why did he hesitate? Doubt clouded his expression. Did he doubt her? Or himself?

"Wilder, I don't understand."

"There are still things between us that haven't been resolved."

A trickle of fear ran through her. She knew the problem. He was thinking about his home. His life was in Homestead, hers here in Eufaula. Wilder was a gentleman, and he didn't want to take advantage of her when he knew he'd be leaving. Instinctively, she started swaying in time to the music. He joined her. His eyes had never been bluer.

"I don't want to think about those things tonight. I know how I feel and what I want. You've said before that I don't need anyone to protect me. Don't try to protect me tonight." She moistened her lips. "Will you dance with me when we're alone?"

His breath leapt, and his arms tightened about her. Slowly, he nodded. "Yes, I'll dance with you."

The music ended. Bethany walked away without saying anything else. Nothing more was needed. Knowing that he'd agreed had its own satisfaction. She felt wonderful, excited, ready to rush the guests out the door so she could be alone with Wilder.

All of a sudden an arm slid around Bethany's back and a hand grabbed hers. Before she could voice a protest, Stanley had swept her up in his arms and was leading her into the midst of the dancers. "I believe

211

this is my dance," he said, smiling down into her eyes.

Momentarily stunned by his presence, Bethany couldn't say or do anything.

"Don't look so shocked to see me. Surely you didn't think that by not sending me an invitation I wouldn't come." He laughed.

Furious that he was actually touching her, Bethany's whole body went rigid. "How dare you barge in here. How dare you presume to touch me."

His hands tightened. He held his teeth together and said, "Try to break away from me, and I promise you there'll be a scene you and The Georgia will never live down."

Bethany pondered what he said as she stiffly allowed him to move her about the dance floor. For the time being, she had no choice but to believe him. She refused to let him ruin this night. Another dancer bumped her, moving her closer to Stanley. "What do you want?" she asked, bristling with contempt.

He smiled leeringly. "Just to look at you, dance with you."

His hand crushed her fingers and Bethany winced from the pain. With his other hand at the small of her back, he applied pressure, trying to force her closer to him. His gaze roamed over her face, down her neck, stopping at the swell of her breasts. He breathed deeply. "I always knew you would be stunning in a low-cut dress." His eyes turned glassy. "You're the kind of woman a man only has to have once, then he can live with the memory the rest of his life. Your breasts are—"

Bethany jerked her hand free of his. It took all of

her control to keep from reaching up and slapping his face. Someone knocked into her shoulder but she stood her ground, seething with anger. "I don't care what kind of scene you cause. I will not allow you to speak to me that way. You can leave right now or I'll call Sheriff Beale over here to escort you off my property."

Stanley laughed bitterly and held up his hands as he looked around the crowd. Several people had stopped to watch them. "Anything you say, sweet Bethany." He turned and disappeared into the crowd.

When he was gone, she put a big smile on her face and turned around so that anyone who was looking could see her face as she left the dance floor. As soon as she was away from the crowd, Bethany wrapped her arms around herself and shook.

It was close to three in the morning when Wilder and Bethany stood on the front steps saying good night to the last guest.

Wilder put his arm around Bethany's shoulder and she looked up at him. "Your parents would have been very proud of you tonight."

She smiled warmly. "That's the nicest thing you could have said to me. Thank you."

"Shall we go in and have that dance?"

At her nod, they started through the door, only to step aside quickly as two band members came rushing out.

"We'll be out of the way in just a minute, Miss Hayward," one of the men said.

"I guess we won't get that dance after all," Wilder remarked.

His statement hung between them for a moment. Was he giving her an easy way out if she wanted it? Was he unsure of himself? A sultry breeze whipped across her face; crickets hidden in the deep carpet of grass chirped loudly. For some reason Wilder was reluctant, but Bethany had made up her mind and she didn't intend for him to change it. The rest of the night belonged to her.

In a steady voice, she said, "I wasn't planning on musicians being around for our dance."

After a moment of silence, Wilder nodded once and said, "You go on up, Bethany. I'll stay down here until these men are through."

When Bethany closed the door to the third floor, she shivered. Wilder had never said he loved her, only that he wanted her. Stanley had indicated he wanted her, too. "No," she whispered over the hum of excitement in her ears. "I won't let Stanley ruin tonight. I love Wilder. I know that he has tender feelings for me. That's enough for tonight. That's enough," she whispered again, knowing she didn't have the right to ask him to love her enough to give up his home in Pennsylvania.

While Bethany waited in the living room for Wilder, she told herself all the reasons why she shouldn't be doing what she was about to do. Her parents wouldn't have approved. She'd been taught better. If anyone found out, her reputation would be ruined. But all those reasons didn't feed the emptiness, soothe the pain, or sate the hunger of desire. Surely her parents wouldn't have wanted her to go through the rest of her life without knowing the love a man and woman share. No, they wouldn't have wanted that for her. At last the door opened, and Bethany unconsciously jumped back.

Wilder didn't speak as he walked into the room and stood close to her, his gaze never leaving her face. He slipped his arms around her, holding her close, giving her the warmth of his body.

"Are you all right?" he asked.

She blushed lightly. "I'm fine. Just a little nervous, a little unsure of—"

"Dancing with me?" he asked, then smiled.

"No. Making love," she whispered.

He squeezed her tighter. The taffeta crinkled suggestively as his hands ran up and down her back. "Bethany, I want you more than I've ever wanted any other woman. I swear to God it's true. But—"

"No buts," she answered softly. "I'm twenty-four years old. I know what I'm doing."

Wilder smiled. "You're so strong yet so innocent, it scares me to death." He lifted her chin, looking deeply into her eyes. "I've never wanted to do anything to hurt you. Do you believe that?"

Again he had a look of pain on his features. Thinking he was talking about buying Grace's half of The Georgia, she nodded.

"You can only hurt me tonight by walking out that door."

"There's no way in hell I'm going to do that," he said, then pressed his lips firmly to hers. The kiss was demanding and without restraint.

"Bethany, I love you. Damn, I do," he whispered against her lips.

Looking up into his eyes, Bethany smiled. "Oh, Wilder, you've made me so happy. I love you, too. I knew you cared for me, but I wasn't sure you loved me."

He kissed her again. Softly this time. "I wasn't going to tell you that until we talked about—"

Her fingers flew to his lips. She wouldn't let him finish the sentence. "I don't want to hear anything tonight except words of love. Tomorrow we'll talk of other things."

"I don't think we should go any farther tonight until we've talked. What I have to say could make a difference."

No, she didn't want to hear anything that could make a difference. Those things could be important tomorrow but not tonight. Bethany swallowed hard. For years, she had put Grace and The Georgia first. Not tonight. Wilder loved her and nothing else mattered. Nothing. She closed her eyes and breathed deeply. She loved Wilder and he loved her. Exhilaration had never been so potent.

"I love you," she whispered back to him, her gaze filled with promises. "Please don't tell me anything else tonight." She lifted her lips to his and touched them reverently at first, but as the pressure increased, so did the fire. He held her so close, Bethany wondered if he could mold his body to hers. The kiss ended, and she pressed her lips to his neck as his hand ran up and down her back, making the taffeta sing. Tingles and prickles left her drifting in pleasure.

As he held her, Wilder started gently humming and swaying, back and forth. He pressed his body as close to hers as their clothing would allow. "I've wanted to do this all evening," he said, leaning into her.

"I've wanted this for weeks," she answered, moving with him, loving the feeling of being so close to him.

"You are so beautiful, so desirable."

Wilder stopped dancing and cupped her neck in his hands. He bent his head and kissed the hollow at the base of her throat. He stuck out his tongue and wiped her soft skin along her collarbone. Bethany felt a building desire in the bottom of her stomach. Wilder's caresses and kisses were making her feel wonderful. His hands slipped to the sleeves of her blouse and he pushed them off her shoulders, leaving them bare for his touch. He covered her upper chest and shoulders with moist little kisses. Bethany ran her hands over his shoulders, down his back, and up into his hair. She wanted to rip his clothes from him and once again feel his flesh against her palms. She wanted to give him the same pleasure she was receiving.

With love in his eyes, Wilder lifted his head and looked down at her. His hands trembled as he caressed the tops of her shoulders, letting his thumbs play in the hollow at the base of her neck. "Satin," he said in a raspy voice.

"Satin?" she repeated, looking dreamily into his eyes.

"I used to wonder if your skin felt like satin, fine cotton, or silk. It's satin."

"I like for you to touch me. I want to touch you, too, but you have on too many clothes," she whispered.

A smile eased over his face and his eyes sparkled. "So do you. Let's do something about that."

In a moment of bravery, Bethany took hold of his hand and led him into her bedroom. The room was bathed in a soft yellow glow from the lamplight. A breeze rustled the sheers that covered the open windows. Their soft movement allowed little more than a hint of moonlight to spill into the bedroom.

"This room looks like you," Wilder said as his gaze drifted from the pillow-strewn bed to the ruffle-cushioned rocker in the corner and over to the rosewood dresser. The walls were papered in a rose and floral print. The bed was covered with a rose-colored quilted satinet spread.

"You'll have to take over from here," Bethany said, not quite sure what the next step should be.

"With pleasure," he answered, and he started shrugging out of his evening jacket.

Her hands were trembling with expectancy as she helped him slip the jacket off his shoulders and fling it over the square post of the half-tester. Her legs weakened as she followed his hands to his bow tie and helped him take it off. As soon as he dropped it to the floor, he pulled her into his arms and kissed her. He kissed her lips, her cheeks, her eyes, her neck, as his hands caressed the firm swell of her breasts. He pushed the sleeves of her dress farther down her arms. His fingers were warm and gentle as they pulled at the material, forcing it to move, to give him access to what he wanted.

Wilder's kisses and caresses were happening so fast she couldn't enjoy one sensation before another took over, sending spirals of desire through her. She wanted to tell him to slow down, yet she wanted him to go faster for fear of wasting one moment of their time together.

"Bethany," he whispered as he held her close and breathed in her rose-scented skin. "I have lain awake so many nights wanting to touch you like this, wanting to look at you."

"I've been doing the same thing," she answered in a husky voice.

"Help me take off my shirt." Trembling and with shaky hands, she helped with the buttons while he pulled his suspenders off his shoulders and yanked the shirt free of his trousers. When he stood before her bare-chested, Bethany smiled. With tentative movements at first, she lightly caressed his shoulders. His skin was warm. No, hot. Slowly, she let the tips of her fingers glide down his chest, stopping briefly when her palm scraped his nipple, then moving down to the top of his pants.

"I like the way your skin feels beneath my hand," she said.

Wilder chuckled lightly. "I like the way you touch me. I like what it does to me, the way it makes me feel. Right now I think I'm the luckiest man in the world."

She smiled up at him. "I feel the same way."

Bethany leaned over and kissed the center of his chest, then sticking out her tongue, she tasted his skin. Wilder breathed deeply and exhaled slowly. Knowing that she pleased him delighted her. She lifted her hands to his chest once again. She had never experienced such wanting. She wanted to touch him, to breathe in his scent, to give him pleasure.

Wilder was doing his best to take things slowly so he wouldn't frighten her, but, damn, he was so hard he was hurting. He couldn't go so fast that it wasn't good for her also, but her touch was feeding an inner fire that had been burning since he first saw her.

Grabbing her wrists, he turned her around and kissed the back of her neck and shoulders as he fumbled with the tiny buttons on her dress, damning everyone of them as he went down her back. As he pulled the bodice off her arms, he turned her to face him. He swallowed hard. Damn, she was beautiful and more tempting than a woman had the right to be. He set about unlacing her strapless corset. When he finished, he threw it to the floor and gazed at the satiny smooth skin of her back. He pressed his palm to her skin, running his hand over her shoulders and down to the small of her back. Her breasts were shaped beautifully and not as small as he'd imagined. With a shaky hand, he reached over and cupped one. Perfect. He looked into her eyes. How long had he wanted her?

"Do you have any doubts?" he asked.

Bethany shook her head.

"Then let's finish getting out of these clothes," he murmured as he bent down, lifted her in his arms, and placed her on the bed.

Chapter Fourteen

Helping each other, they soon lay naked amidst soft pillows and a rose-colored satinet spread. Sometime during the disrobing, Wilder had pulled the pins from her hair and spread it over her shoulders. They kissed and caressed as passion mounted, hunger increased, and desire ran rampant between them.

Bethany had never imagined that a man could make her feel so uninhibited as to allow him to touch her in such a manner, in those places. She never would have believed that the feel of his warm mouth on her breasts would make such funny little noises come out of her throat. She never would have guessed that she'd want to touch a man in his most private place. But she did. Letting her hands leave his back and shoulders, she followed the contour of his body down to the swell of his buttocks. She squeezed them. They were firm. With no sense of fear, Bethany forgot about her own pleasure, slipped her hand around his side, and touched the rock-hard protrusion at the juncture of his thighs. Wonder filled her as she felt free to study the shaft with her hands. It was exalting.

Suddenly, Wilder surprised Bethany by grabbing both her hands in one of his. He lay, half on top of her, his breathing coming in sharp gasps. "You're driving me over the edge." His lips moved against hers as he spoke. "If you don't keep your hands still, I'm not going to make it."

She looked into his eyes. "I want to touch you," she whispered passionately. "I want to know what you feel like."

"I want you to touch me," he mumbled under his breath. "But not now. Not the first time." He lifted his head, his eyes drinking in the desire written on her face, her breasts heaving beneath him. For a moment he wanted to shove himself inside her and take her as wildly and as roughly as he would any seasoned whore. But he couldn't treat her that way.

He ran the palm of his hand down the side of her face, over her breasts, past her waist, then back up again. "Just looking at you, touching you, is all I can handle right now. I want it to be good for you. I want to love you from deep inside me, and I can't do it if you—" he stopped and moistened his lips, "if you touch me like that again. Let me do it all this time. The first time." He kissed her lips tenderly. "Let me bring you to the point where I am, and we'll make— we'll be satisfied at the same time."

Wilder let go of her hands and Bethany gave him a loving smile. Her arms went around his neck, and she settled them in his hair. "Will they be all right here?" she asked in a teasing voice.

"Perfect," he answered. Their lips met and their

tongues probed, sharing, playing, forcing, eager to grant satisfaction.

Bethany had never experienced anything close to what was happening to her. Her body felt as if it were on fire. Her breathing was choppy and erratic. Wilder lay half on top of her, his hands running up and down her body, from her breasts, down to her waist, then over her hips to skim down her legs. His mouth covered her nipple, the gentle sucking causing contractions in her lower stomach. The only thing Bethany knew to do was to lie still and enjoy the sensations wracking her body. His hands caressed her breasts with deliberate movements, intending to feed her desire. He pressed his hips to hers, confirming what he had told her. Bethany closed her eyes and enjoyed his loving.

With every ounce of willpower he had, Wilder held off the joining of their bodies until he knew she was ready to give up her virginity. Even as he entered her, he regretted having to hurt her. He whispered his love for her and caressed her with all the emotion and desire he was feeling. With the tip of a finger, he brought her back to the height she had been before he entered her, and when he heard her gasp, when she held her breath, when her body went rigid, when he was sure she had felt as good as he could make it the first time, he smiled and gave her his seed.

More than their bodies were joined when the climax came. Wilder knew he had to find a way to join their homes and their lives. Bethany might not know it yet, but as far as he was concerned, he'd just taken her for his wife.

"Oh, sweet Bethany," he whispered softly, kissing

her cheeks, her eyes, her neck. "My sweet, sweet Bethany."

The offending words broke like a cutting knife into Bethany's euphoria. *Sweet Bethany.* She froze, turning cold as a mid-winter's day. It was no longer Wilder loving her. It was Stanley! His body covered hers, pinning her to the bed. His cold lips were leaving wet kisses on her face and his hands were pawing her breasts. His fingers were digging into her skin, trying to rip open her flesh.

"No . . . stop! Leave me alone!" She pushed at his chest. His breathing grew louder in her ears. She pushed again. "Don't touch me!" she cried.

"Bethany! Dammit! What's wrong?" Wilder grasped the sides of her head in his hands and held her still. "I'm sorry. Did I hurt you?"

With the light from the lamp, Bethany looked into Wilder's arresting blue eyes. He wasn't Stanley. Thank God! She had thought Stanley was . . . What had happened to her? She lay still, her breath coming in short gasps. What was wrong with her? For a long, horrible moment, she'd thought Wilder was Stanley. How could she? Did she hate Stanley so much that even the man she loved became him when she heard those words?

"Bethany, what's wrong? Did I do something?" Wilder asked again.

His hair fell across his forehead just the way she loved it. How could she have mistaken him for Stanley? "No, it's nothing. I'm sorry," she whispered, pushing her tangled hair away from her face.

"That's not good enough. Tell me why you started fighting me." Danger edged his voice.

Surprised by his roughness, Bethany gasped. "No, I can't."

She tried to move away from him, but he held her to the bed, pinning her with his arms and legs. A sick feeling tightened the pit of her stomach. How could she admit the truth?

"You're not going anywhere until you explain what happened. Dammit, I love you, and I have a right to know why you pushed me away." His voice was so filled with emotion it had a trace of a slur.

"I don't want you to know."

"Tell me!"

"I—you called me sweet Bethany. I hate that!" she said in a raspy voice. "Don't ever call me that again." She trembled.

"Why?" She tried to pull away from him again but he held fast. Bethany struggled for a moment, trying to break his hold. "Tell me!" he said in a harsher tone, demanding an answer.

"Because Stanley always called me that! And for a moment you became Stanley, and I couldn't bear his touch." Her words flew hard and furious, her eyes were wild with anger. "I hate him. I hate the things he always said to me. Don't ever call me that again!" she whispered desperately.

"Goddammit," he said soberly as he pressed his forehead against hers.

Bethany's stomach knotted, and her throat ached. What a scene she had made! She had lost all control over her emotions. Since she'd met Wilder, she'd lost control of Grace, The Georgia, her heart, and her life. How could she have let it all happen?

"Bethany, it's all right. I understand." His voice

was soft, comforting.

"No, you don't," she said, shaking her head, lifting it to him. "I hate Stanley. I hate what he did to Grace, to us. I hate what he always called me. I hate—"

"Stop it, Bethany."

Wilder swore again as he rolled to his side and took her in his arms. He pressed her cheek against his chest. He stroked her hair and held her for a long time before saying, "You're not a 'hate' kind of person, and I know that. You just have a strong dislike for him."

"No, Wilder. Don't try to make me better than I am."

"I'm not." He kissed the top of her head and held her close. "Stanley isn't going to bother you again. And don't worry. I won't ever call you that again. Never again!"

A wave of fatigue washed over her. She let his strength support her. "Oh, Wilder, I do love you. I've loved you for a long time."

"That's good to hear." He kissed her forehead and stroked her hair. "I love you, too, Bethany."

She raised her head and looked at him with luminous eyes. "I'm sorry. I know I've messed up everything. It was a perfect evening until this."

His eyes were filled with understanding. "It's still a perfect evening. The only thing you've done is make me a happy man." He lifted her chin and gently kissed her, running his tongue over her lips before breaking away. "This is the second time I've reminded you of that man." There was a nervous edge to his brief smile. "You're going to have to tell me everything he said, so I'll know what's safe to say."

"Wilder, I know I shouldn't feel the way I do about him, but he—"

"Shhh," he interrupted, then kissed her. "Don't think about him. Is he worth one moment of thought from you?" he asked as he kissed her neck and shoulder, but silently he wondered what else Stanley might have done to Bethany and vowed to get even with the bastard.

Bethany shook her head.

"Good." He rolled her to her back and covered her body with his. "I don't want you thinking about anything or anyone but me. Do you think you can do that?" he asked as he rained moist little kisses over her cheeks and nose.

"I may be persuaded," she said, slipping her arms around his neck and sliding her hands into his hair.

"Maybe this will help," he said as he bent his head and covered one of her nipples with his warm mouth.

Bethany closed her eyes as spasms of delight attacked her insides. "Yes. Oh, yes," she whispered.

Chapter Fifteen

Wilder stopped the carriage in front of a small clapboard house on Ashton Street. It was too early for anyone to be up on a Sunday morning, except that Wilder had not gone to sleep. He'd held Bethany in his arms until she'd fallen asleep, then quietly, reluctantly left her bed.

He'd awakened Seth to find out where Stanley Edwards lived. According to the groundskeeper, Stanley lived in a small apartment on the second floor of the house he now eyed.

It was true that Bethany could protect herself, Wilder thought as he stepped down from the carriage. She'd held her own with Stanley's boorish behavior a couple of times that he knew about. But last night he realized Stanley frightened her more than he'd ever suspected. She was his now, and he didn't intend to allow Stanley's rude and forward attentions toward her to continue. He planned to make sure she never had to see Stanley Edwards again.

Wilder tied the horse to the hitching rail and limped around to the side of the house, spotting the outside stairs that Seth had said would lead to Stanley's apartment. Morning birds chirped as he made his way across the dew-dampened grass. A gray sky promised rain.

Because of all the dancing last night, Wilder's leg was hurting like hell this morning, but he didn't care. He wouldn't rest until he was sure Stanley would never bother Bethany again.

Scowling, Wilder climbed the fourteen steps up to the small landing and knocked loudly on the door. The old boards cracked and creaked under his weight, sounding loud in the still air as he restlessly waited for Stanley to answer. Irritated that Stanley hadn't come to the door, Wilder repeated his effort, only louder. A few moments later he heard Stanley mumbling and stumbling from inside the house.

The door swung wide. Stanley snarled when he saw Wilder. "What are you doing here at this time of morning?"

Wilder eyed Stanley, who was slightly hidden by dark shadows inside the house. "I came to tell you to stay away from Bethany. If you go near her again, you'll have to answer to me."

Stanley laughed as he combed through his hair with his fingers. His plaid robe was belted loosely around a thickening waist that was usually hidden by a waistcoat. "Answer to you?" He laughed again. "I think not."

Wilder drew himself up straighter, his gaze never leaving Stanley's face. He'd known the man would be smug, even offensive. "I only came to warn you,

Edwards. Stay away from her. Stay away from The Georgia."

"As you can see, I'm not the least bit intimidated by your threat." He smiled confidently. "In fact, I had planned to visit Bethany today and compliment her on the success of the ball."

Wilder's breath was ragged with frustration. He was ready to wipe that snide smile off Stanley's face. "I thought I saw you leaving the ballroom last night. I should have known you wouldn't stay away."

"Why should I? Bethany will be my sister-in-law one day."

"Not if I can do anything about it."

"My, my." Stanley clucked his tongue. "I'm beginning to wonder what we have going on in that house. There must be a reason you're so fired up about that woman. What has she promised you—or what has she given you in exchange for your devoted protection? Have you sampled the charms of my sweet Bethany?"

Searing hatred filled Wilder. He stepped forward, his fists clenched. He was trying hard to hold on to his temper. The man obviously didn't know how Wilder felt about Bethany. Stanley wouldn't make such stupid comments if he did. Forcing his hands to remain at his sides, he said, "If you talk to her or even look at her again, I'll be back. And take my word for it, you won't like it."

"I'm not afraid of a spineless cripple," Stanley taunted. "You've had three opportunities to take me on. If the bitch was worth it, you would have already—"

Wilder's control snapped. He caught a glimpse of

a startled expression before his hard knuckles met with Stanley's upper lip and nose. The crunch of splintering bone echoed around him. Stanley howled and fell to a spread-eagle sprawl on the hardwood floor. Blood poured from his nostrils as he groped for the tail of his robe.

Stepping inside, Wilder glared down at Stanley. "Get up!" he demanded.

"I—I think you broke my n—nose, you bastard," Stanley mumbled as he tried to stop the flow of blood by jamming his robe against his nose.

"Get up, you weak-kneed coward," Wilder said again, his voice perilously low.

Stanley's eyes opened wide with fear. "I'm staying right here until you leave." Holding the material over the bottom half of his face, his breathing was nasal and raspy.

Wilder gazed at the pathetic man lying on the floor. How could he smash his face in again if he wouldn't stand and fight? Hitting him once wasn't enough. Wilder wanted to make sure he never called Bethany a bitch again. Stanley was weak. His only strength lay in trying to seduce or frighten women. He didn't want to fight a man. Wilder's stomach churned with anger and repulsion as he reached down and grabbed the front of Stanley's robe, lifting his torso off the floor. He held a tight fist in front of Stanley's face. Stanley's hands trembled with fear as he held the robe to his nose, but he made no sound of protest.

Looking into his terror-filled eyes, Wilder said, "If you ever speak to Bethany again, I'll come back. And I won't mind crawling on the floor, in the mud, or chasing you back into the gutter to get you." Sick of the sight of his whimpering, Wilder shoved Stanley back down on the floor.

"No reason to beat up a man because he wants a little fun."

"Bethany doesn't consider your visits fun and neither do I. Do we understand each other?"

Stanley nodded furiously.

Wilder stared at the sniveling man a moment longer, contempt making him want to force Stanley to stand up and fight. What Stanley had considered fun had destroyed a relationship between two sisters and had almost destroyed his relationship with Bethany last night. He could only guess at the things Stanley must have said to her. At the thought, a tightness grew in his chest. He had to leave before he changed his mind and got down on the floor with him and hit him again. Stanley didn't know how easy he'd gotten off.

Wilder turned and walked out the door, leaving it open behind him.

Stanley lay still until he heard Wilder's carriage leaving. "Goddamned, crippled bastard!" he mumbled as he rose from the floor. He felt as if someone had stuffed a ball of yarn up his nose.

"Ohhh," he groaned as he made his way to the washbowl and bent over it. As soon as he took the hem of his robe away, blood dripped into the dry basin. He swore again, damning Wilder to hell as he poured water from the pitcher into the basin. When he looked up into the shaving mirror, Stanley saw that the bridge of his nose was twisted to one side, and his upper lip was cut and swollen to three times its normal size. Blood stained his teeth and chin and ran down his throat, making him a grotesque sight.

"I'll kill you, you son of a bitch," he whispered into the mirror. "As soon as I catch your back turned, I'll put the long blade of a knife between your shoulders and rip it down your spine." Stanley smiled at the thought of killing Wilder.

"Don't worry, sweet Bethany, your time's coming, too," Stanley chuckled as he dipped a facecloth into the tepid water.

Oh, yes, he'd kill her, too. But first he'd take great delight in telling her how he'd paid Mr. Lester to double-cross her. "Soon," he whispered to the mirror.

Mr. Lester had discovered that Grace spent her first two weeks in Atlanta at The Magnolia Glen Hotel. It was only a matter of time before the detective found out where she was now staying. Then he'd find a way to kill them all. Grace, Bethany, and Wilder. He'd find another town, another woman to marry.

Stanley lightly touched the facecloth to his chin. He winced. Fighting the pain, he chuckled. He'd kill the untouchable Bethany first. And he'd make sure Grace and Wilder were watching.

Chapter Sixteen

Wilder rubbed his bruised and scraped knuckles as he walked up the front steps of The Georgia. Even though his leg hurt like the devil, he hadn't felt this good in years. His only regret was that he'd only struck Stanley once. He hadn't expected the coward to stay on the floor like a snake and not fight him.

He'd been too angry on the carriage ride back to the house to think rationally about anything. He kept wanting to go back and make that gutter-rat stand up and fight like a man. Now he had some decisions to make concerning Bethany. Concerning Grace. Concerning The Georgia.

When Wilder made it to the porch, he stopped and leaned against the great stone pillar and thought of Bethany.

He wanted to hold her.

Closing his eyes, he remembered how she had looked last night with her golden-colored hair spread across her shoulders. He remembered the softness of her skin, the firmness of her breasts, the curve of her waist and flare of her hips. He remembered how innocently she had come to him.

Dammit, he shouldn't have made love to her. Bethany wasn't the kind of woman a man treated that way. He should have insisted they marry first, but he'd let his desire for her rule his body. He wondered if she'd regretted their lovemaking when she woke up this morning. He'd wanted to be there to reassure her of his love, but seeing Stanley seemed more important at the time. Now he realized Stanley was too much a coward to be of any real danger to anyone.

Bethany. Damn, he loved her. He needed her. But did she need him? She had her life well under control. She had The Georgia. Her employees adored her. Did she want or need him in her life? Did she deserve him? Hell, no! Wasn't he keeping her sister's whereabouts a secret from her? What would she do when she found out he'd known where Grace was all along? Would she forgive him? Would she understand that he'd made a promise and felt bound by a code of honor to keep it? Would she realize it was in her best interest that he know where Grace was hiding?

He wanted to hold her.

Wilder opened his eyes, pushed away from the column, and headed inside. He'd take the train to Atlanta this afternoon and see Grace. She wouldn't hold him prisoner in her little game any longer. He would tell her he could no longer keep her whereabouts a secret. She could leave and hide elsewhere if she wanted, but he had to tell Bethany the whole sordid story. He'd make her understand why he'd kept his promise to Grace for so long.

Damn! He would have never made an alliance with Grace if he'd known Bethany wasn't in love with Stanley . . . if he'd known he was going to fall in love with her.

He wanted to hold her.

As he entered the foyer, Margaret came out of her office carrying a piece of paper. "This telegram came for you not ten minutes ago."

As usual, her tone was gruff and cold. When he reached for the paper, he noticed that her gaze dropped to his skinned and reddened knuckles. Margaret held on to the envelope a moment longer than she should have, then she lifted her gaze to his. Slowly, a smile spread across her lips and brightened her face. Stunned, Wilder let his arm fall to his side.

"Seth told me you were banging on his door at daybreak, asking how to get to that Edwards man's house. Looks like you found him."

"Seth talks too much," Wilder answered, but he smiled to himself. It wasn't surprising that the first show of friendliness from Margaret came when she assumed he'd taken up for Bethany. From the first time he met Margaret, he knew that she protected Bethany the way a mother hen protects her baby chicks.

"He sure does." She nodded to the telegram. "Mrs. Stevens said it sounded important. You should read it right away."

Telegrams were certainly faster than letters, but the drawback was that the whole town could know the contents before you did. Wilder was certain it was from his brother. With any luck, Relfe had found the union men who'd attacked him.

"I'll take it out on the patio to read. Have you seen Bethany this morning?"

"Nope. She must be sleeping like a baby. Don't blame her after last night."

"What do you mean?" Wilder asked somewhat hesitantly, trying not to read more into what Margaret had said. He didn't like having a guilty conscience.

"What do you think I mean? She worked night and day on that ball for two weeks. I'm sure she was dead on her feet by the time the last guest left."

"Oh, yes, the ball." Wilder had been so caught up in loving Bethany and getting to Stanley that he'd forgotten about the party. "You're right. She needs the rest." Wilder turned and headed for the patio. He didn't feel like walking three flights of stairs before resting his leg. He dropped into a chair and tore open the envelope.

He scanned the telegram. "Fools," he whispered as the paper shook in his hands. "Goddamned fools. All of them." He read the note again, slower. Atlanta and Grace would have to wait. He had to take the first train to Homestead.

"Wilder."

At the sound of Bethany's voice, Wilder folded the telegram and stuffed it in his pocket. He rose from his chair and turned to face her. She'd never looked more beautiful. She wore her usual white long-sleeve blouse with stand-up collar and dark, flowing skirt. Her hands were clasped together in front of her. Soft hands, gentle hands. Hands that had loved him. His gaze darted back up to her face. An unsure smile trembled on her lips.

"I—I didn't know what to think when I awoke and you were gone."

Wilder gave her a smile that didn't quite reach his eyes, and Bethany knew she'd been right to think that something was wrong when she found him gone from her bed. She should have known it would be like this.

"Bethany, I need to talk to you. Come here and sit down." He pointed to the cushioned rocker.

Startled by his hurried manner, Bethany took the seat without protest. She didn't want to be standing if he was going to tell her that last night had been a mistake.

An elderly couple approached from the side of the house and spoke a greeting to them as they walked past and disappeared into the garden. Wilder took a couple of steps, then turned back to Bethany and said, "Last night should have never happened."

Closing her eyes tightly against the very words she hadn't wanted to hear, Bethany whispered, "No!"

"Yes," he said in an angry tone. "You are not the kind of woman a man dallies with, and I knew that. I—I should have been stronger. My only excuse is that I wanted to make love to you so badly I forgot to think of what it would do to you."

Bethany came out of the chair. "Dallies with?" she asked, shaken by his words. "Is that what you were doing last night? *Dallying* with me?"

"No, dammit! Bethany, I didn't mean it that way. I said it wrong. What I mean is that we should have gotten married before we . . . let things go so far." He grabbed the upper part of her arms. "How could you think I was playing with you? I shouldn't have touched you, and I intend to make amends today. I want to marry you as soon as we can find a judge or minister who'll perform the ceremony.''

Bethany kept her chin high as Wilder's words registered on her brain. He felt guilty for what had happened between them and thought he had to pay by giving her his name. Bethany steeled herself against the hurt.

This morning when she'd awakened and found him gone, she suspected he'd told her he loved her last night only to justify to himself that making love to her would be all right. What he didn't want to admit this morning was that *she* was the one who had insisted on their coming together. For some reason, he wanted to take blame when none was necessary. She'd wanted last night to happen and wasn't sorry it had. Bethany took a deep breath. She wouldn't marry a man who didn't really love her.

"No," she whispered.

"No? What are you saying?"

Wilder's eyes narrowed and a frown appeared on his face. His hands tightened on her arms, and for a moment she allowed herself second thoughts about her answer. She loved Wilder with all her heart. This could be her only opportunity to hold on to him forever. But did she want him if he didn't truly love her and want to marry her? She knew from her experience with John Martin that you could love someone, but not enough to be willing to give up everything to be with them. Did she love Wilder that much? Could she give up her home, her life at The Georgia, for him?

"No, I won't marry you."

"Dammit, Bethany, listen to me. I have to go back to Homestead, and I don't want to leave you unprotected."

A pain pierced Bethany's heart. He was leaving, and he obviously wasn't planning on taking her. That cleared up the problem of whether or not she could leave The Georgia. He wasn't asking her to. She winced inside from the hurt of his words. She'd known he would be returning home, but this was too soon.

Her false bravado was shaky, but it was all she had to rely on to get her through this. She pulled out of his grasp. "I need no protection. You've said so many times. I can take care of myself."

His voice was cold and filled with intense anger when he said, "In some things, yes. But you could be with child right now."

She gasped. She hadn't thought of that. "No, I'm sure I'm not," she said defiantly, willing it to be so.

"How?"

"I just know. A woman knows these things," she answered, wondering where all these words were coming from. Wilder wanted to marry her and he wasn't asking her to give up The Georgia. She loved him. Why couldn't she forget her pride and say yes? What else could she be waiting for? His love. She didn't want his name without his love.

A sharp, jagged streak of lightning split the dark gray sky. Seconds later, thunder invaded the silence.

"Is it my limp?" he asked angrily.

"What!" she exclaimed.

"Is that the reason you won't marry me? You don't want a cripple for a husband?"

241

Bethany took a deep breath and harrumphed. She was furious that he'd think her capable of such. "How dare you think I'm that vain and shallow."

"One woman left when I—"

"I would never leave you if you needed me," she swore with emotion. "Your limp has never taken away from your manliness." Her voice softened. "Surely after last night you know that."

He remained quiet, looking at her. Bethany saw in his eyes that he was hurting. "Wilder . . ." She said his name softly and walked closer to him. Thunder rumbled, and Bethany thought she felt a tiny drop of rain on her cheek. "The way you walk has nothing to do with my refusal to marry you. I wanted last night to happen. I planned it. You've got to understand that I didn't ask for any promises last night, and I'm not expecting any this morning."

Wilder swallowed hard. "I know you love me. I know you never would have let me get near you otherwise. Last night I meant every touch, every kiss, every—" he smiled, "everything about our loving. I don't want to leave you without my name and my financial security. That's why I want to marry you and give you my name before I leave."

Bethany bristled. "I don't need or want your financial security," she countered quickly. "I told you I can take care of myself, and *if* by some chance I carry your child, *I* will take care of him!"

"You make it sound like I'm offering charity."

"You are," she declared.

"Like hell I am. I love you. And I want us to get married today."

Her breath quickened. "You love me?"

242

"Of course I love you. Bethany, I wouldn't have spent the night with you . . . I wouldn't have made love to you if I hadn't known that I loved you. I wouldn't have done that to you. I want to marry you and give you my name before I leave today."

Confusion welled up in her. He loved her, yet he was leaving her. "Today? You're leaving today?" She was stunned. She needed more time to think about what he was saying and what he was asking.

"I received a telegram from my brother just now. There's trouble at the mill. I have to go back to Homestead, and I have to leave right away."

"Why? What's wrong?" Bethany's chest grew heavy, and her words sounded whispery in her ears. Wilder was throwing too many surprises at her. She couldn't think clearly.

"Frick. Henry Clay Frick is the steel mill's plant manager and he—"

"I thought you were the manager," she interrupted, not understanding.

"I am a manager. There's about fifty of us who manage the skilled and unskilled workers. Frick is considered the plant general manager. He's over all of us. The mill at Homestead employs about four thousand workers, with two twelve-hour shifts, seven days a week." Wilder ran a hand through his hair. "Because of a contract dispute with the labor union involving more than three hundred workers who've gone on strike, Frick has shut down part of the mill, putting eight hundred more men out of work. Sympathy strikes have occurred all over the plant."

"Oh, that's terrible!"

"That's not the worst. Frick has hired armed

guards to protect the plant from the strikers when he reopens the works on the sixth of July. I have to try and stop him. There's nothing a steelworker resents more than to see another man take his job."

Bethany gasped. "Wilder, no. You can't go."

"I have to go see if there's anything I can do to stop this madness."

Bethany wanted to grab Wilder and force him to stay with her. Instead, drawing on her strength to remain calm, she grasped the folds of her skirt and held it tightly in the palms of her hands. "I don't want you to go. Union men tried to kill you once. They'll try again."

A dark expression stole over his face. "I have to go. I have to. This is my job. It's my responsibility to be there for my company, for my men."

"Your men? Your men left you for dead. Surely you don't owe them anything." She clutched her skirt tighter. How could she get through to him?

"I said union men attacked me, Bethany. They weren't *my* workers." The uncertainty of his statement showed in his features. He took a deep breath. "This isn't what I wanted to wake up to this morning. You have to understand that I have to go."

Bethany lowered her head. She was acting like a simpering, foolish female. But she feared for him. She wanted him to stay with her. Forever.

Sinking her teeth into her bottom lip, she took a deep breath and tried to gain control of her emotions, tried to regain her aplomb, knowing she couldn't be so selfish as to expect him to stay. She had to think and act. Wilder had trouble. He needed a friend and a helper right now, not a clinging, weepy female. She hadn't asked anything of him before last night, and she wouldn't accept anything this morning.

She raised her head. "If your brother, your employer, and your men need you, of course you have to go." She kept her voice level and looked into his blue eyes. "I'll go with you."

"What did you say?" He gave her an incredulous look.

Dark gray clouds moved briskly overhead. Thunder sounded in the distance, and a fine mist dusted their clothing as they stood on the flagstone patio. The damp, moist air added a heaviness to the conversation. Bethany squared her shoulders and lifted her chin a little higher. "I'll go with you and stand by your side."

"No," he said sternly. "Homestead is not a town for innocent ladies. It's—"

"I'm hardly innocent anymore," she remarked, cutting into his words.

"Don't say that." His voice and expression softened. "Dammit, Bethany, I love you."

Her breath quickened. "I know that now," she whispered.

"I had hoped last night proved that to you." He gazed down into her eyes and placed his hands on her shoulders. "I know you love me, too. Why won't you agree to marry me?"

"I do love you with all my heart. I just can't say yes right now. I need time to think." Her heart pounded. "There are other things to consider, you know. Like leaving Grace and The Georgia and learning to live in your home up north. I want time to think about what it means to marry you. My whole life will change. I can't take that lightly. Let me go with you to Homestead. Let me visit your family and your home."

Wilder pondered her words. She was a determined woman. He squeezed her arms. "Do you really want to go to Pennsylvania with me?"

"Yes," she said softly.

He realized he loved her more than ever. Bethany never failed to amaze and impress him with her strength and courage. How many women would not jump at the chance to marry a man who'd just taken their virginity?

"I guess it's only right that you want to see my home and meet my family before you make a decision. But you won't be going to Homestead. You'll be staying in Pittsburgh with Relfe's wife, at the family home."

She smiled. "All right."

Wilder moistened his lips and asked, "Who will take care of The Georgia for you?"

"There's no one better than Margaret. I'd like to think she couldn't manage without me for a short time, but I'm sure she can."

Cautiously, he brought up a subject he was loath to discuss. "What about Grace? What if she comes home while you're gone?"

Sadness appeared in Bethany's eyes, and Wilder wished he could talk with Grace today.

"I pray with all my heart she will come home. I want so desperately to make her believe I never had any designs on Stanley." She took a deep breath. "If she wants to see me, she'll wait until I return. You come first."

Wilder wrapped her in his arms and held her close. He wanted to make love to her, to sleep with her, to live with her. He knew he would marry her one day soon. But for now, he was relieved by the reprieve. He hated admitting that to himself, knowing it had nothing to do with how much he wanted to make this woman his wife. But when he married her, he wanted to be free of all entanglements. He wanted to come to Bethany with no secrets between them. He wanted everything settled and put in the past—The Georgia, the union men, and his promise to Grace.

Chapter Seventeen

The street was quiet as Bethany stepped out of the carriage in front of a large white colonial house trimmed with black shutters. She glanced around, scanning the area. Impressive houses were jammed so close together they looked as if they were touching. A few trees dotted the landscape. Small shrubs and flowers were kept to a minimum. Wilder's family home was a vast contrast to the acres of grounds and lawn filled with lush flower gardens that surrounded her home.

The late afternoon was shadowed by gray clouds, and Bethany welcomed the cooling breeze that swept across her face. Many times during the two-day train ride, she'd wished for a wind to blow through the railcar and relieve her heated skin.

Wilder touched the small of her back and she walked beside him as they mounted the steps to the front door.

"Are you nervous?" he asked, looking down into her green eyes.

"Maybe a little," she admitted honestly. "I hope your family likes me."

"They will," he assured her.

"I expect things will be different here."

"Not so much. It's a home." Wilder knocked on the front door, then opened it.

Bethany stepped into a wide foyer, with foliated decorations outlining the archways. A beautiful stairway ascended at a right angle and disappeared into a domed wall. She immediately heard the clamoring of feet and the giggles and laughter of children coming toward her. She looked down the long hallway. Two little girls with flying brown curls and white starched pinafores covering their dresses bounded toward them in a headlong dash. Wilder laughed and knelt on one knee. The two girls closed in and jumped him, almost knocking him over.

One arm around each, he hugged and kissed both of them as they said in unison, "I missed you, Uncle Wilder."

"How are my little cherry blossoms?" he asked.

"What did you bring us?" the youngest one asked after giving Wilder another loud, kissy smack on the cheek.

"Don't rush him, Penee," the older sister reprimanded her. "He's just stepped through the door."

Penee answered by sticking out her tongue.

"No need to wait for your surprise. I have it right here in my satchel." Wilder opened the buckle on his brown leather bag and pulled two cloth-wrapped packages from it. He handed one to each of the girls.

Bethany liked them immediately. She was all set to

be nervous and apprehensive, but how could she feel uncomfortable around these two? They had allayed all her fears.

She watched and smiled as they dug eagerly into the packages. While they waited for the train in Atlanta, she'd helped Wilder choose the dolls from a specialty shop. Penee was the first to unwrap her gift, finding a miniature baby doll dressed in a pearl-colored silk christening gown. Both girls squealed with delight and gave Wilder more hugs and kisses.

Deeply touched at how easily, how generously Wilder loved the girls, Bethany knew that whatever the outcome of her relationship with him, she had not done wrong in giving this man her love.

Wilder stood up and said, "Bethany, I'd like to introduce to you Priscilla and Penelope Burlington. Girls, I present Miss Bethany Hayward."

Instantly, the girls' behavior changed from that of children to that of young ladies. They curtsied gracefully as they greeted Bethany. Priscilla looked to be about the age of ten or eleven and Penelope a couple of years younger than her sister. Both girls were beautiful, with streams of shiny brown hair, but while Priscilla had azure blue eyes, Penelope's were the same shade of twilight blue as Wilder's. Bethany found herself drawn to the younger girl.

"Are you going to be staying with us?" Priscilla asked in a grown-up tone.

Bethany nodded. "For a short time."

"We're so glad to have you in our home," she answered properly.

Penelope pulled on Bethany's skirt. "Did you bring us a surprise?"

Priscilla cupped her hand over Penee's mouth. "Mind your manners."

Penee shoved her sister away and jerked her hands to her hips. "Don't tell me what to do."

"Girls . . ." Wilder said in a soft tone.

Interrupting before an argument started, Bethany said, "As a matter of fact, I do have something for you." Penee stuck her tongue out at Priscilla again while Bethany bent over and opened her satchel. She presented each girl with a lace-trimmed handkerchief. As they gave their thanks, Bethany looked up to see a man and woman joining them.

She would have known Relfe anywhere. He looked so much like Wilder, a little older perhaps, but just as handsome. And even though she already had two children, Bethany guessed the petite Ester to be close to her own age. Wilder gave his sister-in-law a generous hug and brotherly kiss on the cheek. Relfe and Wilder shook hands and hugged briefly. A touch of sadness touched Bethany's heart because she and Grace were no longer as close.

"I'd like you to meet Bethany Hayward. Bethany, my brother Relfe and his wife Ester."

Ester smiled warmly and made her feel welcome by saying, "We're so glad you came for a visit. I'll see to it that you have a wonderful time while you're here." Relfe's greeting was more reserved, only giving her a perfunctory smile.

Bethany presented Ester with a handkerchief that had a likeness of The Georgia embroidered in one corner.

"It's so lovely. Such delicate work. And this is your

home?" Ester asked as she led Bethany and Wilder into the living room. "Goodness, it looks so large. Does it really have that many columns?"

Bethany smiled and assured Ester the likeness was accurate. She took a seat on the gold-striped settee. Wilder sat beside her, but Penelope edged her way between them, then Priscilla took his other side.

Remaining quiet like the daughters, Bethany let the other three talk while she looked around the room. Tastefully done, the parlor was vividly decorated in dark reds, browns, and a burnished shade of gold. Hints of pink were found in the floral patterns of the wallpaper and in the velvet-covered chair cushions. The mantel was made from a dark wood highlighted with a marble edging. Brass scrollwork adorned the inner facing. The two settees and three chairs were all finished off with skirts of gold braid. She liked the warm, cozy feel to the room.

Bethany heard her name and looked over at Ester. "I'm sorry. I didn't hear you."

"After two days on a train, you must be exhausted. Would you like to go up to your room and rest before dinner?" Ester asked again.

She was tired, and thinking Wilder might like some time alone with his family, she answered, "Yes, I would like that."

"I'll show you," Penelope said as she jumped off the sofa and grabbed Bethany's hand.

"I should do it. Isn't that right, Mama? I'm the oldest," Priscilla added, to give weight to her words.

"Penee, I'm sure Miss Hayward doesn't want you pulling on her. Now be nice," Ester said.

Penelope looked up at Bethany with those eyes so much like her uncle's. "Am I hurting you?" she asked.

"Not at all." In fact, the warmth of the little girl's hand made Bethany feel warm, accepted. She glanced at Relfe. Well, except for Wilder's brother. She wasn't at all sure how he felt about her presence. His greeting had been reserved. She didn't know if that was his personality or if he took a dislike to her.

"Then I shall take the other hand," Priscilla said in a haughty voice.

"Bethany, you must learn right away how to manage the girls or they will completely take you over," Ester warned.

Looking from Priscilla to Penelope, she said, "I'll remember that should they get out of hand. In the meantime, I'm enjoying this." She turned to Wilder and smiled. "I'll see you at dinner."

He returned the warm smile and nodded.

Ester laughed as Priscilla and Penee led Bethany up the stairs. "She's beautiful, Wilder. We're so happy you brought her with you."

"Yes, she is. And thank you for making her feel welcome," Wilder answered. He was pleased that Ester, Priscilla, and Penee had taken so easily to Bethany. And Bethany certainly seemed to be fond of the girls.

"You should rest, too, Wilder. You're dashing as ever, but a little rest would do you good. Now, if you men will excuse me, I need to see to some things in the kitchen."

"Of course, Ester. We're on our way into the library, where we can talk privately. I promise not to keep him too long and that he'll have time to rest before dinner."

Wilder followed his brother into the library and shut the door behind him. The room was darker than he remembered, with the faint odor of burned wood, beeswax, and leather lingering on the stuffy air. Relfe walked over to a highly polished side table and poured generous amounts of whiskey into two glasses.

"I don't think it's too early for a little nip, do you?"

Not with the way my leg is hurting, Wilder thought, but remained quiet. He didn't want Relfe to know that even though he was walking much better, his leg still gave him a hell of a lot of trouble from time to time. He'd tried to tell himself he wasn't that prideful, but deep inside he knew he was.

"Any word on the men who attacked me?" Wilder asked as his brother handed him the drink.

Relfe shook his head.

Wilder sighed audibly. "It was five damn months ago. You should have found out something by now," he remarked, letting his irritation show in his expression and his words. He'd hoped for some names by now.

Remaining calm, Relfe answered, "You didn't give us much to go on."

"I told you there were five of them. They were all dressed in dark blue jackets and black skullcaps."

"Precisely. You also told us they were all average height. One had a full beard and you think—you think one had a mustache." Relfe spoke slowly. "Do you have any idea just how many of the plant's four thousand employees look and dress like that?"

Wilder checked his anger. It wasn't Relfe's fault the men hadn't been found. He was sure his brother was doing everything humanly possible to find the bastards.

Frustrated, Wilder put his glass to his lips and drank the burning liquid, not bringing it down until the glass was empty. Searing heat rushed up from his stomach, flooding his chest and neck. He coughed and wiped his mouth with the back of his palm. His face and scalp felt as if they were on fire. Damn, he'd forgotten how the good stuff could burn.

He looked at his brother. Relfe had a disapproving expression on his face. "You drank that rather fast. Have you been overindulging?"

Wilder laughed and limped over to refill his glass. "Hardly, brother. Spirits weren't allowed in the hospital and spirits aren't allowed in The Georgia." He coughed again and cleared his throat.

"Speaking of which, we were quite surprised to get your telegram asking us to prepare a room for a feminine guest. Is this serious?"

Wilder sipped the whiskey, taking time to enjoy the taste this time. "I'm going to marry her."

"Really?" Relfe fitted himself into one of the leather wing-backs and smiled. "Strange. You didn't introduce her as your fiancée."

Wilder walked over to the matching chair and sat down. He wasn't in the mood to be drilled by Relfe. Two days of sitting on the train had made his leg stiff and bothersome. He'd take a long walk after dinner. Walking always helped.

"Bethany hasn't agreed to marry me. Yet."

"Interesting. It appears a southern belle has stolen

your heart when none of the beautiful women in Pittsburgh could. Do start at the beginning and tell me all."

"Don't tease me. It was a tiring trip. I'm in no mood for it."

"Who's teasing?" Relfe remained unperturbed, as Wilder knew he would. In a way his brother reminded him of Bethany, trying not to let emotions register on his face and always wanting to be in control.

"I send you to a quiet little town deep in Alabama to recuperate and you come home bringing a beautiful woman with you." Relfe cut his eyes around to Wilder. "I'm curious."

Wilder sighed. He might as well tell Relfe a little so he'd drop the subject of Bethany and get on to the strike. "Bethany owns half of The Georgia which, in case you've forgotten, is the inn you sent me to. We've spent a lot of time together the past few weeks."

"Obviously. Who owns the other half?"

"I do." Wilder sipped his drink and watched as surprise lighted in Relfe's eyes. At last his brother showed emotion.

"Fascinating," Relfe commented. "How did that come about?"

"It's a long story."

Relfe shrugged, showing no signs of giving up on the questions. "I'm not in a hurry."

"All right," Wilder said with rising impatience. "I bought it from her sister because she wanted enough money to leave town." Wilder held up his hand to stop the question already forming on Relfe's lips. "Don't ask. I've said enough about that."

Relfe nodded. "For now. It appears you stayed busy while you were away. Does the withholding of an engagement have anything to do with the ownership of The Georgia?"

"To some extent." Wilder was purposefully evasive. He and Bethany had a lot of things to clear up, not the least of which was the fact that his life was here in Pennsylvania and hers was in Alabama.

"To what extent?" Relfe asked.

Wilder pondered his brother's question while he swirled his liquor in the glass. "Bethany is a very independent woman." He paused. He hadn't come in here to talk about Bethany. "I'll just say that she would have a difficult time leaving her life in Alabama and moving here. A very difficult time."

"I'll accept that for now."

The whiskey was getting to Wilder, making him lethargic. He wanted to lay his head back and take a much-needed nap. But first, he wanted to hear what was going on with the strike.

"Tell me, what's going on at the mill?"

Relfe sighed. "Are you sure you want to know?"

Wilder's response was a tired look.

"Very well. A week and a half ago, Frick enclosed the plant with a three-mile-long board fence and topped it off with barbed wire. As I told you in my telegram, he's hired three hundred Pinkerton agents to protect the plant and the scabs when he reopens the armor-plate and the open-hearth divisions day after tomorrow."

"Damn. Has anybody tried to stop him?" Wilder asked as he moved to the edge of his seat.

"Really, Wilder. All of us have at one time or

another." Relfe gave him an indignant look. "You know how headstrong the man is. He broke the strike in Connellsville back in '90 and he intends to do the same here. Even though I've not heard a word officially, I believe Frick is only carrying out the plans Carnegie laid the groundwork for months ago when he issued the statement that the majority of the Homestead employees were nonunion, and because of that the union must go."

"Does that mean that contract talks are off?"

"Exactly."

Wilder's jaw tightened. "So it's no longer a strike for wages and contract termination. It's a fight for union recognition and collective bargaining."

"From here forward, those will be the real issues. Sad. There's no way the strikers can win."

"Neither will the union. Damn Frick and the workers, too." A sick feeling attacked Wilder's insides. He looked up at his brother but knew he had no answers. "I'll go see Frick tomorrow."

Relfe polished off his drink, then shook his head. "No reason to. It won't do you any good. You can bet Frick had Carnegie's blessing. Strikers have to learn that if they don't want to work for what the company is offering, they're free to go find employment elsewhere. The only thing we can hope for now is that the Pinkertons don't shoot too many of the strikers."

"How can you be so casual about this, Relfe?" Wilder asked, coming out of his chair. "It's not like you to be so complacent."

Remaining seated, remaining calm, Relfe said, "Survival. Unlike you, I have a wife and two

259

children. I can't afford to straddle the fence, as you did. Unfortunately, as Frick sees it, you're either for the company or you're for the strikers. I think you've found out you can't have it both ways."

Wilder's eyes narrowed. "What are you saying?"

Relfe's tone grew insistent. "Only that you've tried to help the workers. You asked Frick to compromise on the contract negotiations and it didn't work. Now it's time for you to stand by your employer." Relfe pointed a finger at Wilder. "I'm telling you, don't go see Frick unless you tell him you're ready to go back to work and teach the scabs how to fire the boiler."

In one gulp, Wilder finished his whiskey and set his glass on the end of Relfe's desk. "You stopped telling me what to do years ago."

Startled, Bethany woke from a sound sleep. She opened her eyes and saw a round-cheeked little girl with both elbows propped on the bed, her chin resting in her palms. It took her a moment to blink the sleep from her eyes and remember where she was.

"I didn't mean to wake you when I touched your hair. It's a very pretty color. I wish my hair looked like yours," Penelope said in a wistful tone. "I knocked on the door but you didn't hear me."

Bethany raised herself up, propping on her elbow. She felt a little exposed dressed only in her sleeveless corset cover and bloomers. "So you decided to come in without invitation?" she asked, trying hard not to smile at the beautiful young girl.

"Yes," Penee answered in a matter-of-fact tone. "Are you angry?"

"No. Did you need something?" Bethany asked as she reached toward the end of the four-poster bed and grabbed her robe.

"I thought you might need someone to help you dress for dinner."

"Oh. Is it almost time?"

Penee nodded and walked over to the dresser. An arched mirror with gilt fretwork was attached to the chest. She fingered Bethany's hairbrush and the silver lid of her powder jar. "This is very pretty," she said, glancing back to Bethany.

"Thank you. It belonged to my mother." Bethany wrapped her robe around her and tied the sash.

"Are you going to marry Uncle Wilder and live here with us?"

Penee couldn't have been more casual if she'd been talking about the weather. Even though she was more than a little surprised by the question, Bethany smiled. She didn't mind that Penee was curious.

"Where did you hear that?" she asked, having no idea what Wilder might have said to the family once she came upstairs to rest.

"While Priscilla and I were having dinner, I heard Mama telling the cook that she wanted her to use the best china and crystal tonight, and to be sure and use the tablecloth she bought in London two years ago. Mama told her that Uncle Wilder wouldn't have brought you all the way to Pittsburgh if he hadn't planned to marry you." Penee turned around and faced Bethany. "Are you going to be my aunt?"

She wanted to scoop Penee into her arms, hug and kiss her, and tell her that she wanted to be her aunt. She wanted to be Ester's friend, too. But . . . There was always a but. "I don't have an answer for you. We haven't made a decision about that."

"Will you know before you leave?"

"I might," she said, then eyed the little girl carefully. "Something tells me you have a special reason for asking." Bethany knelt in front of her and retied a small bow at the neckline of her dress. "What is it?"

Penee pursed her lips and frowned. "Priscilla thinks she knows everything just because she's older."

"And you'd like to be the first to know if your Uncle Wilder and I decide to get married?"

Penee nodded.

"I'll tell you what. If I know the answer to that before I leave, you'll be the first one I tell. How's that?"

A big smile spread across Penee's face. "Then I'll tell Priscilla."

Bethany walked over to the wardrobe and opened the rosewood doors, taking out a violet-colored blouse and matching skirt. She held up the long-sleeve blouse with velvet cuffs and pin tucks decorating the front. "Do you think this is appropriate for dinner tonight?"

"I think it's a very pretty—"

A knock on the door cut Penelope's sentence short. "That will be Mama waking you for dinner," Penee whispered. "Don't let her know I'm in here. She'll be angry I disturbed you." Penee ran to the far side of the bed and ducked behind it.

Smiling, Bethany called, "Come in."

Ester opened the door and stuck her head inside.

"Oh, you're up. Wonderful. I just wanted to let you know that dinner will be in half an hour. Oh, that is a lovely blouse. Do wear it tonight. Just come downstairs into the parlor whenever you're ready. No need to hurry. We'll wait if you're late." Ester smiled and closed the door again.

The petite woman was like a whirlwind. Bethany wondered if she ever slowed down, and she loved the way she talked.

Penelope came running from behind the bed and threw her arms around Bethany's waist, hugging her close. Laughing, she said, "Mama didn't see me. We fooled her."

Caught up in the child's merriment, Bethany threw the blouse on the bed, wrapped her arms around Penee, and kissed the top of her head. Bethany smiled. Her hair smelled clean, her little body shook with giggles.

Oh, yes, she liked Wilder's family. She liked them very much.

Chapter Eighteen

Wilder held his back and shoulders straight as he walked into Henry Frick's office the next morning. He'd never tried harder not to limp, but it was no use. He couldn't hide the lame leg. "Hello, Henry."

"Wilder, son, it's so great to see you. You're looking good as new." Henry shook his hand vigorously and clapped him on the back a couple of times.

That wasn't true. Wilder knew it, and Frick did, too. The months of rehabilitation and recuperation had put back some of the weight he'd lost, but he was nowhere near the excellent physical condition he had been in before the attack. But he would be one day, Wilder vowed to himself.

Frick had never looked better, Wilder thought as he eyed the distinguished man with a full head of silver-gray hair and thick beard to match. Carnegie's right-hand man was always impeccably dressed in starched white shirt, black bow tie, and dark jacket.

"Sit down," he offered good-naturedly. "I hardly

noticed your limp. It appears Relfe was right in not letting the doctor amputate."

A chill ran up Wilder's back and he cringed. He was walking better each week, but he hated being reminded of the time he'd spent in the hospital, fearing each day that infection would settle in the bone and they'd have to remove his leg at the knee.

"Tell me, has there been any progress on finding the men responsible for the attack?"

"No," Wilder muttered quietly, each muscle taut with tension. Every time he was reminded of the men who attacked him, he wanted to get his hands on them and beat the hell out of them.

"I hope you're here to tell me you've fully recovered and are ready to come back to work. We're going to need you in the coming weeks. Yes, I'd say you got back just in time."

Wilder didn't sit down, but he didn't walk around, either. "I'm not here to come back to work. I'm here to talk you out of this foolish and explosive idea of the Pinkerton guards to protect the plant."

Frick looked thoughtful for a moment. "I suppose your brother told you about that."

"It doesn't matter how I heard. It's a deadly solution to an avoidable problem." Wilder's voice remained strong and firm, pleasing him.

"I'm not an immature sapling when it comes to strikes, Wilder. I know what I'm doing."

Wilder was aware of that, and that was what he feared. Frick was known in the industry as a strike-buster. He believed the plant manager expected a confrontation between the Pinkertons and the strikers. Frick had made it clear on a number of occasions that he wanted to crush the union, and he was prepared to go to any lengths to do it. But that knowledge didn't keep Wilder from making a last plea.

"I've kept up with what's been going on. When talks broke off, you weren't far from a settlement. What happened?"

Frick slowly shook his head. "After the way the union men treated you, you're still willing to speak for them, to try to help them. You amaze me, Wilder. But we've had this talk before. Let's not go through it again."

"No, let's do," Wilder demanded, placing both palms on top of the polished desk.

"For what purpose?" Frick rose out of his fine leather chair and walked over to the bookshelf. "You know my feelings as well as anyone. I haven't changed. I'm not going to. Carnegie Company has the right to control its own plants and run them however they see fit. Not the workers. Not the Amalgamated Association." He twitched his shoulders nervously and brushed his beard with an open palm.

"The association wants to work with you, not against you. They proved that by accepting the cuts in jobs two years ago, and a lower piece rate when production increased because of mechanical and technological improvements."

Frick shrugged his shoulders and displayed his hand in a helpless manner. "That's progress, Wilder. You said it well. Increased mechanization in the works has made the union less important. We don't need as many men as we used to. We have the power to call the shots and we will."

"This strike is not about needing as many men. It's about reaching an agreement with the ones we do have. If the workers can accept the decrease in the minimum sliding wage scale and tonnage, why don't you bend on the contract date?"

"Why?" Frick clasped his hands together behind his back. "It's simple. I don't have to. Wilder, it's my plant to run as I see fit. I'm prepared to fight the union in order to give the company as large a portion of the profits as possible. That was my goal when I came here in '89, and it still is. Now, I'm afraid I can't give you any more time." He sat down, then pushed his chair forward. He locked his penetrating gaze on Wilder's face. "One final word. It's time you decided who you want to work for."

Under Frick's steady scrutiny, Wilder only nodded. He found his employer's statement disturbing. Frick picked up his pen and started writing.

Wilder had been dismissed. He headed for the door. What more could he say? What else could he do? If he pressed Frick further, he'd be out of a job, and he feared he was too close to that happening already.

Outside Frick's office, Wilder leaned against the door and pondered. Frick didn't understand him. He was a company man. Settling a contract before a strike was the best solution for the company. Why couldn't Frick see that? There was only one thing left to do, and that was to talk to the leader of the strikers.

Half an hour later, Wilder was walking along the industry-littered banks of the Monongahela River looking for a man he knew only as Corbin. When he'd walked out of the fenced-in area of the plant, the strikers had jeered and threatened him until he asked to see their leader. After a few moments, he was told to walk toward the river and he would meet someone who could take him to Corbin.

Hundreds of smokestacks poured thick ashen-colored smoke into the atmosphere blocking the sun, fouling the air with a repugnant odor that had Wilder wishing he were back in Eufaula at The Georgia, with its clean air, spacious rooms, lush grounds, and beautiful gardens. He recognized and appreciated the need for the steel and textile mills that lined the rivers in the Northeast, and until he went south, he'd never found the industry offensive. It was as if for the first time he was seeing his hometown through different eyes.

Wilder looked up to see a group of four men walking his way, and he tensed. As the men approached, he took the time to look at each face. If there was another attack, he wanted to be able to identify them.

They stopped about five paces from him and stood quietly, letting Wilder look them over. Three of them had their workshirt sleeves rolled up well past the elbow, showing bulging muscles in their upper arms. Their necks and shoulders were thick from lifting beams of steel. Wilder was stricken with a moment of envy. He used to be as muscular, taking pride in working alongside his men in the armor-plate division of the mill. But a week at death's door and two months in the hospital had left him weak as a babe. Only since his stay in Alabama had he started feeling well enough to work again.

For intimidation, one of the men made a fist and hit a hard smack into the palm of his other hand, but Wilder didn't flinch. It was a sure bet that Wilder couldn't best the men if they started a fight, but he wouldn't lie down and refuse to fight like Stanley had.

When several moments passed and none of the men made a move toward him, Wilder decided they were waiting for him to speak. "I want to see Corbin."

"Yeah? Who's inquiring?" asked the one man who'd decided to rip his sleeves off his shirt rather than roll them up.

A couple of the men chuckled.

"Wilder Burlington."

"Hey, aren't you one of Frick's men?" one man asked as he narrowed his eyes and squinted.

"Yeah, I remember. He's the one who got the bloody hell beat out of him," the most disreputable-looking man answered.

"Damn shame what happened to your leg," the sleeveless man said with a lopsided grin. "I heard it was a big hammer."

Sweat popped out on Wilder's forehead, and a painful throb settled in the muscles of his leg. His arms hung loosely at his sides, his hands making tight fists, then opening again. He stood ramrod straight but with his gaze continuously shifting from one man to the other. He didn't know how much more he could take before he broke and hit the nearest man right between the eyes. Wilder was no fool, though, and he knew that if he threw the first punch, he wouldn't come out alive. For a moment he felt as he had many times in the hospital, that he didn't have a reason for living. But as soon as that feeling crossed his mind, Bethany invaded his thoughts. Bethany, with her soft southern voice, gentle touch, and courageous strength. She'd never give up something she wanted, no matter the cost. Her search for Grace proved that. Wilder wouldn't give up, either.

"Corbin," he said again. "Where is he?"

The largest man, the one without shirtsleeves, stepped forward, the provoking grin still in place. He reached into his shirt pocket, pulled out a toothpick, and clamped it down between his teeth.

"Any steelworks' manager who has the guts to come over to this side of the fence and take dirt from these guys has my attention, if not my admiration." The other men booed and hooted their disapproval. "Shut up!" he yelled, almost losing his toothpick. "Let's hear what Frick's man has to say."

Wilder remained firm in his expression and stance. "I want to talk to Corbin."

The man moved the toothpick to the other side of his mouth. "Speaking."

Not willing to believe him so quickly, Wilder watched the man's eyes. His countenance didn't waver. He was Corbin, Wilder decided, and he sensed that he'd intrigued the man.

"You're right. I'm on the wrong side of the fence, but in my opinion there shouldn't be a fence. I'm here to ask you to bring the association back to the negotiation table."

Corbin and his men laughed. "We've tried. Frick isn't interested. Where've you been? We told him we're willing to take a cut in the tonnage and the sliding scale, but we have to have June as the contract date."

"Yeah," one of the men said. "Frick knows we'd think twice about striking in the dead of winter."

Corbin gave the man a cold look. "I'm doing the talking." He turned back to Wilder, the chilling expression still on his face. "Most of us wouldn't survive a winter strike. 'Course, you wouldn't know about houses that are so cold the water freezes around the dipper, or so little bread to go on the table that you only eat once a day, if you're lucky."

"I know," Wilder said in a low voice. "Ask any of the men who work in my division."

"So you gave your men extra at Christmas and helped a few of them get over some rough times. What are you going to do for us today?"

"Yeah!" the other three chimed in unison.

"Give you some advice."

The men laughed and jeered him again, but Corbin remained silent. Wilder was certain he saw disappointment in the striker's eyes. He knew Corbin wanted the best possible contract for his men.

"No thanks," Corbin said, and turned away.

Wilder had to do something quick. Before he could think twice, he said, "Frick has hired three hundred Pinkerton agents to guard the plant. They'll be armed."

A stunned look on his face, Corbin jerked back around to face Wilder. A couple of the men swore under their breaths.

"You better be lying."

Feeling more confident, Wilder shook his head.

"Nose around. Enough people know so that word will get out before the Pinkertons get here. As for that advice, Frick is serious. He's nothing like the man who agreed to your demands three years ago. Frick isn't bluffing. He plans to reopen the armor-plate and the open-hearth on the sixth, and he doesn't intend for anyone to stand in his way. Call off the strike and accept the contract. You can always start planning now for the next one."

"I don't like your advice. We have rights!" Corbin made a fist and held it up for Wilder to see.

Wilder understood, yet he didn't. A man had a right to fight for what he believed in, but he needed to be smart enough to know when the price was too high to pay. Wilder nodded and turned away, wishing he could have accomplished more.

"Burlington!"

Slowly, careful not to make any sudden moves the man might misunderstand, Wilder faced Corbin again.

"It wasn't us."

This time Wilder was the one to step forward. "What are you talking about?"

The provocative grin returned to Corbin's lips. "We didn't beat you up. If union men had done it, you wouldn't have lived."

Wilder had a hard time keeping his poker face. "Denial is easy talk. Back your claim up with names."

Corbin didn't flinch and neither did any of the other men as Wilder searched their faces for any hint that their leader was lying. He found none, but he wouldn't grovel for information no matter how badly he wanted it.

"I didn't think you could do it," he said with a sneer in his voice, then walked away.

But Wilder was disturbed as he limped along the banks of the dark river. He'd just met the man, but he'd bet money Corbin wasn't a liar. If union men hadn't beaten him up, who the hell had?

Chapter Nineteen

Wilder tossed from one side of the bed to the other, throwing off his covering and beating his pillow as he rolled. He didn't know how he'd gotten through the rest of the day and dinner with the chatty Ester and the giggling cherry blossoms. Ester and Penelope seemed to talk nonstop, and Bethany and Priscilla seemed to hang on their every word. Either Bethany was thoroughly enjoying herself or she was more of a saint than he thought.

While they were walking to the dinner table, she'd whispered to him that she was happy to be in his home and so very glad he'd agreed to let her come along.

He'd talked his way out of what he knew would be an unfruitful discussion with Relfe about his visit with Frick, and he certainly didn't want his brother to know about his encounter with Corbin. Relfe wouldn't approve, and Wilder didn't need another reprimand.

When he felt he couldn't lie in the bed a moment

longer, Wilder rose, intending to go for a walk. As he fumbled in the dark, his shin hit the wooden arm of the low-slung slipper chair where he'd draped his trousers. Fierce pain shot up his leg as he fell into the chair, swearing like a drunken sailor who couldn't find his ship.

Within minutes the pain subsided to a dull ache. Wilder lay with his feet stretched out in front of him and his head firmly against the back of the cushion, thinking about Bethany, three doors down the hallway. He needed to touch her, to hold her close.

He'd had a troublesome day. He'd wanted to talk to her alone before they retired, but Ester and the girls had seen fit to keep her busy all evening. In fact, he hadn't had one moment alone with her since their arrival yesterday afternoon.

In the darkness, he tried to make out the time from the clock on the mantel. He rose and walked closer. It was one-fifteen. He wondered if Bethany was asleep. Of course she was, he thought. But he needed to see her. He wanted to talk to her and hold her. No one would know if he slipped into her bedroom and into her bed and just held her for a few minutes.

Not taking the time to change his mind, Wilder stepped into his trousers and slipped out of his room. The hallway was as dark as a midnight sky without stars, but he knew exactly which room had been given to Bethany. Quietly, he felt his way down the hallway until he came to Bethany's door. With the greatest care he opened it, successfully making it inside the room and closing the door behind him without a sound.

Bethany had left her draperies open but the

moonless night offered very little light. On the other side of the room he saw her figure outlined beneath a white sheet and his heartbeat increased. How he'd missed holding her, touching her, kissing her, making love to her.

Wilder slowly eased across the floor until he stood beside the bed. Bethany had her back to him, her golden-colored hair spread out on the pillow beside her. He had the sudden urge to bury his face in its plush warmth. He debated whether to call her name or to simply slide in beside her. Why wake her if he could slip into bed without her knowing?

With care not to disturb or frighten her, he lifted the sheet and gently settled himself on the bed, then slowly stretched his body out the length of hers and snuggled against her back. She stirred, pushing her backside against him. Her body was warm, soft, inviting, and Wilder welcomed it. He smelled the fresh-washed scent of her hair and buried his nose into its silkiness. He was in need of some kisses and caresses. With a soft moan, he pressed his lower body closer, slipping his arm around her so he could roll her over to face him. His hand connected with another body, his fingers tangling in long hair. Wilder popped up and saw Penelope, sleeping soundly on the other side of Bethany.

His startled movements awakened Bethany and she gasped. "What are you doing in here?" She kept her voice a whisper, although her expression was one of great surprise.

"Never mind me! What's *she* doing in here?" he exclaimed in a low voice.

"She came in shortly after I lay down and said she

was afraid of the dark. She wanted to know if she could sleep with me."

"You should have told her no," Wilder said, realizing he had no reason to be irritated at Penee. "I wanted to sleep with you," he complained.

Bethany looked at him innocently. "Were you afraid of the dark, too?"

Wilder grinned. Obviously, Bethany had seen the humor in the situation. He was snuggled too close to her backside to be amused. "I love you, Bethany Hayward."

"I love you, too." She smiled and carefully turned so that she was facing him. "How was I to know that you were going to slip into my room?"

"No, you couldn't have known." Wilder reached up and caressed her soft cheek. Her eyes sparkled in the darkness of the room and her hair shimmered down her shoulders. He grew hard for her. He loved her, wanted her. She was so desirable in her sleeveless nightgown with her face tilted toward him. How could he resist the temptation to kiss her?

He bent his head and kissed her, tenderly, wantonly, letting his lips mesh with hers, giving her his tongue and stealing it back again. With slow, deliberate movements, his hand moved from where it cupped her neck to her breast. She gasped with pleasure. Wilder caressed her, felt her, loved her.

He moved his hand from her breast and glided down her rib cage, past the indention of her waist and over the swell of her hip. Sliding his hand around to her backside, he cupped her buttocks and pressed her tight against his bulging manhood.

"Come to my room with me," he murmured

seductively as his lips left hers and traveled up her cheek to her ear.

"I can't," she whispered.

"Yes, Bethany, I want to love you. I want you." His hands ran up and down her arms, over her shoulders, and up her neck. She had a beautiful neck, beautiful shoulders, beautiful arms. He didn't know why she always hid behind those stand-up collars and long sleeves. As his lips worked their magic against hers, he slid his hand down past her collarbone to find her breast again. He covered the firm mound with his palm, splaying his fingers around the fullness, catching the weight and holding it. She sighed against his lips.

"Come to my room," he whispered again.

Oblivious to all but Wilder's touch, Bethany said, "Yes" against his mouth, letting her tongue wipe across his lips.

A movement on the bed behind her registered and she tensed. Penelope rolled over, threw her small arm around Bethany's waist, and mumbled in her sleep. Coming to her senses, Bethany shoved away from Wilder and said, "No, I can't go. It's not right. Not here."

Wilder had come to his senses, too. His breathing was laborious. "You're right. This isn't the time nor the place. It doesn't lessen my desire, though."

The heat of embarrassment spread over her cheeks and down her neck. "Mine either."

"The truth is that until I touched you, I only wanted to talk to you and hold you. Now I want to make love to you." His voice became husky. "I've hardly seen you since we got here. I've missed you.

Making love to you once was not nearly enough."

His words pleased her, warmed her. "For me either. Why don't we go downstairs into the kitchen and talk."

"I think you're a very smart lady. I'll wait for you outside the door. It's dark in the house and I don't want you stumbling down the stairs."

She reached up and gave him a long kiss. "I'll be right out."

A few minutes later, Bethany and Wilder sat at the kitchen table holding hands. A small lamp in the middle of the table burned low. Bethany liked the way the glow from the light picked up the blue in Wilder's eyes and the golden shimmers in his hair. He was right. They had needed this time to talk, to touch, to be together.

"How are things going with the strike?" she asked, rubbing her palm against Wilder's.

The question caused a frown to crease his brow and she wondered if she should pursue the subject.

"Not good," he said. "Tomorrow night all hell's going to break loose and no one is going to be the victor."

"What's going to happen?" she asked, concern showing in her eyes.

"Frick plans to reopen the part of the mill he shut down when the union workers went on strike. He's hired armed Pinkerton guards to protect the plant from the strikers."

"Is there anything you can do?"

"I've talked to Frick and to the leader of the strikers, a man named Corbin. They're both too stubborn to give in. They both think they're right, and in their own way they are. I'm going down to the banks of the river tomorrow night and try to talk some sense into the Pinkertons. Nobody else will listen. Maybe they will."

She squeezed his fingers. "I want to go with you."

He smiled and kissed her hand. "It's nice to know that you want to be with me, but you can't go."

"Wilder," she said in a stronger voice, "I want to. I want to be there for you."

"No," he answered in a harsher tone. "You don't understand. The Pinkertons will be armed with rifles and the strikers won't be happy about it when they see them. It's too dangerous."

Bethany thought about what he said. It would be dangerous, but for some reason she felt no fear. What concerned Wilder was important to her, too. She wouldn't let him go alone. She didn't want him being selective about the parts of his life he wanted to share with her. She'd come to Pennsylvania to meet his family and was already becoming attached to them. But she'd also wanted to know about his work. This part of Wilder's life was important to her, too. She wanted to know what he faced every day when he went to the mill.

She stood up and pulled the sash of her red robe tighter. "I told you once that I don't run when trouble comes. I'm going with you."

He rose and slid his hands around her waist, pulling her close. "I would never accuse you of running from trouble. But I don't want you to go looking for it, either."

"Aren't you?" she asked.

"That's different."

Bethany looked into his eyes. "No. I'll have to find my own way to the docks at Homestead if you go without me. I plan to be by your side no matter the problem."

He queried her with his eyes. "Does that mean—?"

"It means I love you," she whispered. Bethany reached up and kissed him.

Chapter Twenty

The main street leading to the docks of the Monongahela River was packed with hundreds of people. Bethany and Wilder slowly made their way through the crowd to the plant landing. Men, women, and children came together, ready to fight for their beliefs. Many of the men carried rifles and pistols. Others held only sticks and large pieces of wood clutched tightly in their hands. Word had spread quickly. Frick had hired Pinkertons to guard the steel mill against the strikers.

Wilder had dressed in a torn workshirt, scruffy trousers, and a dark blue cap he kept pulled low over his eyes. He had managed to get Bethany a pair of dark green breeches and a dingy white shirt. She'd arranged her hair up on top of her head and pulled a skullcap on to help hold it in place. Over the knitted cap she wore a soft felt hat with the crown creased lengthwise. Wilder carried a large club cut from the branch of a tree. In the other hand he held a torch. An occasional shout or cry of anger erupted from the throng of people, but most of the crowd remained calm.

About halfway down to the docks, Wilder moved Bethany out and away from the gathering, stopping beside a small toolshed. "Bethany," he said, "the closer we come to the landing, the thicker the crowd gets. There are very few women this close to the docks. I want you to stay here. This building will offer you protection if a fight breaks out."

"I'm not dressed like a woman," Bethany reminded him in an even tone, not wanting to be separated from him. "And even if I were, I can see three women from here."

"I'm worried about you. Things could get rough. I don't want you getting hurt."

Bethany smiled up into his face. He'd let his beard grow the last two days and had darkened it with a piece of coal. Bethany felt it a shameful reaction, but she found herself drawn to his roguish handsomeness. She wanted to kiss him.

Instead, she said, "I haven't come this far to leave your side now."

"Have I ever told you you were a damn stubborn woman?" Wilder asked.

"No, but I like the way it sounds. Say it more often."

Finally, he gave her a smile. "Bethany, against my better judgment, I agreed you could come tonight. I'm afraid the crowd will get violent when the barge arrives. I don't want to have to worry about you getting hurt if things get rough."

Bethany weakened. In order to make Wilder feel better, she said, "All right. At the first sign of trouble,

I'll run for the cover of that building." She pointed to the toolshed not far from them.

He sighed and nodded agreement. "Here." He shoved the torch into her hand. "When we get in the midst of the crowd, I want to hold your hand. I don't want to lose you in this mob. I've got a feeling we're going to have to force our way through from here on down. Whatever you do, don't let go of my hand, but should we become separated for any reason, keep your head low and make your way back here. Don't talk to anyone. Don't listen if anyone tries to stop you. Understand?"

"Perfectly." She nodded. It was important to Bethany to prove that she'd stay by Wilder's side. She wanted to be better than the woman he had been seeing when he was attacked and left for dead.

"All right, let's go."

Wilder grabbed her hand and started pushing their way through the multitude of men and their weapons. The torch was heavier than Bethany expected it to be and her arm grew weak quickly. She wanted to let go of Wilder's hand and change hands to relieve the ache in her arm muscles, but she was afraid to let go for fear she would lose sight of him in the ever-crushing crowd. She lowered her arm a bit to rest it, but soon found that was too dangerous when a man was shoved against her, knocking the flaming rags into her hat.

An ember fell onto Bethany's arm and burned through the thin material of her shirt. She winced from the pain but kept walking. She tried to blow it away. At last the air sucked the fire away and it fizzled out to nothing.

Tense, Bethany kept her eyes on Wilder's back and her hand tightly fused to his. The longer they walked, the weaker her arm grew. She knew that if she said anything to Wilder, he would make her go back to the toolshed. She blocked out the pain, knowing she had to be there if Wilder needed her.

The crowd became so thick Bethany couldn't see anything but backs, shoulders, and arms. She smelled unwashed bodies, burned wood, and the kerosene that was used to ignite the flaming torches. She heard laughter, swearing, angry shouts, and bits and pieces of conversations as she followed Wilder's forging.

The minutes passed and Bethany started to sweat. She felt her grip on Wilder's hand slipping. The bodies moved closer, bumping, knocking, and shoving. Wilder had been right, she thought in a moment of panic. She shouldn't have come. Her arm muscles screamed with burning pain. Bethany wasn't worried about trouble from the Pinkertons, though; she was afraid of being crushed by the horde of men who filed six across in the narrow street that led to the docks.

Her arm and shoulder trembled from the weight of the torch. Bethany was beginning to think she wasn't going to make it. She'd have to tell Wilder she couldn't go on. She couldn't breathe. When she thought she would scream from the terror of being crushed beneath the hot bodies of the men, Wilder jerked out into the open.

Bethany gulped in air as Wilder turned her loose and grabbed the torch. "Are you all right?" he asked. Throwing down his weapon, he placed the tips of his fingers under her chin, lifting her face for his inspection.

"Yes," she answered in a whispery voice, rubbing her aching arm, trying to gain control. "I—I just couldn't breathe very well for a few moments. There are so many people. I'm fine now."

Wilder looked around the dock's landing, then led Bethany away from the crowd and over to a piling several yards from the main landing. Bethany leaned against the large pole gratefully, thinking she might be sick to her stomach. She rubbed her arm and shoulder. She needed to check her burn, too, but she didn't want to do that in front of Wilder.

"I thought I was going to be trampled underneath all those men," she said on a breathy note, trying to calm the quavering inside.

"I shouldn't have let you come. Dammit, I knew better," Wilder reprimanded himself.

"You couldn't have kept me away," she answered, feeling stronger now that she could breathe easily. Bethany looked into his eyes and saw uncertainty in them. "Haven't you realized yet that I want to be here with you?"

"But you shouldn't be here, Bethany. That's the point." His mouth formed a grim line.

Bethany was about to tell him she was a grown woman with a mind of her own, when someone called his name.

"Hey, Burlington, is that you?"

Wilder swung around and saw Corbin walking toward him, this time without his henchmen beside him.

"It's me, Corbin," Wilder said. Turning in a

manner that all but obstructed Bethany from Corbin's view, he walked a few steps to meet him. "I see word got around."

Bethany cautiously positioned herself so that she could see the profile of both men with the light from Wilder's torch. The man he called Corbin was a little shorter than Wilder and quite a bit huskier. The sleeves had been ripped from his shirt, leaving ragged ends and showing bulging muscles. He held a toothpick between his teeth. He was a strong and powerful-looking man, but Bethany sensed that Wilder had no fear of him, so she didn't, either. She settled down on her knees and took her hat and skullcap off, letting the top of her head breathe in the cooling breeze that swept in off the river below.

Corbin laughed. "I asked a couple of questions to the right people and your information was confirmed, including the arrival time, which you failed to mention."

"I didn't have to. I knew you were good enough to find out on your own."

Corbin accepted the small word of praise without comment. He looked behind him down the darkened river. "The tugboat *Little Bill* and two barges should be coming into view any minute now."

Bethany saw Wilder tense, but she remained in the shadows quietly listening to the two men. She wasn't sure she fully understood the strike and all the issues that had brought the Carnegie Steel Mill and its workers to this point. There had never been any trouble at her mill, which she managed to keep open about eight months out of the year. She never had any difficulty getting workers. As far as she knew, they never complained about the amount of work they had to do or their wages. She paid a fair sum and believed the men knew she wanted to keep the mill open year round.

"What are you going to do?" Wilder asked.

"Me? Stand beside my men." Corbin moved the toothpick from one side of his mouth to the other. Sweat had collected on his forehead and on his upper lip. Bethany couldn't help but notice that he looked as tired as Wilder. She had a feeling neither of the men had slept much in the past two days.

"What are your men going to do?"

"Stop the bastards."

"How?"

Corbin eyed Wilder suspiciously for a moment before answering, "Whatever is necessary. If they want to talk, we'll talk. If they fire, we'll fire."

Wilder tensed. "You know that means bloodshed from both sides. It can still be avoided, Corbin. All you have to do is give the word."

The husky man slowly shook his head and moved the toothpick around in his mouth. "We're right. A man don't give in when he's right."

"There's compromise." Wilder tried again to get his point across. "That's what this is all about."

"We tried that. You know we did. Frick isn't interested in anything but union-busting. We don't aim to let him this time."

There was truth in Corbin's words. Truths Wilder couldn't deny. Deep inside himself he knew that what was going on tonight was wrong, but he had no words, no power to stop it. The murmur from the crowd increased.

"Corbin!" someone yelled. "I see the barge coming."

"Quiet the men. I'll be right there," Corbin answered, then turned back to Wilder. "The only thing left to do is show them our strength."

Wilder grabbed Corbin's arm. "There's still time to stop this," he repeated his earlier plea.

"No, but there is time for you to get away from here before they dock. You're on the wrong side of the fence again." Corbin let his gaze fall to the hand gripping his upper arm.

Undaunted by Corbin's words or his stare, Wilder pushed ahead. "It's a fight neither party can win, but you'll be the biggest loser."

"The way we see it, we already are. The plant's closed. We're not working." Corbin wielded the toothpick between his teeth. "Last time we talked you gave me some advice. Now I'm returning the favor. Get your hand off my arm."

Corbin threw his toothpick to the ground, and Wilder stiffened. The two men eyed each other warily. Wilder wasn't afraid of Corbin, but he let go. Corbin had enough men to fight tonight. Wilder didn't want to be one of them.

"Get out of here. This isn't your fight." The striker's tone of voice was soft but desperate.

Wilder realized he wouldn't give up. He felt an unusual camaraderie with this man. He shot a quick glance at Bethany, who was barely hidden in the shadows, then faced Corbin again. "I'm staying."

Corbin eyed him dubiously. "It's your neck." He turned and trotted over to join his companions.

Bethany replaced her skullcap and fedora, then crawled out of the shadow of the piling and hurried to Wilder.

"He's their leader?" she asked as she stopped in front of him.

Wilder nodded. "I think his problem is that in his heart he believes Frick will give in to their demands at the last minute the way Bill Abbott did three years ago. But he won't." His words were choked past feelings of inadequacy. "Frick is an autocratic businessman with an uncompromising grudge against unionism. The strikers don't have a chance."

Bethany knew Wilder was hurting. He'd hoped to avoid a showdown. She wanted to pull him into her arms and comfort him, but she knew that wasn't what he needed at the moment. Instead, she said, "We'll be here if he needs us."

A low rumble emanated from the crowd. Everyone in the horde was looking in the same direction. Bethany and Wilder turned their heads and looked down the river.

The mills and plants that lined the waterway had their lights on, illuminating the darkened waste-filled waters of the Monongahela River. From her vantage point, Bethany could clearly see a tugboat pushing the two barges up the river. It was too dark to see any activity on the barge, but Wilder had said they were filled with men carrying guns, and she believed him. She looked back to the pulsing body of brotherhood behind her and a sudden streak of fear ran up her back. These men were ready for a fight.

Wilder threw the torch down and stamped out the remaining embers. The noise from the strikers grew louder. More men pushed to get nearer the dock's landing. The barges moved steadily closer. Bethany's heartbeat increased. Something dreadful was going to take place.

"Bethany, I want you out of here," Wilder said, grabbing her arm tightly in his hand and ushering her back toward the piling at the far end of the dock.

"No, Wilder, I'm much safer here by your side than I would be trying to fight my way back through that mob."

He swiped his cap off his head and ran his fingers through his hair. "I didn't want you here."

Bethany heard what she hadn't been able to see in his face because of the darkness. He was worried about her. Her love for him filled her, comforted her. "Wilder?" Bethany reached up and briefly touched his cheek, rubbing his stubble against her palm. "You've got to realize I'm where I want to be. I'm by your side."

"I don't want you to get hurt," he whispered in a raspy voice.

"I promise I won't." She reached up and kissed him lightly on the lips. As she drew away, he grabbed her around the waist, pulled her up tight to his chest, and kissed her hard. His fingers slid up the side of her face and threatened to knock her hat off her head. There was desperation in the kiss but there was also hope. Bethany knew there was also the promise of their future together.

"Every man should have a woman like you," he said, gazing down at her with love filling his eyes.

Wilder stepped back and let her go as the first barge came into full view, showing its cargo of about a hundred and fifty men. Each guard had a rifle resting snugly against his shoulder. The other barge was locked to the first, the tug pushing both. The assemblage on the dock became so quiet Bethany heard nothing but the water lapping at the side of the boat and a frenzy of heavy breathing.

The *Little Bill* cast off and a gangplank was pushed ashore from the first barge. Bethany held to Wilder's arm as they watched the first man's foot hit the gangplank. A shot rang out. The man yelled and fell into the water.

Within an instant, a volley of shots rang out from both directions. Bethany screamed. Wilder pushed her head into his chest and crouched behind the pile. Gunshots rang out into the darkness. Angry shouts and swearing filled the night. Bullets hit their marks. Screeches and moans of agony hung in the air. Bethany clutched Wilder to her, fearing he might be shot.

Bullets whizzed past Wilder's head. He shielded Bethany with his body, cursing himself for allowing her to come along. Knowing the Pinkertons would be armed, he never should have agreed. He glanced over his shoulder. The tugboat was already pushing the barges away from the shore. A man standing beside Corbin caught a bullet in the middle of the chest and went down.

"Crazy goddamned people!" Wilder swore into the air as he viewed the pandemonium sprouting from fear. His words were drowned out by the vicious cross fire and shouts of the wounded and grieving.

With his gaze fixed on the front line, he saw Corbin's head snap backward as he took a bullet in the shoulder. Corbin arched his back and winced, then gave his attention back to the man on the ground.

"Corbin's been shot. I have to see how bad he is."

Terror filled Bethany's eyes as she looked up at him. "No! Wilder, you can't go over there. You'll be killed."

He placed both hands to the sides of her face. "I'll be careful. Stay here and stay down."

He pulled away from her, fell onto his stomach, and started crawling across the dock. Shots rang out over his head; the boards scraped his chest and hands. The barges were getting farther away. He knew the gunfire would stop when the Pinkertons were out of range.

"You're hit," Wilder said, coming up beside Corbin.

"It's just a flesh wound," he answered, braving a glance at his shoulder. "Don't worry about it."

Wilder took one look at the amount of blood on the front of his shirt and knew he was lying. He chanced a glance at the back of Corbin's shirt and saw where the bullet had exited. The man was damned lucky the bullet had gone through his body without hitting his lungs or shoulder blades, but he was losing blood fast.

"How bad is he?" Wilder asked, turning his attention to the striker Corbin was helping. As soon as he saw the gaping blackened and red hole in the man's chest, he knew there was no need to ask. Nothing could help the man. Wilder winced. The Winchester repeating rifle was a deadly weapon.

The shooting only lasted a few seconds more as the tugboat pushed the barge farther away from shore. The barge moved out of firing range and the gunshots died away. The crowd cheered, but not

Corbin. He continued to kneel by the body of his companion.

"Let's get this one to a doctor," Corbin rose and yelled to some men standing behind him. One grabbed the wounded man under the arm and another by the feet, and they hurried away with him.

"Goddammit!" Corbin swore angrily. Sweat ran down the side of his face and his eyes were wet.

"We need to be praying, not swearing," a woman Wilder couldn't see called out to the crowd.

"We don't need any help from God. We drove those bastards away ourselves," a man shouted, and the roar from the crowd seemed to agree with him.

"It's my praying what drove those men away," the woman answered. "To God be the glory!"

"Let's get in the water and finish them off!"

"I've got some dynamite!"

"Let's pour oil in the water and set it on fire. We'll burn 'em until they think they're already in hell!"

"I know where we can get a cannon!"

Wilder had been a manager long enough to know that Corbin was losing control of his men. He had to get them back under his command or all would be lost. The Pinkertons may have retreated to regroup and rethink, but Wilder had a feeling they'd be back. Corbin needed to have his men ready.

"Shut up, all of you, and let me think!" Corbin yelled so he would be heard over the roar of the victory-hungry mob. He wiped sweat from his upper lip with the back of his hand and smeared blood across his face. "If any of you have more weapons at home, go get them and bring them here. I want every man who has a gun moved up to the front of the line."

"We know what to do," one of the men replied.

"You need to see about that shoulder," another one spoke up sharply.

Wilder looked around and found Bethany bent over a man who had a gash across his forehead. She was soothing him with words of comfort and wiping the blood from his cheek. She looked beautiful to him, even though he'd never seen her so bedraggled. The time he'd gone up to the third floor and she'd soothed the pain from his leg flashed through his mind. She was so gentle with the injured man. He loved her so much he ached to hold her.

Seeing that she was safe, Wilder turned his attention to Corbin. This might not be his fight, but he was there. "What can I do to help?" he asked.

He wasn't sure what he saw in Corbin's eyes, but it looked like relief.

Wilder didn't get the chance to talk to Corbin again. They stayed busy. Corbin was trying to talk some of the men out of setting up a cannon while Wilder tried to keep another group from throwing sticks of dynamite at the barges. Several men poured a heavy crude oil into the river and set fire to it, thinking the wind would carry the flames out to the barges.

Small patches of fire caused by the burning oil smoked the docks, making it difficult for Bethany to see as she turned away from the man she'd been caring for. She searched the crowd for Wilder. He wasn't where she had last seen him. Her pulse beat erratically as she scanned each face she passed. A man bumped her shoulder, knocking her into the butt of someone's gun. She cried out when the hard wood hit her cheek just below the eye. The smoke became dense, burning her eyes, nose, and throat.

"The barges are returning!" Bethany heard someone shout.

Where was Wilder? Fear spurred her into action. She hurried through the crowd, looking at faces, searching for him. Shots rang out again, and Bethany cringed as men and women started running for cover. She wanted to cry out for everyone to stop the shooting. She wanted to tell them there had to be a better way to settle their differences. She pushed and shoved against the people, desperate to find Wilder.

For a moment, as if fate ordained it, the smoke cleared and Bethany saw a bullet strike Corbin in the upper shoulder for the second time. She watched in horror as he fell off the dock and into the oil-burning water below. Panic rose within her when seconds later Wilder dived into the flames after him. With no fear for her own safety, Bethany crouched low and scrambled across the dock the way she'd seen Wilder do.

Trembling with fear for Wilder's safety, she reached the place where they had gone into the water. She stretched out on her stomach and cautiously peered over the edge. Yellow and white flames came up to meet her. She jumped back as the heat hit her face. Swallowing down her frightened cry, she crept to the edge again. Wilder was in that water and he needed her help. She looked out and, not far from the landing, saw Wilder holding Corbin's head out of the water, one arm around his neck. He splashed and batted the fire away from them with the other arm. Wilder kicked hard with his feet, trying to reach the edge of the pier.

Bethany hung out over the edge as far as she could and called to him. "Closer," she shouted. "Bring him a little closer." She stretched out her arms and soon he was close enough for her to grab hold of Corbin's shirt.

The leader of the strikers was conscious but so weak he couldn't help himself onto the dock. Bethany pulled and tugged while Wilder combatted the oil-burning water.

"I can't pull him up by myself," she shouted over the shots of gunfire and roar of the crowd. "He's too heavy!" Smoke clogged her throat and she could hardly breathe. She coughed, trying to clear her lungs. Heat from the flames burned her cheeks and seared her hands, but still she fought to bring Corbin to safety.

"Hold his head out of the water while I climb up," Wilder said between gulps of smoke-filled air.

Frightened and tired, Bethany struggled to slide her hands under his arms and lock them around his chest. With Wilder's help, she made it. A couple of minutes later they had Corbin lying on the rough planks of the landing. A whispered "thank you" emerged from his lips before he passed out.

"Great Goda'mighty," a man said, breathing on Bethany's neck as he stooped over her shoulder. "I'd have helped you bring him in if I'd known it was Corbin you were pulling out of the river. I thought you were trying to save one of them damned Pinkertons."

Chapter Twenty-One

Bethany had insisted that she and Wilder follow the men who carried Corbin to the nearby doctor's house. She wanted the doctor to look at the burns on Wilder's arms and hands, but she soon realized there were greater emergencies than that. The doctor had just finished removing two bullets from a man who had been brought in after the first attack by the Pinkertons and three more had arrived from the second assault. Corbin, the leader of the strikers, was fourth in line.

They were told that someone had gone into Pittsburgh to get other physicians, but they hadn't yet arrived.

Wilder refused to leave Corbin's side until the doctor could get to him. Bethany found clean cloths and ointment and cared for Wilder's burns, thanking God they weren't as bad as they looked once she'd cleaned them. As more wounded arrived, Bethany and Wilder helped care for the men. When the two new doctors arrived, one immediately started to work on Corbin. Wilder told Bethany to continue to help care for the wounded and that he would go back down to the docks and find out what was happening.

Calming and soothing the fears of the wounded took all her strength, but never far from her mind was the fact that Wilder was back at the docks. The Pinkertons' second attack hadn't lasted any longer than the first, and by the time Bethany and Wilder had Corbin out of the water the gunshots had stopped. But Bethany didn't know when they might start again. The guards could try a third time.

By early evening of that day, all the wounded had been cared for. Most of them had been sent home but five stayed at the doctor's house, three of them critical.

Bethany washed her hands yet again, then splashed the cooling water on her face. She yanked the skullcap she'd worn the entire day off her head and shook her hair out, scratching her scalp where the itchy woolen cap had caused a heat rash to develop. She hadn't heard any shots since before Wilder left and the last wounded man had come in about three hours ago. Bethany hoped Wilder was safe. As she wound her hair back into a bun and pinned it on top of her head, she decided to check on Corbin one more time. Then she would go in search of Wilder.

As Bethany entered the front room she saw Wilder coming in the door. Relief filled her, and she sent up a prayer of thanks. She smiled and he returned it as he walked toward her. He looked tired. His clothes were bloodstained, but he was a most welcomed sight.

"Are you all right?" she asked, taking his hands in hers as they met.

He squeezed her fingers. "I'm fine." His gaze roamed over her face. "You look tired."

"No more than you," she admitted. "Has the fighting stopped?"

Wilder nodded. "The worst is over. The Pinkertons surrendered to the crowd and they are being escorted out of town."

"Thank God," she whispered.

"Let's check on Corbin, then go home and get some sleep."

Bethany didn't let go of Wilder's hand as they walked over to Corbin's bed. She didn't want to ever let go of him again. Trying to stop the battle that had occurred was futile. The feud between management and union had been going on too long, but she loved Wilder all the more for having the courage to try.

Wilder kept a solemn expression on his face as he looked down at the twitching and groaning Corbin. "Does he have fever?" Wilder asked.

"Not yet. The doctor has hopes he'll be all right. Both wounds were clean."

At the sound of their voices, Corbin's eyelids fluttered upward. Wilder bent closer to him and asked, "How do you feel?"

Corbin's dry lips moved but no sound came out.

"Don't try to talk," Wilder encouraged, but understood when Corbin managed to get out the word *water*.

Bethany hurried out of the room and was back within a minute with a glass of water. She placed her hand under his head and helped him drink a few sips. "I just talked to the doctor," she said, giving him a reassuring smile. "He says you're going to be fine in a few days."

He managed to give her a grateful look, then turned his gaze toward Wilder. "How many have we lost?" Corbin asked in a raspy voice.

"A few . . . on each side," Wilder told him, his lips set in a grim line. Damn, he wished he could have prevented the bloody battle. "There shouldn't be any more bloodshed. The Pinkertons are on their way back to Pittsburgh."

Corbin's grunt had a bitter edge to it. "What did we gain?"

Wilder sighed and looked down at the pale man with his chest wrapped in white cloths. "For now, you have control of the mill, but don't expect that to last long. Frick has been on the telephone. The governor has ordered militiamen to come in and take control."

"We'll whip their asses, too," Corbin whispered, then coughed.

"Talk on the street is that there's been enough killing. I don't think the workers are going to oppose the militia."

Corbin closed his eyes and winced. Wilder didn't know if it was because of his words or because of the pain. Even after losing the lives of some of his men and being close to losing his own, Corbin was still ready to fight to keep the union's bargaining power at the plant. It was clear Wilder couldn't change his mind. He found himself at the same point he had been when it all started back in January. He could see merit to both arguments. The hell of it was that the company and the union were right. The problem was lack of compromise from both sides.

"I better go. You need rest."

"No, wait. I—I haven't thanked you for saving my life."

"No thanks needed. I wish I could have saved them all."

"There's something else." He coughed again and Bethany helped him sip from the water.

"You're using strength you haven't got. When you're stronger, we'll talk again." Wilder took hold of Bethany's arm and started to walk away.

"I know who attacked you."

Corbin's raspy words sent a chill up Wilder's back. He stopped short. He turned angry eyes upon the weakened man lying on the bed. Slowly, tremulously, he let go of Bethany and went back to stand before Corbin. Wilder shook. He was so caught off guard by Corbin's statement that he didn't trust himself to speak.

"The way I see it," Corbin said, "I owe you for saving my life."

"Tell me," Wilder managed to say. He felt Bethany's hand on his shoulder, but he didn't turn around and acknowledge her comfort. He was rigid with fear that Corbin might change his mind and not tell him.

"I don't know who the men are by name, but I do know who hired them." He paused.

Wilder didn't move. He waited.

"Frick. The Mr. Henry Clay Frick hired them."

Bethany gasped.

"You're lying," Wilder said in a gravelly voice, but even as he said the words, he knew Corbin wasn't lying.

"Got no reason to lie." He coughed again.

Fear that it might be true caused Wilder's stomach to cramp. "Maybe. Maybe not," he said, trying to remain calm. "You could be thinking I'll turn against Frick and Carnegie and start fighting for the union."

Corbin tried to laugh. "You already have. You just won't admit it." With the back of his hand, he wiped spit from the side of his mouth. "Frick knew it, too. That's why he got you out of the way."

Anger stole over Wilder the way darkness steals over a forest in the dead of winter. It all made sense now. Frick's and his own brother's words about him straddling the fence. A startling thought crossed his mind. Did Relfe know that Frick was the one who had him beat up? Was Relfe in on it, too? No, he wouldn't—couldn't believe that of his own brother.

He touched Corbin's arm. "Swear to God you're not lying to me about this."

Corbin's eyes watered and his lips trembled. "I swear."

Grabbing Bethany's hand, Wilder hurried from the room. She followed him quietly to the carriage. There were many things she wanted to say to him but she knew now wasn't the time. The scowl on his face told her he wasn't in any kind of mood to hear anything. She would talk to him later.

Bethany remained quiet, holding on tightly. She tried not to be frightened by the wild carriage ride to Pittsburgh.

A few minutes later Wilder stopped the carriage in front of a house almost as large as The Georgia. Two armed policemen flanked the front door. Street lamps burned brightly, lighting the entire street. Wilder reached behind the seat in the carriage. He pulled out a wooden-handled hammer and stuffed it inside his shirt.

Shocked, Bethany grabbed his wrist and gasped, "Wilder, don't!"

He looked at her with wild eyes and jerked away from her. "This isn't anything to do with you, Bethany."

"Leave the hammer here, Wilder," she said in a tremulous, emotion-filled voice. "You're not going to use it."

"The hell I'm not."

There was a calmness in his words that chilled her. Bethany was breathless with fear that he might really harm that man. Wilder had never hidden from her his rage at the act of violence that had been committed against him. She grabbed his wrist again with both her hands. "I won't let you do this. You're not thinking rationally," she cried in desperation.

"That man in there crippled me, and I aim to take an eye for an eye. I'm going to make him pay."

The fury she saw in his eyes, the calm she heard in his voice, frightened Bethany more than the gunfire at the docks. Her insides were quaking and her hands trembling as she gripped Wilder's wrist like a vise. "Wilder, no. I've told you I don't care about your limp. I—"

"Dammit, I do!" He yanked his arm away easily and caught her upper arms in his hands. His fingers bit into her flesh. His glare was hostile, his words ground out from a clenched jaw. "I love you, but you've got to stay out of this. It's my fight."

"Wilder!" She grasped the front of his shirt. He let go of her arms and flung her hands away from him.

She tried to grab him again, refusing to give up on him. He flattened his hands against her shoulders and shoved her into the back of the carriage.

His menace-filled eyes glared into hers. His chest heaved, and his hands held her tight. When he spoke, his words were low and succinct. "Don't try to stop me again, Bethany. I don't want to hurt you."

Bethany swallowed hard. Tears collected in her eyes. For a moment she thought she might have gotten through to him. Wilder twisted away from her. The carriage lurched as he jumped to the ground. Bethany closed her eyes, holding back the tears.

Wilder had a difficult time talking his way past the two policemen at the front door. One of the men didn't want to allow him inside because of his tattered and bloodstained clothing. Thinking quickly, Wilder told the guard that he had urgent news about the fighting down at the docks. At last Frick's butler was summoned. He acknowledged that Wilder was known to be an employee of Mr. Frick's.

"Wilder, my word, what happened to you," Frick said a few minutes later when he walked into the foyer where Wilder had been asked to wait.

Wilder looked at his own clothes—steelworkers' clothes—then at the richly dressed Henry Frick. Not a hair out of place, not a wrinkle in his suit. For a moment Wilder was so overcome by his rage that he was calm. But only for a moment.

"You had me attacked, you son of a bitch."

Frick's eyebrows lifted and he took a step backward, pulling on the tail of his evening jacket as Wilder advanced on him.

"You paid men to dress like steelworkers and beat the living hell out of me and bring a hammer down on my leg. Why? Start talking, you bastard."

"Now, Wilder, I—I, let me explain. I only gave word for you to be roughed up a bit. I knew how strong you were and felt sure you could handle yourself with a couple of strongarms. Surely you don't think I wanted you to be crippled for life."

"There were five bloody bastards who attacked me. Four of them held me while one of them brought a hammer down on my leg! Are you telling me they did that on their own?" Shaking with fury, blind with rage, Wilder pulled the hammer from his shirt and shook it in Frick's face. Frick's eyes rounded in shock and his skin paled as he fell against the far wall of the foyer.

"I swear it!" His lips trembled. "You can't blame that on me. I never gave such orders. I only wanted you to stop siding with the union. You were making us look bad. I've always liked you. You know—"

"Liked me!" Wilder snapped. He raised the hammer.

Frick threw up his arms to cover his head, and Wilder saw a frightened old man.

He had always believed he'd want to kill the man who crippled him if he ever got his hands on him. Now he knew it to be true. But Wilder couldn't hit the weaker man. With the force of a steelworker, he slammed the hammer into the wall beside Frick's head, then threw it aside. Wilder landed a hard right blow to the man's jaw. Frick's eyes rolled up into his head and he groaned as he slid to the floor in a crumpled heap.

Breathless, Wilder said in a shaky voice, "If you know what's good for you, you'll stay down. If you get up, I'll kill you."

After a moment of staring at the man, Wilder rubbed his knuckles and walked out.

Frick and Stanley Edwards had a lot in common.

Chapter Twenty-Two

Neither of them spoke when Wilder returned to the carriage. Bethany didn't even look at him. For Wilder it seemed to take hours for them to ride the three miles from the Frick to the Burlington home. He wasn't happy with himself for the way he'd treated her earlier. It wasn't too difficult to imagine how unhappy she must be with him. Damn! He'd never lost control before. His rage had been so consuming he'd been willing to hurt her in order to accomplish what he intended to do. What kind of man had his hatred turned him into?

Relfe and Ester were waiting up for them, but Bethany immediately excused herself and went to her room. Ester stayed in the parlor long enough to hear Wilder recount what had happened at the docks, then left to have the maids prepare baths for Bethany and Wilder.

As soon as she was gone, Wilder said, "I need a drink."

"Splendid idea. After that bit of news, I could use

one myself." Relfe continued talking as they walked out of the parlor and into the library. "With the governor sending in militiamen, it shouldn't take too long to put down the rebellion. Did you say there were about five thousand steelworkers and their families down at the docks when the Pinkertons arrived?"

"At least," Wilder murmured as he ran a hand through his dirty, smoke-scented hair.

"It was foolhardy of you to go down to the docks, even incognito. And to think you allowed Bethany to accompany you!" Relfe shook his head in dismay.

Wilder knew Relfe continued to talk, but his thoughts had already left the tragic, unnecessary scene at the docks. He was thinking about what had happened afterward when he talked to Corbin.

The first sip of brandy went down easy, so Wilder took another. After his third he didn't know which burned worse—the wounds on his arms or the brandy coating his throat, its warmth spreading through him and making him hot.

When Relfe settled into the wing-back facing him, Wilder fixed his brother with an intense stare and said, "I found out tonight that Frick was the one who hired the men to attack me."

Relfe's eyes widened in disbelief. "My God, Wilder, no! Where did you hear such an absurd lie?"

"It's true. He admitted it to me." Wilder watched his brother carefully. He couldn't help but wonder if there was a chance that Relfe had been cognizant of Frick's orders. In one way, Wilder didn't want to know if Relfe had been apprised of it, but on the other hand, he knew he'd never put it to rest until he did. Wilder took a deep breath, then asked, "Did you know about it?"

"Saints alive!" Relfe almost came out of his chair as his foot slammed on the hardwood floor. "Wilder, what in the devil are you talking about? Speak sense, for God's sake. Do you think I'd agree to men beating the living hell out of you and leaving you for dead?"

Wilder shook his head, then put his drink to his lips again. "No, of course not. But I had to hear you say it." He rubbed his eyes. His brother couldn't have been involved. "I'm sorry. It's just that you said something very similar to what Frick had said to me and that gave me a moment of worry."

"What?" Relfe asked aggressively. "My God, I can't imagine what would make you think that. In fact, I'm appalled you even thought for a moment I might have been in on a scheme to have you harmed. Goddammit, Wilder, how could you?" Relfe rose from his chair so fast he spilled his drink on his hand.

"You made no progress in finding the men who attacked me," Wilder said, feeling that he had to justify his doubt. "And you told me I needed to stop straddling the fence. You said I needed to choose whether I was for the company or for the union. Do you remember?"

"Certainly! It's still true. And for that statement I'm labeled a treacherous brother?" Relfe paced back and forth in front of the fireplace. "I can't believe this. I don't *want* to believe this."

Wilder felt a great sense of relief in knowing that his brother hadn't been involved in Frick's machinations and now wished he hadn't mentioned it. He gave Relfe a repentant look. "I'm sorry I even

311

thought it. I was so angry I lost control of my thoughts and my temper. I'm sorry," he said again.

Relfe sniffed, then drank a generous portion of his brandy. "You should be. However, I meant every word of that statement." He pointed a finger at Wilder. "You can't be for both sides. Every clue our detective came up with pointed to the fact that someone other than union men attacked you. Hundreds of steelworkers were questioned and they all spoke highly of you. No exception. But I didn't expect the guilty party would be anyone from the plant, and I don't want to believe it now." He shook his head. Disappointment etched its way into his face and voice. "Not Frick. Surely there's been a mistake."

Wilder swirled the remains of his drink in his glass, then polished it off. "I told you he admitted it to me."

"Impossible!" Relfe rose from his chair and braced himself by placing his hand on the mantel. "I can't believe it's true."

"I didn't want to believe it, either, but I just came from his house."

"You didn't—" Relfe stopped and a stony expression stole over his face.

"Kill him?" Wilder pursed his lips, pretending to think about it for a moment, then chuckled.

"Dammit, Wilder, this is no laughing matter," Relfe scolded.

"He may sport a bruise for a few days, but I doubt I hurt him very badly. It only took one punch to knock him down. He didn't get near what he deserves, considering all the pain and hell I've been through the past few months and the fact that I could limp the

312

rest of my life." Every time Wilder thought about that, a bitter edge crept into his voice.

"I still find it hard to believe. We've worked for the man the three years he's been at the plant." He turned a stricken face toward Wilder. "I've been working for Carnegie Steel for fifteen years, you for ten." Relfe shook his head again. "I'm simply too stunned to take it all in."

"That makes two of us."

"Why? What reason would be good enough to warrant such aggression against one of his own men?" Relfe asked, refilling both their glasses. "Fool! Fool that I am. I should have had some idea. I should have heard talk."

"Come, Relfe. There's no cause to blame yourself. Frick didn't like my pro-union comments. He said he only wanted the men to rough me up a little, giving me reason not to like the union and withdraw my support."

"Unforgivable! This act on you was unjustifiable treachery."

"I doubt Frick will agree with you. In any case, it's a sure bet that after tonight I won't be allowed to remain at the plant even if I wanted to."

"Absolutely. And I won't, either. I'll personally speak to Carnegie and explain the whole ugly business. I'm sure he'll move us to another plant. I won't work for Frick another day."

"No need to upset your life—"

"Wilder!" Relfe gave him a hard look. "This is an affront to my family. An outrage. I couldn't think of staying at the plant after what's happened. I can't and won't work for that man."

Wilder was torn by conflicting emotions. He didn't want Relfe to remain under Frick, but he hated like hell the thought of upsetting his brother's life.

"Maybe—"

"Wilder," Relfe interrupted. "I'm your big brother. When an occasion arises, I can still take up for you. Our ages haven't changed that." He pointed his finger at him. "And this is one of those times. I'll not hear another word about it."

The two brothers hugged, then laughed.

By the time Wilder finished his bath, he had worked out in his mind exactly what he needed to say to Bethany. At first he'd tried to tell himself he could put it off until he had her safely returned home, but in the end his sense of fairness won out. He must speak to her tonight.

He was tired. A twitch had started in his leg and the soapy water caused the burns on his arms to sting like hell. But all that was nothing compared to the way he would feel once he told Bethany he knew where her sister was—that he'd known all along.

Wilder looked at the tray of food that had been placed on his dresser and turned away from it. It was nice of Ester to think of it but his stomach was too jumpy. On the ride from Frick's house to home, he'd tried to keep thoughts of Bethany from his mind by concentrating on the anger churning inside him. Now that he'd had time to sort through his feelings, he realized that in much the same way he was no better than Frick. He loved Bethany, yet he was harming her by keeping her sister's whereabouts a secret.

Bethany had been hurt by the anger he'd directed toward her in the carriage. That in itself was enough to make her decide she'd had enough of his ill-treatment and to take the first train back home. But it hadn't been easy dealing with Frick's betrayal and deceitfulness. And now to realize he was guilty of the same duplicity had his stomach in knots. He had to tell Bethany about his involvement with Grace. And he couldn't wait another day . . . another minute. She'd trusted him to be truthful with her, and he hadn't been because of a code of honor that demanded once he'd given his word he couldn't break it. But where was the glory in keeping his word to one at the expense of another?

He could try to rationalize the whole nasty business by telling Bethany that he hadn't actually lied to her because she'd never asked him if he knew where Grace had gone, but in his heart Wilder realized that wouldn't absolve him. He knew she wouldn't take his news any better than he'd taken Frick's, and he was tempted to leave things at status quo until he could return to Atlanta and see Grace. Whether he told Bethany now or later wouldn't make any difference in the way she would feel about him. But he decided it might make him like himself a little better if he didn't wait any longer.

Shirtless and barefoot, Wilder eased his door open and stepped out into the darkened hallway. The hardwood floor was cool to his feet. A light was still on in Bethany's room, so he knocked softly and opened the door. She was sitting up in bed, pillows stuffed behind her back, a food tray on her lap. A breeze blew through the open window and ruffled the drapes. She looked so lovely, so warm, and so inviting that he felt some of the tension ease from his body.

He wanted to make love to her.

"Do you mind if I come in?" he asked from the doorway.

"No."

He walked to the bed and she scooted over, giving him room to sit down on the edge beside her. She was dressed in her white sleeveless nightgown, her honey-colored hair flowing silkily across her shoulders. Her eyes sparkled attractively. The soft glow from the bedside lamp made her skin look so soft and touchable that Wilder had to fold his arms across his chest to keep from reaching out for her.

He wanted to make love to her.

Wilder realized he should have put on a shirt before coming into her room. The way they were dressed made for an intimate atmosphere and pushed his reasons for coming into her room to the back of his mind. She was beautiful. He wanted to pull her to him and feel the warmth of her body against his.

He wanted to make love to her.

Bethany remained quiet as she cut a slice of peach and handed it to him.

"Thanks," he said. Wilder didn't have an appetite, but not wanting to refuse her offering, he put the juicy sweetness into his mouth and ate it.

"I don't think we've eaten very much in the last twenty-four hours," she said. "It was nice of Ester to prepare a tray."

He nodded as he looked at her beautiful green eyes, rosy cheeks, small nose, and tempting lips. He wanted to kiss the taste of peaches from her lips. Wilder looked away. He had to stop regarding her as the woman he loved and wanted to marry, and get to the unpleasant reason he had come into her room.

"I'm sorry I was so rough with you tonight at Frick's house. I'm sorry I didn't apologize on the way home. Hell, I'm sorry for a lot of things, but my treatment of you was deplorable. I know you were only trying to keep me from letting my temper get the best of me and doing something I'd regret."

She handed him another slice of the peach, and Wilder took it and put it into his mouth. He wiped the juice from the corner of his mouth with his tongue. Bethany watched him. His need for her grew. She hadn't taken her gaze off his lips since he'd sat down. He was hungry for her, and the way she was looking at him let him know the fruit wasn't satisfying her, either. This was going to be harder than he had imagined.

"I have to admit it hurt my feelings, but I understood why you did it," she answered. "You were caught up in the moment of your anger."

And right now he was caught up in a moment of burgeoning desire for this woman. He should be confessing his transgression, begging her forgiveness, but he was too filled with longing for her to force himself to bring up the subject. He'd do it in a few minutes. Right now, he just needed to sit here and talk to her.

He watched as she bit into a slice of peach. A trickle

of juice ran into her palm and Wilder swallowed hard, his throat feeling tight and scratchy.

"You forgot to put salve on your arms after your bath," she said. "Should I get some for you?"

Barely hearing her, Wilder shook his head, trying to get his thoughts back to his original intent. "I'll do it later. I came in here to apologize before you went to sleep. In fact, there are some other things we need to talk about tonight."

Bethany took another bite of the peach, then held it up to Wilder's lips. He saw nectar from the fruit on the tips of her fingers and his desire rose. His breath grew shallow. His lips parted. Bethany fed him. When she took her hand away, Wilder grasped her wrist and carried it back to his mouth. One by one, slowly, he sipped the juice from her fingers, then licked the sweetness from her palm.

"Do we have to talk tonight?" she asked as she pulled her hand away and pressed it against his chest. "We're both very tired."

"There are some things between us that we need to clear up."

She gave him a tentative smile. "Tomorrow should be soon enough."

Wilder closed his eyes for a moment. "Don't tempt me, Bethany. My life is too tenuous right now."

She picked up the tray and set it on the bedside table, then turned back to him. "Let me give you something that's absolute. My love. Stay with me tonight," she whispered softly.

She ran her hand over his cheek and he realized he hadn't shaved. Damn! Her hand moved down his neck, over his shoulder, and across his chest.

"Bethany, that's not why I came in here." He didn't know if his throat was raw from the pain inside him or the smoke he'd inhaled at the docks. He only knew it was tight and constricting. He wasn't saying the things he needed to say. He had to tell her about his involvement with Grace. She slipped her arms around his neck and locked her hands at his nape.

"Do you love me?" she asked, not letting her gaze wander from his eyes.

"Until hell freezes over, then a million years after that." His voice was husky, emotional.

She smiled. "And I love you more than my own life. I would do anything for you. I'll always stand beside you, be there for you."

Wilder reached up and brushed his hand down her hair. He looked into her eyes and said, "I'll always be there for you, but tonight I—"

Lifting a finger to his lips, she whispered, "I need you now. Don't leave me tonight."

When she reached up and placed her lips against his, Wilder knew he no longer had control of the situation. How could he deny her? He would be a bigger fool than he already was if he denied them this night together. He ran his hands up and down her arms, over her neck and shoulders. The touch of her skin beneath his hands felt so good his manhood grew hard swiftly. Fool that he'd been, deceiver that he was, he couldn't, wouldn't deny her.

How could he consider telling Bethany about Grace? If telling Bethany about Grace would mean he would lose her, he'd take Grace's whereabouts to his grave. He'd never give up Bethany. Not for anyone. To hell with Grace. Bethany was his. He clasped his lips over hers with such intensity that they both fell against the pillows. He had to let her know how much he wanted her, how much he needed her, how much he loved her. His hands moved up and down her body, kneading her breasts, cupping her waist, outlining her hips. He was so tormented by his love for her that he was afraid of frightening her with his passion, with his hardness, with his desire to possess her and make her his once more.

He delved his tongue deeper into the sweetness of her mouth. Her taste of peaches mixed with the brandy on his tongue created a heady flavor that enriched his yearning to be one with her. He clutched the hem of her nightgown and pulled it up and over her head, flinging the simple barrier away. Just as quickly, he removed his binding trousers and stretched the length of his naked body over hers. His senses were so acute to her every breath, her maddening taste, her soft touch, that his body trembled. He wanted her so badly he wanted to shout into the air, to let everyone know that Bethany Hayward was his. She was his.

He covered her bare nipple with his lips and fondled it with his tongue, enjoying the presence of it in his mouth. Her soft sounds of pleasure pleased him, heightening his ardor, encouraging him to love her to the fullest.

"You're beautiful," he whispered, his hand working a soothing pattern from her breast to her hip. His gaze drifted from her silky hair to her satiny smooth shoulders, down to her breasts and past her flat stomach with its little indention, then farther. "Absolutely beautiful."

He slipped his hand down to her womanhood. She was ready for him. With sweet words of love and tender caresses, Wilder joined his body with Bethany's.

A few minutes later Bethany smiled beneath the pressure of Wilder's lips. She lay on her side with her breasts pressed against his chest, one leg thrown over his. "I can't believe you were going to deny me your touch tonight."

"Me either," he admitted as his hand caressed the small of her back, down her buttocks and up again.

She looked into his eyes. "I needed your loving."

Wilder brushed her hair away from her shoulder and reached up and kissed her damp skin. "This isn't all that I want for us, you know. I want to marry you."

Smiling again, she said, "If that's a question, the answer is yes. I want to marry you, Wilder."

He looked intensely into her eyes. "Does it matter that I'm unemployed?"

She placed her hands on either side of his face. "How can you say that? Remember, you still own half of The Georgia. When we marry, you'll own part of the mill, too. You know how badly your expertise is needed there. That is, if you'll consider making Eufaula our home."

"Does that mean you'll consider making Pittsburgh your home?"

"The way I feel right now is that I don't care where we live as long as I'm with you."

Wilder kissed the tip of her nose. "I feel the same

way." Circling her in his arms, he said, "You make me feel so good. I love you, Bethany. I can't lose you."

She pressed his cheek to her breasts. "You're not going to."

He held her tightly, burying his nose in the crook of her neck. "Bethany, there's still one other thing—"

"Maybe there is, but we're not going to talk about it tonight," she said as she crawled on top of him and stretched her body over his.

Wilder looked into her eyes and saw happiness, love.

"Let's not waste time talking tonight. There'll be time for that when we return home."

"You're right," he said. "We shouldn't waste the rest of the night."

The quiet opening of the door awakened Wilder. Daybreak lighted the way enough for him to see Penelope slipping into Bethany's room. Damn! Why hadn't he locked the door last night? Because he hadn't planned on staying the night when he entered. Thank God he was covered to his waist, he thought as he rose from the pillow. Penee stopped and her blue eyes rounded in shock. Her lips formed an O. Wilder didn't know how he was going to get out of this one. Thinking quickly, he put his finger to his lips for her not to make a sound. All he needed was for Penee to scream and bring Relfe and Ester running into the room.

But Penee was smart. She followed his direction and put her finger to her lips. Her eyes remained wide with shock and wonder. Wilder glanced behind him and saw that Bethany slept peacefully with her back snug against his. He pulled the sheet over her shoulder in case Penee decided to take a peek around him.

Deciding how to handle this, he motioned for Penee to come forward. With her finger still pressed to her lips, she tiptoed to the bed and stood before Wilder. He had to smile. She was such a pretty little doll in her long white ruffled gown and her tangled hair draping over her shoulders.

"Does Ester know you're out of your bed at this time of the morning?" he whispered.

She shook her head.

"Would she be angry with you if she knew you were in here?"

Penee nodded.

This was going better than he'd hoped. "Did you need something?" he asked in the same soft whisper.

Still silent with rounded eyes, she shook her head.

"I'll tell you what. You don't tell Ester I was in here and I won't tell her you were in here. Do we have a deal?"

Penee nodded again.

Wilder smiled and stuck out his hand. Penee smiled and shook it.

His partner in secrecy exited as quietly as she had entered. Closing his eyes and easing back against the pillow, Wilder knew he had to leave Bethany's room before someone else found him in bed with her.

He didn't want to leave her, though. Not now. Not ever. Telling her about Grace was going to be harder than he imagined because he loved her so much. How could he have kept his resolve last night when they wanted each other so desperately? She had a hold on him like no other woman ever had.

Wilder thought for a few minutes, struggling with the fear of telling Bethany and the uncertainty of her reaction. As much as he wanted to keep his involvement a secret when he was making love to her, he knew that he couldn't treat her that way. But now he realized it would be better to tell Bethany about his alliance with Grace when she was back home. He hoped it would be easier for her to come to terms with the whole thing if she was in her own familiar surroundings.

Yes, it would be much better than doing it now, when she'd have to face saying good-bye to Relfe and Ester. He'd stay in Atlanta and go see Grace and send Bethany on to The Georgia. After he'd talked with Grace, he'd return to Eufaula and explain everything to Bethany. She'd forgive him. She had to.

Before they left, he needed to see Corbin again and close down his apartment in Homestead. He couldn't do any more for the union or the plant. Frick was by nature a fighter and so were the steelworkers. The strike could last for months.

Wilder had been unable to alter the course of events because neither side was willing to make adjustments until a compromise could be reached. He had done all he could for the Carnegie Steel Mill and all he could do for the union. Now he had to concentrate on his relationship with the woman he loved.

Chapter Twenty-Three

A wide smile lifted the corners of Bethany's lips and brightened her face as she stepped out of the carriage and looked at The Georgia—her home. She hadn't realized how much she'd missed it until she'd left Wilder in Atlanta earlier that afternoon. She'd offered to stay in Atlanta with him but he'd insisted she come home, and now she was glad that he had. It was more beautiful than ever to her.

She paid the driver and sent him on his way, knowing Seth could take care of her baggage. After greeting Margaret warmly, Bethany's first question to her was about Mr. Lester. Margaret assured her the man had not even sent a letter. To get over her hurt and disappointment at that bit of news, she spent her first hour home giving detailed accounts of her visit to Pennsylvania, Wilder's family, and the strike at the docks to Margaret, Stilman, Kate, and Seth.

"What kind of business does Mr. Burlington have in Atlanta?" Margaret asked when the others had gone back to work.

"Oh, I didn't ask," Bethany said. "He said it wouldn't take very long and that he'd be back tomorrow or the next day." Bethany saw that Margaret was uneasy. "Why do you ask?"

"Nothing." She started to walk away.

"Margaret, wait. I can see something is wrong. What is it?"

Jerking her hands to her ample hips, Margaret harrumphed. "It's that Mr. Edwards. He's been here twice wanting to know when you were coming back. The second time, I told him I hadn't heard from you and if he showed his face around here again, I was going to tell Sheriff Beale and have him thrown in jail."

A chill shook Bethany. "Thank you for taking care of it, Margaret. I'm sure he won't be back."

"Not inside the house, no. But Seth said he sees him just hanging around watching the place."

Bethany tried not to let her imagination run wild. "Well, I'm not happy about it, but I don't suppose we can do anything if he doesn't come inside."

"I don't like it, either. I thought Mr. Burlington took care of him when he rearranged his nose."

Bethany snapped her head around to Margaret. "What are you talking about?"

"Ooops. I done said too much. Don't pay any attention to me. I'm just blabbing."

"Not enough. What's this about Stanley's nose?"

Margaret relented easily. "The morning after the ball, Mr. Burlington went to see Mr. Edwards. That's all I know for sure. Seth told me Mr. Burlington asked how to get there. When he came back his knuckles were scraped, then three days after you leave

Mr. Edwards shows up here with his nose swollen and purple."

Bethany rubbed her arms as she remembered the night of the ball, when for a few moments she'd thought Wilder was Stanley. Wilder had been so patient with her afterward that it had been easy to forget about Stanley.

With more bravado than she was feeling, Bethany said, "Maybe Wilder will be back tomorrow. If need be, I'll ask him what we should do about Stanley. I don't want him loitering about the property. If he shows up before Wilder returns, I'll talk to Sheriff Beale. Now, I think I'd like to go upstairs and rest."

Early the next morning, Bethany made a list of things she needed at the mercantile and sent Margaret for them, then sat down at her desk to catch up on her work. After being gone for ten days, she had a lot to do. She had hardly begun the paperwork when a shadow fell across the room. Looking up, Bethany saw Stanley leaning against the door frame, a grin lifting one corner of his mouth. Her hands made fists and she gritted her teeth together.

"Before you start with all those 'Go away, no one wants you here, and I'll call the sheriff' cries, listen to what I have to say." He pushed away from the door and walked inside, a silly, knowing grin widening his thin lips. He placed his palms on her desk and bent toward her. "You're going to love me for this, Bethany. I know where Grace is."

Bethany came out of her seat, her gaze making contact with his. "No!" she whispered, afraid to believe him.

"Yes," he answered, his grin in place. "I saw her

with my own eyes yesterday afternoon."

"You've found Grace. Where is she? Is she here with you? Can I talk to her?" She couldn't ask the questions fast enough and Stanley wasn't trying to answer her at all. He just stood leaning over her desk, grinning. Bethany hurried around her desk to stand before Stanley. It was impossible to contain her excitement. "Tell me where she is."

"Not so fast. I'll take you to her, but I thought you might like to know who she was talking to when I saw her."

"No, I don't. I don't care. It doesn't matter. Just tell me where she is so I can go to her."

He laughed. "Oh, I think you'll care when I tell you his name is Wilder Burlington."

She merely stared at him a moment. "What!"

"She's with the Yankee." His hard gaze locked on to her face.

Stunned, she said the only thing that could be true. "You're lying."

Stanley straightened and raised his hand. "I swear to God I saw them together with my own eyes."

"No, you're lying," she said again. Breathless with confusion, Bethany struck out at him. He caught her wrist and yanked her to his chest.

"I'm not lying, bitch! And I'm going to take you there and prove it to you. They're in a boardinghouse about twenty miles this side of Atlanta. I entered through the front door and saw them sitting at a table in the dining room, looking real chummy."

Struggling to get away from him, Bethany said, "I don't believe you."

Stanley grabbed a handful of her hair and jerked

her head back. Bethany bit down on her lip to keep from crying out. "I'm not lying," he said, almost too calmly.

He was too serious for her not to believe him. Bethany quieted down. She was so numb she couldn't hold back the tears as everything started to fall into place. Wilder had decided to stay in Atlanta for a couple of days on business. Was his *business* to see Grace? "He must have found her by accident," she said, hoping to deny the obvious—that Wilder had known where she was all along.

"I don't think so and neither do you."

"O—of course I do," she answered sharply, wiggling out of his grasp.

"I'd wager money they've seen each other often since she left. All he'd have to do is take the morning train up and the late afternoon one back.

"How did *you* find her?" Her voice was rising above an acceptable level, but she was desperate to prove Stanley wrong.

He grinned again. "It was simple, really. Your detective got paid double. After a few drinks and some well-chosen words, he agreed to bring me all the information he gathered. Yesterday when he arrived with the latest, I told him I would make the trip to the boardinghouse to see if the woman was Grace. He agreed it would save us both some time and trouble. I must admit I was surprised to see them together."

Stanley reached up and touched his nose, and Bethany could see it was sitting at an odd angle. Its pale yellow coloring attested to that fact that it had been broken.

"That was deceitful," she told Stanley, but realized the fight had gone out of her.

"It worked. Besides, what that Yankee is doing right now is deceitful, too. Remember that." He combed his hair with his hand. "You expected no less from me, but from him—"

Stanley finished his sentence with a laugh. Bethany couldn't think, she couldn't breathe. She had to get hold of herself. She lifted her shoulders and her chin, her proud air returning to claim her dignity.

"I have a carriage outside. If we hurry, we can catch the morning train and be at the boardinghouse by noon. You can ask him what he's doing there."

Was Stanley lying to her? Was this madness? Did he just want to get her away from The Georgia? Bethany didn't know, but she had to find out. There was no choice. She had to go and see for herself. "Take me to Grace."

Stanley bowed. "I'm ready whenever you are."

"I'll get my bonnet and meet you outside."

Three and a half hours later, noonday sunshine fell across Bethany's face as Stanley stopped the carriage in front of a nondescript house in what seemed to be the middle of nowhere. Her mouth was dry and there was a crick in her neck, back, and shoulders from holding herself so rigidly. For a moment she wondered if she'd acted irrationally in coming to this house with Stanley. It was so quiet she thought it might be vacant.

As they started up the stairs, the door swung open and a woman about Margaret's age said, "Hello. Come on in. My name's Mary," she said graciously.

"Hello," Bethany said, trying her best to be polite as she moved into the foyer. "I—I—"

"We believe we know one of the guests you have registered here," Stanley filled in for her. "Grace Hayward?"

The woman smiled. "Oh, yes, she's here . . . been here almost two months now. Sweet girl."

Bethany's heart pounded. Her hands trembled and her legs shook. "I'm her sister, Bethany."

"I was sure of that. You have the same coloring. She's out in the backyard talking with that nice young man who came in yesterday. Come on, I'll show you."

Striving for composure, Bethany shifted her purse to the other hand and took a deep breath. Her feet felt like wooden blocks as she followed the woman down the hall. Stanley pressed his hand to the small of her back, but she was powerless to move away from him.

Stanley moved ahead and pulled back the curtains as Bethany stepped up to the kitchen window. Wilder and Grace sat at a picnic table. Bethany's heart broke. Trying to sound casual, she said to the woman, "Yes, that's Grace." Her lips trembled so much her mouth didn't want to work properly. The pain was so great she nearly doubled over. A small sound of torment escaped from her throat the first time she tried to speak again. "I'd like to t—talk to her alone. Wait here for me."

She couldn't look at Stanley, but the woman nodded. Her expression told Bethany she knew something wasn't right.

Denial turned to anger. Fury over what she was feeling for Wilder made something inside her snap and fuel her desperation. As she stepped out onto the porch, her only thought was to show Wilder up for the liar he was. At first neither of them looked up from the heated discussion they were having. Then Bethany started down the steps. The heels of her shoes clicked on the boards.

Wilder was the first to see her, then Grace. "Bethany," they whispered in unison.

Bethany didn't stop until she stood before them. She kept her gaze on her sister. "Hello, Grace." The two words she spoke were husky but clear.

Grace folded her hands across her chest in a gesture of defiance. "I knew you'd come eventually." Sarcasm dripped from every word. She turned uncompromising eyes on Wilder. "You brought her here after you promised you wouldn't. You lied to me."

Wilder shook his head but didn't take his eyes off Bethany. "No, I didn't."

"How else could she have found me?" Grace snapped at Wilder.

"No need to be angry with him, Grace." Bethany held her jaw so tight when she spoke that it ached. "I assure you, Wilder never breathed a word to me about knowing where you were staying. Mr. Lester, the detective I hired, and Stanley found you."

"Stanley?" Wilder and Grace said his name at the same time.

Bethany's eyes met Wilder's for the first time and her thoughts betrayed her. She remembered the feel of his hands on her breasts, the taste of his tongue in her mouth. She remembered seeing desire in his eyes and hearing words of love spoken from his lips. She remembered his clean scent of shaving soap. Wilder was so much a part of her senses that even now, knowing what he'd done to her, she still wanted him, still loved him. Bethany felt so heavy she didn't know if she could remain standing.

Gathering strength from her ability to remain calm, she replied, "Yes. Stanley brought me here. Perhaps you should go speak to him, Grace. I'd like to have a word alone with Wilder."

"I don't have anything to say to him or to you," Grace said defiantly.

"Leave us." Wilder's words were issued like an order and apparently Grace decided not to challenge them. She pursed her lips in anger, then picked up her skirts and stomped past Bethany, refusing to look at her.

Bethany and Wilder stood several feet apart, as if some unknown force were wedged between them. In spite of the heat from the sun on her back, Bethany felt chilled to the bone.

Unpleasant scenes. She avoided them, hated them, had an innate reluctance to be a part of one. Now she was forced to participate in one that would destroy her life. She stood rigidly in the grass, preparing for the first strike.

"Bethany," he said again.

That soothing voice. The one that had told of his love and the promise of marriage. No, she didn't want to hear anything he had to say. If he'd loved her, he wouldn't have done this to her. She had to fight her weaker emotions, calm her thudding heart, still her clamoring senses. He'd hurt her too deeply. He wasn't to be trusted.

She took a deep breath, allowing the luxury of air to fill her lungs. At one time Bethany had thought nothing could be more important than hugging Grace and telling her that she loved her. But that was before Wilder. She shuddered inwardly, wishing she could change what she knew the outcome would be. She had to get it over with. "Explain this to me," she said.

Wilder stuffed his hands into his pants pockets. "I've always known where Grace was hiding."

"No," she whispered, even though she knew it had to be true.

"I gave my word I wouldn't tell you."

Bethany already stood ramrod-straight, but she managed to lift her shoulders and chin a little higher. The pain of Wilder's betrayal swallowed her in its depth, allowing her no escape from the truth of his admission.

"No," she shook her head, trying to control her anger and hurt. It wasn't working. Something destructive was building inside her, taking control. "I sold my grandmother's jewelry so I would have enough money to pay Mr. Lester, and you knew where she was all along."

"What do you mean you sold your jewelry? You told me you had your own money to pay for half of the repairs to The Georgia." He eyed her carefully. "Bethany, I assumed you were paying Mr. Lester from the same funds."

Her lips trembled. "I didn't have the money until I sold the jewelry."

Wilder swore bitterly and took a step toward her. "Why? Bethany, I tried to get you not to hire anyone.

I begged you not to hire that man." He reached out to touch her, but she bolted away. "Why wouldn't you listen to me?"

"She's my sister!" she screamed, her anger overcoming her restraint. She swallowed hard, trying to regain control. "How could I not look for her? How could you do this to me? You were supposed to love me. Why didn't you tell me where she was?"

A sob fell from her lips and she quickly bit back the ones that wanted to follow. She was determined that he wouldn't see her cry. No! He wouldn't see her cry.

"Because I had given my word. That used to mean something to me, but right now it doesn't sound like much."

Bethany turned away. "I've decided I don't want to hear this. I can't bear it." Her voice grew softer, while inside she shook. Her ears were ringing. She rubbed her arms. Why was she so cold?

Wilder grabbed her arm and swung her back around. His expression was intense. "You asked me to explain, so I'm going to." When Bethany didn't object, he let her go. "I thought you were involved with Stanley when I gave Grace my word. Later, when I told Grace you were worried about her and thinking of hiring a detective, she told me if I broke my promise to her, she would go into hiding and neither one of us would ever hear from her again. I thought she was young and unstable enough to do just that, so I kept quiet." He stopped with a deep, breathy sigh. Pain was etched across his face. "I knew that if I kept in touch with her, if she ever needed anything, if she ever needed you, I'd know where she was and could let you know. Bethany, believe me, I didn't want to keep this from you, but at least one of us has known where she's been all these weeks."

Bethany's hands curled into fists as she grabbed the soft material of her skirt. Her eyes glared into his. "I'll never forgive you for this."

Wilder's head snapped back as if she'd struck him. "I didn't know I was going to fall in love with you when I promised Grace I wouldn't tell you where she was living. I didn't know she was going to take nine damn weeks to come to her senses." He ran a shaky hand through his hair to calm down. "Saying I'm sorry doesn't begin to make up for what I've done, but I've got to start somewhere."

She didn't know how much more she could take. She was shaking so much she could hardly stand straight. Bethany felt drained. Empty. And oh, how she ached inside.

"I've been here trying to convince her to come back home and talk to you. I told her I was going to tell you of my involvement. I knew I had to before we were married." There was passion in his voice, a soft light in his eyes.

Bethany remained still and quiet while his words penetrated.

"Bethany, please understand why I had to do this," he pleaded desperately.

She drew a deep breath and held it for a long time while they looked at each other. She still loved him and it hurt.

Get away, her mind screamed. *You've got to get away before you weaken.* She sniffled and let the coldness she was feeling overtake her. "No, we won't be married."

336

He took a step forward. "I won't let you leave with this unsettled between us."

"You don't have a choice."

"You've got to know what it was doing to me, loving you, knowing that I had the power to take your pain away yet I couldn't use it. It wasn't easy, Bethany. It tore me apart. I love you. This doesn't change anything. I want to marry you."

She whispered, "It changes things for me. You're no better than Stanley." She kept her voice and eyes free of emotion, in spite of the pain. "No, I take that back. You are more clever. You succeeded where Stanley failed. You have exactly what he wanted. You have control of The Georgia and Grace has turned against me." She turned to walk away, no longer able to bear the hurt, the pain, the bitterness.

"You're wrong." Wilder swung her around to face him again. He held her upper arms tightly, desperation flaming in his eyes. "I love you, Bethany. I swear, I never wanted to hurt you. I wanted to tell you so many times it was eating me alive. I had a decision to make and I made it. Maybe it was the wrong one, but I wouldn't be much of a man if I broke my word to a woman."

She had to fight his logic, the comfort of his touch, the sincerity in his voice. "You chose the wrong woman. Turn me loose, you're hurting me."

"I'm sorry. I don't know what else I can say except that I want us to start over, without anything between us."

"Sorry doesn't take the pain away. The only thing I want from you is to buy your half of The Georgia."

The uneven leap of his breath showed her how

much her demand affected him. Disbelief filled his blue eyes. She watched as hurt and disappointment flashed across them, then finally anger.

"With what?" He almost spit the words. "Do you have more jewelry to sell, or are you going to start on the furniture this time?"

"If I have to," she said evenly, when all she wanted to do was hit him for hurting her so badly. She wanted to force him to take back the deceit, to take back the pain. Anger and bitterness were not easy emotions for Bethany to deal with. They had completely consumed her, shutting out even the simplest form of logic or hint of forgiveness. She was trying to come to terms with the fact that both her sister and the man she loved cared so little for her feelings. She couldn't just turn off her love for them, but she didn't know if she could ever forgive them, either. The pain was too great, the wound too deep.

"Are we back to that, Bethany? Does The Georgia really mean more to you than I do?"

"Yes," she answered, knowing she didn't mean what she was saying but unable to stop herself.

"Has The Georgia ever held you or caressed you? Has it filled that emptiness deep inside you?"

"It's never lied to me. It has never deceived me," she exclaimed.

Silence fell upon them as a gray cloud covered the sun and darkened the sky. It was over. Finished.

Wilder shook his head with dismay. "Keep The Georgia. It's yours and always will be; you don't have anything else."

Wilder turned to walk away but stopped. His eyes narrowed and his breathing became shallow. Stanley stood on the porch pointing a pistol at him.

Chapter Twenty-Four

"Stanley! What are you doing with that gun? Someone could get hurt," Bethany called to him as she took a couple of steps forward.

Bethany had been devastated to find out that Wilder had known Grace's whereabouts. Now she was mortified to see Stanley standing on the porch holding a gun. Because of the trauma of her conversation with Wilder, at first she didn't realize the full extent of what it meant for Stanley to be pointing a pistol at them.

"Come on, Bethany, Wilder," Stanley said as he motioned with the gun. "In the house."

"Stay where you are, Bethany," Wilder countered Stanley's command calmly as he stood on the bottom step, Bethany a few feet behind him. "We're not going anywhere until you put down that gun."

"I think you are." Stanley shrugged his shoulders and sniffed. "We can stand here and talk about this the rest of the day if that's what you want to do, but I think Bethany should see to her sister."

"Grace!" Bethany exclaimed, picking up her skirt

to rush up the steps.

Wilder caught her by the arm and pulled her back. "Wait, Bethany. Let's find out what he wants."

A reckless sensation overcame Bethany. She lashed out at Wilder. "No! Let me go. I've got to see to Grace." She struggled to free herself, hitting him with her free hand. "You've kept me from my sister long enough."

Stanley laughed. "She always was a wild one."

Twisting around to Stanley, Bethany demanded, "What have you done to Grace?"

"Not much," he laughed again, his eyes snapping with the power he felt in controlling the situation. "Come in and see for yourself."

Bethany was finding it difficult to think properly. She knew Wilder stayed by her side as they climbed the steps, but they weren't moving fast enough to suit her.

"Remember, if you try anything funny, Bethany gets the first bullet." Stanley stood to the far side and let them pass.

Wilder stopped and gave him a cold look. "If you touch her, I'll kill you."

Stanley sneered. "I've never known of a dead man killing anyone. And that's what you're going to be. Now get inside, and I'll tell you what I have planned."

As they entered the boardinghouse, Bethany immediately saw the body of the owner lying on the kitchen floor. Blood had puddled beside her. The handle of a knife showed from underneath her body. Bethany covered her mouth to hold in her scream as Wilder rushed over and knelt beside the woman.

"Don't bother," Stanley said without emotion. "She's dead. It's a shame, too. She was a nice woman, but I couldn't have her upsetting my plan."

"You bastard," Wilder ground out between clenched teeth. He looked at Stanley with hatred in his eyes. "There's no way this old woman could have been a threat to you."

"Wrong. She could identify me as your murderer. I had to make sure she couldn't talk. Now into the parlor before I decide to shoot you where you stand."

Seeing the dark red blood seeping from underneath the woman, all rational thought left Bethany. She bolted away from Wilder and ran down the hallway calling for her sister.

Grace sat on a chair in the parlor. A scarf had been used as a gag and covered her mouth. Her hands were tied behind her back. She wiggled, trying to free herself. When she saw Bethany, she started struggling against the ropes that held her and mumbling frantically. Her big green eyes registered terror.

"Grace," Bethany whispered, wanting to strangle Stanley with her bare hands. She rushed to her sister's side and asked, "Are you all right? Did he hurt you? How could he treat you like this?" Frantic with worry, Bethany set out to untie the scarf that corded Grace's mouth and cheeks.

"Leave her be," Stanley said coldly as he and Wilder followed her into the room.

Bethany shook with rage, but still she defied his order. "No. I won't let you treat her this way."

With the gun pointed directly at Bethany's head, Stanley pulled back the hammer. "I said leave her."

Bethany heard a click. Her legs trembled and her

341

hands stilled.

"Listen to him, Bethany!" Wilder's voice was tense with alarm. "Dammit, he's crazy enough to pull that trigger. Get away from her."

Slowly, Bethany turned around. Her eyes darted from Stanley to Wilder. At that moment, she realized Stanley meant to kill them all.

Wilder stood stiff with tension, his hand clenching into a fist, relaxing, then making a fist again. He'd known Stanley was mean, but until today he hadn't known the man was evil. Wilder had to do something. He didn't have too many choices, though. He had to try to reason with Stanley and buy some time so he could think.

"Let the women go, and I'll do whatever you want," Wilder said in an even voice.

Stanley laughed and smoothed back his hair with his hand. "After all these years, the South has a brave Yankee in its midst. I'm impressed, but I don't want anything from you. In fact, you have been the center of my troubles the last few weeks. If you hadn't paid Grace money for The Georgia, she couldn't have run away."

"If Grace hadn't received the money from me, she would have gotten it from someone else. She meant to leave."

"Not before I could have found her and explained that Bethany had been chasing me for weeks."

"That's a lie!" Bethany said, taking a step forward, as Grace renewed her struggle against the ropes that held her hands together.

"Stay put," Stanley warned. "Don't make me use this before I'm ready." He aimed the gun at her chest.

"Do what he says, Bethany," Wilder told her, moving a little closer to her. He chanced a glance at Grace. Her eyes and nose were red from crying, but it didn't appear Stanley had harmed her.

Stanley leaned against the doorjamb, although his attention remained acutely on what was going on in the room. "You know, I didn't want to have to kill all of you at one time, but it has to be." He looked at Wilder again. "If you hadn't given Grace enough money to run away, I would have talked her into marrying me. Then I would have had control of The Georgia and the mill. I could have lived quite comfortably for a time on the money from the sale of those places."

Bethany gasped. "I would never agree to sell The Georgia."

While Stanley talked, Wilder slowly eased himself closer to Grace. He wanted to get behind her if he could and try to untie her hands. He wanted her free to run if he had the opportunity to jump Stanley.

Stanley chuckled. "You still don't understand, do you, sweet Bethany? You wouldn't have been around to agree or disagree with me. I planned to kill you." He gave her an evil smile. "You are just too difficult to handle, my sweet, untouchable Bethany. Oh, but not to worry. I would have made it an easy death for you—maybe like my second wife. All it took was a little shove and down the stairs she tumbled. Everyone in town said, 'Oh, such a pity your dear wife fell, killing her and the baby she was carrying.'" He laughed again. "I grieved for a time, then moved on so I could enjoy her money without the watchful eyes of friends and neighbors."

Bethany gasped in horror. Stanley had never mentioned that he'd been married. She covered her mouth with her hand. He'd killed before. Stanley must be insane.

"My first wife's death was harder." His eyes glazed with remembrance, his voice cold and unfeeling as he continued. "I gave her a drop of poison each day for a couple of weeks. That takes too long and gets messy toward the end when the stomach can't hold down food."

Bethany clutched Grace's shoulders, holding her sister close. Her face was ashen. Stanley was enjoying every moment of their discomfort. Wilder wondered if Stanley was trying to frighten them to death.

"Stop this!" Wilder demanded, forgetting about untying Grace and stepping forward. Stanley fired the gun above Wilder's head, and particles from the ceiling fell on top of him. He stopped.

"Next time I won't aim for the ceiling. Do be patient. I prefer to kill you in my own time, but if you insist, I'll do it now."

Looking at the madman who pointed the pistol directly at his head, Wilder knew one thing to be true: Before this day was over, either he or Stanley would be dead. Infuriated, Wilder decided he'd better hold on to his temper. A dead hero wouldn't be able to save Bethany or Grace. He took a deep breath and backed up.

"Don't look so horrified, Bethany." Stanley's eyes turned glassy. "I would have let Grace live a year or two longer. Long enough for me to sell the mill and the big house and move to another town. It worked so well that way before."

"You're insane," Bethany whispered.

He shrugged. "I don't think so. I've outsmarted the three of you, even though you've tried to keep me from marrying Grace. I needed to marry her fast because I was running out of money. It doesn't last long, you know. After a few trips to New York and St. Louis and one to Paris, it's gone." He straightened his shoulders. "Now listen carefully. Over on the desk, you'll find some paper and a pen. I want you and Wilder to write a note saying that I've bought The Georgia and the mill for fifty thousand dollars."

"You're crazy!" Bethany said, stepping away from Grace. "We could sign everything over to you and you could kill us, anyway."

"You want my promise I won't kill you if you sign the paper? You got it." He laughed.

"Do it, Bethany," Wilder said, taking her arm and ushering her over to the desk.

"Let go of me!" She tried to free herself, but Wilder held tight. "I won't sign. He's going to kill us, anyway."

"Not if I can do anything about it," Wilder told her in a low voice. "I'm waiting for an opportunity to jump him."

"Stop the whispering," Stanley ordered.

Bethany twisted back around to Stanley. "The authorities will never believe I've sold The Georgia. Everyone in town knows how much my home means to me."

"They will when I tell them you planned to move up north with your Yankee lover. Everyone also knows that you followed him to Pennsylvania a couple of weeks ago."

Wilder wanted to rush Stanley and beat him senseless, but he had to be practical. He knew Stanley could get off a shot before he reached him. He had to get closer.

"It took me a while to work it all out after we got here, but now I have it planned. When the paper is signed, the three of you will get in the carriage and head toward Eufaula. About a mile down the road, your carriage will be attacked and you'll all be killed, including my dear fiancée. It will be easy to convince the authorities that whoever attacked the carriage also killed the owner of the boardinghouse and robbed you of the fifty thousand."

"No one will believe you!" Bethany said again.

Wilder had written out Stanley's request while he talked. "Sign the paper, Bethany." He tried to tell her with his eyes to trust him, but he knew by the look in her eyes that she no longer trusted anyone. And he didn't blame her.

"If I sign it, he'll kill us for sure," she reasoned.

"He's going to try it either way. Signing the paper will buy us more time," he whispered, then louder said, "Sign the damn paper, Bethany. For once, will you listen to me."

He was right. They needed more time. She looked over at Grace, then with trembling hands, Bethany picked up the pen and signed her name.

"I see she minds you quite well. I guess there was hope for me after all had I been willing to take her on. Now go help Grace stand, both of you."

Wilder and Bethany flanked Grace and helped her rise from the chair. Keeping the pistol trained on them, Stanley picked up the paper and glanced at it. Apparently satisfied, he said, "Now very carefully walk outside to the carriage. And don't try to be a hero, Wilder. If I have to, I'll kill you here and drag your body to the carriage later."

Wilder made his plans as they walked down the front steps. Once they got in the carriage, they'd all be sitting ducks for Stanley to pick off one by one and make it look like a robbery. Their only chance would be for Wilder to spook the horses and make them run. There was a farmhouse about five miles back down the road. If they couldn't find help there, maybe they could find cover.

"I want to untie Grace," Bethany said.

Stanley shook his head. "I'll untie her later. I think I might have a little fun with her before I kill her."

"You're a horrible, despicable man!" Bethany yelled at him.

Grace struggled and mumbled frantically. Wilder held his teeth together tightly and said, "Be quiet, Bethany, and get in the carriage."

Wilder helped the two women into the carriage. He tried to maneuver closer to Stanley but couldn't get near enough to jump him. From the corner of his eye, he could see that Stanley was taking the time to fold the piece of paper and put it in his jacket before climbing on his horse. This was his chance. He rammed his shoulder into the flank of Stanley's horse, causing the animal to rear and bolt.

Without glancing back, he jumped into the carriage and slapped the reins on the horse's rump. "Lay low," he called to Bethany as the carriage jerked and raced away. Wilder didn't try to look back to see if Stanley's horse had left the yard. He could only hope it had.

With her hands tied and no way of supporting herself, Grace fell forward into the floor. "Untie her!" Wilder yelled to Bethany as the carriage sped along the dirt road.

Bethany followed Wilder's orders and crouched on the floor beside her sister. The scarf was easy to untie, but the knots in the rope had tightened and Bethany found it difficult to work them around Grace's wrists as the wagon wheels jarred over the rough terrain. When at last she was untied, Grace threw her arms around Bethany and held her tight.

"He's crazy! He wants to kill us, Bethany! What are we going to do?"

"Just keep your head down and everything will be all right." Bethany said the words Grace needed to hear, but she wasn't sure she believed them.

They didn't get far before Wilder heard shots. Moments later, bullets started hitting the cab. A quick glance told him Bethany and Grace were huddled together on the floor. "Stay down," he called to them.

Sweat popped out on his forehead as he beat the reins on the horse's back harder and harder. The ride was bumpy and he thought his teeth would pop out of his mouth, but he allowed no slack from the poor horse and continued the wild beating. They had to make it to the farmhouse.

Stanley brought his horse up even with the carriage and moved in closer for a better shot. Wilder scooted farther down onto the seat, hoping to avoid Stanley's bullets, when the carriage was jerked backward as one of the wheels hit a hole. Wilder flew up into the air as the vehicle toppled, throwing all three of them to the ground.

Bethany got to her feet quickly and looked around. Wilder was trying to rise. Stanley was jumping off his horse, but Grace lay on the ground not moving. Bethany picked up her skirts and ran. Bruised and battered from the fall, she also had a burning ache in her side.

"Grace!" she exclaimed as she fell on her knees beside her sister. Bethany lifted her head onto her lap and breathed a sigh of relief when Grace opened her eyes. "Thank God you're alive," she said joyfully. "Where do you hurt?"

"I—I think I'm all right. I just lost my breath for a moment."

Thankful she wasn't hurt badly, Bethany brushed strands of hair away from Grace's face. "Don't try to talk. Just lie here quietly."

A shadow fell across her.

Bethany swallowed hard and took a deep breath. Her mind was clearer than it had been since she first saw Stanley standing on the porch holding the gun. She knew what she had to do. She wasn't strong enough to wrestle the gun from him, but Wilder was. Even though Grace and Wilder had hurt her more than any two people could have, she loved them both more than her own life. She had to save them.

"Don't leave me," Grace whimpered. "I'm scared."

"Shhh. Don't be frightened. I'm going to take care of you," she soothed.

Rising to her feet with her purpose in mind, Bethany faced Stanley. An angry smirk twisted his face. A quick glance told her that Wilder had reinjured his leg. He was hobbling toward them as fast as he could. Her heart constricted. She was doing the right thing. She moved a little to the left, putting herself between Stanley and Wilder.

"Thanks for the carriage accident," Stanley said confidently. "Makes my story about robbers all the more believable."

Wilder had twisted his knee and wrenched his back when he was thrown from the carriage, but he'd finally managed to stand. What kind of damned hero had he turned out to be? he wondered bitterly as he limped closer to Bethany and Stanley. He had no choice now. He had to take his chances and try to wrestle the gun from this madman. As he drew near to the two, Bethany turned around. The expression on her face told him she was about to try something foolish.

"No!" he yelled, and grabbed for her as she lunged for Stanley. The gun fired. Bethany gasped as the force of the bullet hit her upper shoulder, knocking her backward. She heard Wilder yell and Grace scream. Pain seared into her flesh and darkness threatened to engulf her. Through blurred vision, she saw Wilder struggling with Stanley. He would save Grace and himself. She closed her eyes and crumpled to the ground.

Rage consumed Wilder as he grabbed Stanley's wrist with both hands, trying to control the gun as it fired into the air. Stanley gouged his thumb into Wilder's eye, trying to pop it from its socket. Wilder cried out and threw his head back as far as it would go. Stanley's thumb had him blind with pain, but still he didn't release his wrist. He continued to force the gun in the direction he wanted it to go. At last he embedded the barrel deep in Stanley's gut. He slipped his hand down to cover Stanley's trigger finger with his own, then squeezed. The gun fired. Stanley's eyes widened in shock, then in horror, as he slowly slipped to the ground.

Wilder pulled the gun from Stanley's lifeless hands and threw it as hard as he could, then rushed to Bethany's side. In his haste to get to her, he knocked Grace out of the way. "How is she?"

"I—I think she's alive," Grace said, tears washing the dirt from her face.

Grace had already torn the white blouse away from Bethany's shoulder and packed the wound with strips from her petticoat.

Bethany mumbled and her eyes fluttered open. "Grace," she whispered.

"I'm here," she answered, bending over her sister so she could see her. "I'm all right, and you're going to be fine, too."

"It's over, Bethany," Wilder whispered in a husky voice. He caressed her cheek with the tips of his fingers. He loved her so much he hurt inside. He wanted to yell at her that she was foolish for stepping in front of that gun; he wanted to hold her and tell her how very proud of her he was. Instead, he said, "Stanley's dead. And you're going to be all right."

A spasm of pain flashed across her face. "Take me home," she whispered. "I'll be all right if you take me home." She groaned and closed her eyes.

Wilder removed the petticoat bandage and looked at the gaping hole in Bethany's white shoulder.

Goddammit! He hoped Stanley was burning in hell! He wanted to kill him again.

The bullet was high enough to have missed her lungs. Gently, Wilder slid his arm beneath Bethany and lifted her up to check her back. He winced. It hadn't been a clean shot. The bullet was still lodged somewhere in her chest. Fear grew inside him. He had to get her to a doctor quickly. He looked around. Thank God the shaft hadn't broken and the horse was still hitched to the carriage.

Rising to his feet, Wilder started running as fast as his battered body would allow. He prayed the axle hadn't been broken when they hit the hole.

Chapter Twenty-Five

Six days after the shooting, Wilder sat at the small desk in his office at The Georgia with his feet propped up on the windowsill. His arms lay across his chest and his hand supported his chin. The draperies were open, showing a cloudless summer sky. Bethany was safely settled in her bedroom upstairs on the third floor.

Wilder and Grace had stayed by her side the five days she spent in the hospital in Atlanta. The medicine the doctor gave her caused her to sleep most of the time, but they never left her. On the fifth day, the doctor had declared her well enough to make the train ride back to Eufaula. She was weak but grateful to be back home in her own bed. Margaret, Stilman, Kate, and Seth had been there to welcome her home. When Grace took Bethany's dinner tray up, Wilder went to his office to look over the paper he'd asked his lawyer to prepare. All he had to do was sign it.

His reluctance to do that kept him staring out of the window as twilight descended and faded. Once he handed the document to Bethany, his relationship with her would be severed.

Bethany had risked her life for him. He chuckled ruefully. He couldn't lie to himself. Bethany had risked her life for Grace and it had simply benefited him along the way. Wilder's hand made a tight fist. Dammit! He should have taken that bullet.

There was no way he could ever be exonerated. Even with Stanley out of the way, Bethany had plenty of reason to be angry with him. To hate him. How could he expect her to forgive him for all that he had done? It was asking too much of her. He knew that, but still he wanted her to. She was too honorable to accept less than complete trust in a man and he had blown any chance of that the night Grace ran away.

How could he have known that he was going to fall in love with Bethany? That she was going to become the most important person in his life? He had been attracted to her when they first met, but he had no way of knowing it was going to turn into love.

If he could do it again, he'd do it differently. But what was the use in thinking like that? Since she had awakened from the surgery to remove the bullet, Bethany had treated him as if he had a plague. She'd been polite. Bethany didn't know how to behave any other way. She'd answered his questions with a yes or a no, but she wouldn't really talk to him. Her wound was healing as expected, but inside she hadn't begun to mend.

He knew there was no way Bethany was going to give him another chance. And he couldn't blame her. He should have told her where Grace was living the minute she'd insisted on hiring James Lester. He sighed. All hindsight did was leave him riddled with guilt.

Wilder swung his feet down and swiveled back around to his desk. Picking up his pen, he quickly signed the piece of paper and stuffed it in an envelope. The emptiness inside him grew. It wasn't easy to give up Bethany. He placed the envelope into the box he had for her and headed for the long journey up the stairs. He'd be all right, he thought, once he lost the urge to smell the faint scent of roses, once he forgot how gracefully she walked, how good she felt in his arms, how easily she loved him. He'd be all right when . . . "When hell freezes over," he muttered, and continued up the stairs.

"May I come in?" he asked from the doorway a few minutes later. She was propped up on her pillows, the same way she had been that night a few weeks ago in his brother's house. She had on a long-sleeved nightgown and her arm was bound to her chest with a sling. She'd never looked more beautiful. He'd never wanted to hold her more.

Bethany drew a deep breath and held it for a moment while they stared at each other. She still loved him, and it hurt.

"I wanted to return these to you before I leave," he said as he stopped beside her bed.

He was leaving? Her chest tightened. She wanted to ask him not to go. She loved him. She needed him. But fear and that nagging sense of betrayal forced her to remain quiet.

"What is it?" she asked, taking the box from him.

"What little the jeweler had left of your grandmother's jewelry."

"Oh," Bethany gasped, her heart filling with love, her throat clogging with emotion. "I don't know what to say." She looked away from his penetrating stare. "Thank you. You didn't have to do that."

He sat down on the edge of the bed. "I wanted to. It should have never been sold." He waited for her to look at him. "Bethany, I want to do so much more for you. I love you."

"Wilder, don't."

"Don't what?" His voice was husky with feeling. "Don't tell you I love you? Don't thank you for standing beside me, taking a bullet for me?"

"Stop it," she whispered, and looked away. "I only did what I had to. I knew I wasn't strong enough to take that gun away from Stanley, but you were."

"You're the bravest woman I've ever met. Dammit, Bethany, I want to stay here with you."

"No," she said quickly. "Too many things have happened. Too many things," she repeated.

"I know," he finally said. "I even understand. But I couldn't leave without telling you one more time that I love you. That I'm proud of you."

Bethany couldn't speak. If she did, she risked asking him to stay. And she knew that wouldn't be fair to him until she'd settled some things in her heart. She remained quiet.

"The doctor says you're going to be fine." He took a deep breath and stood. "I've rented a small house in Columbus, Georgia. I won't be far away if you should need me. I'm sure I'll find work in one of the mills there. Grace has the address if you should ever need it."

Her throat was so lumpy with clogged emotions she couldn't speak.

"Good-bye, Bethany." Wilder turned and walked away. And he didn't look back.

Several hours after Wilder left, Bethany opened the package and lovingly fingered the jewelry. At the bottom of the box she found an envelope. She opened it and saw the deed to Wilder's half of The Georgia. Bethany closed her eyes and wept.

"I'm not hungry."

"Well, you're going to eat if I have to spoon-feed you. Now sit up so I can put this tray over your lap."

"I'm really not up to eating anything," Bethany told her sister as she struggled to make herself comfortable against the pillows.

"You haven't been up to eating since you were shot. It's been over a week now. I'm tired of bringing this heavy tray up, only to take it back down hardly touched." Grace lifted a spoon of mashed potatoes to Bethany's lips. "Take a bite."

Bethany was not accustomed to this take-charge attitude from her sister and she wasn't sure she liked it. This new Grace was going to take some getting used to. "I can feed myself, thank you," she said in a terse tone, and took the spoon from Grace.

"Then prove it by eating all those potatoes and at least half of the chicken I cut up for you."

Reluctantly, Bethany started eating the potatoes. Stilman had added cream and they were delicious. She picked up her fork, pierced a small piece of the chicken, and put it in her mouth. "Are you going to stand there and watch me?" Bethany asked when Grace didn't move.

"No, I'm going to sit and watch you."

Bethany ate as she watched Grace pull the pillow-stuffed rocker over to her bedside and sit down. Something Wilder had said to her a long time ago flashed through her mind. *Grace is going to need a sister when she comes home, not a mother.* Looking at Grace now she knew Wilder had been right. But how did one learn to let go?

"Why are you looking at me like that?" Grace asked.

"Like what?" she asked, then put the last of the potatoes into her mouth.

"Like you're trying to see through me or inside me. It makes me nervous."

"I didn't realize I was—"

"Yes, you did," Grace interrupted.

Bethany shouldn't have tried to deny it. She placed her fork down. Grace had come home, but she wasn't the sister who'd left.

"I think it's time we talked," Grace said, removing the tray and setting it on the nightstand. "You're well enough now."

Bethany looked at her confident-sounding sister. "I'm fine. There's very little pain in my shoulder anymore." But there was much pain in her heart.

"I know you're not completely well, but the least you could do is pretend you're happy I'm home."

Months of anger and bitterness surfaced, and Bethany felt tears gather in her eyes. "If you knew what I went through to try to find you, Grace, you wouldn't say something as unfeeling as that."

"You haven't gotten over your anger, have you?"

"I'm not sure it's anger I'm feeling. I think it's disappointment."

"I know," she admitted softly. "Wilder told me about you selling the jewelry and hiring that detective. Oh, Bethany, I know I was horrible to you, but I was so mixed up. It was so easy to blame you for ruining my life. I couldn't see that I was the cause of all my troubles. You were right about Stanley, and I was wrong about you. I want you to forgive me. I'm sorry for holding Wilder to that stupid promise and for running away in the first place."

Bethany squeezed her eyes shut. When she opened them, she saw a tear running down Grace's cheek. "So many things have happened."

"I know," Grace said quickly, moving to the edge of the bed and sitting down. She grabbed Bethany's hands and held them tightly. "I'm sorry for everything that's happened. I've got a lot of explaining to do. Don't turn away from me, Bethany. I love you."

Grace slipped her arm around her. Bethany responded by returning the hug. It didn't matter what had happened between them; they were sisters. Grace would never know the hell she'd been through. The heartache, the pain, the emptiness, the worry, and how it had all multiplied when she discovered Wilder had known all along. Even thinking about it now tore at her heart.

"Grace, I know why you ran away, but I don't understand why you stayed away. There wasn't an hour that passed that I didn't worry about you and wonder what you were doing. Why did you refuse to let Wilder tell me where you were?"

When she spoke his name, Bethany had a sudden urge to see Wilder, to touch him, to smell his scent. She had missed him. She'd missed his gentle, soothing voice. She'd missed his presence in her room.

"I was angry and I was jealous. I truly believed you wanted to take Stanley away from me."

Bethany shook her head as flashes of memory spiraled through her mind. "Stanley was insane," she whispered.

"I know that now. But at the time I didn't. He was so charming. I can't believe I didn't see through some of that facade."

Bethany didn't really want to talk about Stanley, but if it helped Grace to understand him, she'd suffer through it. "I hope you know now that he set out to tear us apart."

Grace shivered. "Well, enough said about that. I guess you'd like to know what I've been doing the last two months."

"Yes, I need the answers to a lot of questions."

Grace rose from the bed and fiddled with the dishes on the dinner tray. "I stayed at a hotel in Atlanta the first couple of weeks. I loved the shopping during the day, but I was always lonely when night came. I liked being away from you, but I didn't feel safe in that big city all by myself.

"Wilder came to see me and explained that he'd have to tell you where I was if I didn't come home. I told him I'd leave and no one would ever find me if he did. He realized it would be better if one of you knew where I was, so even though he wanted me to come home, he agreed I should move to this boardinghouse where you found me. Mary was nice to me. She reminded me of you. I'm so sorry Stanley—"

"Don't say it," Bethany interrupted, not wanting to face the pain of remembering the innocent woman's death.

"No, I won't." Grace returned to the rocker. "I spent most of my days helping her stitch two quilts she was going to sell in Atlanta. I was always good with a needle."

"Yes, you were," Bethany replied when Grace paused.

"When Wilder showed up at the boardinghouse and said he had to tell you where I was because he wanted to marry you, I got angrier. I was so jealous. I couldn't understand how you could attract a man that handsome without even trying, when I was doing everything I knew how to please Stanley and couldn't keep him from looking at you."

There was a dull ache deep inside Bethany and it wasn't coming from her shoulder. "Let's not mention his name again. He's out of our lives now. That's all that's important."

"I'm sorry I keep mentioning him. It's just that he was so much a part of what happened."

"But I was the biggest problem. I cuddled and coddled you for so long, I didn't realize you were growing up. I'll take the blame for spoiling you, for overprotecting you, but you should have let me know where you were."

"I know. But I was hurt and I wanted to hurt you.

When Wilder told me he loved you and wanted to marry you, I was so jealous I couldn't see straight. You seemed to be doing so well, having it all. You had Wilder who loved you. And you had The Georgia. I was determined to see that you didn't get me, too. I was miserable and lonely spending my days quilting. Wilder tried to tell me that you needed me. I knew that wasn't true. I always needed you but you never needed me. You never needed me."

"That's not true. Grace, you've been my whole life since Mama and Papa died. Of course I needed you."

"I understand that now. I know how much you did for me and I hurt you so badly. I'm sorry, Bethany. Can you forgive me."

Clearing the lump in her throat, she said, "I already have." It felt good to be able to say that. Bethany knew it to be true. It would take longer than a few days to forget all the pain, but the healing had begun.

"Are you sure you can forgive me?"

"What kind of sister would I be if I couldn't?"

"Thank you," she whispered. "I know you wouldn't say it if you didn't mean it." Grace paused and ran her hands down her cotton skirt. "I have something else to tell you, and now is as good a time as any, I guess."

There was something about Grace's tone that made Bethany raise up from her pillows, holding her bound shoulder with her free hand. "What?"

"I'm going to be leaving at the end of August."

"No, this is your home." Bethany tried to remain calm, but inside that old familiar hurt started again. Threads of resentment attacked her.

"Not anymore. I've never cared for this place the way you do. I know what it means to you, but to me The Georgia is just a big old house."

"Don't say that," Bethany said, appalled her sister would feel that way about their home.

"Why not? It's true." Grace sat forward in the chair. "Listen to yourself. You're trying to tell me what I feel. I don't want to live the rest of my life here in this house. I want to go places and do things."

"Go places? You just told me you didn't like Atlanta. You didn't feel safe there." Bethany couldn't let her leave again.

"That's because I didn't plan that trip. When I left, I didn't know where I was going or what I was going to do. This time I do." Her voice softened. "You're right in one way: The Georgia is my home, and thanks to you, it always will be. Wilder has arranged for me to visit his brother and sister-in-law in Pittsburgh."

Bethany stiffened. Wilder certainly knew how to take care of Grace.

"Ester has just found out that she's pregnant, and she's not feeling well. I'm going to be a companion and chaperone for her two daughters, Priscilla and Penelope."

"When did this come about?" Bethany asked in a tight voice, stinging from the knowledge that Wilder and Grace had made plans without consulting her.

"Wilder kept in touch with Relfe by telephone when we were in Atlanta. They were worried about you. Relfe told him they were looking for someone to care for the girls. Wilder mentioned it to me, and I asked him if he'd recommend me. He didn't want to at first. He said you would need me when you came home. I told him you'd have Margaret and the rest of the staff stumbling over themselves to take care of you."

Thinking of how kind Relfe and Ester had been to her softened Bethany. And if Grace was determined to leave, she couldn't pick a nicer home to live in. Wilder's words came back to her. *When she comes home she'll need a sister, not a mother.* Grace had changed. Independence had been good for her. Bethany marveled at her sister's assertiveness. Leaning back against the pillows, she realized it was time for her to do some changing, too.

"It was very kind of Wilder to arrange everything for you, but do you have to go so soon?"

It was bittersweet, but Bethany found she could finally accept Grace had to live her own life. The sense of loss was fading; rebirth was crackling the air. They fell silent for a short time.

"You'll love the girls," Bethany said. "I know it's not polite to have favorites, but Penee is so warm and friendly. She reminded me of you at that age. You won't regret spending time with them."

"I'm looking forward to it." Grace rose from her chair. "You look tired. I think you should go to sleep now."

"I am tired." Bethany was glad her sister was back, but Grace couldn't fill the emptiness inside her any more than being at home could. Wilder was missing from her life, and she wouldn't be whole without him.

"Before I say good night, I want you to promise me you'll speak with Wilder."

"I really don't want to talk about this. What's between Wilder and me is no concern of yours."

"After all that's happened, how can you say that? I'm the one who broke you two apart. I've apologized to him for taking advantage of his kindness and using his honor to get at you. I want to see you get back together. He won't come back here. I begged him to. He thinks you have all you want or need wrapped up here in this house. Don't let it be true, Bethany."

No, it isn't. I love him. I need him. I miss him. "I can't talk about this right now," she whispered, evading her sister's probing eyes.

"Do you love him?"

Bethany bristled at Grace's question. "That's none of your business. You have no right to ask about my personal life."

"Yes, I do. You and Wilder would be married by now if I hadn't been so childish. I want to help you get back together."

"It's not that simple." Bethany closed her eyes briefly. "I'm not sure I can trust Wilder."

"That's an unbelievable statement coming from you. You could trust Wilder with your life. He's proved that. I've never met a more honorable man."

Her words caused a flash of anger. "You can say that because he kept his promise to you." The wound opened, the hurt she'd held inside eased to the surface. "I can't forgive him for that. His honor went to the wrong woman." Damn him! It hurt so bad.

Color stained Grace's cheeks. "You're not being fair. Try to put yourself in his place," she pleaded. "At the time, he did what he thought was right. Does that sound familiar? How many times did you do

365

what you thought was right for me? He's not the kind of man you let walk out of your life. You gave up one man for The Georgia. Don't do it again."

The conversation dangled unfinished while a breeze ruffled the curtain lace, the silence hanging heavy between them. Bethany turned away from her sister, unable to think clearly. She wanted to cry out from the loneliness and emptiness. She wanted Wilder to hold her.

"Don't let my mistakes ruin your life. Neither of us will ever be happy if you do." Grace walked to the door but turned back to Bethany. "Wilder is a wonderful man. I did the two of you an injustice when I refused to see you or let Wilder tell you where I was. Don't blame him. Don't punish him any longer. I know he loves you. He thinks all you want or need is this house. This house! As if this structure could make you happy. Let him know that you love him and need him."

Bethany stared at her sister as a chill ran through her. It was time to make a decision and she wasn't at all certain what that decision should be. She loved Wilder. There was no shadow of a doubt about that. She missed him, but could she forgive him and accept what he'd done? Could she go find him and marry him?

A late afternoon wind swept across Bethany's cheeks as she watched Grace's carriage drive away. The house would be quiet without her.

Over the hours of restlessness the past month, Bethany had tried to lay the blame on Stanley,

Wilder, and Grace, but when all was said and done, it rested on her shoulders alone. She couldn't blame anyone for her unhappiness, and she couldn't depend on anyone to make her happy. It had to come from inside herself.

Margaret was standing by the file cabinet when Bethany walked back inside. Her large frame was covered in a lavender print dress. "Grace gone?" she asked.

"Yes. She seems excited about this new job of hers. I know she'll love Relfe and Ester's girls. She just hasn't been home long enough." Bethany couldn't deny a twinge of sadness. She'd always hoped Grace would one day work at The Georgia, but that wasn't going to happen. And even though it made her sad, now she understood.

"Don't worry about her," Margaret said, her tone sounding something like a reprimand. "Grace is going to be fine. She's just trying her wings again. Now wipe that forlorn look off your face."

"Grace's leaving isn't the only reason I'm sad. There are some things you don't know, Margaret."

"I know all I need to know," the older woman said gruffly. "Grace told me some, Mr. Burlington told me some, and I figured some things out for myself. I've done had my say to both of them. I told them both that weren't no way to treat you, making you worry all those weeks not knowing where Grace was. It wasn't right."

It surprised Bethany to discover that it didn't make her feel better to know that Margaret agreed with her. Maybe both her wounds had healed.

"I know that Wilder wanted to tell me about

Grace. I think he even tried to on a couple of occasions." Was she actually defending Wilder?

Margaret walked back to her desk and sat down, the chair squeaking from her weight. When she looked back at Bethany, her lips were set in a firm line. "So why are you telling me this now? I can't do anything about it. Maybe I could have if you'd told me a long time ago."

"I'm telling you because you've been a part of The Georgia for a long time. It's important for you to know that I love Wilder."

"What he did to you wasn't right," Margaret said again.

"No, it wasn't. But we all live by a different set of rules, and because of that I'm beginning to understand why he acted as he did. Once you understand something, it's easier to forgive."

Margaret let out a deep breath and harrumphed. "Don't go asking my advice because I don't have any. It wouldn't matter if I did because you wouldn't listen to me. If you want to forgive that Yankee, go ahead. It's no concern of mine. Now get on out of here. I've got work to do. All you're doing is hindering me."

Bethany stood and looked down at her friend. "Margaret, I'm going to see Wilder. At one time I thought I could let him go. I thought I could live without him. I tried to convince myself that he wasn't the kind of man I needed in my life. Now, I know that's not true. The hurt has faded." Bethany rubbed her shoulder. The pain was gone. "With Grace's help, I understand more about what went on between the two of them."

"You do what you have to."

"And what will you do, Margaret?" Bethany asked, knowing the woman had never liked Wilder, knowing she could decide to leave.

"My work. Same as I've always done." Margaret finished by giving Bethany a rare treat: She smiled.

Chapter Twenty-Six

It was two days into September and there was the slightest chill to the late afternoon air as Bethany stepped out of the carriage in front of the address Grace had left her. She didn't know what she was going to do if Wilder wasn't home or if he refused to see her. Even after she had mended her relationship with her sister, Bethany still felt empty inside. Wilder was missing in her life. She could have tried to reach him by telephone, but what she had to say needed to be said in person.

She finally realized she had to accept her part in the deception. If Wilder had told her where Grace was hiding, she would have gone after her. Her sister had needed that time alone to do what Bethany had never allowed her to do—grow up. Grace was now a strong, capable young woman, no longer the spoiled girl she had been when she ran away. And Bethany had done some growing up, too. She now knew that losing control of someone didn't mean you lost them forever.

As she stood outside the door of the small frame house, she brushed the wrinkles from her rose-colored dress, trying to buy more time. At last she knocked. When the door opened, Bethany's breath caught in her throat. Other than his surprised expression, Wilder was as handsome as she remembered. Excitement and relief danced along her spine. How had she stayed away from him this long? Her hands ached from clenching with the effort not to reach out and touch him, feel his warmth.

"Bethany," he said calmly, his gaze fastened on her face. "It's been a long time."

"Yes." Her voice was a mere whisper. She was so pleased to see him that she felt she wanted to look at him forever.

"How's your arm?"

She threw her shoulder forward slightly as her hand covered the place where she'd been shot. "It's not giving me any trouble."

"I'm glad." They looked at each other for a moment, then Wilder said, "Come in."

Feeling as though a lump the size of an apple was in her throat, Bethany followed him into the living room. He motioned for her to sit down on the velvet-covered settee, but she couldn't. She was too nervous to sit still, even though she'd had days to practice what she was going to say to him.

"No, thank you. I'll stand," she managed to say in an even tone.

"Suit yourself." His words were clipped.

"You're looking very well," she said softly. She laid her wrap and gloves across the end of the settee while keeping her gaze fixed on him.

"Your concern for my health has always been touching." His brief chuckle held a mocking hint of sarcasm. "And to get it out of the way, my leg couldn't be in better shape. Thank you for asking. Now what can I do for you?"

The pain in his voice was reflected in the tightness of his mouth. Worry lines radiated from the edges of his eyes. She wanted to lift her hand and smooth them with her fingertips. He wasn't making this easy. Maybe she did want to sit down after all, she thought, looking at one of the burgundy-colored armchairs. Tension was building up in her throat, making it tight. She had to hurry and say what was in her heart, before her courage failed and her emotions jumped out of control.

Bethany fumbled with her purse, finally pulling a large white envelope from its depths and handing it to Wilder. "I believe this is yours."

Wilder took the envelope from her and opened it. She thought she saw his hand tremble.

"I don't want it," he said harshly. "The Georgia no longer holds any interest for me." He extended the deed toward her.

She searched his eyes, the twilight blue eyes she loved, and only found anger. Yes, he had a right to be angry. She'd refused to forgive him. Somehow, she had to make him meet her halfway. "It's yours," she stated quietly, refusing to take the document.

"What's the matter?" He threw the paper on his desk and stuffed his hands in the pockets of his dark blue pants. "Have you run out of money again? Don't you have anything else to sell now that most of your jewelry is gone?"

Bethany's green eyes registered hurt and a chill shook her body. "That's not fair," she whispered.

"Life's not fair, Bethany," he said, showing no sign of relenting. "Haven't you figured that out by now? I don't want The Georgia. I never wanted it. You said the only thing you wanted from me was that house, so take it. It's yours. It's all I have to give you."

The light of anger glinted in his eyes, making her hot. "I was hurt when I said that. I didn't mean it. I don't want it, either. The deed has your name on it." Her voice was husky, sincere, her eyes filled with promise. She swallowed painfully, making an enormous effort to control the emotions raging inside her.

"Then take it off. I told you I don't want the damned thing." He paused as his eyes searched hers. Suddenly, he turned his back on her and said, "I wanted you, Bethany, not that house."

Bethany refused to be rebuffed by his words. She wouldn't take no for an answer. "I can't live at The Georgia without you, Wilder. I've never stopped thinking about you. You're on my mind all the time. I love you and I miss you, and I don't want to go home without you."

He faced her, whispering desperately, "Don't do this to me, Bethany. I'm just now learning to live without you in my life. I know what I did to you was a mistake. I've apologized. I can't do more." He slid both hands into the pockets of his pants.

Her green eyes held a steady gaze on his. She couldn't lose him again. "It's true that for a long time I thought your keeping Grace from me was unforgivable. I didn't think I'd ever get over the fact that you didn't break your promise to Grace. Now I realize it was for the best. By keeping us apart, both Grace and I did some growing up."

"That would have happened, anyway."

She took a step closer, shaking her head. "No, it wouldn't have. I—I had an unhealthy attachment to Grace and The Georgia. I didn't know how to give them up. I didn't even know how to share them with others until you came along." Her voice grew softer. "Because of all that's happened, I can accept the fact that Grace has her own life to live and you own half of The Georgia."

Silence stretched between them, with neither speaking. Bethany didn't know how to get through to him. She took another step, her eyes pleading. "I miss you. I'm not happy without you. I want you to come back to me."

"You don't know what you're saying." His breathing became ragged, and his eyes greedily searched her face.

"Yes, I do."

"If you're trying to put me through hell, don't bother. I've already been there."

"So have I."

He slowly took a step toward her. His eyes narrowed and a muscle worked in his jaw. "I knew where Grace was for two months and didn't tell you."

"I know."

"I could have told you at any time and saved you the sorrow and pain you went through."

"I know."

Another step from him left only inches between

them. "I'm without excuse."

"I know. And it doesn't matter anymore," she whispered. "I was wrong, too. I lied when I said The Georgia was more important than you. That's not true. It was never true." Not wanting to wait, she rushed into his arms. They circled her slender body and brought her up close to him.

When she lifted her face to his, their lips met in a hard, demanding kiss that took her breath away. Bethany's hands roamed up and down his back and through his hair as she pressed closer and closer to him. She received his tongue and gave her own in a loving exchange. He had never felt so good! His kisses had never been so sweet, so powerful, so satisfying.

"Oh, Bethany, my love, you smell so good!" he murmured against her lips. "I've missed you." He cupped her face in his hands and looked deeply into her eyes. "I love you."

"And I love you. I'm sorry it took me so long to work things out. I've never stopped loving you, needing you, or wanting you. I don't want to go on living without you," she whispered into his ear.

Bethany held him tight as his lips traveled over her cheeks and down the slender column of her throat. The heat of his kiss was a blessing. His hands sent delicious ripples of delight up and down her back as they caressed and pressed her breasts against his hard chest.

"Tell me this isn't a dream. Tell me you're really here and I'm holding you, loving you."

"It's real. I'm here. Oh, Wilder, my pride was so strong, but thank God, my love for you overcame it."

She kissed him with tender passion.

"You feel so good, you taste even better, and you wouldn't believe how I've missed the smell of roses." He inhaled deeply.

Bethany opened her eyes and placed her hands on each side of his face. "I've missed you. We've all missed you. Even Margaret has been wearing a sad face."

Wilder chuckled. "If Margaret is wearing a sad face, it's because she knows you've been unhappy."

Bethany's eyes turned serious. "I meant it when I said I wouldn't go back home without you. I want to be wherever you are."

He lifted his eyebrows and grinned at her. "Are you telling me that you'd leave The Georgia and stay here in Columbus with me?"

"Yes, if you'll let me?" It wasn't an easy question for her to ask.

With their bodies pressed close together, Wilder continued to rub her back. They rocked gently from side to side as their gazes held. She meant it. She would live anywhere in the world as long as she was with him.

"I think you have changed." He smiled, then lightly and gently ran his tongue over the sensitive skin of her lips. "I don't want to live here in Columbus," he whispered against her mouth.

"Does that mean you'll come back home with me?" Love shone in her eyes.

He held her tightly in his arms, his hands running lazily, sensuously up and down her back. "Yes, but, Bethany, I meant it when I said The Georgia belongs to you. It's yours, free and clear."

Her heartbeat raced. "Don't you understand that without you there it means nothing to me. It's only a big old house," she said, using Grace's words. "Wilder, I want to be with you, no matter where we are."

"Then I guess I'll have to accept half of it as a wedding gift. That is, if you'll marry me today."

"Do you still want to marry me?"

His hand tightened about her waist. "That's my question. Yes, Bethany, I want to marry you. I want to marry you today and take you back home."

"Can we do it so fast?" she asked as she snuggled close and breathed in the soap-clean smell of him.

With the tips of his fingers, he lifted her chin so he could look in her eyes. "If I promise you we can get married today, will you say yes?"

There was a dancing light in her eyes. "Yes, yes, yes!" she promised, and claimed his mouth with hers.

It was late in the evening before Mr. and Mrs. Wilder Burlington arrived at The Georgia. When they made it to the third floor, Wilder picked up his bride and carried her into the living room.

"I've always wanted to do that," he said, a possessive quality to his voice. He kissed her briefly. "Which way to your room?" he asked.

"You already know that." Bethany smiled, then kissed the base of his throat, just above his shirt collar.

He laughed. "I know, but that was something I

always wanted to ask."

Wilder carried her into the room and laid her down on the coverlet. Reaching over her, he lit the lamp. Yellow light fell across them, yielding a soft glow, casting their shadows across the room. He settled down beside her and pulled her to him, throwing one leg over her protectively.

"Have you missed your home in Pennsylvania or the mill?" she asked.

"Sometimes, but not right now. Anyway, I expect I'll be so busy upgrading your mill that Homestead will seldom cross my mind again." Wilder caressed her cheek, then let his hand slide down her chest to rest on her breast.

"Have you heard how Corbin is doing?"

Wilder reached over and gave her a gentle kiss. "He's well. There's dissension among the strikers. He's trying hard. He knows that once their unity is broken, the end is inevitable. Relfe feels it's only a matter of time before most of them give up the cause and go back to work."

"Will it have all been for nothing?" she asked as she started unbuttoning his shirt.

"Standing up for what you believe is never nothing. Now enough talk about that. I want to get you out of these clothes and have the pleasure of looking at you for the rest of the night," he said softly.

Bethany replied by raising her head and kissing him. They clung together for a moment in a long, deep kiss.

"How do you feel?" he asked on a sighing breath.

Bethany gazed into his eyes. She smiled and touched his cheek. "I feel wonderful," she assured him.

"How do you feel inside, Bethany? What we just did was forever. Marriage can't be taken lightly."

His seriousness caused a lump in her throat. "Are you having second thoughts?" she asked, almost afraid to hear the answer.

"Lord nò! Not me. You?" He brushed at her hair with the back of his hand, then rubbed his thumb across her lips. "I had time to think on the ride from Columbus. I guess I'm having a little trouble believing you've really forgiven me for keeping Grace from you."

"I have forgiven you. I meant it when I said I understand now that you did what you had to do at the time. You stood up for what you believed in— your honor. How could I hold that against you? It's just that for so many years, I was afraid if I lost control of Grace and The Georgia, I'd lose everything. But I finally realized the only way I could lose was by not winning back your love." She smiled. "Grace and this house are important to my life. But you *are* my life. Now I don't want to hear another word about it."

"Then maybe you'd like to hear this: I love you."

"And I love you."

With ease, she reached and pulled his suspenders off his shoulders, then let her hands glide down the front of his trousers. There was an uneven leap to his breath. She spread his shirt open and let her hands and lips touch his hot skin. She planted several kisses on his chest before her lips found his small nipple and sucked on it.

"That feels wonderful," he said, pressing her tightly against the length of his body, clasping her head to his chest. "I can't take too much of that, my love. It feels too good."

A tiny moan escaped from his throat when his lips covered hers with hungry pressure. She found the button on his pants, but Wilder's hand caught her wrist and he whispered against her lips, "Not yet. Ladies first."

She slid her arms around him and hugged him close. "Love me, Wilder," she whispered into the crook of his neck.

Much later that evening, Bethany lay snuggled in the warmth of Wilder's arms, the wrinkled sheet entwined about their legs. Her hair lay across his shoulder, her breast against his arm. Contentment cloaked her. If it were possible, she loved Wilder more now than ever before.

Propped on his elbow, his gaze searched her face. Her hands played in the hair on his chest, twirling little curls around her finger. She couldn't stop touching him. She'd never tire of being near him, of feeling the warmth of his body so close to hers. She hugged him tightly, their naked chests touching, caressing.

"Oh, Wilder, I love you so much I want to touch you everywhere."

"Be my guest." He grinned and kissed her softly, running his tongue over her lips and down her chin.

Bethany ran her hand up and down his chest and looked up at him, savoring the feel of him.

"You know, when I left for Columbus, I really

thought I'd lost you for good."

"For a while, so did I," she admitted, then rolled on top of him.

Wilder brushed her hair away from her shoulder, exposing her scar. The doctor had done a good job. He reached over and kissed her shoulder and whispered, "I don't intend to stop loving you until twilight."

With a loving look, she gazed deeply into his eyes. "I like the sound of that. I've always thought of your eyes as twilight blue."

"And yours are the most haunting shade of green I've ever seen." He kissed her hungrily.

"Bethany," he asked a short time later, "will you make love to me in the rose garden?"

"What?" she asked, astonished. "Right now?"

Laughter rose from deep within his chest. "I don't mean tonight, my lovely wife. Next spring, when the roses are in full bloom and their scent is so heavy in the air we can taste it. I want to put a rose in your hair and drop silky petals all over your beautiful body."

"Wilder, are you serious?" she asked with anticipation already leaping through her.

"We'll find out come next spring." A deep throaty chuckle rumbled in his chest. "And I can hardly wait!"

Author's Notes

Even though The Homestead Steel Mill Strike of 1892 was lost by the end of November and set labor in Pittsburgh back for years, history praises the strikers for their solidarity.

Henry Clay Frick never recognized the union and was determined to break it at any price. Public opinion condemned Frick's actions in hiring the Pinkertons, but two weeks later he regained a small measure of sympathy when a man overpowered him in his office and shot him twice.

I took some liberties with Frick's character. In my research, there was no mention of Frick hiring thugs to attack any of his employees. I reasoned that any man who could hire Pinkertons to fire upon the strikers could have been capable of arranging a violent attack on a rebellious employee.

CATCH A RISING STAR!

ROBIN ST. THOMAS

FORTUNE'S SISTERS   (2616, $3.95)
It was Pia's destiny to be a Hollywood star. She had complete
self-confidence, breathtaking beauty, and the help of her domi-
neering mother. But her younger sister Jeanne began to steal the
spotlight meant for Pia, diverting attention away from the ruth-
lessly ambitious star. When her mother Mathilde started to return
the advances of dashing director Wes Guest, Pia's jealousy surfaced. Her passion for Guest and desire to be the brightest star in
Hollywood pitted Pia against her own family—sister against sister, mother against daughter. Pia was determined to be the only
survivor in the arenas of love and fame. But neither Mathilde nor
Jeanne would surrender without a fight. . . .

LOVER'S MASQUERADE   (2886, $4.50)
New Orleans. A city of secrets, shrouded in mystery and magic.
A city where dreams become obsessions and memories once again
become reality. A city where even one trip, like a stop on Claudia
Gage's book promotion tour, can lead to a perilous fall. For New
Orleans is also the home of Armand Dantine, who knows the secrets that Claudia would conceal and the past she cannot remember. And he will stop at nothing to make her love him, and will
not let her go again . . .

SENSATION   (3228, $4.95)
They'd dreamed of stardom, and their dreams came true. Now
they had fame and the power that comes with it. In Hollywood,
in New York, and around the world, the names of Aurora Styles,
Rachel Allenby, and Pia Decameron commanded immediate attention—and lust and envy as well. They were stars, idols on ped-
estals. And there was always someone waiting in the wings to
bring them crashing down . . .

*Available wherever paperbacks are sold, or order direct from the
Publisher. Send cover price plus 50¢ per copy for mailing and
handling to Zebra Books, Dept. 3814, 475 Park Avenue South,
New York, N.Y. 10016. Residents of New York and Tennessee
must include sales tax. DO NOT SEND CASH. For a free Zebra/
Pinnacle catalog please write to the above address.*